Monumental

Books by Adam L. G. Nevill

Novels

Banquet for the Damned

Apartment 16

The Ritual

Last Days

House of Small Shadows

No One Gets Out Alive

Lost Girl

Under a Watchful Eye

The Reddening

Cunning Folk

The Vessel

All the Fiends of Hell

Monumental

Short Story Collections

Some Will Not Sleep

Hasty for the Dark

Wyrd and Other Derelictions

Monumental

Adam L. G. Nevill

Ritual Limited
Devon, England
MMXXVI

Monumental
by Adam L. G. Nevill

Published by
Ritual Limited
Devon, England
MMXXVI

www.adamlgnevill.com

© Adam L. G. Nevill
This Edition © Ritual Limited

The right of Adam Nevill to be identified as the author of this work has been asserted by him in accordance with the Copyright, Designs and Patents Act 1988. All rights reserved. No part of this publication may be reproduced, stored in a retrieval system, or transmitted, in any form, or by any means (electronic, mechanical, photocopying, recording or otherwise) without the prior written permission of the publisher.

Cover artwork by Samuel Araya
Dust jacket and cover design by Peter Marsh
Text design by Peter Marsh
Ritual Limited logo by Moonring Art Design
Printed and bound by IngramSpark
ISBN 978-1-0684470-1-3

NO AI TRAINING: The Work may not be used or accessed in any manner which could help the learning/training of artificial intelligence technologies.

Without in any way limiting the author's [and publisher's] exclusive rights under copyright, any use of this publication to 'train' generative artificial intelligence (AI) technologies to generate text is expressly prohibited. The author reserves all rights to license uses of this work for generative AI training and development of machine learning language models.

For Tim Durrant, who taught me how to paddle and took me onto the water. And to all of my mates and peers at Paignton Canoe Club, with whom I've shared many adventures.

'The nameless, forgotten ones . . . They have gone back into the still waters of the lakes, the quiet hearts of the hills, the gulfs beyond the stars. Gods are no more stable than men.'

Robert E. Howard (from 'Shadows in the Moonlight')

I

[2–3pm]

Then came the terrible scream, splintering from high on the valley's western slope. A cry smelting the utmost terror from deep inside a woman. There was no faking that.

She was hidden in the trees above the meadow; a barrier of woodland extending from the wide mouth of the estuary, then along each side of the valley that the group had paddled into.

During their journey here by kayak, they'd watched the estuary basin shrivel to wetlands and a creek, before the waterway eventually broadened again to become a tree-enshrouded river, the shallow, clear water now murmuring alongside the meadow in which they were setting up their tents. Continuing deep inland, the marching parallel columns of trees on the valley sides tapered and obstructed a view of anything further up. Whatever lay on the other side of the forested slopes, they couldn't see either.

When they heard the scream, the five kayakers near the river's edge all stopped what they were doing. They remained stricken to a standstill by their surprise, their fear.

Moments without breaths elapsed.

No one managed to remove their eyes from the bulge of woodland on the high ground.

But nothing moved. Nothing at all. And the trees resumed their silence.

2

Before

[Noon–1pm]

*O*nly once the six kayakers had paddled from the chaos of the sea and glided into the Wyrm Valley did the wind drop. The atmospheric change was so abrupt, the effect was akin to scurrying indoors to flee a storm. Some felt a sense of having crossed a border. A profound but invisible demarcation had separated a hostile sea from the uncanny tranquillity now engulfing them.

Climbing out of the rocky promontories of the twin headlands crumbling into the sea, the steep slopes of the combe deflected the gale away from the glimmering estuary. A vast, shallow mirror on the flat floor of the valley's belly. Choppy water, the hue of iron filings, had now calmed and paled. Here, the surface was glassy enough for impressions of clouds to shimmer on placid water. Below the crystalline skin of the estuary, on either side of their cockpits, sand became visible. White shell fragments glowed from a seabed the colour of unbleached sugar. Drowsy air thickened, syrupy, the temperature balmy, sub-tropical. In early October, in England.

Bottom layers, sodden with perspiration, clung to ribs. Greenhouse humidity, trapped inside cagoules, encouraged six pairs of fingers to yank down zippers. Sweat trickled from beneath hatbands and helmet rims.

Marcus's first impulse was to congratulate his five companions for not only remaining upright in their sea kayaks but for simply being present. Most of his relief was reserved for Mary and Jane, neither of whom had swum. But the other paddlers were too spread out to hear him. They'd all washed up separately, the morning's formation having been broken by the powerful northerly that gusted at noon.

Relief surged to joy, and Marcus wanted to laugh and whoop. Then he wanted to thank God aloud, because the six of them were still alive. No one had been left behind. None had been separated from boat and paddle in the sea's churning swell. Too easily, now, did he imagine one of their boats upside down. He'd have cried out, 'Swimmer!' to alert the others. But his call would have been drowned out by the boom of the wind, then scattered by its whips. The swimmer would have been there, then not there; visible, then lost between rising and falling waves; a colourful splash of waterproof, swept back and forth and up and down. A pale hand raised.

He also visualised the struggle to reach the swimmer: the effort to turn his boat about in breaking waves and to stay upright himself, before commencing a battle with the sea to reach the capsized paddler. Fighting his own panic, and trying to remember how to perform a deep-sea rescue, he'd have soon questioned the feasibility of such a procedure in those conditions. Imagining this made him feel cold and delicate. He'd never called a lifeboat out in ten years of regular sea kayaking. But there was always a first time, waiting in the wings like an unpopular cast member.

Stretching his back, he shook off the feeling of dread about what might have been and leaned back over the stern deck. Behind his buoyancy jacket, his heart issued a muffled knocking, slowing as he relaxed into his seat. Thawing tension in his neck and arms melted to warmth. Giddy from adrenaline and exertion, he scooped up water to splash his face. A tug freed his drinking bottle from the deck lines near his cockpit. Gulping the contents, he squeezed the sides of the bottle as if life's very strength was being restored to a body made so insignificant by the tumult of surf and wind.

Having been transfixed by a fearful concentration while tossed about by the rough stuff, only now, in sheltered water, could he assess his recent performance. Support strokes – at least a dozen low braces, that he'd executed in a blur – had kept him the right way up. His feet, legs and hips had not tensed against the hull as they had once done. Instead, they'd loosened. A steady forward paddle, with sweep strokes to keep him on course, had taken control of his arms. He'd not had to think. He'd felt his way out of danger.

You're always better than you think you are, when you have no choice but to be better. During his first season on the sea, an old paddler had said that to him. And here was a rare moment to acknowledge his own experience, gathering interest in a personal kayaking vault.

Gradually, the group re-formed inside the estuary. Each paddler stroked the flat water, or sculled, to reunite like friends separated in a boisterous crowd. Marcus could see everyone's teeth. All of his companions were smiling.

'I thought that rising north-westerly looked dodgy this morning,' he called out, suppressing a note of accusation that would sharpen his voice. He angled his boat closer to Julian and Nigel, rather than the three women, to make his point.

Nigel had planned the paddle and was leader. Julian had advised Nigel, because he always did, regardless of whether his advice was sought.

Nigel grinned at Marcus as an unfeeling coach might confront an injured boy who'd been thrown, unprepared, into a contact sport. 'Bit bumpy. But if you were worried about a little weather, why did you come?' Even in small talk, Nigel possessed a remarkable ability to convey judgement in everything he said.

Stung by the provocation, Marcus's breathing caught and remained shallow as if the incoming air was being squeezed through a straw. Of late, he'd driven home from paddles writhing with suppressed anger, his teeth grinding against all that he hadn't risked saying to Nigel, whose resentment appeared inexhaustible.

Any opportunity that Marcus might have taken to respond to the man's goading was swiftly stolen by Julian. A smirk crawled through the older man's beard and his little blue eyes twinkled at the chance to contribute. 'You've got to account for tidal flow. Incoming tide crossing the flow, with a reef below. On top of that, you've basically got wind against water.' A veteran in his third decade, Julian treated Marcus as if he were a beginner. He would never recognise him as much of a paddler.

'I know,' Marcus said, and felt churlish for saying that much. 'I've been in worse.'

'So, what's the problem?' Nigel said. 'Are you suggesting that you are the only person capable of leading a paddle like this?'

A broader smirk wormed the aperture in Julian's beard wider, revealing peg teeth. 'That wouldn't be remotely accurate, if that's what he thinks.'

Marcus's face flushed. Even on open water, he felt cornered by the pair. He wasn't pretending to lead and had made an effort not to undermine Nigel. But he'd remained silent that morning, before they'd launched, when he should not have done. He'd held his tongue about the forecast and now disliked himself for having done so.

Several paddlers had noticed the tension between him and Nigel growing over the last few summers. They laid the lion's share of the blame at his door, not Nigel's. A favouritism that incited Marcus's paranoia. He suspected that Nigel had shared a grievance.

But which one?

They would be out here together for three days. Marcus would mingle with the others and keep Nigel at an arm's length. He shouldn't even be here; he should never have joined the trip. That had been apparent from first light when they'd met; his presence had elicited no warmth from Nigel and Julian, and not a trace of camaraderie. But the original idea to paddle the Wyrm Valley had always been his. No kayaker that Marcus knew had paddled the valley further than the estuary mouth. A three-day tour was required to reach the Wyrm, paddle the interior and return. He'd suggested this very expedition last summer. Nigel had since taken ownership of the plan and organised his own trip. *This one.*

And Marcus would never let Nigel paddle the Wyrm before him. Never.

The pressure to make the expedition a success, however, was now all Nigel's. Not an enviable prospect, particularly since it was the first group paddle he'd planned and led. That was showing. Nigel had made the mistake of not breaking himself in gently with a few local paddles. By choosing a tour as ambitious as the Wyrm Valley for his debut, he'd multiplied and elevated the risks for a group of mixed experience.

Nigel's navigation, and particularly his reading of the flow and tide, had been acceptable. But he'd chosen the date of the trip weeks before, irrespective of future conditions, and had simply hoped for the best when the time came to launch.

When he'd reached the car park at six that morning, Marcus hadn't liked what he'd seen on his phone's Windy app. More weather than was predicted the previous evening was forecast to blow from NNW at noon. The day before, the forecast had suggested a rising, gusting northerly, though nothing resembling what they'd just escaped: at least a force six gale, a hard six too. The squall had built from eleven o'clock and continued rising. But no one should have been surprised; the potential for strong wind and hazardous conditions had been there for all to see at first light. Long before they'd set out.

But Marcus had stayed quiet.

Prior to their scrambling into this sheltered estuary, they'd been mere minutes from disaster. Had they left Scarlet Cove in Brickburgh any later that morning, Marcus doubted they would have reached the Wyrm. Or, at least, not all of them would have made it.

Earlier, as they'd carried their boats across the pebbles of Scarlet Cove to the shoreline, then prepped the kayaks, Nigel had barely glanced at Marcus. Instead, he'd fussed, territorially, around his wife, Sophie. Or he'd bantered with Julian. He'd ignored Marcus's attempts to chat through the timings and route dictated by the changing conditions. There had been no briefing either. Had he led the paddle, Marcus would have executed a quick, informal discussion and equipment check. *Who has a towline? Who has a radio? PLB? What channel are we all on? First-aid kits? Anyone?*

Lowering his voice to stifle his temper, Marcus said, 'It's not about me. Or you.' He nodded at Mary and Jane, who'd rafted up and were talking excitedly about what they'd just paddled through.

'I wouldn't let anyone come on this trip who couldn't handle a bit of wind,' Nigel said.

Bit of wind. Blown apart and forced into varying tacks, it had been every man for himself for thirty minutes that seemed to pass like three hours. Any longer in those conditions and they would have lost each other. Some of the group would have paddled to the estuary to seek cover. Others, probably Mary, would have been weather-cocked towards the Atlantic. They'd have been routed.

Marcus would have followed anyone blown off course to keep them in sight. And he'd still be out there now.

He raised his voice to counter Nigel's and Julian's conspiratorial grins and their exchange of knowing glances. 'You had no idea what that wind would do to the water down here. You've never paddled this far before, Nigel. And I'll bet you've never crossed Creel Point in that much wind either Julian.'

Nigel pulled away and showed Marcus his back. 'We're here, aren't we? Got us here, didn't I? And on schedule, give or take half an hour.'

Marcus had only caught word of the paddle from Sophie and only after she'd added him to a Facebook group that Nigel had set up to organise peer paddles. Trips, Marcus suspected, that were intended to exclude him and rival those that Marcus had organised for the last four years. Most kayakers were happy for him to lead. Hard-won trust in him had accumulated.

Following his habit of supplying irritating embellishments, Julian added a footnote to Nigel's dismissal of Marcus. 'There's an element of risk on all paddles. You have to account for adverse conditions. Part of the sport.'

Nigel nodded enthusiastically. 'Exactly,' he muttered. The two men had formed a familiar faction.

Encouraged by his confederate, Julian raised his voice for everyone's benefit. 'If you waited for no wind, you'd never go anywhere. The most risk you've faced today was driving to Scarlet Cove.' He finished with the characteristic titter that Marcus found odious. A rash of heat flooded his scalp.

Julian's contrived nonchalance about danger and his arrogant insouciance wearied Marcus as much as Nigel's one-upmanship. Amidst the heaving swell, he'd glanced across at Julian and seen a bloodless face, the whittled teeth bared in a grimace of terror. Julian had panicked. He was the most experienced paddler in the group, but had immediately abandoned the others and lit out for the estuary mouth to save himself. Instead of toadying around Nigel, Julian should have stepped in and called the paddle off that morning.

Sophie wasn't taking sides with Marcus – he was certain of that – but she never missed an opportunity to berate her husband in front of an audience. She paddled towards Nigel's kayak from the side, threw her head back and roared. 'It's the first and last time I'm going on a trip that you put together! Stupid bastard! That was bloody terrifying!' Her voice dropped, the tone more insistent, her words more potent.

Monumental

'We could have lost Jane and Mary. What were you thinking? Did you even look at the forecast? What would we have done if someone had swum? I knew this would happen. Why do you think I put Marcus in the group?'

Marcus imagined himself occupying Nigel's skin at that very moment, and withered. Though his empathy wasn't without a wicked sense of satisfaction.

Nigel looked away from his wife's fierce expression and angled his head down, as if in shame. The one person he never snapped at was Sophie. He used to do so but had restrained himself for a couple of seasons. Damage control was the consensus.

Sophie's fury still possessed a force capable of bewildering Marcus. He'd been on the receiving end of it more than once and now wished that he hadn't mentioned the conditions. He felt implicated and responsible for the deepening conflict. Hostility on the water could turn viral. And, in case other things were said that could not be unsaid, he fretted with an urge to intercede and appease.

Julian, however, was quick to fill the uncomfortable vacuum that followed Sophie's outburst. He regularly deceived himself into believing that his sagacity was required in all situations, including the marital strife of others. His inability to read a room, or a group of kayakers on the water, was a social deficiency that never failed to surprise Marcus. Grinning, and without taking measure of Sophie's fury, nor how humiliated her husband was, Julian proceeded to counsel her. 'It's the only way a paddler gets to the next level. It's the sea! There's always wind! We've all got to fill our boots at some—'

Sophie twisted around in her cockpit, discharging the pool of water that had collected on her spraydeck. Her formidable eyes stopped Julian mid-sentence. 'You'd even lecture the bloody coastguards, wouldn't you, as they pulled us out of the sea? Some of us were frightened out there. For our lives! So don't take this as an opportunity to deliver a sermon about people filling their fucking boots!'

Marcus angled his boat to avoid seeing her pale face – the lips aquiver, a tremor in one eyelid. An admonishing glance from her could burn the skin of his face as if his head were pressed against ice. Not for the first time, he felt sympathy for the children she taught in secondary school. Instead of looking at her, he watched the grin petrify inside Julian's scratchy beard, the facial hair made whiter by purpling cheeks. A silly titter escaped the beard accompanied by a 'Sorry' that was barely audible.

'Don't be sorry,' Sophie shouted. 'Just don't be a twat! Can you manage that until we get back to Scarlet Cove?'

This final blast, Marcus suspected, was directed at all three male paddlers.

Because they had all been just that: twats. One had insisted on their going this week, despite the forecast conditions; a second had failed to employ his experience and call time on the paddle; a third had waited until it was too late and then begun a blame game. Him.

Of late, however, Sophie was becoming angry often enough to appear unstable. When she missed trips, Marcus wasn't alone in feeling relieved. Others were made nervous by her volatility, like Mary and Jane, who buddied up on the water and only spoke to Sophie hesitantly. But Marcus feared far more than being scolded by her; he feared that her loss of restraint might lead to disclosures that could never be retracted.

Fatigued from struggling through the swell, and now visibly perturbed by the argument, Mary and Jane drifted closer to the other paddlers, yet maintaining distance from Sophie.

'Well done, you two,' Marcus said, nodding at them, glad of the distraction the women presented. 'Pat yourselves on the back. I'll check my phone in a sec, but that was easily a force six, possibly a seven.'

When Jane smiled at Marcus, her green eyes brightened and his heartbeat filled his throat. Even her casual attention thrilled him, though he suspected that little was casual about her interest in him now. His excitement, however, was immediately tempered by discomfort. Her interest in him incited another kind of tension in the group; something else he'd prefer to avoid on this trip.

Julian, Nigel and Sophie had taken to observing even slight interactions between him and Jane. And Sophie didn't need to say anything to express her disapproval. A look usually sufficed. Julian, however, on account of his proprietary yet deluded fascination with Jane, was prone to act out. And he was bristling now. Not even being chastened by Sophie's scolding could restrain him from shorting-out any current that sparked between Jane and Marcus. He felt compelled to contradict Marcus. 'Bit of an exaggeration. On the Beaufort Scale, that was somewhere between five and six.'

He then squeezed his boat between Jane and Marcus's kayaks to erect a physical boundary. As he did so, his paddle blade clashed against Marcus's. A collision that drew an accusing grimace from Julian, as if the collision was the other party's fault.

Trying not to laugh at Julian's ardour and clumsy jostling, Jane eased her boat away while feigning interest in a distant valley slope. Oblivious to her desire for space, and like a duckling pursuing its mother, Julian steered his boat after her.

The noisy clash of paddle blades drew Sophie's attention to Marcus. He sensed that not all of her ire had been expended on Julian, or her husband. Plenty remained for anyone else that displeased her.

When Nigel noticed where his wife's attention had drifted to, his little eyes darted about beneath thickets of eyebrow, until settling to cast an accusing, defeated glare at Marcus. 'Let's crack on,' he said. 'We can post-mortem the bloody conditions later. We're here for the night and the best part of two days! Let's get ashore. Get dry. Get a bite to eat. Put the kettle on. Everyone's tired. No one's thinking straight. We don't need any bloody dramatics.'

Marcus shrugged at the man's attempt to cool boots, which he thought was always better imparted in softer tones, without invective or blame. Pitying Nigel, he looked away from the man's plump features, sweaty and squashed beneath the peak of his cap. This would be the last paddle they took together. Ever.

'Look at this! Look at where we are. It makes it all worth it,' Mary gaily offered, to signal her aversion to the squabbling. Her matronly impatience was often sparked by the competitive manoeuvring of the other paddlers, and was always expressed in a tone that made the offenders feel foolish. 'It's so beautiful here.'

3

[Noon–1pm]

*M*ary often wondered which paddle would be her last.

She'd made it to sixty-eight. Just. Four summers before, this distance would have been comfortable for her, though she'd never liked swell. But if this wild camping trip proved to be her last, and she suspected that it might, then she must cherish every second. Or at least try to, if she could stifle the pain.

She wouldn't say anything to the others about how fiercely her right shoulder hurt. By insisting on carrying two of the boats, from the car park to the shore at Scarlet Cove, she'd inflamed her arthritis. Then she'd turned her left ankle on the pebbles. Pressing her left sole upon the foot rest inside her boat on each stroke of the paddle had sent flickers of lightning to her hips. Then, for hours, the sparks had exploded into a firework of pain; a green-blue light flashing across her pelvis. Paddling harder to cut through the swell had aggravated both ankle and shoulder. She now dreaded putting weight on either joint. And when they eventually landed, the others would notice her hobbling.

Of more concern, had she capsized and swum, she'd have been incapable of getting back into her boat. And she knew it.

She forced herself again to believe in what was becoming her daily mantra: that she would not be a burden to the group. For as long as they remained on the water, she would make herself cope.

On land, however, she didn't imagine she'd be venturing much further than the tents. A hike up the Wyrm Valley had been mooted during the planning stage. If a walk went ahead, she wouldn't be taking part. So, she would compensate by managing the camp. Rather than hold the others up, she would prove how useful she could make herself with the camping arrangements. No one would regret her participation.

Right up until her husband Geoff's first stroke, and six months before he passed, she had toured Devon, Cornwall and France with him in their camper van. She'd cook her speciality camping dish tonight, a bean chilli. Geoff's favourite.

Long after her ovaries had been removed two years previously, and most of her lymph glands, and the secondary tumours in one lung, no one could have convinced her that she'd ever paddle again. But she'd gradually rebuilt her stamina and strength on numerous peer paddles with Jane and Marcus. He'd organised them to assist her return to the water.

But Nigel still didn't want her here. And God only knew why Sophie had invited her. Perhaps to spite her husband. And she'd overheard Julian suggesting that they'd arrive at the valley later than was desirable, because Mary was not only the slowest paddler but 'glacially slow'. Nigel had rolled his eyes in acknowledgement of his sidekick's wry comment and muttered something about him and Sophie 'only having childcare covered for three days, not a fortnight'.

Overhearing them, Mary had been disoriented with humiliation. A shame that had flushed her entire body with a horrible warmth. She was certain that everybody else had heard the remarks too. In the online group, too, they'd barely concealed their disapproval of her inclusion on the tour. What had not been said felt far worse than what might have been.

Julian was clueless, an autodidact and an irredeemable bore, so she made allowances for him. But Nigel was cruel. A bad-tempered, silly man, clinging onto Sophie, who clearly couldn't stand him. Her own husband. The pair had always been difficult to manage in a group situation, but after lockdown they'd emerged more brittle and spiky than they'd been before. Mary still harboured hopes the couple would behave on the trip, for everyone's sake.

On balance, however, she wasn't sure which dynamic was worse: the antipathy between Nigel and Sophie, or the tension festering between Nigel and Marcus. The latter pair were as bad as each other. Always locking horns. Compelled to contradict each other. Forever competing. This whole paddle had been Marcus's idea. So, of course, Nigel had to steal his thunder. But something else must have occurred between the men to account for the incessant spats all summer long. The uncomfortable atmosphere they'd introduced into every paddle was becoming intolerable. Neither would give an inch of ground. Hadn't they once been friends? Listening to them, no one would guess.

Marcus didn't think she was fit enough for the trip either. That hurt her the most. In the car park that morning, as they'd taken their boats off the roof-racks, Marcus had smiled at her in that manner of his that made her beam and feel spoiled by his attention, and he'd asked her if she was sure 'that she wanted to paddle so far.' She feared he'd see her as a lame duck that he'd have to supervise. And he wouldn't want to linger at the back with the slowest paddler while Nigel put on a display of performance paddling out front.

Marcus had been so kind to her all year – though she now suspected that his helpfulness was partially motivated by a desire to get closer to Jane, who only ever showed up if Mary was paddling. Perhaps he'd become frustrated with Jane's elderly chaperone, as if she were some maiden aunt and an impediment to his amorous intentions. Jane was a grown woman who could make up her own mind, though Mary, as tactfully as she could, had warned her younger friend about Marcus's reputation. He'd already had to leave a club in Dorset, and Jane was so terribly naïve and trusting. She was clever and pretty enough to pick and choose. She needn't settle for a scoundrel.

Mary forced her attention away from the troubled group and her discomforting thoughts. Both were exhausting her. She admired the estuary instead. Wide, glittering. Dense woodland coating each valley side. This is what she was here for. She'd never paddled anywhere so beautiful. She doubted that anyone in the group had either. The Wyrm – with its tidal estuary, wetland and river – was virgin water for them all, even Julian.

How could such a paradise be kept hidden? A sylvan arcadia, exotic and seemingly unique amidst the intensively farmed landscape that surrounded it, yet every inch was private land. Steel fencing corralled the woodland's entire boundary, from shoreline to the peak of the valley on each side. There was no public access, not even a track for walkers. The sea and a shallow estuary protected the mouth. What justification could there possibly be for this privacy? She thought it immoral.

Then, as she gazed at the vista of the Wyrm Valley and its gentle waters, the delight she had felt in them gave way to sadness, as she thought of Geoff and how she would have loved to share this with him. Such rumination opened another door in her mind, leading into a room furnished with health concerns. Another appointment with the oncologist loomed. She was due for a scan in two weeks.

Her eyes moistened. She touched the side of an eye to dab away a tear.

There was no better place for her to be. She must remember this. Being here was a blessing. And she would not take a single day of remission, and of not being sick, for granted.

She wouldn't let anything spoil this trip.

Perhaps the last of a lifetime.

4

[Noon–1pm]

'We have crossed the line and are now trespassing,' Julian said, grinning, paddling close to the stern of Nigel's expensive Cetus. 'Trespassing on one of only three estuaries in the British Isles where even the water is private and off limits!'

No one responded. Marcus sighed wearily and hoped that he'd been heard. Julian had repeated the same fact online; that morning too, as they prepared their gear; and often during the paddle, whenever they could hear themselves above the wind. The information hadn't needed to be repeated, because Marcus had already known. This valley being private property was an additional incentive to paddle it, as far up as possible. The exclusion of the general public from such an expanse of green space, and from the actual water, had always rankled with him.

'You need written permission to set foot here. I've never known it be granted. Did anyone remember to apply?' Julian guffawed and snorted as he repeated once more what they were all well aware of.

Jane placated Julian's excitability with a thin smile. Though Julian now tailed Nigel closely, most of his attention was directed over his shoulder at Jane. His conspicuous need to impress her, Marcus surmised, would be sustained until the trip was over. The possibility of a conversation with her, without Julian's interference, seemed unlikely. Maybe that wasn't such a bad thing. There would be better places and times to manage the situation with Jane; to disentangle himself from what he'd impulsively started. To avoid what he most wanted was the best strategy for him and her now. As well as for the others in the group. The beginnings of the trip had not been auspicious. Why add another complication?

If he achieved anything on this paddle, it should be a calming presence at a safe distance. That's what he'd decided: to behave. To simply be better.

Shallow around their coloured hulls, the estuary water appeared soupy as the level dropped. Glossy strands of eel grass sprouted. Other than where their pointed bows creased the surface and spread neat V shapes behind the boats, the estuary remained unruffled.

Peering over the side of his cockpit, Marcus spied a plethora of shattered crab shells, mere feet beneath his hull. He'd never seen so many broken crabs. A major food source for the birds here, though he hadn't seen one yet, not even a gull. That surprised him. There was a wetland here and the whole valley was an area of conservation. The water should have been teeming with birds.

The estuary's wide entrance gradually narrowed towards the marsh, and a wetland became increasingly visible; a spiky brown line, straight ahead and in the sights of their bow toggles. Somewhere in the middle of the tapering valley, seawater flowed into a tidal river, mixing with fresh water that poured from distant moors, north of Plymouth.

On either side, the valley's flanks rose. As far as he could see ahead, there was no break in the forest. From estuary mouth to wetland to the obscured inland portion of the valley, there was no evidence of mankind's usual depredations. No buildings visible. No land cleared for more of the continuous farmland that patchworked the earth around this crease in the coastline.

'Tide's going to turn soon. We should push on and get as far up as we can before we run out of water,' Marcus called out to the group.

Jane and Mary nodded and deepened their paddle strokes.

Nigel didn't react, nor did his silent wife. They continued to fume in silence, paddling apart from each other, in the lead.

Annoyed at Marcus's observation about the water level, Julian smirked inside his beard. 'More importantly, we don't want to be paddling against an outgoing tide.' A predictable, obvious, inevitable footnote. But at least the tempo of the older man's paddling increased.

As the group moved more swiftly through the slowly emptying estuary, the north wind soundlessly swept above the valley and pushed the gloom further south. Charcoal clouds partially cleared from the sky over the sea behind them. Dismal shadows, cast onto the gunmetal waves, lifted and vanished like sooty wraiths. In their place, a previously hidden sun spread a golden light down the valley and across the water, warming the backs of their tired necks. They'd paddled without much of a pause for five hours to get this far. The change in the weather and atmosphere felt like a divine reward. Nothing less than a welcome.

'I wonder,' Jane said, giggling, 'if the landowner has already seen us through binoculars. From up there, somewhere. What if he tells us to bugger off? What would we do? It could get embarrassing. We won't have enough water to paddle out for another twelve hours. Julian can explain it to him.'

'Sure he'd relish the opportunity,' Marcus muttered.

Julian's contribution was inevitable. 'We'll be camped at the bottom, well away from the buildings at the top. They're miles away. As long as we don't light a fire, they won't have a clue we're here.' He smacked his lips.

'Just as well,' Jane said. 'Because I doubt the police have a trailer big enough to tow six kayaks out.'

At that, they all laughed. And it felt good to laugh after the exertion of the paddle, the unwanted excitement of the storm that had nearly put an end to their trip, or worse, and the bickering that had erupted the moment they'd arrived on this great watery tongue.

5

[1–2pm]

From laughing at Jane's jest, they suddenly fell silent, astonished, even shocked, at the sight of the trees.

White trees.

Dead trees.

So many bleached trunks and limbs spiked and clawed upwards from the expanse of mudflats. Though the trees were scattered, no two standing close to each other, the sparse arrangement of the ghostly copse continued into the distance. A natural cemetery at the base of the estuary, where the sea ended in a wetland.

They drew closer. Most of the pallid dead stood straight and forlorn in their devastation, but Jane could see that a few trunks were tilted, while others twisted on the ground, part submerged, green with algae, horribly contorted.

At the unfolding sight of the stricken wood, Jane was beset by a sudden, abstract idea – the kind that she often experienced but rarely shared with anyone. She wondered if the anguished poses of the trees suggested the skeletons of unworldly creatures; wretched fossils from a distant past, of things that had once suffered petrifaction during a sudden cataclysm. The accursed population must have since remained in place, like the lifeless preserved citizens of Pompeii.

These trees had grown for years before the earth around their roots was claimed by the sea. Twice each day, the roots and smooth trunks of the dead wood, their very bones, were still covered by incoming tides.

Around the hulls of their kayaks, brackish water the colour of strong tea moved sluggishly. They'd entered a creek that threaded a serpentine channel through the arboreal graveyard. Unbroken across the opaque surface ahead of them, reflections of perished timber and spindly branches loomed in ominous stillness, like sentries. Or warnings.

At the waterside, the wizened limbs and crooked twig fingers suggested intent – one that was unclear to Jane, until she interpreted it as clutching. The branches groping at the air, so eager to catch the eye, might be seen as pleading to whoever floated below. Were they beckoning? Was there a message to impart? These trees might possess hungry ghosts that were eager, at a rare sighting of the living, to confess woes and share torments. Or was the lifeless wood suggesting a hazard? Should they venture further into these swampy vestiges of land? Perhaps these forlorn husks acted as a deterrent.

None of these morbid ideas did Jane share with her companions. Though, as she entertained them, she recognised the private dark thrill they created inside her, one that she felt all the way down to her tailbone.

Out front, Nigel guided the party between the muddy banks that enclosed the creek's languorous swill. Shallow, murky water moved against them, albeit slowly; the first stirrings of a turning tide in slacker water; a pause before an entire waterway gushed for the sea, like some giant bathtub emptied of its dirty dregs. They needed to be off the water soon.

A hint of sulphur singed the unmoving air. In places, smaller tributaries snaked away, their destinations obscured by turning banks. More fallen logs appeared. Mosses covered them and draped from uplifted branches like the cerements of the dead. In other places, patches of glossy grass leaked from the distant woods, and bewigged clumps of earth raised themselves into mounds.

At one time, Jane realised, the dead trees would have been joined to those still living on the valley sides. The wood might have once reached the very banks of the creek. Against the distant verge of the surviving wood, the bleached and sunlit timber of the vanquished trees appeared more stark and despairing. Jane now imagined the dead trees rushing horizontally from the slopes. A starving crowd of bony children and adults. All fleeing. Into extinction.

Maybe the desiccated corpses had once been panicked by something up there, and fled for the perceived salvation of the creek. Their surge would have been slowed by the deep mud. There, they would have been forced to wade, becoming exhausted before eventually sinking to their knees and coming to a halt. Mired in the bog, spent and breathless, they had succumbed together, just short of the water they'd once thought was an escape route.

Where on earth do these thoughts come from? Her mother used to say that. Now Mary said similar things to her.

Her reverie was broken by Julian's latest broadcast. 'Salt water. Trees can't survive it. This lot were reclaimed by the sea. From the roots up they were, effectively, poisoned. No green shoots, leaves or anything on them at all. Clear evidence of rising sea levels—'

When Sophie said, 'Here we go,' Julian stopped talking.

'Strangely, eerily beautiful,' Marcus offered over his shoulder to Jane.

'Isn't it!' She nodded enthusiastically. It was one of a growing number of things that had made her fall for Marcus: he had imagination. She wanted to encourage that side of him, while also sharing the very same quality in herself with him, and more often. Not just on the water. 'I've never seen anything like it. Have you?'

Julian answered for Marcus. 'Once. In North Wales . . .'

To escape another anecdote, Jane paddled forward and drew level with Marcus. He greeted her with a faint smile and eye-roll.

Immediately, from behind them, there was an eruption of splashing as Julian pursued Jane. But there wasn't room in the narrow channel to allow for another boat, for which she was grateful.

'But no birds,' Marcus said.

'A cursed place,' Jane said.

'And we're camping inside it.'

'Do we have to?'

He laughed but not for as long as she would have liked. He'd quickly looked away too. She'd noticed how self-conscious he became in her company. He often appeared shy, or uncomfortable. Maybe he was embarrassed that their affinity was being noticed by others – particularly Sophie, who made him wary. Nigel also made Marcus reluctant to engage with her; he was prone to butt in, as was Julian, and contradict anything that Marcus said to her. Whatever his reasons, Marcus's withdrawals from her smarted and left a small ache in her stomach. He wasn't the kind of guy that she imagined being influenced by others. He seemed to have figured things out for himself, as much as anyone could. But there was a noticeable reticence in his attitude towards her. Even after . . . *the kiss*.

'My word, will you look at that,' Nigel said from around a bend in the creek. Jane couldn't see him but in such undisturbed air she heard him clearly. He might have been sitting beside her.

Sophie, who was also out of sight, asked, 'What the hell?'

'Why would anyone hang them up there?' Nigel said, sounding baffled.

This enigmatic discussion, ahead and out of sight, made Marcus paddle more swiftly to see what Nigel and Sophie were talking about. Jane followed him but slowed her paddle strokes. Apprehension exceeded her curiosity.

Unruffled, Sophie continued to lecture her husband. 'Local kids. A prank. I'm quietly encouraged by the idea that young people might want to hang bones from trees, to spook people like you.'

'Who though? No one's allowed in the valley. And they'd have one hell of a hike to reach this place on foot. You'd sink to your thighs in this mud. You'd also need a ladder to get them up there.'

'All the more reason to praise their handiwork. Some of them still get outdoors and shin up trees. Especially down here in the remote communities. Broadband is slow. They can't play Fortnight.'

By the time Jane finally rounded the bend in the creek, entering a section in which the banks steepened, and the channel widened, the married couple had stopped paddling and were softly feathering the water with their paddles to keep their boats still. She couldn't see their faces. They'd craned their necks to peer up at the lower portion of a dead tree. The trunk was long, and listed as if weighed down by the weathered remains that hung from two dry branches.

The curved spinal column of a large animal. The intricate ladder of joints appeared intact. Accompanying the backbone, on a neighbouring branch, a hoary skull suggested prehistoric origins. Deep eye sockets glared despite being empty.

Each artefact had been secured to the ghostly tree limbs with a wispy but durable brown twine, from which fibres peeled like stray hairs. Certain thicker branches, extending from the middle of the trunk, had been selected to dangle these bones over the water's edge. And, like ghastly wind chimes, the installations seemed eager to broadcast a strange, hollow clacking. Mercifully – because Jane was repulsed by the mere notion of the bones knocking against each other – there wasn't a wisp of a breeze.

'Cow or horse, I'd say,' said Julian, when he joined the others. Grinning triumphantly at the mild concern on his companions' faces, he seemed to regard them all as gullible children who needed their nonsense dispelled by paternal wisdom. He tried to whistle the theme tune of the *Twilight Zone;* a dullard's response, Jane always thought, to anything inexplicable or mysterious. She wished she had the confidence to tell him to shut up. He was spoiling a real moment. How often in life was one confronted by something genuinely weird?

'Too big to be human. Thankfully,' Marcus said.

At that Jane chuckled, as did Mary. Judging by the anxious frown lining Mary's forehead, a dose of levity was not unwelcome.

'Livestock. They fall over cliffs, all along the coast.' Julian spoke directly to Jane, as if she was in particular need of reassurance. 'You've got to remember, it's all farmland around this valley. There are always bones in the coves. Kids have collected them and strung 'em up. That's all.'

After taking pictures on the phones they had stowed inside waterproof cases and tucked into the pockets of their buoyancy vests, they gradually became more used to the display. Their shock dwindled into puzzlement.

But the unexpected – and, for some, unwelcome – novelty of the spine and skull had not entirely worn off when they were confronted by more hanging bones. A great many more, lining the banks of the brackish creek, round the next bend.

Awaiting them was a veritable palisade of gibbets, festooned with more desiccated spines, skulls, femurs and even entire ribcages, hung like the keys of glockenspiels. For another thirty metres or more, on either side of the narrow waterway they traversed to cross the mudflats, the skeletal installations hung in empty air, poised and resplendent with a simple horror.

Beneath their pallid scaffoldings of dead tree branches, the bones had weathered. They'd been here for some time. Some were even discoloured an unpleasant brown.

Mary's surprise was evident in her sharp intake of breath, audible to all.

Nigel's grimace expressed distaste.

Jane's revulsion verged on shock. 'Oh, God. So wrong,' she muttered. It slipped out before she had time to think.

After that, no one, not even Julian, had anything more to say. They were silent for some time. This stasis, the absolute stillness, was profound enough to discourage anyone from making a sound. As if they didn't dare to.

Overwhelmed by the aisle of animal remains, oppressed by the close air so tightly contained by the creek banks, forced to squint under a sun emitting the heat and light of another season, Jane detached from the group, drawing inward. In the seclusion of her mind, she suffered a strong impression that the marsh was trapped in some form of suspension, outside the world from which they'd just paddled.

More than the absence of any movement upon the mudflats, it was the oppressive silence she found most uncanny. Save for the near imperceptible rippling of the creek against the hulls of their kayaks, and the odd splash of a shortened paddle stroke, the airless marsh uttered not so much as a sigh from any direction. No birds cried out. Not even from the distant valley sides.

'Got it all,' Julian said, holding up his Go-Pro camera, which he'd unclipped from his helmet to zoom in on a fleshless pelvis drooping above their concerned faces. 'Captured for posterity. Someone can make sense of all this when we get back.' His voice was even more annoying and unwelcome than usual. Impudent, too, in this landscape made grotesque, and altogether stranger and less knowable, by this display of the limbs and heads of dead beasts.

'Ssh! Julian, please. Will you be quiet? Listen,' Jane said. The tone of her voice surprised her even more than it surprised Julian, whose expression slumped from startled to dismayed.

To Jane, studying this section of the creek, the marsh might even have been holding its stale breath. As a predator might when studying prey. The land seemed content to watch and listen to them. If a hunter remained hidden somewhere beyond the marsh, it would be able to peer between the petrified trees and observe what was moving so slowly along the creek. This thought made her think of their group as a herd of colourful animals. Beasts too long and cumbersome to turn themselves around in the narrow channel and escape by the way they had come in.

'Listen to what?' Sophie asked. 'I can't hear anything.'

'Precisely,' Jane said. 'I can't even hear the sea. Where's the wind gone? Have you seen a single gull?'

'Oh stop it, Jane. Don't,' Mary said from the rear.

From the front of the group, Nigel turned his head, though the look of bewilderment in his eyes offered none of the reassurance intended by his words. 'Just sheltered here, that's all.'

Marcus cleared his throat. 'I wonder . . .'

'I'd rather you didn't. Honestly, you and Jane, you're making it worse,' Mary said.

'This place. Ahead of us,' Marcus said. 'The old manor was a sanctuary of sorts. Mind, body, spirit place, with a craft programme. And things like that. There was an artisan colony here too. The estate doubled as a retreat, you know, for artists. So, I wonder if these bones in the trees are something that they made. You know, like sculptures.'

'Therapy? This?' Jane asked.

'I don't know. Kind of a bone garden. Or something.'

'Well, someone's been working something out of themselves that I think is bloody awful. Can we get out of here, please?' Mary said.

The seriousness of her expression and tone, however, had the opposite effect on her companions. An infectious wave of giggling passed through the kayakers. When the laughter reached Mary, even she couldn't restrain herself and joined in.

Everyone laughed except Jane.

6

[1–2pm]

For the group, an end to the mudflats was a welcome distraction from hanging bones and the spidery, bleached trees. Jane's respite was brief, however, and dissipated not long after they entered the reed bed. A marsh entirely filled by a crop of brown stalks that shot up to the height of a tall man. Save for a narrow band of bright sky directly above the feathery, oat-coloured tips of the myriad stalks, and the brown water on which they travelled, nothing of the valley could be seen in any direction from below in the creek.

A new but imperceptible air current stirred the dense bushels into a papery rustling. This hushed discourse above her head flowed forward from the unseen outer distances of the wetland. And, as she listened, she found it hard not to suspect that the whispering plants had engaged in discussion and were murmuring about what had dared creep among them. She wasn't involved in this conversation. But she felt that what she heard was indiscreet. It was meant for her to overhear. It was about her.

Silly. Ridiculous to think this way. But that's how she was made. And she often wondered if this was how her instincts used abstract thinking to warn her.

The plants grew from the same glossy mud in which the dead trees had made their final stand, yet the reeds created a unique environment and changed the atmosphere again, from morbid to claustrophobic.

The further away from the sea they ventured, the stranger the estuary grew. She wanted to communicate this notion to her companions but didn't know how to without sounding crazy. At this point, she also entertained a notion that they were being pulled, even sucked, towards the valley interior – a place they had yet to glimpse. Though the slack water was just beginning to trickle in the opposite direction, her boat encountered no resistance within the shallows sliding about the hull. She found it too easy to paddle forward.

When the creek widened and darkened beneath an overhanging arch of trees, the beginnings of the river felt disproportionately welcome, as if an unseen danger had now passed.

7

[1–2pm]

Here there existed two near identical worlds: the world above the river, and its depiction on the surface of the water. Until the pointed bows of their boats broke the illusion, the world reflected on the river formed a perfect image of the reality that blossomed, with a near unworldly vibrancy, above the waterway. Bulrushes and the overhanging branches of the impenetrable palisade of trees lining the banks were reproduced in photographic detail around their hulls. Even the vibrant green of the foliage leaked into the water like a dye.

The creek worming between the oppressive reed beds had finally delivered the group onto the dark glass of the river. A good fifty metres of a straight, pristine watercourse became immediately apparent. Nothing beyond the riverbanks, however, was visible. Here was another funnel and channel from which they could not see what was beside them, nor where they were headed. The valley led. The Wyrm guided. They were going where it chose to take them.

But, though enclosed, at least the river was broader and more colourful than the creek. The width even allowed them to paddle three abreast. This improved morale.

Under the arching trees and amidst dappling shadows, ribbons of river were touched by sunlight, producing clear shallows that slipped over sand. Pebbles shone like buffed

Monumental

gold. Dragonflies darted in and out of the verdure; sparks of green and blue between wisps of whirring wings. Dust clouds of gnats erupted from marshy pockets near the banks, where fallen debris composted. Alder, birch and willow draped the water, the leaves unruffled in the drowsy atmosphere. In patches, the air itself misted with puffs of visible pollen; a gossamer so fine not even gravity could make it fall.

And yet, here was a beauty that Nigel could not enjoy. Something else took his breath away. The same thing that had choked him all morning.

Since the argument about the conditions, an unspooling of his painful ruminations had been impossible to restrain. Was seeing this river valley not worth the acceptable risk of the gale? And no one had anticipated a wind so strong. *Marcus* certainly hadn't. Why hadn't *he* mentioned it in Scarlet Cove? Hindsight was such a wonderful thing.

What a prick.

Here, in this astonishing valley, Nigel suspected that his rage might have intensified.

The bucolic wonders that he'd led this group to discover should have softened Sophie's rancour and pulled her gently towards him. But the distance between them since they'd arrived was as broad as the estuary behind their boats. Even here, she'd taken *his* side.

Just as well I invited Marcus. Isn't that what she'd said?

She was a stranger. How was that possible after twelve years of marriage? Even his attempts to touch her, playfully, innocently, now felt inappropriate. She demurred. Slipped out of reach. Tensed. Even recoiled. She snapped.

Cold, unfeeling eyes. There was not a trace of warmth inside them for him. That is, if Sophie even looked at him. Which was not often these days and only through necessity when managing their son and domestic affairs. She looked at him with little besides scorn. Even contempt. *Yes, genuine contempt.*

They existed under the same roof, yet he struggled to remember how she had once looked at him. She'd even desired him once. Unthinkable now. Nothing resembling arousal was ever returning to her eyes.

Not for you.

Because of him.

He couldn't bear to hold the man's name inside his mouth. The very word exuded a tremendous power, capable of cursing him into deeper wretchedness. That his wife had invited *him* had ruined the expedition before he'd selected a paddle from the garage.

He couldn't bear to turn around in his cockpit, because his sight would always find the generous width of Marcus's shoulders and his hard arms, tanned the colour of syrup. Merely being within sight of *his* arms made his own flabby appendages feel as if they had withered, bloodless and limp. The man's perfect teeth chewed at his mind and gnawed his thoughts. That smile he wanted to smash like a bottle.

Beside him, *you're unsightly. A source of revulsion for your own wife.*

The man never tired. In a kayak *he* had the balance of an acrobat. The way *he* rolled and came back up in seconds, shaking jewels of water from glossy black hair. Showing off to make Jane simper.

Jane now too. Had *he* had *her* as well? There were rumours. People shared uncomfortable silences. Truth lay in the silences and in the flicker of the eyes that averted from his baffled misery.

Just friends, others said. *He* couldn't be friends with anyone. *He* was an addict. *He* was diseased and *his* disease had laid waste to several relationships.

The tapered, hard belly. His *fucking belly!* Just a glimpse of the man's firm waist – as narrow as a twenty-year-old's – and the sweaty belt of fat around his own waist would bulge, even quiver. His groin felt like a nappy filled with dough. He couldn't abide his reflection in profile, and, at home, he'd moved the standing mirror into the spare room.

You need to lose a few pounds. Get in shape. Look at Marcus. You're the same age.

It'd been three years since his wife had said that. At the time, he'd not been able to breathe. Had felt nauseous, then strangely limbless. His consciousness had trembled, shimmered, then detached from its moorings within his skull. He'd had to sit down; he'd not felt that terrible since his first heartbreak, as a fresher at university, twenty years before. But Marcus, the bastard, owned a gym! How could anyone keep up with that? Since hearing his wife's remark, every time he'd taken a shower her casual comment had scalded his hairy back like a cattle brand.

Even that far back, *he'd* been on her mind. Three years.

He knew now. That horrible cold penny had dropped. And he'd since remembered more and more. One thing related to another. The past was a forest of mirrors, one reflection revealing another. Each contained an image he'd rather not look at.

Glances from her to *him*, leading to asides that he'd sometimes overheard; all occasions impregnated with new meanings. What had she said that time, as *he'd* offered Sophie the use of his new paddle? *Careful where you put that. You'll get me in trouble. More trouble.* It was the 'more' that cinched it and closed the deal. His wife hadn't realised how close he'd been to her boat.

Other revelations winded him, running ice down his nape. The paddles she'd wanted to go on; *he'd* been on every one. She'd started buying the same brand of gear as *him*. *The same colour boats!* Her laughter at everything he'd said. *Remember that?* Followed by that period of feigned uninterest in *him*, evidenced by insincere criticism that came across like provocative flirting. That was after pretty Sandy and Heather had joined the paddling community. She'd been jealous of Marcus's instant camaraderie with the younger women. That was four years ago, not long after he and Sophie had taken up the sport.

So far back. Even four years ago?
She must have sunk to all fours right around then.
Like a pig.

That long ago?
Had they?
She doesn't think you know.
Would she even care if you did?
She's such an angry bitch because he *rejected her!*
He *must have had his fill, then tossed her away.*
For Jane.

A feeling came over Nigel. An insidious warm creep that sweated him from scalp to ankles and left his breathing shallow. He might have been suffocating inside a sauna. A squeezing hand closed around his heart, making it smaller, harder.

Stop it. Stop it.

Briefly sobering from a rage that nauseated and fatigued him, he remembered how he always buried these unendurable sensations under the heavy soil of a continuous loathing. A peat and loam of wretchedness, sown with a persistent stitch of resentment. The stitching would often split, though, and out would flop the steaming horror of what his mind forced him to confront and endure. About her and *him*. Together.

He wouldn't go *there* this weekend. He wouldn't. He had to get past this because, whenever all three of them were on the water together, he could no longer tolerate being on the verge of releasing a thin lunatic scream. Or would it be a bellow that tore his lungs free of his mouth?

Stop it. Stop it.

But how is it possible? He's *here. That fucker! On my paddle. Pissing on my shoes. Again.*

From Scarlet Cove to the Wyrm, Sophie hadn't stopped thinking about *him* either. *He* was on both of their minds, always.

No. No. No.

Momentarily, Nigel lost all sense of the river and his paddle strokes and even where he was. His consciousness dispersed and re-formed with a clear image of *his* head, broken apart like eggshell. The handsome face deflated into a rubber mask.

Nigel grinned.

Monumental

Again and again, he would bring the . . . *what? A rock!* A rock smoothed by the tides. He would bring it down, again and again, until he was pounding and splashing pulp. He could do it. And would leave *him* unrecognisable. If Sophie wept, he'd do the same to her. He'd feel no guilt.

Is that where you are now?

Oh, Christ.

The idea of smashing them both apart was too good to let go of. He felt the stirrings of an erection.

To the authorities he'd express remorse, but he knew he'd come alive with a secret ecstasy about what he'd done until the end of his life. But whose fault was that? They'd made him like this.

How many times have you destroyed him, physically, in your thoughts? And mentally and emotionally and financially? The castration fantasy that he'd entertained for a few weeks last year now appeared behind his eyes. Cutting all that sloppy flesh free from between *his* legs. *That one* had first erupted from the whitest heat of his anger. The last time he'd entertained *that one*, he'd smashed everything in the dishwasher and stood over the sink with a knife pressed into his own throat. He hadn't recognised himself at all.

He worried he'd made himself susceptible to seizures. The eczema was back, all over his face and across his belly. *He* had manifested on Nigel's very body as an infernal itching; a scabrous, unsightly disfiguration.

Pathological.

You wanted to chew the skin from off his *face.*

How many times have you run him *over?*

Punctured his *hull and left* him *to drown, two miles out? You even carried a chisel in your kitbag last summer, in case an opportunity presented itself.*

You actually bloody did! A chisel!

Fucker!

How often have you broken his *neck with a single punch?*

With your hands, you have crushed the rings of cartilage inside his *throat, one hundred times.*

The bad reviews you left on Google about his business. Does he know?
And yet, you have said nothing to either of them.
'Will you give me some bloody room!' Sophie cried out beside him.

Nigel broke free from the terrible black pressure, and the bright red streams that spilled through his head. As if rousing from a heavy sleep, he returned his attention to the river.

The water and trees blurred. He'd made himself dizzy. Nigel blinked his sight clear and unclenched his jaw. He mustn't break more of his own teeth. His entire head now ached horribly. Not concentrating, he'd drifted too close to his wife's boat.

'Sorry,' he said, sullenly, barely able to release the word.
Why are you apologising?
Wife? What a joke.
She remained at his side because of Harry, their little boy, because she needed him to provide for their family.
But you can't even do that now, either.
What the storm hadn't destroyed, thieves had picked over, gutting his café on the seafront in less than twenty-four hours. They were now living off Sophie's teaching salary, while encumbered by the massive debt that he'd incurred to start the business – a commercial endeavour that few had encouraged. *He'd* even had the temerity to advise Nigel against the business too!

Marcus tried to tell you . . . Sophie had screamed, the morning after the storm that destroyed their lifestyle and security.

'It's wonderful. So pretty!' Mary called out from the rear. 'I'm so blissed out.'
Oh, fuck off. Save it for Instagram.
'There. Look. A river meadow! We have to camp there. The flowers are still out!' This from Jane, just behind Nigel's boat.
I'll decide on that, if you don't mind. And I hope Sophie hears you swallowing his sword tonight.
Bitch.

8

[2–3pm]

*M*arcus had been the last kayaker to come ashore on an inlet of the riverbank beside the meadow – a crescent of shingle, where pebbles formed a small beach. Waiting for enough space to slide his kayak among the other five boats, he'd plucked his spraydeck from the cockpit and sat in a wet seat, legs draped over the bow. He'd waited while Mary had struggled out of her boat, assisted by Sophie and Jane.

Mary had not wanted anyone to touch her shoulder. 'It's a bit tender,' she'd said. Nor had she been able to place all of her weight on one ankle. These were new injuries collected that day. Cancer that she'd survived the year before had withered her body, so she wasn't heavy. But her helpers, while coaxing winces out of the oldest member of the group, had still struggled to get her upright.

Marcus watched with dismay; Mary wouldn't be shaking this off. He'd keep an eye on her. Make sure she didn't overexert herself. They still had to paddle back, and if her shoulder didn't improve they'd need to take turns towing her out.

Julian had been the first paddler ashore and had leapt from his boat in a sprightly manner. He'd always land first, to direct a group about where to moor their kayaks. As usual, he'd offered criticisms masquerading as helpful suggestions.

'No, you'll need to pull your boat up higher than that! When the tide comes back in, you'll not want to be wading downstream to retrieve it.'

Nigel was the paddle leader. He'd decided on the area in which to make camp, though any of them could see that this was the perfect spot. Mary had called it first. Perhaps this was the only spot. Not since they'd entered the estuary, a couple of hours before, had they seen anywhere suitable to pull ashore, let alone camp.

After the marsh and its dead trees twisting from the mud, and the enclosure of rustling reeds, they'd eventually emerged onto the broad river. On either bank, the foliage had remained unbroken until the tight tunnel of willow and alder had thinned to unveil floodplains. This was a world seemingly from the past. Above perfectly rendered on the water below. A halcyon depiction of an English river lost almost everywhere, save in those memories that had been preserved in the landscape paintings that hung in galleries.

Dazzled and enchanted, the group of six had then glided into this explosion of sunlight. An expansive blue sky had been waiting; a broad, flat meadow presenting itself. The sight had left them stunned and blinking.

By the time Marcus was ashore, unzipping his buoyancy vest, stepping out of his sodden neoprene spraydeck and popping his hull hatches to retrieve his tent, kit and supplies, the others were already in the meadow, inspecting the ground.

Long, coarse grass, festooned with the last of the summer's wildflowers, offered a level surface; a dark green pelt, sprayed and swaying with white, buttercup, scarlet and purple splashes, that reached from riverbank to the treeline of the valley's western side. They might have been making camp in a Monet painting. But the presence of the flowers aglow in sunlight was unnatural enough to present as uncanny; this was October and Autumn hadn't even chilled the ground.

'More evidence of climate change,' Julian had remarked. 'Everything's out of sync.'

By the time the meadow grasses were whipping Marcus's wet shins and he was sweating under the weight of his gear, Julian had already unfurled his tent like a parachute after landing from above. Near where Nigel and Sophie had dropped their bags, Julian straightened his groundsheet to form a rectangle, claiming his spot beside the paddle leader and spouse. That end of the campsite, Marcus would avoid for three good reasons.

Pitching his tent too close to where Jane was fussing over Mary, who had presented her injured ankle to the younger woman, felt presumptuous. He'd give the girls ample room too. Setting up too close to Jane would trigger Julian's competitive twitching and bitching. And yet Marcus didn't want to position himself too far away from the others and appear anti-social.

Once he'd decided on a patch of thick grass, a dozen strides to the left of where Jane and Mary had dropped their rucksacks and extraneous bags, Sophie had paused in what she was doing. Frowning, she'd watched Marcus's deliberations. 'You'd think we smell,' she'd said, though loud enough for all to hear.

'He's all right there,' Nigel had replied. He was finally pleased about something; in this case, the physical distance between himself and Marcus.

'Yes. Yes. He won't be getting in the way over there,' Julian had said, and tittered.

Marcus had briefly indulged a fantasy of punching Julian's old, bearded face really hard. Instead, he'd said, in as dismissive a tone as he could conjure, 'Don't tempt me to paddle a mile further upstream, or to head for those trees, for a bit of peace from your continual streams of B.S.'

Sophie struggled to think of a riposte. Julian had seemed surprised that Marcus had taken the teasing badly.

'And I'd join you up there, Marcus. I can't wait to see inside that wood,' Jane had said. 'It's massive.'

Blushing, Marcus had looked down at his kit, though not before catching sight of Julian's wounded expression.

Despite his discomfort, he'd been tempted to expand on Jane's comment about him and her in the woods together, to antagonise Julian. But he didn't speak again.

As if she were in need of protection or guidance, and to endorse his claim on the much younger woman, Julian had then abandoned fussing over his groundsheet and ambled towards Jane. A big beardy grin had lit up his narrow, self-regarding face. Marcus had then heard him offering to put her tent up. 'One of the benefits of fitting so many boilers. Tents are child's play in comparison.'

Marcus had smothered a groan and unpacked his gear. His recalcitrant memory had then refused to release the information he required, regarding how he'd erected his tent in the past. He'd bought himself time by arranging the pegs and poles in the grass. If he could see every component, the correct sequence for their assembly might be revealed. He would not ask for help. Any pause in his preparations might draw further criticism from Julian.

As he'd hunted for the mallet that he knew he'd packed – the second entry on the long list of what he needed that he'd made for the three-day expedition – Jane must have wandered off and entered the woodland. She hadn't said anything to anyone. He would have heard her. He later assumed that she'd needed to pee. Women that he'd camped with before were as stealthy and discreet as cats when nature called.

A little later, while inside his tent and clipping the inner mosquito net into the flysheet, Mary had said, 'Jane's been gone a while.'

Any mention of Jane always summoned a response from Julian, who'd offered something to the effect of 'Well, she can't get lost. Just needs to head back to the river.' *Titter, titter, titter.* 'Just let her stretch her legs. I intend to do the same in a minute. I'll find out where she's gone.'

'She'll love that,' Marcus had whispered, and clicked two sections of a tent pole together.

9

[2–3pm]

*S*wallowed by a wood as sombre as the interior of an old church built from stone, Jane guided herself up the slope and between the trees. The atmosphere was dark enough to prevent her looking directly into the penetrations of light that smarted against her eyes; shafts that speared the canopy and lit up patches of bracken and leaf fall carpeting the loamy soil. After her first hesitant steps inside the wood, the smells of the river and pasture disappeared completely. A sodden mulch, from the earth's perpetual composting and mushrooming, became overpowering. But the rot of the earth also mingled with a thinner, cleaner air at head height. Moist bark and the tang of pure rainwater soon rubbed at her sinuses.

Another boundary crossed in the Wyrm. From the brightness and warmth of the river meadow to a cold darkness. Slipping inside had made her shiver. She'd suffered the sensation of a thick drape falling behind her shoulders, sealing the entrance. Already, the expanse of meadow and river, only visible at the wood's edge, seemed too far behind her. The voices of her companions, as they set up camp, failed to reach her.

Another unique realm within the same valley. A placid estuary. An orchard of dead trees. Windless mudflats. A labyrinth among reeds. The enchanted river.

Now this, a true riparian river woodland cloaking the valley slopes. Individual worlds occupied the Wyrm. The area couldn't have been more than ten kilometres long, but each section possessed a unique flora, texture, atmosphere, fragrance. Each had startled her, commanding the full attention of her senses.

Further up the incline, myriad ferns tottered around her knees but grew no higher. Where the fronds parted, dead wood consumed by moss, grey scale and corruptions of white fungus formed cross-stitched thickets of decay. Old bones rising from shallow graves.

Ferns and fallen branches entirely carpeted the hill as it climbed and ended in a greater darkness higher up. From the meadow, she'd seen the tops of ancient oaks, thrusting out from the summit of the valley. Around these giants, crowds of holly and hazel elbowed with leafy branches, striving for the sun. She'd no sense of where the wood ended. The boundary she would only discover by venturing higher. From there, she hoped to climb something to look down on the entire valley. The desire to do so stirred a tingle through her belly.

She moved on, upwards, in a winding meander that involved careful stepping between fallen debris and explosions of nettles.

As she wove about, from side to side but ever higher, the effects of the valley reached inside her more deeply, probing what lay beneath the busy surface of her consciousness: the instincts and impulses surviving in her species for millions of years.

With the exception of the hushed and hushing sound of the reeds, the vast silence of the Wyrm continued beneath the tree cover, heightening her apprehension at being observed. At being in the presence of something not yet immanent that issued an even greater feeling of exposure than she'd known in the wetland. Amid this night-time of trees, the watcher had drawn closer.

There was no one here but her. Yet the sense of a curious scrutiny grew with each careful step upwards. She soon likened the effect to walking into a crowded room, in which every unspeaking face had turned, in expectation, towards her.

The curse of an imagination.

Her own species was conditioned to be afraid of such places. Or, at least, wary. She knew that. This accounted for her mood, and the anxiety would pass. Unease did not possess a monopoly over her feelings either, because she also felt great excitement – the surprise and wonder of engaging in a true adventure. This exceeded caution. She was a child again. The little girl that ran ahead of her parents during family walks. Back then, the feeling of hidden eyes observing her would always bring her to sudden, fearful stops. A greater openness to the air, and a leaking of the strength from her legs, would always keep her small form still until her parents were in sight again.

Jane continued to pick her way across patches of clearer ground, between the thickets of fern and the occasional battlement of shadowy holly. When the gradient steepened, either she reached for hanging branches or they reached for her like arms, offering helping hands.

Halfway up the incline, her chest hurt and seemed full of cold stones, pressing against her lungs, shortening her breath. Her thighs burned. Sweat on her scalp and between her shoulders cooled. She shivered, stopped to rest again and looked back the way she'd come. Obscured by verdure, the treeline had entirely disappeared from sight.

She wished she'd waited for Marcus to finish erecting his tent and asked him to come along. But he was being weird, and Julian would have tagged along too. And that was the last thing she wanted.

Once she'd regained her breath, she pushed herself away from a trunk and continued towards what appeared to be a plateau above; a flatter area, or a clearing, with a solitary tree growing from it, as if a ledge had been cut into the slope. There she'd rest again before pushing to the summit.

After a momentary and horrified gape, Jane tore her eyes from the cattle carcasses. The stench of their decomposition hit her moments before she saw them.

Three animals hung from a tree limb extending over the clearing. Their rear legs were tied with the same coarse twine as had been used to suspend the bones on the creek bank. Few other details of the butchery did she allow herself to examine.

Her eyes flitted over other features in the glade. Yet she failed to make sense of what confronted her. With one hand clamped over her mouth and nose, she eventually focused upon a stone trough: a rectangular cistern, similar to what is found at the corner of a pasture on dairy farms, or – once intended for horses – outside country pubs. The trough in the clearing was hewn from stone, weathered but crudely ornate. Though clouded by green and black lichen, a swirling pattern was visible, etched into the squat ends and along the flat sides of the container. That reminded her of caskets discovered in dusty tombs and the prows of Viking ships.

Inexplicably, the white fluid brimming inside the receptacle appeared to be milk. Gallons of milk.

Moving hesitantly, Jane inched back to the trees she'd come in through, withdrawing across what she realised was well-trampled earth.

Black soil, tufts of grass and a scattering of miniature ferns, growing in disorderly plots, floored the flat clearing. Between these outcrops, the earth was compressed as if by the weight of many feet. But on her way up through the trees, she had discovered nothing even vaguely resembling a track, let alone a path. So where had so much congress emerged from? Around the glade and above it there was nothing but unmanaged foliage.

It was dank and only dimly lit from gaps in the overhead canopy, but she could see enough to understand that the shadowy plateau had not formed naturally. This ledge had been cut into the steep gradient of the hillside. Trees felled, stumps removed, the ground levelled, for earthworks that had occurred in the past. Though how distant a past was another mystery. The flat area was not maintained yet was still used for these grim and inexplicable operations involving farm animals. And milk.

Her memory returned to the creek and her recollection of the skeletal installations lining the banks. She thought, with something approaching hope, that the gruesome spectacle of the hanging cattle here was nothing more than a practical curing process, to provide materials to hang on branches within the dead wood. But then, the aisle of bones that she'd paddled through was hardly decorative; it was primitively sinister. So, on balance, even if this glade was employed for some process of reducing flesh to bone, the purpose and intention of the endeavour offered no comfort at all.

Evidence of the function of this manmade platform revolted her. Yet her revulsion was exceeded by the horrifying effect of the glade's overall aspect. Only a few stunned seconds here had been required to trigger a long dormant sensitivity; a fearful aversion that might have been a vestige of the spirituality remaining from her childhood, and her religious education in a strict Church of England primary school. Her senses cried out that she now stood in an evil place.

Once her thoughts had settled on the notion of the clearing being malignant, the very air around her seemed cooler than that of the surrounding wood. Even without the presence of the dead cattle, it seemed plausible that the morbid and ghastly atmosphere would have existed anyway, as if malevolence exuded from the very earth.

When she spotted bits of obscured stonework, at the rear of the plateau, what she'd first thought was a dreadful woodland abattoir soon assumed a pagan character. Jane adjusted her position, moving sideways around the glade's perimeter to better see these stones or rocks.

At the back of the glade, a greening stone lintel became visible. A sturdy arrangement of limestone blocks supported an arched entrance, shaping a black oval. An entrance that gave her the idea she was standing in something far stranger than a site of mutilation. The notion of a temple came to mind. And sacrifice.

As if the obscured tunnel belched an icy breath across the glade, her body temperature dropped even lower.

Though mostly obscured by brush and fallen branches, a tangle of ivy and a poisonous froth of nettles, there was a black hollow beyond the detritus. A hollow or cavity. Or the dark mouth of a lightless tunnel.

A second glance made her hope the structure was merely an old lime kiln. It certainly resembled one. Perhaps the conical roof had been consumed by verdure and soil. On either side, the sloping earthen banks had been entirely covered by moss and small plants and now blended into the woodland floor surrounding the glade. The colour of the shadowy ground even matched the stone arch and camouflaged it. Had the cows and trough not been present, she might not have noticed the tunnel behind the debris.

The notion that cattle, trough and hole were all connected by design prompted her to leave and descend the slope.

As she turned to go, Jane noticed parallel lines of rusted metal, protruding from scattered leaves and fallen twigs. Rails. Tracks extending from under the foliage blocking the mouth of the tunnel. As they crossed the clearing, the corroded tracks disappeared then reappeared in two other places.

Train or tram tracks. The miniature version used by mine wagons to ferry raw materials out of a mine. She'd seen similar on Dartmoor. Marcus had mentioned a mine in the Wyrm Valley – either in the Facebook group or during a discussion on the water, she couldn't remember which – but now understood that the area in which she found herself had been fashioned into the hill for the specific purpose of mining. It had since been repurposed for reasons that she wished to remain ignorant about. And even if she was curious, how could a site of industrial archaeology be connected with milk in an old trough? How did a closed mine fit into the practice of stringing up withered cattle, their flanks so deflated they looked as if they had starved to death on some desert plain?

Reluctantly, she returned her attention to the carcasses.

All of the surprise and terror of their ghastly demise remained fixed within the bulging, murky eyeballs. Though spotted with flies, the bluish orbs hadn't entirely dried out. Three pairs of gaping jaws further attested to an unpleasant end, the final bellows, the shuddering gasps of these creatures. All were too easily imagined.

On the shrivelled hide of the nearest carcass, she noticed lesions. Peppering one side of the beast was a cluster of holes. On the ribcage, belly and the punctured sack of the mottled and blackening udders, the wounds spread like a rash. She wondered if the beast had been killed with a shotgun. The throat had not been cut.

Whatever the cause of the animals' demise, she needed to leave the glade and go back down and tell the others about what she'd found. She must also insist that they all leave the valley without delay. But when she turned to flee the appalling glade, the enigma of the strange, beautiful and ghastly valley was only set to continue. And in a manner that paralysed her with shock. She never took more than one step.

Such was her bewilderment and fright at what had gathered around her, the breath that she'd sharply sucked in was released as a thin cry. A sound too feeble to be classed as a scream but within the same genus. She hauled in another breath and automatically said, 'What do . . .' to all of the small, pale figures that had appeared, or emerged soundlessly from wherever they had been hiding and watching her.

At first, without singling out an individual in the silent, motionless crowd, she took them all in at once. That sight was horrific enough. But it was only after she'd paid close attention to the form nearest to her – the one rising from a crouch – that Jane found herself unable to speak again.

Nothing but a scream would have formed an adequate response to what soon stood upright and close enough for her to smell it.

So Jane screamed.

10

[2–3pm]

Once his tent was up and he'd finished assembling his Jetboil camping stove, Marcus had knelt in the grass and sorted through his chilled bag for coffee. He'd bought a special cafetière that would screw onto the stove. He rummaged for the device and felt a flood of joy at the prospect of a hot cup of coffee. And that was when the scream tore the still air of the meadow in half.

In a single heartbeat, the commotion of the busy campsite became a still life.

Until Mary said, 'That was Jane.'

'Jane!' Sophie bellowed, and her raised voice broke them from their respective trances. Marcus's ears even hurt inside, though he was over ten metres away.

Mary was the first to move. She raced a few yards forward, away from the mess of a half-assembled tent, only to pull up. Gasping with pain, she raised one foot from the grass.

Marcus stood, stared at the trees and swallowed to relieve the constriction inside his throat. He waited and waited for Jane to make another noise.

She didn't.

Julian called out his own version of 'Jane', but his voice sounded frail and questioning.

'Jesus,' Nigel called out. Perhaps this was in reaction to his wife's bellow so close to his ear. Or maybe it was a delayed reaction to the frightful scream. It was hard to tell. His call was also akin to a statement of disbelief, because something else had gone wrong with the trip that he'd planned and was leading.

Marcus was running a moment before he realised he was running. Once free of the smattering of coloured tents, sleeping bags and rucksacks, he picked up his pace. Behind his back, he received an impression that Nigel and Julian were following him and joining the race across the meadow towards the trees.

Marcus only glanced back once. Nigel stumped his short legs as quickly as he could. He looked ungainly and wheezed like an asthmatic. Julian skipped about as if avoiding potholes, or the patches of dried cow dung half-hidden among stalks of grass. Mary hobbled after them. Hands on hips, Sophie stood among tents that looked half-collapsed at such a remove.

They were all so far away. Whatever had happened to Jane, Marcus would see first.

A vast wall of leaves and branches soon bloomed above him, rising up the sides of the valley to scrape at the sky. From the shadowy interior, a cold miasma of mulch and shadow sighed. And only when he was close to the wood did he realise how much time would be required to find someone inside it.

He hauled in a deep breath and, from the pit of his belly, called out, 'Jane!'

She didn't reply.

II

[2–3pm]

There seemed to be no end to the slope, no summit visible. The sides of the valley had not appeared to be so vast from the estuary and river, more like verdant strips. But all of Marcus's assumptions about the Wyrm thus far were flawed. If the way out were not determined by a steep gradient, he would have become lost. Beneath the tree canopy was perpetual dusk. Though it had only just gone two, he too easily imagined what the naked eye would see inside the wood once the sun went down. Not much.

Weaving between trunks and stepping over land mines of sharp, brittle wood, with the sea of concealing ferns whisking his shins, he was both elated and surprised when he glimpsed Jane. After no more than twenty minutes of desperate heaving and floundering amidst the undergrowth, he had located her.

At a distance, to his right on the valley slope, he fixed on the shock of her blonde hair flashing between entanglements. Hints of silver were also discernible. That was her shirt. She'd already passed his position as he made his way up, yet Jane was struggling to get down, limping or stumbling as if intoxicated with fatigue, or hurt. But at least she was descending towards the river meadow.

Bent over, hands on his thighs, Marcus called out to her. She didn't respond.

He straightened his back. Moving horizontally across the face of the slope, Marcus hurriedly zigzagged towards her. Avoiding the torrents of stinging nettles, he tore lymph and blood from his shins and calves on the bracken, twigs and thorny vines that slowed his feet. Forcing his way through the scrub angrily, he tripped twice, fell once. A thin branch stabbed inside an ear. Obstacles resembling trip wires and pits and clutching hands lay in wait beneath the ferns. He swore and sweated and kicked out, wasting energy.

By the time he was almost upon Jane and calling to her every few steps – though she'd taken no notice of his voice – she'd been reduced to a crawl to pass herself between trees and weakly clamber over obstacles. And she was crying.

Finally, he came within reach of the bedraggled figure and muttered, 'Oh, God.'

Long scratches on her uncovered arms and legs had bled for some time. Some of the blood was smudged into covering large areas of skin. Other rivulets dripped from her elbows.

This looks much worse than it really is, he told himself, in an attempt to allay the wooziness that overcame him at the sight of her distress and blood. Dragged out in clumps, her hair appeared backcombed and sprayed in place.

'Jane. Jane. Jane,' he whispered, crouching before her face. He took her hands inside his own. They were soft and moist and trembled like small white animals. 'It's me. Marcus. You're okay. We found you. You're fine . . .' He cut his reassurances short when he noticed the front of her vest. The fabric glistened blackly. That couldn't only be sweat making the blood from small cuts worse. The edges of the broad stain were scarlet. Her vest was sodden with blood. All down the front. *Blood. Shit. Blood.* But he couldn't see a gash, only a cluster of holes and runs in the fabric on either side of her sternum. Perhaps she'd fallen and impaled herself on a sharp stick. There were more than enough, artfully scattered about the woodland floor, to skewer a body. He'd cut one of his legs deep enough for his own blood to pool around the ankle of a paddling boot.

'Jane. Where are you hurt? Hey, Jane, what happened?'

She didn't appear to recognise him. She was in shock.

'Come on, come on, let's get you up, kid.' He'd never called her that before, but that's what she made him think of: a child.

As their faces drew closer together, as they had done that one time that they'd kissed for a long time outside of the Old Creel pub, he noticed her eyes. They weren't right, but dreamy and intent on something in the air that was causing her great concern. Marcus looked up and over his shoulder but saw nothing unusual.

'It's going to come from up there,' she said, or he thought she said.

'What?'

'It's all inside of me. I'm in the air. Up there.'

Gibberish. Delirium. Shock.

Marcus slipped his hands under her damp armpits and raised her to her feet. Once she was upright, there was little rigidity in her legs. She couldn't walk unassisted. He bowed and slipped one forearm behind her knees, then threaded his other arm under each of her armpits. Bracing himself to the core – and making sure that his back was straight – he rose with a groan, dead-lifting the young woman.

How could one so slender weigh so damn much?

'Guys! Nigel! Julian! Over here! Found her!' Marcus called, then panted to regain his breath. Carefully, he took one step down. Then another. He needed help, or it'd take forever to reach the meadow. He couldn't descend in a straight line because of the fallen branches and impenetrable thickets of brush. His own limbs jumped with adrenaline. He became terrified of stumbling, of dropping her.

In the distance, a murmur of the other men's voices rose. A snap of wood rang out from that direction. Like a gunshot, the noise seemed to bounce between far-off trees. Neither of the men appeared to have moved far from the bottom of the valley. Marcus wasn't sure they'd heard him. He called again but elicited no response and continued down.

When he finally stumbled into the meadow, he collapsed to his knees and laid Jane on the grass. As she came away from his front, their wet rash vests peeled apart. Mingled sweat evaporated from where their bodies had clung together for so long, leaving his stomach clammy. Her blood was smeared across his chest and arms. His wet thighs jumped, two pillars of pain.

Marcus lowered his sopping head. Working his lungs like bellows, he hauled oxygen into his brain. Motes of silver pricked his vision, descended, went out like sparks on wet ground. His arms were numb and chest tight as if bandaged. He'd never carried an adult body so far.

Slumped beside her, on all fours, he peered along the border of trees. Leafy branches groped out, curling to earth like breaking waves. Nigel and Julian were nowhere to be seen. They'd not reached him, perhaps not even heard him. They'd not assisted him carrying an injured member of their group down the uneven slope and around myriad obstacles. He didn't know what they were doing but hated them both, blackly, for not being here. When he coughed, his phlegm was sharpened by blood.

The colourful meadow was empty, save for Mary. In the distance, the oldest paddler plodded like a lame pony. Hands weaving like a tightrope walker, peering at the ground and engrossed in where she placed her feet, she hadn't even noticed him and was still ten metres shy of the valley slope. She'd hobbled towards the place he'd first entered the wood. An utterly futile gesture. She must now laboriously limp all the way back to the campsite. On that ankle, she couldn't assist with carrying Jane. The group now had two injured paddlers.

Eventually, and by the time Marcus had recovered sufficiently to sit up and attend to Jane, Julian appeared. Stepping out of the treeline, he emerged as if delicately alighting from a bus, some way off. When he heard Marcus call his name, he stopped and looked in the right direction, then returned his attention to the trees and said something that Marcus never caught.

'Hurry up!' Marcus roared. 'She needs help! She's bleeding!' He was too winded to get more out.

Julian gingerly stepped about and moved slowly, either as if he didn't want to arrive, or as if he was taking great care not to twist his thin ankles.

Marcus blinked sweat from stinging eyes and peered across the meadow in the direction of the campsite. That was visible, about one hundred metres to his right. He couldn't see Sophie and had no sense he'd moved that far, sideways, along the valley side. He couldn't have done, surely? He'd ascended, more or less, straight up. He'd then worked his way, horizontally, across to Jane. But surely not so far from where he'd entered the trees. What did it matter? He had her. They were in the open.

'What happened to her?' Julian asked in a voice bordering a whisper. His blanched, pointy features gleamed with sweat, and he wafted a hand at the tiny flies orbiting his ear.

'How would I bloody know? I just found her. Up there, trying to make her way down. She was crawling. She's bleeding. Chest wound, I think.'

'Chest?'

'Yes, chest! Where's Nigel? We need to get her back to the tents and get help. Carrying her down that slope nearly finished me. Did you not hear me calling you?'

Julian looked away, over his shoulder, and shrugged. As if on cue, Nigel barrelled from the trees and stumbled into the grass. He emerged close to where Julian came out.

'I don't have my phone,' Marcus said, breathlessly. 'Call 999. Ambulance. Now. Coastguard's no good because the estuary's low. She'll have to be flown out.'

'My phone's by the tent,' Julian said. 'Like yours,' he added, to defend himself against the glare that Marcus threw at him. 'Anyway, a phone's no good. There's no signal here. Nothing at all.'

'Well, get on your bloody VHF. This is an air ambulance job.'

They couldn't be reached from the sea for another nine hours. He'd once liked the idea of being so isolated, because it made the expedition more of an adventure. The estuary was too shallow for yachts or power boats. At low tide, he guessed that it would be possible to wade across the channel on foot. So, another of its chief attractions for Marcus was its unsuitability for anything but sea kayaks. Despite this, if their timings had been out, they would have been forced to drag their boats for miles, across the shallows at low tide, to get onto firm land. An ordeal that would have included traversing the soft, sinking, stinking mud of the wetland and creek to reach the inland river. Their planned route had only been feasible for one third of the incoming tide.

Nigel had got the navigational elements right. Marcus had made sure to check his readings of the tidal flow, tides and the distance at an average paddling speed of three miles per hour. Each variable had needed to be precisely calculated for them to hit the vital period of high water, with sufficient depth to cross the estuary and reach the river. They had made it. But only just.

Now, there was this situation. And they couldn't paddle back out until around midnight.

'What is it? What's up with her?' Nigel asked, as he drew nearer, though his tone was dismissive as if Jane had merely done something stupid that was now inconveniencing him. The man was sweating so much that his hair was plastered to his scalp and gleamed like a shower cap. His rash vest would need wringing out like a wet flannel.

'Injured,' Julian said to his friend. 'Chest wound, apparently.'

'Chest? How?'

'He doesn't know. Hasn't got a clue,' Julian said, as if Marcus was, somehow, at fault.

'Where the fuck were you two?' Marcus roared. 'Did you even get up that bloody slope?'

Nigel glared at him, his eyes shrinking to shards of jet, embedded inside a crimson face.

'I've just carried her all the way down. Could have used some bloody help!'

'Well, you shouldn't have just taken off,' Nigel said, in a quiet, sullen voice.

'What?'

'Jane! Is she all right?' Mary called from where she was now dragging one leg towards them.

'No!' Marcus called back. 'She's hurt.'

'What?' Mary cried out, and then again, 'Oh, God! How?'

'Bleeding. She's in shock!' Marcus said. 'Julian, run and get on your VHF. Tell Sophie to get my first-aid kit. Rear hold. Green bag.'

Julian looked to Nigel as if for permission to leave.

'Did you hear me?' Marcus shouted. 'Move! Now!'

Julian finally took off, though not as quickly as Marcus would have liked. 'Run, for God's sake!'

Nigel chewed the moustache hair extending over his top lip. His body was at a standstill but panic inflamed his small eyes. He was studying the wet mess that was Jane's bloodied chest.

Marcus stripped off his rash vest. His shirt might stop the bleeding. Blood still pooled in the crevices of Jane's shirt. The girl was breathing but her eyes had closed. He wasn't sure when she'd passed out.

Carefully, he peeled the sodden fabric from her stomach.

'What? What are you doing?' Mary screamed from where she'd managed to hobble, while being too far away to see what was going on. The note of alarm in her voice suggested that she suspected Marcus of impropriety.

Beneath his fingers, the polyester peeled then slopped off Jane's bare tummy. Her abdomen was pinked with smears and droplets of watery blood. Marcus tugged the sopping vest up further, eased it around her ribs and tucked the hem into her armpits. A process similar to peeling a wetsuit from soaking skin. As he'd worked the drenched cloth off her chest, the voices of the others had continued to bark. Cries that infiltrated his frantic thoughts and lit new fires.

'What are you doing? Marcus, stop!' Mary had screamed, from where she fell about in clumpy grass after an attempt to hobble faster.

Nigel did little more than turn his head to bellow, 'Chest wound!' at the older woman.

Mary, her face a chalky mask of horror and shock, muttered, 'How? But how?' before her voice died away.

As if stained by berries, Jane's sports bra was purple. The true colour of the garment was flesh-toned; Marcus could see the straps. But it was the punctures on her breasts that made him dizzy.

From the curve of her bosom to the top of her bra, Jane might have been repeatedly stabbed with nails. Punctured. Pairs of deep holes clustered around her nipples. Black pits that welled with blood so fresh that Marcus felt sick to his boots.

Bites. They were bites.

Marcus covered Jane's chest with his wet rash vest and applied pressure. Jane didn't respond. Her cheeks and forehead were speckled with a milky sweat. Hair was plastered to her forehead. Around her ears the strands were dark. 'Water. You have water?' Marcus asked.

Nigel didn't answer.

Mary finally reached them. To traverse the last few metres of ground, she'd been reduced to shuffling across the grass on her backside. Marcus realised her ankle must be in horrendous shape. He shook his head. She should not even be here. Her recent serious illness aside, Mary's inclusion had most surprised him because of her paddling speed. She'd always been sluggish, and this trip required two five-hour tide-sensitive stretches. But Sophie liked her and must have insisted on her inclusion, as well as his participation. The previous year, Mary had lost her husband. No one had the heart to question her being there.

Their problems were multiplying. Thank God for VHF radios. They had three in the group: his, Nigel's and Julian's.

Once Jane's horrible wounds had been covered, Nigel inched closer. He bent forward and winced. The man looked spent; his face drained to the colour of cream cheese.

Marcus drew in a deep breath and swept his mind of broken glass. 'We're two men down. You'll have to help me carry her back to camp. Yeah?'

'Of course,' Nigel said, abruptly.

'Air ambulance. That's what we'll need for her. Someone can come back for Mary.'

'Stop panicking!' Nigel suddenly barked. Saliva speckled Marcus's face.

Marcus blinked, then frowned. 'I'm trying to—'

'You're making everything worse with your guesswork! You don't have a clue what's wrong with her! You probably shouldn't have moved her! And stop telling me what to do! Are you the paddle leader? No, you are not! Stop trying to take over! I'll handle the rescue from here. Get her under the arms. I'll take her feet.'

The easy bit.

Much of his shock had switched to how unstable Nigel appeared in the situation, but this was no time to argue. With his biceps looped under her armpits, Marcus lifted Jane from the ground. And, at least, in this position, he wouldn't have to look into Nigel's furious face.

Under the blue firmament, in a silence broken only by their gasps, they carried the unconscious woman across the flower-strewn meadow.

12

[2–3pm]

'Music, is it? Can you hear? Up there. We're going. Up... to the mountains. Graves. Houses? Made of stone...' Jane's eyes had briefly opened. As she stared at the sky with the intensity of a fanatic, the blue of her irises seemed too pale. 'I don't want to go.'

'It's okay, my love. Okay. Just relax,' Mary said, and applied a dampened travel towel to Jane's burning forehead. She was moistening the fabric with water from a drinking bottle. 'She's got a terrible temperature,' Mary said softly to Sophie, who knelt on the other side of the injured girl. Jane had been placed on a thin inflatable mattress and covered with a sleeping bag. Marcus's first-aid kit was open beside Jane's hips.

By the time Mary had limped into the campsite, Marcus and Sophie had stopped the bleeding with gauze pads, affixing them with surgical tape. They'd also covered the bitten area with an antiseptic salve that Marcus could still smell. A scent from his childhood signalling the end of fun.

On arrival, Mary's maternal compassion had kicked in and she'd become proprietary. She'd nudged Marcus aside.

'Keep giving her water to sip,' Sophie said.

Now that the two women were attending to Jane, Marcus's spirits marginally improved because of the sheer relief he felt.

He was grateful for being able to stand up and move away from the dried blood, clammy skin, the alabaster face, the wide, unfocused glare. Mary had two grown-up sons; Sophie a three-year-old boy. There was a confidence and ease in their ministrations that his gingerly efforts lacked.

Once the exertion of carrying Jane to the campsite had ended, he'd squatted and sweated next to her unresponsive body. His mind had been like a table covered in delicate crockery, some stacked. The table had been knocked hard. The contents, like his thoughts, had tumbled and scattered. Items had fallen from the top and smashed below. As he'd tried to retrieve and straighten the bits of his reason that remained unbroken, the barrage of questions from the others, which he had no answers for, had distracted him. The table was knocked over again.

Gaining a little space from Jane and the concerned frowns of the other two women, he could finally breathe. Even think. And that was paramount, so that he could figure out what to do next.

Marcus was forced to reconsider the place in which they now found themselves marooned by crisis. The Wyrm remained as wild as the remotest areas within the county. Like the other coombes in South Devon, between prehistoric ice ages, thawing tundra and moor ice had created epochal landslides of stony rubble. Vast torrents sweeping towards a primaeval sea. Debris had worn this groove into a younger earth. His knowledge of how managed the valley had been since, beyond a brief timeline, was scant. But there was a manor house somewhere. Further up.

From the Countryside Trust website, he'd gleaned, from a mere four paragraphs devoted to the valley, that there had been mining in the 1800s for tin. An estate had once encompassed all of the Wyrm Valley. A family seat for the Waddetons after the arrival of William of Orange in 1688. From then until the Second World War, when the property became a military hospital, the property had changed hands repeatedly. Agatha Christie had once been a frequent visitor to the manor. Some of her stories were said to have been inspired by the Wyrm and the estate.

The valley changed hands again in the 1950s and the manor house was converted into a luxury hotel. That didn't last much further than the middle of the next decade, when the defunct hotel was repurposed as a private care home. That had better luck and endured for several decades.

Subsequent owners of the valley, in the mid-90s, turned the manor into an organic farm, twinned with a mind-body-and-spirit retreat. It was also a home for artisans and artists who were granted residencies. The studios and wellness facility had since closed, though the mothballing was recent. But around this time in its history, the valley was classed as an area of conservation.

Now, the land and the actual water were in private hands once again, those of an entity called Green Leaf. The valley was still listed as an area of conservation and a rewilding project but had also attained the classification of a site of scientific study. Some version of the mindfulness programme had continued for a while, under the auspices of Green Leaf, and then closed.

Green Leaf's business address was listed near Totnes. Marcus knew nothing else about them other than that they didn't allow visitors. But he suspected that the paucity of online information about the company was deliberate and served to discourage outside interest. He'd not imagined rich hippies from Totnes, however, being militant about private property. Another hunch that had encouraged them to paddle here.

As he wiped another wave of sweat from his face, Sophie roared at her husband, 'Have you got that bloody radio working?'

Nigel stood beside Julian, near the boats, twisting the switches on top of his radio, or jabbing small buttons, before pressing the unit against an ear, desperate for static. Beside him, Julian held two smartphones skyward, praying for a signal.

Against these futile gestures, the width of the river shrank with the outgoing tide. Under the opposite bank, wet shingle now lay exposed, gleaming golden. The door on paddling out of the estuary had closed some time ago; probably while Marcus was stumbling on the slope, with Jane's inert body in his arms.

'There's no reception,' Nigel muttered. 'At all.'

'Nothing,' Julian added. 'Dead zone. Just crazy. Phones, I understand. No signal down here is not unusual. But radios? I just don't get it!'

'PLBs?' Marcus called out to the group. 'Because I think this would be the time to set one off.' He didn't own a personal locator beacon, but Julian did.

As if he hadn't heard Marcus, Julian kept quiet for a few seconds, before muttering, 'We'd have no clue if the signal had been received. They're one-way—'

'Yeah, I know what they are, Julian,' Marcus said, his voice on the edge of shouting. 'But this is why equipment checks are useful before people set off on three-day paddles!'

Nigel's back stiffened. He didn't turn around.

'Well, you could buy one,' Julian said, smirking humourlessly. 'Instead of relying on me all the time.'

Marcus wanted to tear at the man's beard until the valley was filled with the sound of ripping Velcro.

'Must have been a snake,' Mary said, her voice breaking. 'Bleeding's not stopping and now she's swelling up. Sophie, look.'

Sophie shook her head. 'It'd have to have been a whole nest. She's covered in bites.'

'Adders?' Mary asked. 'Aren't they poisonous?'

'But why all over her chest and nowhere else?'

'Adders are very rare and shy,' Julian chipped in, from the riverside.

'Then what the bloody hell did this to her?' Sophie shrieked at Julian. 'She's covered. They're deep.'

Julian flinched. 'Have you considered venomous pet snakes? People release them into the wild. They breed.'

Even if there had been any validity to Julian's speculations, his theory felt inappropriate, misplaced and diversionary.

'I don't think it was a snake,' Marcus said.

Sophie and Mary peered at him, expectantly, awaiting elaboration.

'Her upper arms. On her triceps and forearms. The back of her arms. I noticed the marks when we cut the rash vest off her. Indents. Little bruises. Like fingermarks.'

'What?' Mary cried out. She and Sophie immediately raised Jane's arms and began inspecting her skin.

'Here,' Mary said. 'I can see. But she might have just banged herself.'

'And here,' Sophie concurred. 'No. Someone . . . It does look like someone held onto her.' She looked at Marcus in a way that made him uncomfortable, hot and defensive.

'What?' Mary cried out again. Then peered at the valley side. 'But who would . . .'

'If hands made those marks, they must have been bloody small,' Marcus said. 'Like . . . baby hands.'

'I've heard it all now. I think you better keep quiet, Marcus.' Nigel said this without turning his head. 'I've told you before. You don't know what happened to her. So just shut up.'

Marcus took a breath, then turned his back on the fraying discussion. He walked into the meadow, his fists clenched so hard that he was in danger of cutting his palms with his fingernails.

He peered into the sky. No air ambulance was landing here for a while. That much he'd already accepted. They'd told a few people in other kayaking groups about where they were heading for three days. No paddling peers, or his colleagues at the gym, would even raise an eyebrow until late on the third day, or maybe even the fourth day. That much he knew. Sophie and Nigel's childcare arrangement would trigger an alarm when Mum and Dad didn't arrive on time. But that was still two days away. Nonetheless, he would now keep all thoughts and speculations to himself.

Either that, or they'd all be looking at three injured paddlers once he'd punched Nigel out of his shoes.

One of them needed to run for help.

He'd do it.

Marcus peered up the valley. If he were to climb one of the valley sides and eventually emerge from the woodland, he had no idea where he might find the nearest occupied farm building outside of the Wyrm. Apparently, there was a fence corralling the valley. Someone had told Mary; one of her friends who'd once tried to hike in the valley.

He needed to head upriver to the top of the valley and the buildings.

The northern side of the meadow ended in a cascade of scrub, candy-pink buddleia, willow and alder trees. This border stretched from the wooded slopes to the river's edge.

Cows used this meadow. He'd seen their dung. There must be a gate or cattle path that led out of the pasture. The river levels would soon be too low for a kayak to paddle any higher, particularly with the current pitted against the boat. Running would be quicker.

His sense of the valley's dimensions and contours was mostly derived from coastal maps and apps. He'd referred to them again, the weekend prior to the trip. Shallow water and wetland in the estuary had been marked with symbols on both paper and digitised charts. As was the weir, deep inside the valley, at its northern peak. Somewhere up there was also the business end of the Wyrm: the manor house and several outlying buildings that must have once been used as a hospital, hotel, care home, and for guests of the latter-day retreat.

At the peak of the valley, he'd also noticed a thin white line on an ordnance survey map, indicating a single, probably private, road. A minor road that scored its way down from between two distant villages to the top of the Wyrm Valley. He knew what those minuscule white lines meant in Devon – hedge-choked sinuses, pot-holed surfaces, insufficient passing places. Progress in and out would be slow.

And how would paramedics get from there to Jane down here? Beyond this service road, the only feasible access into the valley was from the air. The sea was no longer an option.

The emergency services would have to either land a chopper in the meadow or drive down that scratch of a lane at the top of the valley.

He surmised that there must be someone in the manor house, and a landline. An air ambulance could be called from there. He didn't know, with any precision, how far away the buildings were; but they couldn't be, from what he remembered of the map, more than a few kilometres north.

He took a deep breath and called, 'Nigel?'

'What?' Nigel replied, sharply, without turning his head. He was fiddling with the second radio.

'You have a map? Of the valley?'

Nigel didn't answer.

'Fuck's sake. What about you, Julian? Map?'

Julian looked at Nigel and was thinking of saying something about him not being the paddle leader and that having a map was, therefore, not his responsibility. He demurred and instead said, 'Did you not think to bring one either?'

Marcus clenched his jaw. One of them should have carried a map; though now, to be fair, with everyone so over-reliant on phones, he saw few paper maps on paddles.

From his memory of the valley's topography, the manor house had been positioned close to the river, though he couldn't recall on which side. But there was no other option: he must find the building on foot. 'I'm going to jog to the estate buildings. Someone must work or live onsite. This conservation project must have staff. Cows are kept here. I've got their shit on one leg. The owners will have a phone. A building of that size can't be derelict. I'll take my phone. See if I can get a signal higher up.'

No one answered him. Annoyed, Marcus turned towards Nigel and Julian. 'Hey! The radios are useless. Phones too.

They're not going to start working because you're waving them around like magic wands. I think we've established—'

Julian cocked his head back and squinted to deliver a correction. 'A message might still be received. There could be a flicker of a signal without us knowing.'

'Fine. Well, send a bloody text message into the void. I'm going to find help.'

Mary asked, 'Can you be quick?'

Marcus sighed. 'I'm not going to stroll. I'll run.'

He'd already paddled for five hours, carried Jane down the valley side, then borne most of her weight across the meadow, while Nigel had huffed and puffed, merely holding her ankles. Adrenaline and deep reserves of energy would be required to power the next leg of the ordeal.

'I'll come with you,' Nigel announced. He threw all three radios onto the ground and turned, his face white with anger.

The idiot might have just broken the radios, but Marcus restrained himself.

'Careful,' Julian shrieked, and fell upon his discarded handset.

As much as he wished to, Marcus didn't say: *the last thing I need is a fractious, competitive, out-of-shape man holding me up.* Instead, he said, 'I'll be quicker on my own.'

'Not your decision!' Nigel roared back.

Sophie and Mary jumped and turned their heads.

'Mary can stay with Jane,' Nigel barked. 'It doesn't need bloody five of us. Julian can stay here and keep trying the radios.' He turned to his friend. 'Maybe you should get up the valley side and try for a signal higher. Yes, now I think of it, get on that, Jules.'

A wounded expression transformed Julian's face, as if a betrayal had just been inflicted on him. He was aghast at the suggestion that he should enter woodland in which Jane had been savaged. 'There? I don't think anyone should go near the trees until we can establish what—'

'Cross the river then. Try the other side. It can't all be full of bloody snakes, or whatever the fuck bit her! Sophie and I will go and get help. As leader, I'll make the report.'

Monumental

Marcus walked to his half-unpacked gear. He dropped a water bottle in a dry bag. Added his phone. He then collected his radio from where Nigel had cast it down in a tantrum. Slipped it inside the dry bag. 'Let's shift it.'

Sophie stood up. 'How far away is this bloody hippy retreat, or whatever the hell it is?'

'A few kilometres, from what I can remember,' Marcus said. 'Maybe five, but not much more, at a guess.'

Nigel shook his head. 'That's all it is. A guess! I think we've had enough of *guesses*. I think it's longer.'

'If you'd brought a fucking map, paddle leader, we'd fucking know!' The outburst roared from between Marcus's teeth before he could rein the comment back in.

Nigel turned to Marcus, his shoulders and thick neck tensing. As if violence wasn't far away, his hairy arms bent at the elbow and tensed. His purpling face dipped, as if he were a bull preparing to charge. 'If I'd had my way, you wouldn't even be here! You are obstructing a rescue! You need to step aside and stop causing panic!'

'Oh, for God's sake, Nigel! Will you give it a rest?' Mary screamed.

They all stopped moving and speaking, and stared at Mary. They'd never heard her raise her voice before.

'Jane is seriously hurt. She'd still be in those bloody trees if Marcus hadn't found her. And carried her all the way out. So stop bloody contradicting him and listen to him! And get going! I'm not leaving her for a moment. I'll be here. So go! Now!'

13

[3–4pm]

*H*e'd been running at a swift trot before the sudden appearance of the vast stone dome brought Marcus to a standstill. Astonishment left him dazed.

He bent over. Depleted lungs inside his aching chest forced him to heave at the air to catch his breath. Against the palms of his hands, his thigh muscles quivered. But he never took his eyes off *it*.

What was it?

Wonder soured to unease.

Since they'd crossed the estuary, his reservations about the valley had evolved into a persistent anxiety. But neither the orchard of bones, nor the fact that Jane had been bitten into insensibility and was gravely ill, was an adequate primer for *this*.

Running ahead, he'd left Nigel and Sophie ten minutes before. After they'd set off from the campsite, with Marcus out front, the couple had stopped jogging almost immediately. Winded and red in the face, Nigel had been reduced to a shuffle. Sophie had stayed with her husband but seemed displeased with the arrangement. Had she run off with Marcus, the tense situation, and everything else between them, would have been made far worse.

As they readied to leave camp, Nigel had said, 'We should stay together.' He'd also adopted a stern expression, intending to bring Marcus to heel. His request had nothing to do with rescue protocol, Marcus knew. Nigel simply couldn't abide the idea of Marcus making decisions or playing a more prominent role in the crisis than him. *Because, even now, in this mess, his resentment continued.*

'Jane's in a bad way. We've wasted enough time,' Marcus had replied and launched into a sprint. Once clear of the first meadow, he'd slowed to a trot.

The valley had narrowed as he'd headed north. Crossing acres of river pasture, neatly sectioned into plots by natural barriers of trees and scrub that functioned like hedgerows, he'd kept the river on his right. The fact that the land was managed and used for grazing had encouraged him about finding help and enabled him to run faster.

Thickets of alder and willow had resumed their monopoly of the riverbanks. Only glimpses of the water had been possible; the surface was black with shadows cast from the banks. To his left, the wooded slope had drawn nearer as the valley narrowed into an arrowhead. A nervy wariness that he'd fought to suppress had grown as the treeline encroached; he'd passed close enough for half-lit spaces to become visible, tunnelling between pale trunks and rifling upwards and into darkness.

At the end of the river meadows and grazing, he'd picked up a dusty track. An avenue of sloe and larch trees formed an arch, their canopy dimming the sun. Bushes, nettles and coils of blackberry vine marshalled his jog. Either side of the furrow, the parched soil was rutted by tyres. Evidence of narrow vehicles that bumped up and down the valley. More reassurance that human occupation was near.

He'd not trotted far through the juvenile wood, however, before a clearing widened ahead of him. It was when the dirt track had concluded, and his feet sank into lush grass, that he was brought to a standstill. He'd simply sleeved the sweat from his brow, bent over and stared.

At *this*.

He'd thought of the discoveries made by conquistadors, as they'd hacked through South American jungles to find temples swallowed by vines. But this was England and everything above ground had already been discovered, and he simply couldn't guess what the purpose of the structure was, nor what it depicted or might contain. Not at first sight. Nor after staring at it for a minute.

Before he'd entered a circular area of grass containing the edifice, Marcus hadn't seen the top of the conical structure. Scrub had blocked his line of sight. He wondered if anyone walking up the valley was supposed to suddenly happen upon this place, behold it and be startled to a reverent awe. If this had been the architect's true intention, then he had succeeded.

The Wyrm continued to be a haven of undisclosed spectacle. The valley kept its curiosities secret. An extraordinary achievement in a county festooned with walkers' paths, holiday lets and villages.

The monument of silent stone suggested that it was an imitation of a construction from another, earlier period, though from what era was an additional mystery. A lustre, not yet tarnished by age and weather, glowed beneath the cloudless sky. The stone blocks were relatively new. The curved walls hadn't stood for aeons.

Limestone. Built like a cairn. A giant cairn. Or was it a kiln? As tall as the highest oaks of the valley's slopes, the mound of interlocking stones commanded a height of at least twenty metres. And so distracting was the sight of the stone mound, squatting in maintained grounds, that a few more seconds elapsed before Marcus noticed the wooden posts.

Wooden pillars, at equal distances apart, formed a ring, enclosing the oval paddock. A ceramic planter had been placed at the foot of each pole.

Marcus kept close to the perimeter and inspected the nearest post. A tree trunk, as high as a telegraph pole, the branches cut away. Stripped of bark too, to allow for the design to be carved into the unclothed timber. Spirals and concentric circles. Each visible pole was decorated in the same way. Cement anchored the totems into the earth. A wooden henge that encircled the windowless stone structure.

To what purpose?

Marcus also noticed what the large bowl that had been placed at the foot of the nearest pole was filled with: milk. A glazed clay container filled with milk. Unpasteurised, he suspected. Going scummy and pestered by flies. The next bowl and the next and the next and the next contained milk. At least ten litres in each bowl.

The ground here was tended with care, even reverence. The grass had been neatly shorn around the posts and, what increasingly reminded him of a vast stone hive, this great centrepiece with no discernible purpose. He'd never come across a building like it before, let alone one surrounded by a wooden henge and bowls brimming with milk. He struggled to associate the shape of the structure with agriculture, or industry. Kilns he'd seen, but they were a fraction of the size of this giant. Maybe it was used for storage? For storing what, though? Grain? He could see no doors.

The arrangement and symmetry of the site and its artefacts were artful, clearly planned to appear ceremonial. But the construction had the air of a replica – though what had been recreated? Something pagan, or Neolithic?

Outside of the totems, the trees and scrub grew wild, forming a second circle. But the entanglements had been cut back to prevent the wilderness encroaching upon the clearing. At the verge, between the two circles – the inner demarked by the staves, the outer of trimmed foliage – a shallow ditch had been dug and since clothed with a pelt of short grass. A sort of moat, separating the timber dolmens from the slow onslaught of nature. He assumed the trench, like the totems, encircled the entire paddock.

Here, the woodland on the left side of the river was connected to the valley slope. But the foliage was younger.

He suspected that the scrub and trees had been encouraged to grow unruly and erase the meadowland that extended to the wetland. If his hunch was correct, with the exception of the circular paddock and moat, this area had been rewilded.

After the wetland and the suffocating reed beds, they'd paddled through thick riparian woodland. To Marcus, each of these unique areas now resembled natural defences. Travelling from the direction of the sea, the lower layers of the valley were like successive walls enclosing a castle keep, or this dome. And here, the overgrown wood's encroachment offered the curious structure another natural concealment, from each end of the valley and from either side. This place had been created, then hidden. It had been camouflaged by rewilding.

As Marcus continued to gaze and dawdle about the clearing, he heard Nigel and Sophie's feet scraping the dirt track that had delivered him here. Louder scuffles were soon followed by the noise of Nigel's wheezing.

The idea of another confrontation added weight to Marcus's fatigue, so he set off to inspect the structure. Aware that he'd become distracted from getting help for Jane, he planned to be quick, but soon hesitated again, and before he'd reached the nearest section of curved wall. Because of the stench.

A miasma of decomposition.

14

[3–4pm]

'What the hell is this?' Sophie called out, as Marcus appeared from behind the far side of the dome. She and Nigel were standing on the turf between the structure and where they'd entered the clearing.

Marcus nodded at the cairn. 'I don't advise getting too close. Smells as if something died inside. Recently.'

'What is it?' she asked.

'No idea. There's a door on the other side. It's padlocked.' The sole entrance was made of thick wood; the top, bottom and each side of the door flush with the frame; the hinges drilled deep into stone.

Marcus had also noticed a series of small apertures randomly patterned across the curving walls and slotted in at various heights. They reminded him of the slits designed for archers in castle walls, though he wasn't inclined to brave the stench and peer through one of the vertical fissures. Little of the vast, unlit interior would have been visible anyway. He presumed the holes were for ventilation.

Nigel ambled to the structure, peering up, as if in awe at a site of antiquity. 'Impressive feat of stonemasonry.'

'I'm going to carry on,' Marcus said to the couple.

'We'll come too.' Sophie looked directly at him, her eyes lively with . . . *what?* Marcus tried to read her expression. It was stern, as usual, but he sensed the presence of a playful disbelief, as if she were surprised by his behaviour. Mocking, he thought, his attempts to create distance between him and them. The couple were odd fish; each of them had a default setting of disagreeable and provocative, yet still expected folks to stick around and accept being on the receiving end of it.

Marcus turned to the far side of the paddock. An opening in the trees and scrub was visible, wider than the one at the opposite end. What he could see of the path out was neat and grassy. On either side of the prospective exit avenue, carved wooden staves, planted at regular intervals, continued to poke at the sky.

'Dear God!' Nigel called, drawing back from the curved walls. 'Bloody stinks.'

'I did say,' Marcus muttered.

Nigel hurried away from the cairn, one forearm covering his nose and mouth. 'What the bloody hell are they doing here?'

'Let's find out,' Marcus suggested, heading for the path out.

Sophie followed Marcus. 'It must have some connection to all of those bones,' she offered to the two men. 'I mean, skeletons hanging from trees? It's disgusting. All of it. What on earth possessed them to do this? It's . . . barbaric. Savage.'

'Let's hope they're sane enough to use phones. I still can't get a signal,' Nigel said.

Marcus didn't have one either; he'd felt compelled to check his phone after catching a whiff of the reeking cairn. His radio offered nothing but static on any channel. No phone reception: *that*, he could understand – this was rural Devon – but, as Julian had posited, an unresponsive VHF was inexplicable. He'd never known his radio fail to get a signal, even three kilometres out at sea. They had three unresponsive units inside the valley.

'Animals. There must be dead animals in there. Do you think?' Sophie pressed, casting another look over her shoulder. 'You said there's a door. Locked?'

Unable to avoid doing so, the two men exchanged glances that made them both uncomfortable. 'Even if it wasn't locked, I don't think I'd have opened it,' Marcus said.

'Jesus Christ,' Sophie said, her irritation resurfacing. 'How long is this bloody valley? Jane could be—' she paused '— much worse and we wouldn't even know.'

'We're doing all we can,' Nigel said, irritated by his wife's suggestion that such eventualities had not been planned for.

Marcus kept quiet. At this point, he felt that anything he said would incite one of them, maybe both of them, to launch into accusations and contradictions. He was feeling the strain too: of worrying about Jane, of constantly being startled by what the valley contained but also confounded by it.

'I thought this was supposed to be a retreat for hippies,' Sophie said. 'Bloody commune or something.'

'That closed. That's why I planned the paddle,' Nigel said, as if compelled to defend his arrangements. 'It's a long valley—'

'Tell me about it!'

'I thought if we camped by the estuary, we'd not be noticed. Not be doing any harm.'

Nigel was almost quoting Marcus, verbatim, from when he'd first proposed the trip, during the previous summer. Had Jane not been lying beside a river and gibbering, covered in sweat, with a swollen, bitten chest, he'd have been even more irritated by Nigel's taking ownership of his ideas.

The further away they ventured, the more he thought about Jane and what else they might have done to ease her condition. No matter how hard he rinsed his memory, he couldn't remember anything useful, or related to her injury, from the multitude of health-and-safety, first-aid and rescue courses that he'd taken in the last ten years. He'd covered hypothermia, dislocated shoulders, unconscious paddlers with lungs full of seawater, even heart attacks and strokes on the water. For bites and an infection, he had nothing.

'There's almost no information available about this place,' Marcus said. 'I've looked a few times.'

'It's private property. They don't have to disclose anything,' Nigel said.

Sophie threw her hands into the air. 'Is it any bloody wonder they don't?'

Marcus suppressed an urge to laugh, to relieve the tension oppressing his mind. 'Nothing lasts or sticks here. So fuck only knows why this and the bones are here. Far as I know, Green Leaf started a rewilding project. And I can see where they've made a start on that. But I've never even seen a picture from inside the valley on Instagram. How is that possible?'

Nigel raised his hands in exasperation. 'That thing back there, the dome, wasn't built in a day. Must have cost a fortune to put up.'

'Agreed,' Marcus said. 'And look at this.' He pointed out the grassy avenue they now hurried along. Perfectly groomed banks, of an identical height, ran along either side of the path. At the foot of the raised earthen banks, the wooden totems reared, each etched with more rings and circles. Behind the raised banks, the crowding verdure had been cut back to prevent any extension of greenery over the neat path. 'Earthworks. This ground has been levelled. Banks built. A henge installed. A path running through the middle. But hidden within the greenery. The aisle has a name. It's called a . . .'

'Where's Julian when you need him? He'd bloody know,' Sophie muttered.

'I've seen one in Dorset. Neolithic, I'm sure. A cursus! That's it. That's what they're called, I'm sure. And this isn't original. It looks new and it's maintained. The originals had a ceremonial purpose. It's thought they were used for some kind of procession. But no one really knows.' Marcus pointed at the sides of the path. 'Tyre treads. See? In the grass. Here and here. So, something is driven along here to that cairn thing.'

'Quad bike,' Nigel said. 'We had one for the business.' He nodded ahead. 'Looks like the valley opens up a bit. See it?'

The enclosed avenue concluded thirty metres or so ahead of them. Beyond the avenue, part of a field or pasture was visible.

Monumental

'Finally.' Sophie checked her watch. 'We've been walking forty minutes! Please let this bloody manor, or whatever it is, be here. It's got to be.'

At exactly the same time, they all broke into a trot.

15

[4–5pm]

As they trotted out of the cursus, they forgot about their various discomforts: the sweat making their shorts and vests cling, the blisters that had formed and burst on feet still encased in wet paddling shoes, their tired legs, and even, in Nigel's case, breathlessness. At the end of the grassy avenue, between the raised banks and the attendant wooden poles and curtailed scrub, the Wyrm Valley broadened into a verdant floodplain. Marcus imagined that they'd stepped into Middle Earth. Or, at least, back into Devon between the wars. A vista exalted by unseasonal sunlight.

Sheltered by woodland to either side, the upper portion of the valley was entirely cultivated. Across the river to the east, the land was divided into neat squares. Rows of crops grew from red soil. Fences corralled two orchards.

On their left, on the western side of the valley, pasture for grazing extended to the treeline and slopes. Wizened cows turned their heads and considered the group with weary eyes. Marcus wondered if their emaciated condition was indicative of breed, or if they were ill.

In the distance beyond the grazing, the broad, flat facade of a manor house stood sentinel over the valley: three storeys of yellow and brown stone, glittering with mullioned windows. Chimney stacks bristled among dull slate tiles. Two wings with peaked roofs flanked the centre block. The former family seat of the Waddetons. In other times, this vast building must also have served as the military hospital, hotel, care home and retreat.

Stone steps, cut between two columns, led to the darkness of an open door, capped with a triangular pediment. The property would contain two dozen rooms. Or more. Behind the building, and on each side, green waves of woodland surged from the valley slope. A large rock – perhaps even a sculpture, or large Neolithic standing stone – had been placed on the front lawn.

The face of the building was angled towards them. As if intuiting scrutiny from the many panes of black glass, Marcus felt uncomfortably conspicuous. Since they'd landed at midday, he had been aware that they were on private land but untroubled; now he was fully conscious of their trespass. Guilt crept coldly through his gut. Shame warmed his skin. They weren't supposed to be looking at this. And they weren't, he suspected, supposed to have seen anything inside this valley. Perhaps, Marcus mused, we English are programmed to feel deference before the grand and majestic. Was there any greater signifier of the class you did not belong to than property? Whoever lived here possessed enough wealth, and entitlement, to buy an entire valley, as well as the water that ran through it.

As if experiencing a similar discomfort, Nigel said, 'I know we have a critically injured paddler, but this could get embarrassing.'

'At least we bloody found it. I thought the valley was never going to end,' his wife added, breathlessly, though even her tone was subdued.

Nigel walked on. 'Come on, let's get this over with. House is still some way off. But at least the bloody door's open.'

They walked rapidly, almost jogged, along a worn path of lighter grass, close to the riverbank. The water was shallow, snaking over pale stones and smooth boulders; practically a stream this far up the valley.

'Raspberries, there,' Sophie said, pointing across the water. 'Blackberries and gooseberries too, I think. That's what they're growing. Soft fruits. And that bit, facing south, looks like a bloody vineyard.'

'Market garden or something. These types are into that sort of thing,' her husband contributed, wheezing.

'Too bloody big for that,' Sophie said. 'It's a farm. Probably more further up that we can't even see. Spuds in that field. Broad beans over there. They must sell it.'

'Back to civilisation. That's the main thing,' Nigel said.

Marcus couldn't have identified any of the crops. But he wondered if the unhealthy-looking cows had somehow provided the milk he had seen by the dome. The idea inexplicably undermined the reassurance that the sight of the house had initially offered. As much as he wanted to, he couldn't persuade himself to share Nigel's confidence.

They came to a standstill when they saw the three children. Three youngsters, on the other side of the river, standing amidst rows of plants.

Sophie was the first to speak, though only after a pause in which they all tried to fathom why the children were wearing sunglasses, broad-brimmed sunhats and so much clothing. Even gloves. With the exception of the pallid portions of their faces, visible below the eyewear and hat brims, and not concealed by the straight whitish hair that they all wore bobbed at their narrow shoulders, all of their skin was covered. A silvery sheen oiled their sickly cheeks as if they had been coated in zinc.

'Triplets, you think? They're identical,' Sophie remarked before calling out to the three small figures. 'Hello! Are your parents in the house?' She pointed towards the distant building.

The children watched her without moving or speaking.

'Can you fetch an adult, please? It's very urgent. We need help for someone who is hurt.'

With hidden eyes, the children continued to watch them.

The impassive posture of their thin-limbed bodies, and what could be gleaned from their blank expressions, betrayed no reaction at all.

Marcus suspected their disposition might be explained by bewilderment, mingled with a touch of fascination, as if they had been surprised and didn't know what to make of the people intruding into their afternoon. Not even Sophie's innate classroom and playground authority made an impression on the trio. 'They might be mute,' she muttered, somewhat dejectedly.

But an adult had been summoned. A thin woman came into view at the edge of the nearest orchard, upriver. She stuffed a tool into a pocket on the front of the apron, then kicked off what looked like Crocs. As if panicked, the wiry figure wasted no time running towards them, barefoot, and at a speed that Marcus found strange, even alarming. Her legs flapped and flared in some kind of baggy washed-out orange trousers that made him think of Hindus.

'We have an emergency—' Nigel called to her, before his wife cut him off with a more strident tone.

'Someone is injured! Badly!' she shouted.

'Have you a phone?' Marcus called out.

They were all talking over each other, their voices frantic, yet also tight with the embarrassment of trespassing.

Without Marcus being aware that the children had moved, the three little figures had somehow dropped to a crouch, behind the small bushes of the row they'd been standing inside. It took Marcus a few moments to relocate the tops of their sunhats and the reflective lenses of their glasses. They had been there, then not there. Partially hidden, they continued to stare at the red-faced paddlers with a persistent studiousness.

Marcus realised why the kids had not been visible to them as they'd entered this clear portion of the valley. When they'd emerged from the avenue, the children must have been crouching among the raspberry bushes just as they were now.

A concealment he thought odd, though he didn't have time to examine the feeling because the woman was not racing towards them but to the three children. And as she neared them, she appeared both angry but also stricken with fear, as if the children were in danger.

'What's her bloody problem?' Nigel muttered. 'Think I've had enough of this.'

From inside the orchard that had produced the first person, an engine growled into life. Soon after, a quad bike shook itself from the treeline. The vehicle was ridden by another woman, also wiry, her arms coated in the same skin-tight shirt of dark cloth as the first. She also wore baggy faded-orange trousers. A fawn apron completed what now resembled a uniform. She rocked and skidded the bike down the riverbank, fishtailed it about in the water, then accelerated up the other side, before heading towards the manor house.

'Where's she going?' Sophie asked Marcus and Nigel.

'You shouldn't be in here!' the first woman called from across the water, in a voice breathless from exertion and deliberately hushed, as if she was taking care not to be overheard. As she'd approached the children, she'd whistled to them. The children had fled to her and clung to her legs. She then crouched and protectively encircled the children with her thin arms. And she wasn't wearing a blue blouse with tight sleeves, as Marcus had first assumed; her arms were densely inked with tattoos. As was her throat to the chin.

Late middle age, Marcus thought, her lined face sun-baked and leathery. Wild blue eyes and crooked teeth were the most distracting features, beneath wiry salt-and-pepper hair, tugged into a ponytail. She stared at the visitors with undisguised, even brazen, hostility.

Nigel stepped forward and bellowed, 'We have a seriously injured person near the mouth of the river! Would you please get us to a phone!'

'You cannot be here!' she said, again in that suppressed tone of voice. 'Not at this time. It's just not right. You can't. This is private property!'

'Yes, we know, but we have an emergency!' Nigel roared. 'We need an air ambulance!'

'It's very serious!' Sophie chipped in.

'We have no signals here. Our radios don't even work! Do you have a landline?' Marcus pressed her.

The woman stood up and backed away, the three odd youngsters clasped to her waist. They remained attached to the fawn-coloured apron she wore, peering up at her with their odd, delicate, identical faces. 'Lower your voices!' the woman insisted, her voice a hard whisper.

'Why?' Nigel demanded, raising his arms in frustration. 'Did you not hear what I just said? We have a seriously injured person!'

Her voice broke into a desperate hiss. 'You are in a temple. Lower your voices.'

'Temple? What fucking temple? That bloody smelly igloo-thing back there?'

Alarm, and maybe even fear, registered on the woman's already harried face. 'The entire valley is sacred.'

'Christ alive,' Nigel muttered to Sophie. 'Are we still on planet earth?'

The woman continued to back away, pulling the children along with her. 'You have intruded upon a strictly private time in our calendar.'

'What?' Nigel asked, shaking his head with exaggerated disbelief.

'How did you get in?' As she asked the question, she glanced towards the valley slopes, downstream. Then returned her frantic eyes to them.

Marcus stepped forward. 'We kayaked up the estuary.' He spoke softly and apologetically. 'And we're really sorry to have intruded. But one of our friends is hurt and sick. Almost as soon as we came ashore, on your land, she was bitten by something.'

The woman's reaction – alarm, even shock – was evident and prevented him from saying any more.

'The house has a phone?' Sophie asked.

The woman retreated towards the orchard with all three children now clutching her thin blue arms.

'Hell is wrong with her? Bloody loony tunes, or what?' Nigel said to his wife.

'Let's get to the house,' Marcus said, and immediately broke into a trot. 'Mary must be going out of her mind.'

16

[4–5pm]

By the time Marcus, Sophie and Nigel reached the front path that divided a perfect lawn before the grand front doors, four people had gathered at the foot of the stone staircase, barring the entrance.

The quad bike that had roared from the orchard was parked on a gravelled area, outside the inner lawn, and the rider now stood among the quartet. She must have alerted the occupants of the house. Marcus assumed the older grey-haired woman had been the distant rider. Her scrawny chest rose and fell, and her cheeks were flushed from exertion, or emotion. To Marcus she also appeared agitated, or angry. A strange and disproportionate response to three sweaty people appearing on foot, albeit uninvited, and wearing kayaking clobber. He didn't imagine they could be much cause for alarm. Little more than a mere nuisance, surely. He judged her to be in her early sixties; similar in age to the woman who had herded the odd children about herself and ushered them away through the fruit crop. She wasn't present and nor were the kids.

The bike rider's ire also appeared to have infected those that she'd joined. A younger woman, as statuesque as a catwalk model, peered at them coldly. Her chin was raised, as if in provocation, and her posture betrayed the tension of a body made alert by a threat.

On the uncovered arms of each woman, similar tattoos to those of the orchard worker were displayed. These intricate circular patterns, identical to the designs impressed into the timber posts of the henge, added a tribal flavour to the pair. The older woman's arms were black with ink. Not so the younger woman; her markings were fewer and more graceful.

Each woman also wore the same loose orange trousers and vest over her slim, rangy frame. Muscles knotted at the side of their jaws. Collarbones protruded. They reminded Marcus of a yoga instructor he knew, of Krishna monks, even prisoners. All-weather tans darkened their skin and made their clear eyes sparkle arrestingly. Not a trace of cosmetics or hair dye enhanced the hair or skin of the two women.

They flanked a tall, bearded man with a ruddy, freckled complexion. What was left of his hair on top was an uncombed sandy red. Remnants of long and haphazardly groomed hair at the sides and back were pulled into a baggy ponytail that he might have spent a few nights sleeping on. He wore a fleece, the same baggy orange trousers as his companions, and flip-flops on his gingery feet. An air of arrogant wariness, or even suspicion, was evident in a stare so intense that Marcus struggled to meet the man's eyes. There might even have been contempt in the fierce gaze that the man levelled at him and Nigel. Peeking above one collar, the inked tail of a tattoo suggested that a lizard might have crawled inside his clothing.

The man's face also triggered a sense of recognition in Marcus, though it was too vague for him to recall where he'd seen the man before.

A second male, also bearded but shorter, with his black hair pulled into a topknot, had appeared last after pulling the front door shut. When he trotted down the steps, he didn't avert his sullen eyes from the visitors, particularly Marcus, as if he'd been singled out as the primary threat. His hands, hooded top and orange pantaloons were stained with oil and soil. Rings of black ink wormed around his throat and neck.

There wasn't a joule of warmth within the welcoming party and Marcus didn't doubt that their trespass was the reason for the chilly reception. Though they bore the aspect of a sect or cult with agrarian pretensions, they were probably employees of Green Leaf, the corporation that owned the Wyrm. And they simply stared at Marcus, Nigel and Sophie, as if expecting an excuse or apology. But the interrogatory bearing was made keener by the surly edge; a warning that whatever explanation the intruders offered was unlikely to be satisfactory.

Trespassers will be prosecuted.

What he'd just heard from inside the building, before the door closed, heightened the acute discomfort that had plagued him since they'd emerged from the henge and cursus. During the few moments after they'd come to a stop and their feet had ceased crunching the gravel of the path, Marcus had heard muffled sounds of distress. A woman crying inside the building. On the ground floor, he presumed.

The closing of the door silenced her.

Marcus had glanced at Nigel and Sophie, to see if the cries had registered with them. They seemed so committed to the task at hand, he couldn't be sure that they had heard. Or cared, if they had. His abiding hope was that those who had been inside the house – three of the curious tattooed figures before them – had been attending to someone in distress, rather than being the cause of their pain.

Marcus peered again at the large rock that stood amid perfect, shorn grass. Like a shard of a meteorite, the massive block of stone appeared to have fallen from space and just missed the house. The placement couldn't have been natural. Someone had put the great rock there. He couldn't imagine why. Before the architectural magnificence of the house, the crude, misshapen stone was incongruous. Weathered, antique markings were visible among the rashes of green and black lichen and bore a close resemblance to the visible tattoos of the valley's occupants, as well as the carvings on the totems.

Nigel grinned with a mixture of apologetic obsequiousness and an urgent desire to be heard. 'Do you have a phone? We need to call for an ambulance. One of our group is injured. Seriously, we believe.' He chattered while the crowd around the steps watched him without reacting. As if awaiting his response, both women and the man with the topknot eventually side-eyed the tall, bearded man.

'How did you come to be here?' he asked, the tone of voice soft, not at all confrontational, but imperiously bred.

Again, Marcus tried to remember from where he knew the man. He recognised his voice too.

'Kayaks,' Nigel said, grinning. 'We were caught in a bit of weather and came into the estuary.'

Marcus glared at the side of Nigel's face and hoped that he wasn't going to claim that the only reason they'd paddled up the valley was for shelter. Because the humourless and intimidating people who stood before them would soon see the tents and camping paraphernalia.

'We thought we might stay a night,' Marcus said. 'By the river.' But as soon as he'd spoken, he wished that he hadn't. Some of the group confronting them noticeably stiffened. Others perceptibly shifted, though not much. He thought he heard a few concerned breaths.

'Oh, you did, did you?' the tall, bearded figure asked, his tone derisory. And as if he were eager to deflect a repetition of lies that he must have heard before, his tone gradually sharpened with an edge of provocation. 'On strictly private property? The entire valley is off limits. Are you going to tell me that you didn't know?'

Marcus answered. 'We knew. But had heard the facility was closed. None of us have ever paddled this valley before. We just wanted to see it.' The unwavering penetration of Topknot's questioning glare pinned him in place. These were the kind of eyes he'd expect to encounter in the faces of violent criminals, as a prelude to a savage beating. For an alarming moment, he believed this figure capable of anything, and that real violence was not far away. 'We wanted to see the river. We hadn't expected . . . We didn't know . . . there'd be . . .'

Nigel turned to Marcus. He looked sweaty and nervous. His expression communicated a desire for Marcus to shut up.

As if impatient and weary with the entire situation and everyone involved, Sophie took over. 'We weren't doing any harm! One of our golden rules is to leave no trace. You wouldn't have known we'd even been here. But one of us is now hurt and we'd like to use your telephone. Please! So, if you wouldn't mind—'

'What is the nature of the injury?' the man asked Sophie. Her husband answered. 'A bite, we think.'

'We don't think,' Sophie snapped at Nigel. 'There's no doubt. She's covered in bites. All over—' she passed one hand across her chest '—her front.'

Marcus received the impression that the group standing before them, who'd initially betrayed their feelings by tensing, were now committed to not reacting to the new information. A practised, contrived indifference was employed, for a few seconds of absolute silence, before the group fidgeted and looked to the tall man in expectation.

'May I ask where she received this injury?'

'In the woods,' Nigel said, eagerly, his tone placatory. 'We pulled in on a floodplain, where the river opened up. She went into the trees.'

The man before them nodded. 'That explains it. Bats,' he said, drolly. 'The bats. They're not to be disturbed. Nor have they been in this area of conservation. Your friend must have gone fairly deep inside the wood to have come across the mine and disturbed the bats.'

Around the speaker, the others seemed to exhale and relax. The tall woman almost smiled.

'Bats?' Marcus said. 'I've never heard of bats attacking people. And they're nocturnal, and she's been bitten multiple times. There are also bruises.'

As the man turned his attention to Marcus, the look in his eyes couldn't have been mistaken for anything but barely suppressed rage at having been contradicted – something he didn't appear accustomed to. 'Bruises from where she crashed about, probably panicking and disturbing an environment in which no human foot is supposed to tread. An immaculate environment unlike anything in this county. Perhaps even the entire country.'

'How bloody quaint!' Sophie barked. 'Well, your bats have bitten the shit out of our friend, who has lost consciousness! She must have rabies!'

'Shock. I doubt it's more. Must have been traumatic for—'

'Phone! Please! The phone,' Sophie said, raising her voice even higher. 'It's taken us forty minutes to run up the bloody valley to get here. We can't get a signal! We're wasting time! We must get Jane help.'

'She's alone?'

'No, we left two of our group with her,' Nigel said.

'Six. Quite the party,' he said and dismissively turned his back on Sophie. 'One moment, while we decide about what to do with the problem that you have so kindly shared with us.'

The others, who keenly watched their elected speaker or leader, smirked once his sarcasm, as if it had been some type of Pavlovian signal, had given them permission to do so. The tall man guided Topknot and the statuesque woman to one side, out of earshot.

As he whispered, the handsome woman's blank expression hardened to what Marcus interpreted as concern. The smaller man narrowed his eyes and nodded his head. The discussion continued for a length of time that made Marcus uncomfortable and Sophie even more impatient. 'Did they not hear what I just said? Isn't it illegal not to offer help? Someone is seriously injured on your land!'

Nigel stared at Sophie and made placatory gestures with open palms, whispering, 'Let me handle it.'

'You,' the tall man ordered Topknot, in a raised whisper that Marcus overheard. 'Understand, Vine? You do it.' Without waiting for an acknowledgement, the tall man turned, approached Nigel and issued a single demand: 'What is your name?'

'Nigel. I'm. I'm...' he cleared his throat. 'The paddle leader.'

'I see,' the curious blend of aristocrat and hippy intoned dismissively. 'Vine and I will show you inside. We'll put in a call to the appropriate authorities.'

'Finally,' Sophie muttered but loudly enough for everyone present to overhear.

Vine beckoned for Nigel to follow him up the stairs.

The tall man stared at Sophie and Marcus. 'I'm sorry about your friend but this really is most inconvenient. You've caught us at a tricky time. And you shouldn't be anywhere near here. I've every right to prosecute.' He turned and skipped up the stairs. The tattooed ladies stayed behind, Marcus presumed, to stand guard.

17

[4–5pm]

Marcus no longer cared about the people of the manor, or the fact that his group had trespassed. The tattooed figures in their odd orange pyjamas had evolved, in his thoughts, to a source of annoyance; a self-inflated, ridiculous entourage. He just wanted to get out of their valley. Picking over the injustice of such a freak show owning so much land, and the water, was something he would indulge once he'd made sure Jane was safe. He'd also never felt so much affection for his home in Divilmouth as he did now: the wet-room, his huge bed, the view of the sea from the living room, the new kitchen that seemed to have improved the quality of the food that he cooked. He desperately wanted to go home.

His back hurt and the day's continuous exertions and shocks had taken a toll that registered in his muscles and sinews as an assortment of aches. Dehydration and stress had created the equivalent of bruising at the back of his brain, which issued a persistent ache behind his eyes.

Now that the call to the emergency services was in progress, he dared to relax. Yawning, he ambled to the low wall that corralled the gravel forecourt and sat down. He dropped his head between his knees and closed his eyes. All over his skin, the sweat, a residue of dried seawater and the trickles of blood on his legs, cracked. He was a mess. He thought of his hot tub and intended to spend an entire evening inside it, bubbling water lapping his chin, a bottle of wine within reach. But, more than anything, he wished and wanted and wished for Jane to be all right.

Sophie sat next to him. 'At long bloody last.'

Marcus sighed. 'How long do you think it'll take for help to get here?'

She shrugged. 'Medics seem to get to places quickly, though I have no idea where the nearest hospital is. Plymouth, I think. But I've hit my limit. I'm sick to death of over-thinking this and speculating. The uncertainty of it all. I'm done. We just have to wait now for it to be over.'

Marcus nodded his acknowledgement. 'I hear you.'

'Do you think . . .' Sophie started to ask.

'What?'

'Jane. She looked terrible. Just bloody awful. She'll be all right, won't she?'

'Don't,' Marcus said. He took his radio out of his dry bag again and turned it on. No reception up here either. 'What else could we have done? Help is on its way.' He scanned the valley around them. 'But this place. What the hell is going on here? This lot? Those kids?'

'Who should be in school. Whole setup is weird.'

'A bit sinister too. I really, really want to get out of here. I wonder what else they're growing, like that lot in Brickburgh who were using the caves as dope farms. They have mines here. They've got druggie cult written all over them. I get the feeling they're hiding something.'

'No shit, Sherlock.'

Marcus checked his watch. 'Eight hours, or not far off, until high water. I'm not staying here any longer than that. We're paddling home tonight. Those that can. If the wind's dropped a bit. Though how would we know inside the valley? But Mary can go in the ambulance with Jane. I'll tow her boat back to Scarlet Cove. Julian or Nigel can tow Jane's kayak. You can choose between a lift with emergency services or a night paddle.'

'Hang on, the paddle leader will want to make the final arrangements. You're overstepping the mark. He'll want to fine-tune your ideas, then pretend they were his all along. For posterity.' She didn't have the strength to laugh at her own jest. 'What a joke.'

A silence fell between them. Sophie didn't look at him. Her concentration soon drifted. Her lips never moved but her eyes were faintly smiling. 'It'll be dark soon,' she eventually said.

Marcus was surprised at how vulnerable she appeared. He continued to study her troubled, drawn, tired but still sensual face. Difficult, disappointed, desirable: often his undoing.

She was having a hard time; this he didn't doubt. Nigel too. The paranoia that he bore some responsibility for the couple's current strife made him uneasy, even a little breathless. He really wished that he hadn't come. Joining the expedition had been reckless and foolish. Though, if he had not, he wondered what chance Jane would have had.

Marcus drained his water bottle and ate a cereal bar. Sophie refused the half he offered her. As he stretched his back, he said. 'What's keeping them? How long can it possibly take? If he's not out in a minute, I'm going to check.'

Sophie stared across the river, until she sucked in her breath and said, 'I was going to tell him.'

The sweat remaining in the small of Marcus's back chilled. When his mind thawed, his pulse thumped between his ears and inside a dry throat. 'What?' he said, though the word came out raspy and strangled, as if a pair of fingers had pinched the sound at the back of his throat. He knew precisely what she was referring to.

She didn't remove her eyes from the far side of the valley. 'Get it all out. He has a right to know.'

'What the hell, Soph? No. No. No.'

Sophie smiled, though her expression was far from pleasant.

'Are you out of your mind?' Marcus pushed.

'I can't think of a better place.'

'I can. I really can.'

'With us all together.' Her voice softened, the intonation adrift from the gravity of what she was suggesting, let alone the consequences.

Panic dropped Marcus's temperature. His mind lurched from fright into flight. He struggled to catch his breath and scratched through the wreckage of his thoughts for excuses, reasons, anything that might persuade Sophie to change her mind. 'Think of Jane,' he blurted. 'Can you do that?'

'Oh, I do. Jane. Jane. I can see that you do too. Can't tear your eyes off her.'

'Hey. There's nothing—'

'Carrying her out of the woods like that. Her hero!' Sophie giggled. 'Are you fucking her yet?'

'What? No. It's not like that.'

'Liar. And then you'll be worming your way out of that too. Bit flaky for you, isn't she? Or is anything that moves fair game?'

'Sophie. Stop it.'

'Why? You've been seeing her all summer.'

'Jealous, is that it? You haven't taken your eyes off her, or me, since we left. Jane and I are both single. You're married but jealous, because of some ancient history that you've been more than happy to leave buried for years.'

Marcus only had time to blink before her hand collided with his cheek.

His eyes brimmed with tears. Between his ears, the sound of her hand impacting against his face rang out like dropped crockery. After a moment, half of his head seemed to have strayed too close to an open fire.

Hot with humiliation, yet chilly from shock, he instinctively peered over his shoulder. Both of the tattooed women by the steps had seen the slap and continued to watch the situation, keenly.

Sick and white and breathless, Marcus wanted to run, blindly, away from the building, up the service road. He would keep going until he was clear of the valley, the paddlers, his life, everyone who knew him.

Love lasts as long as memory. And his memory had possessed, from adolescence, tremendous powers of suppression. Until it didn't.

He'd always hated the guilt. He likened it to a freezing, ashy rain, that often fell in monsoons, without warning. The slap from Sophie and the gush of adrenaline that followed seemed to break a dam. Recollections of his old girlfriends spun through his mind in an odd carousel of wreckage. Bomb damage. He didn't think, however, of his brief time with Sophie. Not right away. Instead, and oddly, he thought of the others. Or some of them. Who wept, screamed, sighed, smiled, trembled with fury or sent him text messages, all over again.

No memory could hold as much as he'd done. But one thing always related to another, and every mirror in the soul showed another reflection of some other mishap and past shame. There were times when he looked back at his own love life as if it were a film; not a great one either. One hundred scenes of pornographic lust mostly followed by tragedy. What had been accomplished but misery? Had Sophie known how many indiscretions there had been before her, she would never have touched him. She'd have prodded him away with a long, spiked pole.

Only the exciting parts, preceding and immediately following the peak of conquest, had ever fascinated him. After seduction and sex, he'd inevitably see a previously undisclosed facet of his lovers, and, in a heartbeat, he'd assume that he and they were destined to become two people who were going to make each other exhausted and miserable.

The idea that he'd kidded himself, that he'd always get away with such profligacy of the heart and such narcotic promiscuity, only now astonished him. Or seemed to. He wondered why the penny had taken so long to drop. *Because here you are.* No, he was wrong; it had dropped before. But he'd continued.

Monumental

As he sat on the uncomfortable wall, a familiar fatigue crept down his spine and limbs; a peculiar despair manifesting as a weariness that, he suspected, only compulsive philandering could produce. The cold shocks from these confrontations, his inevitable withdrawals into loneliness, those desperate returns to the fray: all of that hit him like a cardiac arrest. He felt horribly dizzy and weightless, drained of blood.

Sophie had been terrifying. Only now did he think of her. Crazy, unpredictable, violent Sophie. In her, he'd seen the inferno that must finally incinerate him. *Surely he'd seen that?* She'd also been exciting and erotic; at least twice, he'd almost passed out from pleasure when he'd been buried inside her, outdoors. In the sand dunes, where they'd first met in secret, he'd also seen her second face – calculating and perhaps cruel.

This year, Sophie's unpredictability had escalated. He'd been keenly aware of that too, and he'd been unsettled by the change in her; wary of her impulsive incursions that might cross his borders. He'd simply hoped for the best and kept a safe distance from her, as far as was feasible. Surely she had too much to lose, like a marriage and her family. That's all he'd had to go on. And he'd never envied Nigel. Not once since Sophie had called their affair off, four years before – to his immense relief.

Sophie had been so good with Jane earlier too; calm, proficient, tired but accepting an essential responsibility to assist another in need. That had given him comfort. But how she'd just changed, when finally alone with him, wasn't only unnerving; Marcus realised that he was frightened of her. She was frightening. Always had been. That had been a huge part of the appeal too, if he were honest with himself. He'd even eroticised the evidence of danger within her. Courting self-destruction offered its own high.

But Marcus also feared for her. She was unwell and he'd suspected that she had been so, years before, when they hooked up; reckless, impetuous, terribly unhappy, prone to rage, looking to create chaos. He hadn't ruled out self-destruction as one of her unacknowledged motivations.

And he'd contributed to her illness, or pathology, or whatever it was, in order to extract his own pleasure.

In times like these – and there had been a few – he detested himself. The preceding year of enforced celibacy that he'd managed to adhere to had felt like a decade. But abstinence hadn't changed anything. Because he was again compromised by an indiscretion committed years before. History: it never leaves you alone.

He'd been backsliding with Jane; flirting, fraternising, paddling with her all through the summer. He'd been manoeuvring himself, again, into a thrilling, risky tryst. The narrowing distance between himself and temptation had been intoxicating.

Such ruminations always peppered him with a rash of mortification. A drizzle of sweat freckled his brow. Yet his disbelief and loathing of his incautious, impulsive nature might just as quickly switch to a recall of the precise details, images or words spoken during his affairs, which might engorge him with arousal. He was an addict who deliberately needled himself.

From the age of fourteen, when his compulsion to seduce began, another act that he'd mastered was to effortlessly uncouple reason from his impulses; to give the future no thought.

Jane had set Sophie off. *Jane*. It had to be Jane. Poor Jane. Had Sophie been harbouring delusions about him and her getting back together? Was the prospect of him being with someone else so unbearable to her, even after so long? Four years. He wasn't tempted to flatter himself. Sophie knew the score and she was a mother now. But then, if he were honest, and this was a time for accepting brutal truths, he had suspected that she'd never let him go.

During the intervening summers, even long after their affair had concluded, he'd noticed her eyes on him, from near and far. But had he liked that? Hard to admit, but he thought so. Part of him had relished that kind of attention; of being wanted, desired. For long periods, too, she'd ignored him.

Monumental

Then she'd resumed a mild interest, one knowing and edged with provocation, when others were also within distance of hearing her. She'd been playing roulette; she'd been letting him know that at any time she could bring the roof down on both of their deceitful heads.

Earlier in the summer, when his roof-rack had come loose in a car park near a jetty, his boat had clattered down the side of his car. She'd said, loudly enough for Mary to overhear, 'Can't think what I ever saw in you.' When she'd read the panic in his eyes, she'd smiled with the preening satisfaction of a natural tormentor.

Though only one kiss had ever passed between him and Jane, he'd been indiscreet in getting too familiar with her, right under Sophie's nose. *What were you thinking?* But he had made his vow of celibacy and kept to it. He was in recovery. He was trying to change. That's all he had. And he'd stepped away from Jane after that one kiss. That was new for him. He'd felt stupidly proud of such a minuscule triumph.

You're confusing Jane and baffling yourself.

Jane. Marcus moaned and caged his face with both hands. Recalling the bites on her pale skin made him nauseous. A repulsive desecration of beauty, of her perfection, her essential goodness. He wanted to clutch her as if she was an injured child. His child. If such terrible things could happen to Jane, then what was the point of anything? He felt like crying.

The peak of his panic passed. Fear dwindled but left a stain of dread. These feelings came and went, came and went. A constant. The only continuity.

What had he stuck at? What was the point of him?

He still felt unable to move his burning eyes from the turf between his feet, though he couldn't really see the ground. Sophie and Jane had turned him to stone.

He cleared his throat. 'When this is over, when we're back home, we'll talk, but not—'

'I'm leaving him.'

Marcus carefully slid out of reach of her hands. 'That's between the two of you.'

'You're in this. Balls-deep, if you must know. Why should I go through this alone, when you're as much to blame?'

'Blame? It was years ago. Four. There is nothing between us.' He ventured that hopefully. 'Nothing at all,' he repeated, to convince himself. 'Why are you doing this?' That came out as despair. 'To me? To him? Why?'

'Oh, there is plenty still going on. A great deal unresolved. Much more than you know. Some things you can't walk away from, like some feckless bastard who's had a bit of fun.'

'I can see that you're upset. Angry. But you're not irrational. You're not cruel.'

'Aren't I? I fucking hate him.'

Marcus released a long breath and felt as if the very last of his strength was passing away with the exhalation. 'He's an easy man to dislike. But you married him and you've been looking for a way out for years. That's got little to do with me.'

An impression of the blow still glowed over half of his face. He wore an incomplete mask of sunburn. The imprint of a knuckle against his cheekbone thumped. Anger stirred and left him restless. Now, he wanted to retaliate. Spite added acid to his throat and tongue. 'But you want me punished. Is that it? Maximum drama. Maximum damage. Scorched earth. That's why you wanted me to come this weekend. To do this? To exhibit it all? Spite. Malicious spite. Why don't you make your confession about one of the others? Or is this just about punishing me? I wasn't the only one. You told me.'

That surprised her: him daring to bring that up. She didn't like resistance from her men. He remembered how sharply and decisively she would put his small insurrections to the sword. During the affair, they'd met one evening each week, for two months, and turned back the clock one million years to a time of animals fighting on the ground, one atop the other. Almost immediately, he'd tried to knock the liaisons back to once a fortnight – his usual non-committal sideways shuffle towards the exit.

But there was no rain-checking Sophie. Penalties paid for denying her had been severe. Text messages and calls on the hour. She must have been sending the messages while teaching classes at school. Repeat visits to the gym, his place of work, until he relented and did what she demanded. She'd never respected any boundaries; access all areas from the first flirtation. Any suggestion of another woman in his life had triggered her rage. She'd even begrudged him a sister, of whom he was very fond. She'd been rude to the women he employed as trainers; they'd looked at Marcus in dismay, at such a lack of quality control in his not-so-private life. *Married too. Oh, Marcus.*

Sophie looked at him now as if she was ready to punch him, rather than just slap his face hard. She had punched him twice, back when they were seeing each other. Puffed up one of his eyes and cut a lip against his teeth. When he'd started to flinch around her, usually after sex, when she would begin to interrogate him about the women at the gym, he'd become frantic to escape her.

Nigel probably had no idea that Marcus was the reason he and his wife were kayaking at all. Sophie had made them take up the sport so that she could be close to Marcus. She'd pursued him deep into his hobbies. To Marcus's immense disappointment, Nigel had taken to the sport. Marcus had sometimes even thought of giving up and selling his boats and kit. But that would have been the equivalent of a signed confession.

'That was different,' she said. 'I told you. They're irrelevant.'

So that's it then: they're irrelevant. But I'm not. I will be the one who is sacrificed for all of your indiscretions and who triggers the break-up that you've wanted for years. He wanted to say all of this but worried that if he did so, she'd start swinging her fists on the lawn outside of the manor house.

Her voice became a whisper that broke. 'Did it mean nothing to you?' A glimmer of moisture filmed her eyes.

Manipulation or grief? He didn't know. Never had done. *How many times have you been played in this game? Are you flattering yourself by feeling guilty about the damage you inflicted on her?* He suspected that what he was being confronted with was emotional opportunism. He could not overcome a paranoia that this was a displacement of her unhappiness and resentment onto him. Backdated. But he couldn't abide female grief, particularly when he'd played a part in causing it.

Another wave of cold remorse washed over his seawall, drenching his spirits, black and sopping. His heartbeat might have slipped out of synch and his defences collapsed like a shelf of snow. He suddenly wanted to hold Sophie's hand, apologise, beg for forgiveness.

What he then said sounded fake and odious. But he did mean it. 'Sophie. It was four years ago. Four. A mistake. Exciting, yes, at the time, I'll admit. One of those things that shouldn't have happened but did. We agreed that it was wrong and stupid and reckless. Impetuous. I was. You were too. I disappointed you. God knows, I've regretted it all since.'

'Bastard.'

He'd thought he might have just regrouped enough and gathered his forces, even mustered sufficient composure and the good sense to talk her down, by explaining himself and crawling from this terrible mess that she'd disinterred like a still-ripe corpse. He wasn't succeeding. Not at all. He felt as if more than his reputation depended on what he said next: his life seemed to be at stake.

If news of the affair got out – or was it already tainting the wind? – he'd never be able to show his face again on a paddle. His social life would be drowned at sea. Such things had happened to him before; at jobs he'd worked prior to owning the gym, in clubs, societies. He'd soiled them all.

Marcus softened his voice. 'Had things been different. Circumstances. Then who knows? Who knows anything? But we agreed, did we not? Years ago? You have a family now.'

No extrication from the string of illicit liaisons in his life had given him more of a reprieve than when Sophie had tearfully ended their affair. When she'd explained that she couldn't see him again, because she and Nigel were 'working things out', he'd half-collapsed in his living room. With relief. When she cut him loose, he believed he knew something of the last-minute pardons from firing squads, and the profound experiences of salvation that they provided. But the break-up had never really been more than a temporary amnesty. At the time, he'd feared as much.

Marcus tried again. 'What you have is much bigger and far more important than what happened between us. Which was two people being briefly fascinated with each other. I never wanted to hurt you. And I hate myself for doing just that. I honestly don't like making people unhappy. Sometimes, I just don't think it through. That's what I meant about regret.'

Now she was crying, silently. 'I didn't want any of it. With him.'

'Please. Sophie. Not here. We're in enough trouble as it is.'

She dabbed her eyes and sniffed, stood up and walked away.

Had he talked her back from the ledge? Or could anything happen now?

Nigel and the two men reappeared together and shuffled down the front steps. Nigel's face was consumed with a big grin that made him look immature, excitable, even slightly unhinged. Nonetheless, he was pleased with himself. The two other men appeared preoccupied, or committed; to the rescue on their land, Marcus presumed.

18

[5–6pm]

Nigel had ignored Marcus. Need-to-know basis: a matter for the paddle leader and estate owner only, it seemed. Aware of him but excluding him, Nigel had come out of the manor house holding two glasses of wine. One of which he'd passed to his wife. The couple had gulped the contents as they'd walked to the waiting quad bikes. The skinny tattooed woman had collected their glasses, as if they were wedding guests at a reception. Nigel had then gleefully clambered onto one of the bikes, to sit behind Vine with the topknot.

Sophie had sat, morosely, behind the scrawny older woman they'd first seen riding the bike, and had ridden away too, behind her husband, away to Jane and the campsite. Sophie hadn't looked in Marcus's direction again. Nigel had not said a word to him. They were glad to be shot of him.

The feeling was mutual.

There were only two quad bikes.

Marcus had desperately wanted to ask Nigel when the emergency services could be expected, and in what form. But after Sophie's revelations, he'd become reluctant to communicate with either of them. He'd kept his distance, paced the lawn and waited to be apprised of the rescue details. As if he were irrelevant, they were not offered.

Monumental

Typical of Nigel: to know things that Marcus did not, to be ahead in the game, to hold something over him, to lower his status in the hierarchy. And yet allowing himself to be irritated by the man's scheming made Marcus wince with shame, considering what he'd already done to Nigel.

The statuesque woman had then disappeared inside the impressive house with the tall man; he was the authority here. They'd not returned since. Before he vanished indoors again, the aristocratic hippy, in a dismissive aside, had curtly asked Marcus to wait outside. This only made Marcus more inquisitive about the interior, the rescue arrangements and all that was being concealed from him. Which was everything.

On the other side of the valley, the woman and the three weird kids weren't visible and hadn't reappeared.

Half aware of the great boulder that he circled, as if it were eager to listen to his preoccupations, Marcus peered more closely at the random circular patterns chiselled into the uneven face of the rock. Same style as the wooden totems, though these carvings, as he'd assumed before, were severely worn and much older. He wondered what significance the patterns possessed to have motivated the freak show that lived here to permanently transcribe the ancient markings onto their flesh. Why was the boulder even on the front lawn?

He sensed a commitment to beliefs in the Green Leaf organisation, and to ideas and values incubated in isolation, that he would almost certainly consider absurd, perhaps even dangerous to its own members. He didn't like the look of any of them. Cold, hard, unfeeling eyes, to a man and woman. Their attitude and demeanour did not seem compatible with their pastoral affectations, the conservation and rewilding. He simply didn't get them.

Left alone with his teeming thoughts, his confusion soon warmed to irritation, sharpened by anxiety; for Jane, but also for what Sophie might do next.

He loathed the terrible power she held over him. The possibility of her telling Nigel about the affair tormented him into occasional bursts of panic that left him giddy and clammy.

He decided that the chances of her doing so were high, if not certain, now. The looming confrontation would be terrible. The embarrassment would be crushing. Mary's disapproval of him would be worse than Nigel's reaction. Though what form the latter might take was hard to predict. Black-faced, spitting bluster, perhaps. A fearful, bloodless silence, maybe. He doubted it would get physical. Not Nigel's style.

Part of him also wanted to get the confrontation over with. *Start over.*

Again.

Pinching his clothes away from his chest and stomach, Marcus shivered. His rash vest was moist and made his thin, long-sleeved mid-layer damp. He'd left his wet cagoule on the bow of his sea kayak to dry and hadn't brought a fleece. Now that he'd stopped moving, the cooling air found the wet parts of his body. For the first time since they'd landed, he felt cold. In an hour it would be dusk. He'd need warm clothes before the sun went down.

Marcus squinted at the sky hoping for a sign of a chopper. A signal that this ordeal would end. He had no idea if help would arrive from above or by road. The light was perceptibly dimming. He remained in the dark, waiting for the dark.

'We might as well have a drink.'

Marcus started. He hadn't heard the door open, or the tall man's footsteps as he came outside. He'd changed his footwear to a pair of hiking boots. The man carried two elegant glasses in one hand, a bottle of wine in the other. He showed the label. 'One of our own. Nothing but the best for a guest. Four years old.' The smile the host offered him was vague, yet knowing.

Marcus was simply relieved to see some effort at conviviality. 'Your vineyard?'

He nodded. 'I bet you could use a glass.'

'God, yes,' Marcus said. 'Very welcome and very kind, considering. I am truly sorry for what we've dumped on you today. It's my fault. My curiosity about this valley caught on. I didn't organise this trip, but I lit the fuse.'

'I'll admit to being angry and inconvenienced, but we now have a situation. With your friend. That changes everything. At least it's brought strangers together. You know, we humans have a natural instinct, an urge, to help each other.'

'I'm assuming help is on its way?'

The man nodded.

'Thank Christ for that.'

'They should be here soon.' He looked away and at the magnificent house.

Marcus thought of the crying woman. He wondered if he should ask after her.

'What's done is done,' the man said.

'I'm afraid that not even bones hanging from trees are a sufficient deterrent for sea kayakers.'

The man returned his attention to Marcus. 'They're still there?' He seemed surprised.

'A veritable orchard of animal remains. You didn't know?'

'Haven't been down that far for a long time. We don't like the wetland being disturbed. We don't allow anyone in there. Including ourselves. That area is in a critical stage of regeneration.'

'Why put them there?'

The man shrugged. 'You're asking the wrong person.'

'I thought it might have been one of the artists, when this was a retreat.'

'A fair guess.'

Marcus waited for an answer but the man didn't elaborate. He didn't want to engage with Marcus, or even meet his eye. The indifference, Marcus suspected, was contrived. 'Earlier, you said you were having a difficult time?'

'Private matter. I'm Clement, by the way. You're Marcus, I'm told. Nigel mentioned your name.'

And it was then that recognition dawned and ended Marcus's mystification about where he'd seen the man before. *Clement*. They'd never met, but he'd read about the guy in the news. He'd even seen him on television. 'Clement... Colman, is it? Thought I recognised you.'

'Been a while since I've been in the public eye. Not something I miss.'

'So that's how you managed to own an entire valley.'

Clement's thin smile humoured his comment.

'Entrepreneur, wasn't it? Tech. Apps. AI?'

Clement shrugged. 'Selling the company enabled me to do something that mattered more. To me. I once had homes all over the world. But I never leave here now.'

Marcus's knowledge was vague, though he'd Google the man when he got home. What he did recall was that Clement Colman had sold his tech business for millions. It might even have been billions. Like syrup over pancakes, venture capital had poured money on the man for years. But there had been controversy, a great deal of it, a few years ago. About the company being overvalued. Marcus hadn't retained much information, but he recalled something about an inquiry and legal issues about deception regarding what the tech's bots had been trained on. Intellectual property rights had been infringed, copyright desecrated. Several broadsheets and news organisations had sued Colman's company.

He was hiding in the valley. Had wanted to disappear then? How was it not general knowledge that a derided tech entrepreneur owned a big chunk of Devon? Marcus decided not to mention any of this. Instead, he accepted a top-up of white wine and opened his arms to the valley. 'You invested your fortune wisely.'

Clement smiled. 'I think so.'

'Impressive spot.'

'We've rebuilt what was once here. Planted what should grow again. Something simpler. More natural. Less destructive. This project began as a sanctuary for those seeking a more meaningful way of thinking and living. I took that over and took it further, by evolving a well-intentioned but inefficient and near bankrupt idea into this – a protected environment that we continue to refine. The orchards, crops and the pastures for domesticated animals are back in the very places they occupied in Neolithic times.'

Monumental

'Really?' Marcus peered, with more interest, at the array of crops on the far side of the river. 'How can you be sure?'

'Archaeology. We found the evidence. With teams from three universities. What's been here for six millennia, some of it even longer, we revived and restored. You could say that we're undoing the vandalism that began with the Roman conquest.'

'So, you turned the self-help retreat into an organic farm, based on Neolithic agriculture?'

Clement glanced at Marcus. His lips and eyes thinned as if he'd been insulted.

Marcus's tone might have been irreverent, but he hadn't meant any harm. Clement was touchy about his valley. Marcus added, 'You're self-sufficient?'

'Almost.'

Marcus laughed. 'It's a kind of compound then? For the super-rich?'

Clement almost smiled but without warmth. He didn't like being teased either.

Perhaps it was the wine, or just relief from the ordeal of the day, that made him push his luck, but Marcus was also fascinated by the idea of owning an entire valley. What might that feel like? 'I've read about these operations in Hawaii. New Zealand put a stop to it, I think. Small kingdoms, fenced off, strictly private, owned by tech and energy billionaires. A new feudalism as the earth's climate changes. Island fortresses and hoarded resources. Which makes you a king. And me a peasant poacher that belongs on a gibbet.'

At that, Clement did laugh, and with enthusiasm. 'I saved this environment, so don't let resentment get the better of you, Marcus. And I spent a fortune doing so. Way back when the care home folded and the lease was up, the Wyrm was going to be covered in luxury flats and a private golf course. Did you know that? Had the estuary not been too shallow for the marina that they wanted for mooring yachts, this entire valley would already have been developed before I could save it. All of it. Covered in cement, glass, steel and landscaped grass.

Another green desert. Now that would have been a compound. A gated community for bigger rich wankers than me.'

It was Marcus's turn to laugh. He stopped to swallow another deep draught of the delicious cold wine.

Clement was pleased to see this. 'What do you think?'

Sweet-sour, tangy and a little bubbly; so much so that the wine filled his eyes with tears. 'I will put my class rage to one side and admit that you have fermented an absolutely excellent wine.' He gulped another mouthful.

'Isn't it dreamy?'

'Like a perfect Prosecco. You sell this?'

'A little. Not much. But some to local farm shops. It's mostly for our own use.'

'Hard to believe it's British.'

'Thank you.'

'I bet you don't want lifestyle journalists and wine buffs crawling all over this place.'

'Precisely. The more people who know about our project in the valley, the more intrusions we will have to fend off. Which means that our focus will be distracted and the less successful the rewilding project will be. Always happens. People and their self-interest are inevitably drawn to success and novelty. Believe me, I know all about that. We don't want distractions. We grow everything for our own needs. If there's a surplus, we distribute the excess to where it's needed. Locally.'

'A benevolent ruler. Philanthropist.'

'You mock. But you've now seen most of the valley, so tell me where you've seen a place in the county, or even the country, as wild and undisturbed as the Wyrm.' Clement let Marcus ponder the question, then grinned widely, revealing all of his perfect teeth. 'You can't. I made the valley an area of outstanding beauty. We've been thinking of introducing auroch and wild pigs next, on the valley slopes. I found a place in Kent that breeds the nearest thing to what once roamed here. Otters are coming, Marcus. Otters! In another hundred years, this place will be perfect. An ark for British flora and fauna.'

Monumental

'Or covered by the sea. I saw the dead wood.'

'Oh, no! We never thought of that, Marcus! More?' He offered the bottle.

'Please.'

Clement poured Marcus a second glass. 'Sea defences. All in hand for stage three.'

'It is an incredible venture. My only problem is that no one else can see or enjoy what you have restored and achieved. Only you and your rich mates.'

'Public access would destroy the valley. You know that. Imagine it filled with litter. Plastic refuse. Bin bags. Dogs and their shit. Disposable barbecues. Tents. Paddle-boards. Bloody kayakers.'

'There you have a point.' Marcus took a sip of wine rather than a gulp. He'd already made headway through the second large glass that had been left brimming by his host. He'd drunk it too quickly on an empty stomach jumping with nerves. The alcohol coursed through his depleted bloodstream and left him dizzy. His skin felt warm again and he was growing stupidly happy. Worst of all, he realised he was coming close to liking Clement Colman. 'The henge? And that stone mound? I'm intrigued about how they're connected to the rewilding and conservation. What's that all about? It also stinks, Clement.'

'Can you keep a secret?'

'I'm actually pretty good at that.' His own remark made him think of Sophie enough for fear to pinch his gut.

'When we began the rewilding, mid-valley, we found more than we bargained for.'

'That building was never there?'

'No, but something near identical had been. Once. You see, we found a code. In the ground. That's how we think of it now. A message eight thousand years old. A blueprint we deciphered. That took a while. But with the help of the team who excavated the Brickburgh Caves, we eventually understood that this was once a very special place. A sacred place from so long ago that it's a complete head-fuck.

'We found the first gateway, a little higher up the valley than the temple. That's where a procession once began, before moving between parallel columns of wooden staves. You must have walked through them to get here. Wooden staves that marked an avenue. A ceremonial pathway. A processional avenue. That led us to evidence of a ring of staves, circling the old tennis courts. The courts and pavilion were dilapidated. Relics from the hotel. The courts had to go, so that we could return the ground to a natural state. Rewilding, you see. This reclamation process uncovered all of the crop marks of the staves of the processional cursus and the original timber circle.'

'Insane.'

'All of the original positions of the staves we eventually replicated with timber from the valley. But, for reasons that eluded us at the beginning, there was once a procession down this valley. And that led into a circular henge. Whatever the henge encircled was underneath the tennis court. As we cleared away the court and old summer buildings, we intended to erase all evidence of a human presence. The irony won't escape you, because, by doing so, we found evidence of the first people to settle in this valley. In 6000 BC. When we ripped the cement out, we found the foundations of an early Neolithic structure. Made of wood and stone. An incredible find.'

Marcus felt a need to interrupt. He'd kept one ear open to the sound of a helicopter's rotors, or an ambulance's siren. He'd heard neither. 'One of our paddlers – Julian – would love to hear this. It's right up his street. But, on that matter, can you check on the air ambulance and when it's coming.'

'Sorry, I'm something of an enthusiast for this valley. I get carried away.' Clement jogged back to the house and disappeared inside.

Marcus exhaled and studied his wine glass. At the sides of his vision, a judder and a flicker became apparent. He blinked and shook himself. He felt as drunk as he would be after drinking six glasses quickly, not one and a half. The floor of the valley seemed to be subtly moving.

When he stared at a point on the ground, or in the distance, the world stopped swimming. Pouring wine into a near empty stomach, and into a body depleted by exhaustion, had not been wise.

'Chopper's on its way,' Clement called from behind him. 'Just checked with the coastguard. As for Jane, I can't help you there. Radio and phone signals are blocked in the valley. We only have the landline, I'm afraid.'

'How?'

'Masts along the ridges of the valley.'

'That's crazy. What if one of your people had an accident?'

'Not being able to just call for help makes one particularly careful with one's own safety. But I can tell you that she'll need to get herself checked over. We've seen similar nasty bites on the cows in the lower pastures. I fear she's going to need rabies shots.'

'Shit.'

'I've heard they're horrendous.'

'But bats, really?'

'What else? I've seen one slow worm in seven years here. Never an adder.'

Marcus was about to take another sip of the wine, to take the edge off a new prickle of stress, but paused. 'So, you spoke to the coastguard, not the ambulance service?'

Clement nodded. 'Chopper's minutes away, apparently. You've brought the whole works down on us.'

'Bloody hell. We'll never live this down. Sorry. And, I interrupted. You were going to tell me about that mound. The dome. Cairn, would you call it?'

'Temple.'

'Temple? It smells like a tomb. Don't tell me you're burying your dead? Would that even be legal?'

'I'll come to that. Because that is the best part of this story.'

'Okay, so the temple . . .?' His speech slurred. Marcus frowned at his glass then let it hang beside his hip.

'A temple. Oracle too, perhaps. At least an impression of one. In the earth. Remnants of the materials used in the construction were buried. But the original dimensions of a building still existed as a map impressed into the earth. Deep down, it was; right under the feet of the old hotel guests, who'd played mixed doubles and even picnicked on a site of antiquity. And that's what we found, the floor plan of an extraordinary Neolithic site, within the ring of staves. A structure had once stood in the heart of this valley, constructed from local stone. You know, the foundations were two thousand years older than the first pyramids.'

'You're shitting me.'

'Amazing, isn't it? How could I not fall more deeply in love with this place?'

'I can see that.' Again, Marcus's words tripped, dragged. He was embarrassed enough to pause and make a determined attempt to concentrate on not slurring. 'Sorry. Feel a bit squiffy. This is bloody potent.' He raised his wine glass with an arm that felt both too heavy and numb. Liquid sloshed onto his shin. 'Shit. Sorry. Do you mind if we start walking down to the campsite? They might need help . . . organising our evacuation.'

'Of course. But we'll have to walk. I can't call a bike back.'

'I need to use my legs.'

'I'll come with you.'

'Cheers. But I still don't get why you think the remains were part of a temple.'

'Well, what had been in the middle of the henge was the most important bit. The stuff that went on inside the circles, that's always been the great mystery for historians. Lost to us now. Places get repurposed and used for all kinds of things over expanses of time. But many archaeologists believe that wooden or stone rings, arranged in a circle, served to contain a sacred purpose. And, in our centre, we found something even more interesting than what surrounded it.'

'Gold. A hoard.'

'No. Something far more valuable than precious metals, or the artefacts of lost races. In the foundations of the building, we found bones. So, so many. When we dated the soil and the other materials, some of the bones had been deposited at the very start of the site's usage. They must have been placed there for religious purposes. So, we assumed that this had once been a burial site. An ancient one. A big one. Concentrated in some kind of structure. A massive tomb-shrine. Made of stone long gone that might have been carted off in the Dark Ages to build hovels, or the mining interests of the eighteen-hundreds used the materials. We don't know. But no one, not even the landscapers of the old hotel grounds, destroyed all of the evidence. Because we went really deep. Deeper than anyone who'd ever owned this valley before me. Down through many, many layers to find the bones and stones.

'And these remains were not from a Neolithic barrow, as we'd suspected. Because there were no tools, no potsherds, no ornaments, no sword hilts. Nothing like that was ever buried at this site. Only bones existed from the very beginning of the site's usage. The remains were taken away by a university and studied. That's how we arrived at the earliest date of activity at the site.'

Marcus's dizziness was getting worse, and he felt too hot. He was listing to the left and nearly bumped into Clement. His vest and mid-layer had re-soaked with sweat. He wanted to take them off but if he moved quickly, or even looked down, he believed he might fall. Unless he kept his eyes level with the nearing treeline, he was also sure that he'd throw up. 'Do you mind if I sit down? For . . . for . . . a second.'

'No. Go ahead. I should have warned you. Our wine's strong. You drank it pretty quickly.'

'Had good cause. It's been one hell of a day. But the others will kill me if I show up half-cut. And at a time like this.' He struggled with the zipper to open his rucksack, then remembered that he'd drained his water bottle on the way up the valley. 'I could use some water. You have any?'

'Not on me, no.'

Marcus stumbled and sat on the grass. He shook his head. 'I have some by the boats.'

Clement sat beside him. 'Okay, but let me finish this bit. The best bit.'

'Tomb. Bones.'

'Human and animal bones, Marcus, had been deposited together for thousands of years. As I said, the tomb-shrine, or what we thought of it initially, was built in 6000 BC. But the henge came later. Around 2000 BC. An addition, not long before whatever was going on here all stopped. Completely. That was around 1000 BC. But the site had already been active, with or without the henge, for five thousand years. And for five millennia, the bones of people and animals had been chucked inside this building. No valuables. Just bones. That's a long period of time. A similar pattern to the charnel character of the Brickburgh Caves, and they're not far away. Though, unlike in Brickburgh, no remains of prehistoric animals were found. Just domesticated sheep, goats and pigs here. And people. A lot of people. The constructions and the deposits in this valley were solely the work of early man from 6000 BC. The remains were placed here by people.

'So, this site had never been repurposed as a barn, or king's tomb, or a home. Nor afterwards in Roman Britain. No one ever lived in the original structure.'

Marcus leaned backwards on an elbow. It felt necessary. His head was heavy enough to lollop about his shoulders. His legs sprawled. Had he not felt so dizzy, he might have been more embarrassed. When he tried to speak, he struggled to align his thoughts. His jaw seemed to have detached, and the movement of his tongue was sluggish. He swallowed and only found his voice by a tremendous act of will. 'Time, gentlemen, please. I need water. Burning up.'

Clement giggled. The laugh made him sound younger than his years. He was amused. 'So, what were these relics telling us, Marcus? The bones? What kind of heritage was this? In my valley? A ring of staves erected around a building in which the dead were interred. For five thousand years.

Monumental

A massive tomb-shrine? Maybe. It was possible, though unlikely. But because of the procession down the cursus, between the staves, that led to the circle, then the original structure might have possessed religious significance. Might it have been a place of sacred mystery, and not a mere graveyard? Was there worship here? The academics we had here thought it likely.

'So, for early people, how did this place function as a site of transformation, of life into death, and to whatever lies beyond death? I tell you, I couldn't think of anything else until we found the answer. And to better understand and visualise what had been here, we reconstructed, from the impressions we'd gleaned from what once stood here, the staves and the temple. We brought the past back.'

Clement reached across and pushed Marcus's shoulder. 'Still with me, brother?'

Marcus toppled sideways and his face bumped grass. A smell of soil filled his head. 'Careful,' he slurred, and couldn't draw the saliva back inside his mouth. Now that he was lying down, one arm felt hopelessly trapped beneath his body. But he hadn't the strength to free the useless limb. Beyond his splayed feet, the lower valley moved, surged closer, then backwards, then forwards, again and again. The river and the wooded slopes swam from side to side, this way and that.

Marcus closed his eyes. The darkness inside his head swirled into a whirlpool. From outside of his disorientation, Clement's voice drifted from a greater distance than was possible.

'Guess what we found next? Please pay attention. You'll want to hear this, Marcus. It's really important that you do, so that you will understand. The next thing we found, deep down, was a door. And we unblocked it. We had to get a crane down here to remove the massive stone. You've seen the rock. At the house, on the lawn. That was a lock on the door.'

Marcus tried to focus on the distant mouth of the avenue that had brought him here, but the trees jerked from here to over there, up and down. The very earth seemed ready to leap into the air.

Clement's voice penetrated his stupor: quiet, then loud; distant, then close. Soon he was behind Marcus's eyes. 'What did it all mean, Marcus? The staves and stones and bones and the rock? Well, it was the valley itself that finally filled in the missing pieces. The bits absent from our knowledge. About what was once done here. The purpose of it all. You wouldn't believe how these hills murmur with stories. About old ways.

'This is where our mindfulness training really came into its own. With some old Hazzard meditation techniques. A little psilocybin concoction played a part, I'll admit. The diaries of the family, the Waddetons, who built the house played a crucial role too – the written historical record. But meditation was the primary means for making contact. Or how we were *reached*.

'There were no songs or stories or poems left, to tell us what to do. Or pictures. Nothing like that. Nothing was written down or depicted, not from way back then. If the druids had left anything, the Romans obliterated it. But an influence persisted. An atmosphere. Feelings. Suggestions. Glimpses. Presences. Marcus, what has always been possible here is the potential to see other times and places, once an inner vision has been cultivated.

'My word, the stories we heard about that old care home too. The things the residents experienced. People thought it was their dementia, or the powerful medications they were prescribed. But no one was hallucinating. They were *seeing*. Seeing what was already here, from before. Things that had remained closer than you can imagine. And this lingering influence, if you like, that we made ourselves susceptible to, led us to the mine. The next piece of the puzzle!'

Clement's voice dropped to a whisper that scratched inside Marcus's skull like static. 'Another door. There is a world behind these doors. This valley has many doors and chambers, Marcus. The doors we couldn't hope to walk through. But *they* can, from the *other side*. The Little Priests.

'We called them messengers. In the beginning. And from *them*, we learned about what the temple once looked like, what it was for and what it needed from us. And the Little Priests also told us what to put into the belly of the Wyrm Valley.

'So, this is how we knew that we had a temple in this valley. *They* showed us what it was, its purpose. These were the original Priests. And that was no tomb-shrine under the tennis court. We were reconnecting with something far greater, far more important. Something monumental! And that, my trespassing paddler friend, is why the temple fucking stinks.

'Every single bone we found inside there was once part of a sacrifice. To a god. A bloody god, Marcus! An actual god. And every bone that we've since added has also been part of that legacy of sacrifice. You picked the wrong time of year to trespass, my rude friend.'

Marcus couldn't lift his head. He burped. Then burped again and was sure that he would soon be sick. Hands rolled him onto his side. A distant voice came and went, came and went. 'We brought it back. Doors, Marcus . . . They open onto passages . . . Or holes . . . that start in other places and . . . We've lost sight of all that, with our self-importance. I was worse than most . . . We're really not a big deal . . .'

Marcus heard no more. His mind rolled into darkness, then dropped away altogether.

19

[5–6pm]

So many trees, an unbroken green wall fencing the valley from upriver to the sea, unnervingly still and silent. The woods should be alive with drifting birds, singing birds. Mary hadn't seen or heard a solitary bird in or near that inscrutable, dense canopy that concealed the darkened slopes on either side of the valley. A place in which Jane had been hurt. Marcus had remarked about how lightless he'd found the woods, how chilly, and that cool darkness now hid whatever had punctured poor Jane's skin. Alone, in half-light, she'd been engulfed inside that wood. Bitten frenziedly.

Mary closed her eyes and suppressed the thought.

From inside the trees, she could be seen down here, sitting in the meadow beside the river. Nothing impeded a view of the plain from high up, or from the foot of the woods. Between her and the treeline, open ground yawned. The scattering of bags and half-assembled tents of their campsite lay entirely exposed. They might have camped inside an arena, or chosen a place in which an ambush was most likely to occur. Though, an attack from *what* she didn't know. But the longer she'd sat beside Jane, holding her hot hand and listening to her disturbing monologues, her notion of a surreptitious scrutiny had grown and worked on her already excited nerves.

Monumental

It was the evidence of the infantile fingers, bruised into Jane's upper arms, suggesting that small, determined hands had gripped and held her, that Mary could not expel from a rumination that grew more anxious with the passing of too much time spent in silent contemplation. There was still no sign of the others who'd gone to find help.

Apes? Could there be apes here? With sharp teeth? But wouldn't I have heard them by now?

How she'd admired the beautiful, exotic valley earlier. A scenic backdrop for a night under the stars. Or so she'd thought as they'd clambered, laden with gear, into a meadow weighted with promise, and the thrill of the novelty and innocent pleasure of wild camping. On arrival, tears of joy had stung her tired eyes. Friends – or just about – together here, blessed by warmth and light. A cool dusk ahead of them, with a hot meal and a fiery mouthful of the brandy that Marcus always carried. Scents of the earth and drowsing flowers, the far-off ripple of the river across smooth stones, and her body cocooned in the fleecy warmth of a sleeping bag, the night's cold air cupping her face. What a cruel joke.

For a few days, each of them should have been shrived of their tourniquet of stress, of petty shackles. Wishful thinking, because they'd paddled here with their grievances on board; more baggage than the holds of their boats could contain. Too many had arrived tense, prickly and sullen, or defensive. Other than poor Jane, she'd thought her peers incapable of appreciating the beautiful valley.

Perhaps the trial of the swell, the strange quiet of the placid estuary, followed by the ghastly spectacle of the bones strung from bleached branches, had provoked their pettiness. It had been hard to get here. But it was even harder to be here. Everything about the valley had proved deceptive. Getting out now presented itself as the hardest task of all.

Beneath her, cross-hatches of spiny grass burned her buttocks. Her ankle bone had disappeared within a thickening tube of swollen skin. A shard of pain penetrated her foot to her toes. Under her aching shoulder, the corresponding arm rested on her stomach as if it were already inside the hammock of a sling.

The light was dimming. Her clothes were mostly dry but the warmth of the air had thinned. She felt uncovered and more helpless than at any time since their arrival in the Wyrm. Any optimism she'd felt when the others left to fetch help, had dwindled to a sickening uncertainty. Now worry drained her more than the ordeal of the paddle.

She was bleakly aware of Marcus, Sophie and Nigel travelling a great distance upriver to get help that still hadn't arrived. She couldn't possibly have followed them. She imagined herself hobbling to the visible boundary of trees that bordered this meadow, then crawling, only to find another expanse of grass and wildflowers on the other side. Until help arrived, she wasn't moving.

'It doesn't end,' Jane said, after a gasp. 'The round stones aren't graves. Houses . . .' The young woman's eyes were open but what she looked at, and with such intensity and fearful wonder, was not here. Not in the meadow. Nor in the sky. Though Jane seemed convinced that it was, as if she was looking at an altogether different place.

Of growing concern was the pallor of Jane's cheeks and forehead, each pimpled with a greyish sweat that Mary continually dabbed away with a wet towel. The young woman's blond hair was black at the fringe and around her ears. Drenched. 'That isn't the sky,' Jane said. 'Ours is different.'

Mary applied the teat of the water bottle to Jane's lips. 'All right, love. It's all right. Come on, drink this.' She thought of her husband, Geoff, before the end; the shrunken head inside the woollen hat, the worn face, the odd word and gasp.

You're ill, or you're caring for the ill. You never see it coming. Then, quickly, that is who you are, and all that you do.

Julian returned from the boats. 'No good. Nothing. It's definitely not the batteries.' He'd repeated the same information more times than she could remember, or even guess.

'If you say that once more, they will hear my scream in Plymouth.'

Julian's wounded expression suggested that Mary had made a greater criticism than the one she was justified in expressing. But he couldn't abide being wrong or disagreed with. Mary often wondered if Julian believed himself incapable of error. She wasn't surprised he'd never married. They'd paddled together for ten years and he'd never mentioned a relationship. And though his infatuations with women were manifold, she wondered if he'd ever been involved with one in a meaningful way.

He hadn't crossed the river either, to try for a signal on the other side of the valley, as had been suggested, or ordered, by Nigel. Julian had remained near the boats: pacing, fretting, unwilling or unable to look at Jane.

'I think I should probably head out, while there's still a trickle in that creek,' he said to himself more than to her. Announcing this appeared to give him relief.

'What, just leave?'

'If the weather's blown south, I might get a signal on the radio. Outside the estuary, I can alert the coastguard.'

'Is that a good idea? It'd take you ages to get out of the estuary.'

'Well, I've got to do something. And you're not going anywhere.'

That sounded like both accusation and censure. He looked away as soon as he'd said this, then paced to the only erected tent – his own. Mary had asked him to finish assembling it, in case Jane needed shelter. Her skin had been too warm for a stuffy tent, but Mary wanted the option when the sun dipped and the temperature plunged.

Julian backed out of his tent, trying to conceal a toilet roll. She was seeing too much of his eyes behind his spectacles, as if the lenses were now magnifying the fear that filled them.

She'd noticed his demeanour change during the last thirty minutes. He was fidgeting or marching about with more intensity. His preoccupied stare had grown too wild for her liking. He was beginning to remind her of a panicked animal. When he wasn't speaking to her and repeating himself endlessly, he was muttering to himself. She guessed all that she'd heard were the lines that he'd been rehearsing, internally, for two hours. 'The valley's a lot longer than anyone thought,' he declared, not for the first time. 'Must be! They've been gone hours! Where's the bloody air ambulance! We'd hear it. Where the bloody hell is it?'

Mary groaned and closed her eyes. 'Can you change the record? You're really not helping.'

He glared at Mary. 'Well, I'm not just hanging around! We're getting nowhere.'

'High tide's not till midnight.'

'Closer to one a.m., actually.'

'You'd have to drag your boat to the end of the estuary.'

'It'd be a slog but not unfeasible.'

'How would you get through the mud? In the reeds and wetland, it'd be up to your thighs. You get stuck, that's three of us in trouble and you cut off from us. You're the only one here who can still bloody walk.'

Julian scurried to the cover of the trees extending from the riverbank. He'd already been inside them twice to urinate. She'd seen him and heard the distant tinkle of water against the undergrowth, as if he was now pissing with terror.

Mary knew that he suspected Jane might die and he didn't want to be here when it happened. Mary didn't rule the eventuality out either. What had been fever and listlessness had degenerated into an unnerving immobility, punctuated by outbursts of mystical gibberish. The woman was insensible, her pulse faint, her limbs paralysed. She barely blinked and was unresponsive to anything but trickles of water that Mary slipped between her bloodless lips. Despite the strange utterances escaping her delirium, and the near imperceptible rise and fall of her chest, it wasn't hard to imagine her completely lifeless. And soon.

Mary was no stranger to waiting for the end. Even her own.

20

[5–6pm]

*M*arcus briefly wondered if he were lying atop a train carriage and sliding from side to side on steel. When the locomotive careened around the bends, it would pitch his body upwards, until there was only air beneath his shoulders. He'd then clatter down and endure painful bumps against metal so cold that it burned his naked flesh, as well as bruising his back, buttocks, hips, loose arms and thumping heels.

No, he was not on top of anything because there were sides to the container that he was being scattered across. He was within something, like an iron box with no lid. Up there was the sky. His eyes could not be still enough to notice much of it, but the sky was there – blue staining to indigo, without a wisp of optimism.

Violent though his transport was, the flashing and the rapidity of his bright but muddled thoughts was somehow worse. As soon as a notion formed, it dispersed, making way for new, random suggestions to appear and vanish in turn. Memories erupted only to cool black. New fragments of recognition struggled to unearth themselves from the void. Almost familiar faces opened their mouths before being erased.

As the journey continued, he tried harder to stitch his mind back together from a scattered jigsaw of colours and partial pictures, spilled onto a dark red carpet. A broken stained-glass window. Shards of recollection. No full picture, no light of reason shining through. But slowly, amidst the chaos and mess of his head, he grasped and held smaller details until one image suggested another and the pieces clicked together.

His red kayak. Carrying a tent bag. A black, square chiller bag in the other hand, a sleeping bag roll clutched between his teeth. Into the meadow he'd struggled, on which a vast bannered army of wildflowers amassed. Meadow. Water, river water. Thin, cold, clear, the colour burnished by the glossy rubble of a pebbled bed. Up the curling faces of grey, froth-tipped swells he'd risen. Before the meadow? Yes, before the flowers, the sea had tossed him. Lifted him as if riding an elevator, his stomach dropping the other way. Tippy in a kayak, thrashed by ocean air. Waves, salted spume peppering his face. Seeking others in the troughs below a grey sky.

Friends.

Paddling.

A group.

The shingle of Scarlet Cove and ox-blood sand. Morning. That morning. All together. Some laughing, laughing at dawn. Him uncomfortable.

Now this. Naked on metal, thrown from side to side, under a vast and swallowing sky. His stomach a slopping bucket of nausea.

More memories flashed awake, for moments, before triggering other urgent recollections. A pockmarked skull hanging from a white branch. Glimmering mudflats, holed by crab tunnels, spread between skeleton trees. Orchard of bones. Great walls of living trees on either side of a creek. Water between slimed banks narrowing like an arrowhead. A vast stone beehive, or igloo, with a terrible stench puffing from it. A grey mound rising from pea-green grass. A circular lawn tended like a bowling green. Fenced by poles. Swirling patterns carved into the timber.

Marcus turned his bouncing face to one side and poured out a slurry of sewage, the gastric odour as foul as the hot stink of the innards seeping from the dome's stone slits.

Temple.
Clement.
Sweet wine gushing into his mouth. Eyes dewy with ecstasy, he'd wolfed it.

He turned, but when confronted by the other side of the shuddering, oily trailer, his guts turned themselves inside out again. From the cellars of his stomach, he retched. He shook, belched and coughed himself empty.

A feeling of choking and suffocating followed; and the sensation of impending death. In panic, he flopped onto his stomach. Face down in a tinny, scratched trailer bed that ran with his bile, he sucked air through acid-seared pipes to inflate his lungs with the smell of the metal workshop in secondary school.

But the vomiting cleared his mind of teeming shoals of notions lasting no longer than raindrops.

This skin he wore was now mostly dark. Crusty as black tar. He was sticky, his flesh drying. All of him was creosoted with rust and salt, down to his stained toes. He'd been blooded, from head to toe.

Injured!
Air ambulance!

Was he hurt, without any memory of the accident that had befallen him? Was he now being ferried to hospital at reckless speeds?

Inside a trailer?

What was left of his reason frantically scanned his body for pain, incisions or tears wide enough to coat a man with his own blood.

There were no cuts. There were only bruises and the slopping, surging nausea; incessant greenish waves drowning his mind and making his limbs limp. How he wished to be still, to be unmoving. But into the air he was tossed again as the trailer struck a bump.

For a moment, there were bushes and trees watching him pass. And he remembered being asleep in the grass.

Waking. Before this. And feeling terribly sick, his skin moist and chilly, as slippery hands had rubbed his naked limbs and tummy. Around his neck, a woman's hands had spread the slippery filth, and behind his ears as if she was soaping him with liquid gel. A bucket's metal handle had rattled against plastic. Smooth fingertips had daubed his face, swirling in circles as if moisturising his skin. The basting liquid had stunk of beef joints resting in pans as the oven warmed. A cloacal aroma. Foul hormones, spiced minerals. Meat. Cold meat. Old, cold meat. Slippery in buckets.

Red to the elbow, two pairs of arms had kneaded him on the cold grass like he was dough. They'd spread the sauce, marinating him until he'd dripped, then crusted. They'd knelt and massaged gore into his pores until he was the crimson of burned bacon. They were smiling. The decorators of his flesh had been elated. Two women who'd laughed like children drunk on sugar and excitement, had worked and slathered and smeared. Their eyes weren't right. Clement was a sadistic boy, driven by boredom and resentment to torment a weaker child. He'd stood behind them, watching. The tall woman he'd thought beautiful had a face of scissors, hollows and cartilage, and was as deranged as an inmate who'd chiselled extremities from hinge joints. He thought of killers pulling ribbons and sloppy organs out of open torsos.

The older quad bike rider, who'd alerted the household to the trespassers, had nothing but a skull on her thin shoulders, but she'd plastered him with an enthusiasm that he now realised was a form of derangement. Her arms and neck were inked with woed. Savage, swirling blue curves, etched like the giant stone in the garden and the timber staves chiselled with circles that swirled to a tight centre. The mere memory of these patterns triggered spasms inside Marcus's gut, belching a cow's foamy cud across his cheeks.

The trailer thumped over a lump in the road and Marcus was airborne again. He almost sat up that time, inside the trailer, like a crash test dummy without a seatbelt, thrown into accidents to measure damage. He hardly broke his fall with arms that were so heavy and legs that were as dead as posts. Before he flopped back onto the wet steel bed of his carriage, he spotted the rider of the quad bike, the vehicle that towed the trailer that he rolled within, soiled and reeking and naked.

Marcus rolled and pushed himself onto his elbows, for long enough to unleash a fresh cascade of watery vomit that splashed between his elbows and onto the chipped metal bed of the trailer. A curve in the track pitched him sideways and into sheet metal. The side of his transportation pen boomed like a bass drum and nearly knocked him senseless.

The rider of the quad bike was a man. Red wisps streaming. Bushy beard making his head rectangular. *Clement*. A band crossed the back of his skull. A halo of long feathers fluttered around his strange head.

Tree branches, impossible tangles of bushes, darkening sky, wet metal, his rusted arms, his cock and balls encrusted black with old blood – all of this turned and swirled and swilled and shook and vibrated.

Just breathe, Marcus told himself. *Just breathe.*

By pushing his dead-meat feet into the corners of the trailer bed, and his weak-fingered hands into the sides, Marcus arranged himself spread-eagled, face down. But, as if they'd traversed another speed bump, he was thrown into the air once more. His face landed first, unbroken by hands, and seemed to connect with the blade of a spade, swung by hairy arms. *Cacunk*! On impact, a tooth chipped. As hard as a diamond, the fragment stuck to his tongue. Around his limbs and over his face, filth cracked. A mud mask. Salted with iron. Tenderised by hammer blows. Taken to market in a metal trailer. A side of glistening beef.

The jolts, the swaying, the shaking, the sudden thumps, abruptly stopped. The trailer's tyres hummed and rumbled across a smoother surface.

Dazed, Marcus struggled onto elbows as bruised and tender as they'd been when he came off a bicycle as a kid. He raised his smarting face from the shuddering trailer bed and peered back the way he'd been dragged. Between timber poles, he had travelled down the grassy cursus. The ancient processional path.

A second quad bike followed. Ridden by the older woman who was tattooed blue, her limbs as rangy as a marathon runner. The papered skull of her face was gone. That had been replaced by an oval mask. Bearded with feathers, furred with feathers, plastered with ashen charcoal feathers, her nightmare head was ruffled by the wind. Deep inside the eyeholes, a buried glimmer of a cold glare.

Marcus glanced the other way, to where he was being driven.

A small mountain of stone blocks lay ahead. A place resurrected from the deep, from foundations embedded in Neolithic earth. A brutal cathedral dug up from beneath a tennis court. Windowless and grim. Crudely imperious. Implacable. A cruel, ugly shrine.

The temple.

As well as being appropriately clothed in blood to enter an unhallowed interior, Marcus realised that he reeked of the building's incense. He already smelled of death.

21

[5–6pm]

Had more of the interior been discernible, Marcus suspected the stench might have been visible as a toxic mist, off-white in colour like an oily maggot.

Engulfed by the unbearable corruption, his dizziness worsened. The miasma of decomposition was poisoning his lungs, settling inside his stomach, clouding behind his eyes. A saturating rot, absorbed by the skin to leave indelible stains. He feared that he'd never smell anything else again but this. Forever, it would mottle his sinuses and hang inside his folds. He barked as much as coughed and soon wished that he'd sucked in more of the clean valley air before they'd shoved him inside the 'temple'.

Marcus could now do little more than cover his mouth with a stained forearm and stop breathing through his nose. Peering up, his bleary eyes and spinning mind grasped at the source of what illumination there was here, and for the origin of what served for air. For he must have air. If he didn't find clean air, he'd surely pass out.

Through a circular hole in the underside of the domed roof, a disc of bruised sky. So high up. So far away.

Around the circular perimeter, the dome's walls were obscured by shadow. But enough of the day remained to trickle into the middle of the structure. Periodically, the slits in the exterior of the great stone dome thrust a few dusty cross-shafts into the hollow space.

Like tree roots uncovered by a lowering tide, racks of ribs, cluttered with stiff rags of black flesh, emerged from out of the gloom. He counted four limbless carcasses on the earthen floor, haphazardly heaped near the centre. Rounded like the skeletal remnants of ships' hulls, the ribcages were tipped on their sides and lay as if glimpsed through the silted murk of an ocean bed. Dead cattle left to rot. Detached from spinal columns, as if the animals had swallowed explosives, leg bones and the faint lumps of skulls lay scattered elsewhere. There was little flesh on the carcasses, but enough viscera must have remained to produce the infernal stench.

His throat was on fire. Thirst lit salted embers through his gullet. He needed water even more than clean air. Marcus coughed and coughed and staggered sideways until he could rest on the damp stones of the nearest wall. His shoulder held him upright beside the wooden door that he'd been manhandled through.

To get him inside, Vine had twisted his arm up his back. Outside in the grass, when the pall of rot had first buffeted his face, the grips of his captors had tightened. The bony, tattooed female ferret who'd followed the trailer on a quad bike had clenched a spidery hand on his forelock and tugged him forward by the hair. Unnecessary precautions and subduing techniques, because he could barely stand upright. He could have been guided, simply, like an ox to slaughter. They'd even needed to drag him out of the soiled trailer. Once on his feet like a foal slopped with afterbirth, his legs had failed. But the assault had been executed sadistically; there had been an element of enjoyment and satisfaction in his tormentors' actions.

Trespassers will be prosecuted.

Now that he was shut inside, disorientation continued to interfere with his limbs. As if a wire was pinched between vertebrae, his numb feet could do no more than plod. If he attempted walking in a straight line, he would go down like a felled tree. What he might land on didn't bear consideration.

Monumental

Compared to how he'd felt during the journey, down valley, inside the metal trailer, his confusion wasn't as severe. Feeble though it was, a growing awareness of his situation had crawled back inside his skull. Nausea had sweated him cold and weak, and, though the substance must still be contaminating his blood, his stomach must have purged a portion of the drug that had spiked the wine. A potent narcotic to have made him so unwell.

Marcus didn't touch the door behind his back; he'd seen the bolt and padlock on the other side. Once he'd been incarcerated, he'd heard the metallic snaps of the barrier being secured. No handle protruded from the inside of the door; there was only hard wood for hands to slap against, in despair, before merely nudging at the impenetrable surface. He'd not give his jailors that satisfaction.

A natural refrigeration chilled his blood-mired flesh. Individual hairs ripped free of the clots plastering his skin and extended like feelers into the foetid air.

His bleary vision groped around what else could be seen of the temple. The walls were of irregular stone blocks, cemented together; a sturdy curvature, patchworking to the heavens, passing in and out of shadow. Unbroken, uniform contours and textures extended from the soil to the visible disc of sky.

Puritanical by design or as utilitarian as a sewer, the stinking dome allowed no decoration. The grey tones of this mound were never intended to please the human eye. And yet this structure was considered sacred. Who in their right mind, he wondered, would hold that view.

Compacted soil formed the floor in all directions, though not in the centre; that was missing. Light falling from directly overhead was swallowed by a circular hole. A firepit, perhaps; that was his first thought, but as he stared at the anomaly, the greyish light revealed the uppermost part of a shaft, constructed from the same stone as the surrounding walls of the dome. Around the rim of the hole, the masonry was neater than elsewhere in the temple. He was reminded of a culvert in a castle, used for draining slops into a moat or river.

Directly above the pit, a horizontal beam crossed the entirety of the vaulted dome. Blackened by smoke, or stained by creosote, the discoloured timber was darker than the carved staves of the cursus and ringed henge.

Because it traversed the building several metres above the ground, he assumed that the beam, or joist, supported the walls. The way it crossed the circular pit made him think of a well, though no bucket on a rope descended from the beam. For which he was glad; he didn't want to think about what might be drawn out of that darkness.

Inside the black temple, he soon detected murmuring.

A voice.

Then another. Two voices. Some way off. But inside the dome with him.

As Marcus turned, his knees sagged. Spreading his hands on the wall, he dropped his head over his smeared chest and waited for the spinning to stop.

He glanced to the other side of the structure. Directly across the dome, a shadow moved up the wall before it became a body, head and shoulders. The silhouette of arms emerged into the furthest reach of what light pooled beneath the flue. A black figure, the limbs too whittled to be clothed.

Marcus thought of wretches fed on carrion and held captive for years. A notion that almost made him issue his first genuine scream since infancy. Somehow, he stayed silent. Only his breathing quickened.

A second shadow tried to stand beside the first one. Pawing itself up the stones, the figure eventually got to its feet, though it remained hunched over.

'Who is it?' a woman whispered.

'How would I bloody know?' the man answered, his voice made louder by irritation and carrying to Marcus. The man's words and tone prompted recognition. Nigel.

'Nig—el?' Marcus asked, though the sound was more of a stutter, divided into two syllables.

'Marcus?' Sophie whimpered, her tone elevated by disbelief, or perhaps hope. Desperate hope.

22

[6–7pm]

As he squatted to relieve the painful gassy pressure that had been expanding and popping inside his bowels, Julian imagined his exit strategy. And as the fantasy became more vivid, the river downstream formed in his mind as if it were before his very eyes: the pale stones and tendrils of green weed passing beneath the hull of his moving boat; his kayak gliding away from Mary's grim face and Jane's wild eyes in the half-assembled campsite; the very symbols of this expedition's ruin.

If he kept his boat stripped of weight and set off equipped only with his paddle, buoyancy jacket and radio, he'd make quicker progress on the river section of the valley. The water levels were low. But if he didn't hang around and he pulled his kayak along the shallow bed, there might be enough water to keep the boat partially afloat and reduce drag. He could follow the deepest channel. All he needed was a few inches to get as far as the wetland.

Now, the marsh would be tough and messy. From the reed beds downwards, he'd be sinking at least to his knees before yanking his feet up and out. And for miles with the incoming flow against him. Sliding about, for sure, caked in mud. He could take his boots off to wade the creek bed, sliding the kayak through the shallows before him; or he could drag the boat by the bow toggle. And he'd be doing so in the dark with a head torch. Gruelling, but eventually he'd be washing the mud off in the salt water of the estuary. When he reached it. He could rest there, try the radio again.

And at least you'll be moving in the right direction: out!

In a few inches of water, over a firmer surface of sand and broken shells in the first section of the tidal estuary, progress would be much easier. Somewhere near the estuary mouth, he'd be able to get into his kayak and paddle out. Paddle out of this mess. A shallow depth of seawater is all he'd need to get afloat. A few centimetres. That was the beauty of these boats. The Inuit hunters were geniuses. His boat didn't weigh much and neither did he.

This plan was for the best.

For everyone, of course.

Something must have delayed the party that left the camp hours before. No sign of relief or rescue had arrived. Not from above. Not from any direction. Obstacles must have appeared. Or a greater distance to walk, than was envisaged, had delayed Nigel, Sophie and Marcus.

The silence of the valley was driving him crazy. Those bones in the trees that he'd been so dismissive of, he now associated with the punctures all over poor Jane's swollen chest. What the connection might be between the two horrors, he hadn't the imagination, or the will, to surmise. He'd be embarrassed to even suggest a link between them. Those that went in for morbid rumination he'd always considered a bit weird and weak-minded. That was the only thing he didn't like about Jane. But privately, while refusing to speculate about and dwell on the unpleasant and grotesque aspects of the evidence, he couldn't rid himself of a feeling that there had been foul play in the valley.

What he'd always managed to uphold – and he was proud of it, if he could suppress the insidious doubts about self-deception – was to eschew the irrational stuff that flowed through people and life, and to focus on practical solutions instead. He had an ability, which he often considered remarkable, to maintain almost any appliance.

Any mechanical thing he could tinker with, understand its processes, identify faults and repair it. This skill, combined with his extensive knowledge of most practical matters, would free him once more from difficulty and chaos. Right here. And his growing suspicion that something was seriously awry here, he saw only as a reason to change things, take initiative, alter the plan.

You're not running. You're making an informed decision, based on a thoroughly considered crisis, with multiple moving parts. Once the initial strategy fails, your priority is the welfare of the majority of the group, ensuring their safety. From the start, you'd have done things differently. But if people won't listen, then you're not to blame.

As uncomfortable as Julian was in acknowledging it, Marcus was still their best chance of attracting attention. He was the fittest member of the group. Even after carrying Jane out of the woods, he'd had sufficient stamina to run for help. The guy owned a gym and, for once, his strength and fitness had come in useful for something other than impressing women.

But he'd also been gone hours. If Marcus was still running, or had only just arrived at the manor house, more precious time would elapse as he tried to raise help. On arrival, he might have found the building empty and shuttered. He would then have had to leave the valley to locate the nearest farm building or village, or come within range of phone and radio reception. That could take him an age while moving up and down undulating hills and across uneven ground.

Somewhere in the rear, Nigel would be plodding along on his rickety knees, huffing and puffing and bickering with Sophie.

And it doesn't need two people to watch Jane. There's nothing you can do for her. Mary can't walk. She shouldn't even be here! You've got to go. You! Go for help. Get on the sea. Call the coastguard. If Marcus has got word out and the emergency services are already aware of the situation, then so be it. No harm done. The group has split. We're out of contact and sight of each other. A second attempt to raise the alarm has to be made.

Julian, I really wish you'd gone earlier.

And if he left now, he might be the first person to summon help. He could almost hear people saying, and for years too: 'Thank God Julian dragged his boat through that wetland and estuary. If he hadn't, Jane wouldn't have made it.' This might be a sure-fire method of deepening the connection he assumed he and Jane shared. That idea flickered awake inside his meagre frame, and soon this notion of being a saviour surged hot and electric, thrilling him so much that his pulse thumped hard.

Until, between one heartbeat and the next, every internal deliberation ceased.

After a moment of bewilderment came disbelief.

Then, at the threat of imminent danger, paralysis. His entire scalp froze stiff. His throat seized.

When terror's grasp eased a little, Julian stood up. His paddling shorts remained around his ankles.

He dropped the toilet roll. It bounced and tumbled down the camber of the bank, before disappearing into the undergrowth.

He'd not heard anyone approach. Not a sound.

And within the time it had taken him to stand up, the speckled head, without making so much as a rustle, had disappeared. But the horrible feathered face had definitely been there. From inside the cascade of willow that screened him from the river, the head had appeared. And he had been regarded by it.

Moments later, however, he was uncertain that he'd seen an actual face. He must have encountered a mask instead. A facial covering that had featured an appalling pair of pink eyes, with tiny black pupils, buried inside layers of feathers. And from the position of the head, if the figure had been standing upright, the body below must have been small. About the size of a toddler. Either that, or someone had silently crept up to him, on their hands and knees, wearing the loathsome headdress.

He wasn't sure which option was worse.

23

[6–7pm]

When Marcus called, 'I'll come to you,' across the interior, the cavernous dome swallowed his frail voice and he felt even less substantial.

Like a blind man, he guided himself around the walls, palming stone and huffing pinched breaths in a vain attempt to inhibit the stench assailing his very existence. Bewilderment drove the headache conjured by the toxin and dehydration. Occasionally, in the murk, he stepped over a particularly evil-smelling lump. The scattering of parts over such a wide area continued to confound him. But not knowing why he was here, or why this had been done to him, was a greater drain on his strength and his focus than the imprecise hobble he made around the clammy walls.

Despite his disorientation, Marcus tried to recall some of Colman's monologue about archaeology. The owner of the valley had spoken about ruins. A dig. Codes in the soil. Foundations of a temple discovered beneath a tennis court.

A temple – this stinking abattoir?

The tech billionaire and AI charlatan turned organic farmer, the baron in his compound ruling mad peasants, had bragged about ancient sacred purposes. This much Marcus remembered. Though Colman had remained enigmatic about the role that the monument of the ages had played in the valley, right up until Marcus had lost consciousness, the man had definitely said something about a 'god' and 'sacrifice'.

He'd been too preoccupied with staying conscious, while fighting nausea, to pay much attention to Colman's ridiculous claims. Being inside the dome, however, horrified and frightened him enough to reconsider what he'd been told when outside it.

Had the authorities even been notified about Jane's dire condition?

Nigel had come out of the manor house grinning. The paddle leader claimed to have taken control of the crisis and executed calls to the appropriate parties. So, he must have spoken to someone. But the colony at the Wyrm Valley had since drugged and abducted three strangers. This wasn't the behaviour of people who would have let Nigel summon the emergency services. Exposing Colman's operation to the authorities would be an act more counterproductive than opening its gates to the general public.

Marcus shuffled to where the other two leaned and struggled to remain upright. He must know what they had learned, because he doubted that a person drugged and forced inside this reeking mound was going to be granted an opportunity to leave it anytime soon. He was already certain that what they were enduring was no lesson designed to deter trespassers from returning to a private area of conservation and outstanding natural beauty.

None of this could be happening. Not really.

And yet it was. He was inside *here*. Now.

Jane's chest, moist and puffy, pocked by punctures, streaked with blood and the shadows of a woodland canopy.

Dead radios.

No signal.

A pendulous skull hanging from a withered tree branch above a brackish creek.

Dear God.

He must revive himself. And think.

You must. You must.

Despite having struggled to find any fellow feeling or affection for his imprisoned companions today, Marcus nearly wept with relief when he finally reached them. Sophie felt the same and, tearfully, tried to clasp him.

But even in hell, Nigel staggered between them. 'What's this bastard doing?' he demanded. A patter of saliva speckled Marcus's face. They'd not been this physically close for a long time; not since deep-sea rescue practice in the early days of the couple's sea kayaking. He and Nigel had since contrived to avoid even carrying each other's boats to and from the water. Ferrying Jane's body across the floodplain had been the first physical burden they'd shared in years.

A glimmer of neat teeth and the whites of two small, angry eyes, was all Marcus saw of Nigel. He asked nothing of how Marcus felt. He couldn't bring himself to entertain even a smidgen of sympathy for his plight. Marcus wondered if the man's loathing of him was capable of any moderation. He'd seemed repulsed by Jane's dilemma too; irritated that she'd been injured.

Does he know?

'The wine. Poisoned us,' Sophie whispered, her words papery and breathless.

Marcus coughed then swallowed three times to lubricate his throat. He scratched out a few words. 'Clement. Clement Colman.'

'What?' Nigel wasn't as inebriated as him or Sophie. He'd never been a big drinker. He couldn't have swallowed as much of the valley's glorious wine.

'Bloke at the manor house. He's that tech guy. Owns all this. Claims this is a temple.'

'Temple! What fucking temple?' Nigel bellowed.

Marcus stepped away from him. 'I don't know.'

'Well, you're not much bloody use then, are you?'

Despite his misery and delirium, Marcus's face flushed hot with irritation. 'They found something—'

'Found what?'

'Nigel! Shut up!' from Sophie, her exhausted voice moistened by grief.

'They dug up foundations. For this thing. The henge too. Some place that was here before. They think it's ceremonial. Neolithic. They erected all of this, recreated what they think was here before. That's what he said to me. I was out of it. Head swimming. I don't remember much. But these nut jobs think its provenance is ancient, sacred—'

'Provenance? Provenance, my arse! Why are we inside it? Bloody nonsense!' Nigel's familiar roar had not only returned but seemed likely to remain his basic setting. 'What's it got to do with us?'

'They worship a god here. Make sacrifices. That's all I can remember.'

That shut them both up. Sophie gasped. Nigel's murky silhouette stiffened.

'Ambulance. You called 999?' Marcus pressed through Nigel's silence. 'For Jane? The call was made?'

In the ensuing silence, Marcus might have counted to four.

'He didn't,' Sophie said.

'I was going to. But—'

'The stupid bastard let that tosser make the call.'

'He insisted!' The weight of humiliation and remorse in Nigel's voice was painful to hear.

'The line was probably dead. Or he called the fucking speaking clock!' his wife screamed.

'Christ,' Marcus said. He'd expected as much but hearing it confirmed felt like being told that he had cancer. 'Oh, Christ.' He sank to his knees and placed his hands on the damp soil that he could not see.

'Why did they paint us in blood?' Sophie asked him. Through the darkness, from where she squatted, her face nudged closer. Her hair seemed to be missing, but it was plastered, blackly, about her skull. She looked as if she'd been burned. And in such thin light her eyes were seared of more than hope.

Abject and filthy and reduced to your knees. All of you.
Marcus shook his head. 'Fuck knows. I was out of it when they covered me with this slop. But it can't be good.'

'Thinks he's teaching us a lesson!' Nigel roared. 'Scaring us! They're bloody crazy! They don't live in the same world as anyone else! That's bloody obvious! This is all a fantasy! They've involved us because we paddled up their creek without permission!' He laughed, the sound unpleasant, the tone vindictive. 'I'll have this whole valley shut down. Police crawling all over it! I bet they're growing drugs like those maniacs in Brickburgh. Fucking cave hippies! Throwbacks! Didn't those arseholes cover themselves in blood and worship a bloody dog?'

'A hyena,' Sophie muttered. 'In caves filled with human remains.' Her voice trembled and she stifled tears. 'Nigel's in denial, Marcus,' his wife added.

'I am bloody not!' he roared back at her.

'You are,' Sophie said, as her indistinct but gore covered face edged even closer to Marcus. Like him, she'd been sick; he could smell it on her breath. 'We're not leaving here, are we?'

The question might have slid ice all over Marcus's stinking, dirty skin. He had no answer ready, nor could he make even a feeble attempt at reassurance.

'There's a body, Marcus,' Sophie said, her voice dropping to a whisper.

'What?' he asked, raising his head and moistening his desiccated throat again with saliva. 'What did you say?'

'A person. In here with us. Dead.'

Without disbelieving what she'd said, Marcus still repeated, 'What?'

'It's not just cows in here. They killed someone. A person.'

'You don't know that!' Nigel shrieked. 'I bloody told you! They put dead things in here. That's all. One of the hippy twats must have died. This is some kind of new age open grave. These types do this. Stick themselves under trees and ... and things like that. They think it's natural. They think oils and herbs can cure diseases. Did you see those kids? Probably never been to school. They're all wacko!'

Marcus almost laughed. Had he done so, he knew it would have placed him at the top of a slippery slope, with madness waiting at the bottom. He considered stumbling back across the dome to the other side. This pair were making everything worse. *In life, so in death.*

Sophie did laugh. And she didn't stop. Her dry voice cackled and cracked and rose through the octaves until it disintegrated into a shrill wail. Then the noise she made plunged and disintegrated into sobbing, or dry heaving. It was too awful to listen to. 'My Robbie,' she screamed.

Their son. Their little boy. Three years old. He was with his nan while Mum and Dad enjoyed couple's time on a paddle. But his parents were now stained with animal blood and trapped inside a dungeon reeking of death.

Marcus was feeling as weak as he'd ever been, but this new and terrible awareness made him feel even worse.

They have a kid. Oh, my Lord, they have a kid.
The joke has to end.
It's time to let us out.

The true nature of their plight was overcoming him in stages. Notions of their fate slid around his muddled head, then expanded until imagining them further became unbearable. Staggered revelation. His thoughts had not moved much faster than the stumps of his legs when they'd attempted to walk. But terror now lit a stronger fire than mere fear under his consciousness. Inside the temple, the slow return of sentience had few advantages. 'This body . . .' he started to ask.

'Torn apart!' Sophie screamed. 'I stepped on a face. In the dark. The face slid off the fucking skull! I can still feel it on my foot. The nose . . . in my instep . . . The smell!'

'Stop it,' Nigel muttered at his wife.

'There's a hand over there! How is that a natural death, you bloody moron?' she screamed at her husband. 'That poor bastard was ripped apart!'

'Shut up. Shut up, Soph. Please. It can't have been. You think this Clement imbecile has a tiger, or something?' Nigel said, pleading with her to calm down, as well as needing to persuade himself that his wife's wild assumptions were incorrect.

Marcus clawed himself up the wall and staggered inwards to where more light fell upon the centre of the space. Coughing as he moved, he plugged the lower half of his face with a forearm. Blood cracked and flaked from his skin. Still unsteady on his feet, he didn't get too close to the stone shaft that plunged into the greatest darkness.

Turning about, Marcus assessed the walls above his head. More specifically, he tried to focus on the cracks between the blocks of stone. As if his eyes were already guiding his toes and fingertips, he instinctively looked for fissures. The inner surface of the temple was not entirely smooth. The depth of the visible crevices remained to be tested, but the gassy smudges of light filtered through gaps and probed the interior all the way to the crest. Even across the underside of the domed ceiling, the slots continued. Marcus wondered if it would be possible for a climber to make a fist inside a slot, to support a body's weight; this might even allow the extension of another arm to reach the next slit, and so on.

To work on his physical and core strength, during the winter months, he often used the indoor climbing wall in Exeter. These walls suggested some equivalency with the hardest route he'd ever attempted, though this climb would be twenty times longer, with the ceiling presenting an impossible overhang. There was no safety harness or rope at his disposal either.

A fall from that height would break an ankle or leg, even a back.

It might be possible to reach the beam. But to what purpose? Even if he were able to stand upright on the spar, the beam wasn't high enough to allow him to clutch at the hole above in the underside of the roof. And even when dimly visible at such a remove, that curved, sepulchral ceiling was enough to trigger his vertigo. Yet he could not help imagining being forced to make a desperate attempt to climb the stinking walls, before he expired of thirst.

He shook his shaggy, mired head and slumped onto his heels. He wasn't thinking rationally.

'Soph, you have to be strong,' Nigel muttered from near the wall. He was stooped over her. 'For Robbie. We will see him again. Our boy.'

She answered with a deep sob, her agony resurgent.

'You should listen to your wife, Nigel. She's way ahead of you on this,' Clement Colman said, from the other side of the wall.

24

[6–7pm]

After Clement Colman broke his silence, none of them spoke. All were struck dumb. For the entire period they'd been installed within the stone mound, Clement could have been outside, listening. Had Marcus, Nigel and Sophie been able to see each other's faces in any detail, they'd have witnessed a mutual dawning of this realisation.

The landowner's first words betrayed an attempt to contain guilty excitement. His breathless tone also indicated a suppression of nerves; perhaps in anticipation of something significant. Whatever that revelation might be, Marcus assumed it was not in their best interests. And now that he was better able to consider the man's behaviour, he'd suspected this same underlying agitation in Colman's demeanour earlier. On the lawn of the manor house, when first confronted by the three troubled trespassers, the landowner had appeared disproportionately cagey. His initial irritation had turned into a contrived indifference, to mask what must have been a fear of discovery, of the exposure of malign activities being conducted on his private land.

On account of his own growing desperation, and he knew it was nothing more, Marcus still clutched at the idea that their doping and confinement were an elaborate stratagem; that Colman was merely punishing them and making an example of those who dared to intrude on his land. According to this swiftly dispersing wishful fantasy, their ordeal would soon end.

'I need you all to change your thinking. I cannot change your circumstances. I sincerely wish that I were able to, though you may not believe me,' the valley owner said, from the far side of the thick, curving wall. 'All I can suggest is that you consider your dilemma to be a unique privilege. Because you are now part of a great tradition. You've nearly completed a journey that was once taken inside this valley for millennia. The ground beneath your feet is saturated with the remains of animals and people who in the past completed the very same procession as you. A few of our own have walked in your footsteps too. Unwittingly of late, it has to be said, and this is regrettable.' For a moment, the man's voice weakened, almost cracking on the final syllable, until he cleared his throat. 'But if you can alter your perspective and view your participation as part of a great cycle, I hope that some understanding can be drawn from this unfortunate bind that you're in.'

'Oh God,' Sophie muttered, but loudly enough to be heard by Marcus, who hadn't moved from the centre of the structure. 'Is he saying . . .' She must have been reminded of what she'd trodden on in the dark, and of the impression that part of a human face had left on her soft instep.

A wave of nausea broke over Marcus. He closed his eyes, bent forward and placed his hands on his begrimed thighs. He could do nothing but listen to the madman, who now circled the mound while holding forth.

'Now, this might be hard to take in, at present, but a full enlightenment is only a few hours away. You see, an actual god's feasts are scattered about where you stand. Incredible. Preposterous, you might think. And I don't expect you to believe me. Not yet. But, I'm very sorry to say, your own bones will soon join the remains of the people who first made this unique journey, through this valley, eight thousand years ago.'

'What?' Sophie screamed.

Monumental

As if in awe at what his own thoughts suggested, Clement Colman sucked in his breath. When he spoke again, his voice trembled. 'A legacy.'

Marcus imagined Colman's bearded face on the other side of the exterior wall. The freckled features would be sweating, but, despite what sounded like genuine remorse in his tone – though it might have been nothing more than a squeamish shame – his little eyes would have narrowed and developed the faraway, beatific aspect that Marcus had noticed earlier, when the man had first lectured him about the significance of the archaeological discoveries in the Wyrm. The lunatic's narcissism was, once more, reaching for the grandiose.

If he wasn't mistaken, what Colman was disclosing also implied a gleefully sadistic, even inhuman, quality in this relishing of the power that he held over them. What was even more appalling than any satisfaction that Colman derived from the situation was his belief that he was entitled to imprison and execute strangers. Actual people. This was the hardest thing for Marcus to acknowledge. He'd heard and read about such people, but he'd never expected to encounter one. Not in this life.

Once the wave of nausea had ebbed, Marcus opened his eyes and followed the direction that the voice of their tormentor took. The speaker was padding more quickly around the circumference of the dome, moving south.

Sophie stumbled sideways, with one hand pressed against the stones for support. She seemed anxious to follow that voice.

'What? What's he saying? He's insane!' Nigel cried out.

'It sounds crazy, Nigel,' Clement said, and so good-naturedly that the inappropriateness of his tone felt as shocking as the befouled, putrid interior. 'I get that. Why you'd think that. I really do. It took us a few years to grasp the importance of this valley and of what still exists here. But the truth of the matter is now unequivocal. And you will come to understand this too. This very evening, in fact, as we mark a grand cycle and tradition. You see, for thousands of years, people and animals went inside the original building alive. But they never came back out in the same condition, none of them. What we discovered during the excavations, Nigel, were the remains of sacrifices. Inside a temple. Or, if you prefer, a banqueting hall for something extremely old. The temple was never more than a receptacle for a miracle.'

'This can't be happening,' Sophie said to the others inside, then swung her head at a slit in the wall. 'Are you fucking insane? Joke's over!'

Clement ignored her. 'A gateway between states, between places. That is where you are standing. I'm just trying to explain. You deserve that much. A door, you see, between here and someplace else, exists inside the temple. I tried to tell Marcus earlier – but he was feeling a bit squiffy. But I told him that the heart of the whole edifice, the interior of this design, was never intended for the living to occupy. Or not for very long. What we never realised, until it was too late, was that by digging down so far, and knocking on some very strange doors, we were establishing, shall we say, a continuity, or service, in our stewardship of this great but terrible valley.'

'What's this bloody idiot gabbing about?' Nigel seemed to ask of himself as much as his fellow captives. He was still prisoner to his own astonishment, disbelief and outrage. Marcus felt that he, at least, had moved on. Strangely, he envied Nigel's mystification.

Clement Colman's voice continued to rotate around the curved stone wall. He was reciting his own epiphany, as if only repetition would help him believe himself. 'The purpose of the inner sanctum was reserved for the presence of the supernormal. Something that was being worshipped. Right here! A god. And on your side of the door, right where you stand, gods have been known to eat.'

'You wretched, mad bastard!' Sophie even thumped her fists against the stone wall, though, so dense was the masonry, her blows made no sound at all. 'Get that bloody door open now! Now! Do you hear what I am saying? You crazy bastard! Open it! Now!'

'Alas, Sophie, if only dear Jane had not stepped into those woods, I'd have let you all paddle home with a bottle of our finest wine. I'm afraid, however, that what would have been found in her bloodwork, folks, pretty much sealed the current deal. But, at least, after your untimely intrusion into the rite, one of our own will be granted a reprieve. So, there's that. Some good will come from the sacrifice that you are making tonight. And you'll buy me more time to figure out how the rest of us dig our way out of this mess, once this year's rite is finished. So that no one else has to . . . well, you know, stand in your shoes.'

'What the hell are you talking about? Get that damn door open now!' As Nigel roared, he made quick work of crossing the earthen floor towards the wooden door. Marcus watched him stagger yet maintain a reasonably direct trajectory.

Clement ignored Nigel's rant. 'Jane, unfortunately, must have disturbed the old priesthood.' Their host was too absorbed by his embellishments and sheepishly delighted by the sound of his own voice; the reclamation, Marcus presumed, of status and power lost when the tech industry showed him another kind of door, from his former position, from which he'd unleashed other high-risk products without regulation, antidotes or any meaningful thought about consequences.

'Jane received their mark. Their blessing. Crude, perhaps, but there's nothing that can be done once someone has been *kissed* by a wight. Let me tell you that from personal experience. You know, it was the Little Priests who put an end to the care home and the hotel. The mining too. Nothing could ever stick here. Because the valley was not being administered, was not being used properly for its intended purpose. The Wyrm Valley's destiny, you could say, was written in stone. If you look back far enough, and I dug as far back as 6000 BC, you'll find evidence of the much misunderstood and maligned priesthood of the mine. Because of them, the whole valley was believed cursed for thousands of years. For good reason too.'

'What the hell is wrong with this freak?' Nigel bellowed.

'Your timing was impeccably wrong, Nigel. That's all. When you paddled up my estuary, you stuck your bloody beaks in at precisely the wrong time of year.'

'Let us out!' Nigel kicked at the door with the sole of a bare foot. His blows made no sound beyond a feeble thumping. And that concluded when he hurt his foot.

Marcus finally broke his silence. 'Others will come. People know we came here! It's not too late to turn back, Clement. There's always a choice. Don't make this worse than it already is.'

'Yes!' Nigel roared in agreement. 'If we're not back by Friday, you'll have the bloody coastguard here!'

Marcus gritted his teeth. Though this might have been the first time in years that the two men had found agreement in anything, he desperately wished that Nigel had not revealed their plans. He should have lied and said that the paddling group was expected back on Thursday morning. That would have restricted Clement Colman's timeline, and his opportunity to enact more of this psychopathic nonsense, by twenty-four hours.

'Oh, Marcus. That self-assurance might get Sophie all hot and bothered. And I'll let you explain that to her husband in the time that you have left. To settle your affairs, as it were. I'm afraid your wife has been indiscreet, Nigel. Was overheard earlier, while you were inside my house. And do you all think we're stupid? We who have done nothing less than make contact with the divine? An actual god! We've always had a plan for just such an occasion as this – an intrusion at precisely the most inopportune time. By the end of the rite, there'll be little or no evidence that any of you were ever here.

'I've arranged for your boats and kit to be dumped way out in the channel, once high water returns. Money can't buy everything, but I've found that it will motivate a couple

Monumental

of blokes I know, who own a crab boat. The tidal flow will disperse your belongings to the east. I'd expect them to make landfall in Dorset, in about one week. Nor will there be any sign of the miracle that we've unwittingly returned to this valley, for the second year running.

'Though we've a bit of tidying up to do in there, we're shutting the shit-show down and aim to be long gone soon. It's time to throw the towel in. And we won't be the first in the valley to do so. Sometimes, acceptance is a bitch.'

'You cannot . . . CANNOT KEEP US IN HERE!' Sophie roared. Marcus doubted that even the most badly behaved children in the school where she taught had ever heard such fury explode from her.

Clement continued to try to justify why they'd been drugged, abducted and imprisoned. Ultimately, their objections only appeared to encourage him, because his lecture continued in more of a self-regarding, amused and smug fashion, as if he were delivering a TED talk. So assured was he of his arrangements, he never raised his voice, in which Marcus better detected a trace of an American accent, or an affectation from all of the time the man must have spent out there.

'If only you'd come a couple of weeks ago, you'd have been fine. Even if you'd shown up next week, then none of this would be happening. The window in our annual calendar is very narrow, but the October rite must be observed. Whether we like it or not. Had we known how things were going to pan out, and that we'd all be standing here like this, we'd never have removed the capstone or built the temple. But I've always been a bugger for smashing ceilings.'

'I'll smash your bloody ceiling! And to hell with your October rite,' Nigel bellowed. 'You can shove it up your arse! You need to think about damage limitation. All of you. Do you hear me, you other freaks, creeping about out there? If you believe anything this lunatic says, you're deceiving yourselves. Greatly! You all need to start creating a distance between yourselves and this criminal. He's responsible!

Kidnap. Maybe worse than that!' Over by the door, Nigel ranted himself hoarse, breathless and into what sounded like hyperventilation.

Outside, silence fell. Perhaps, Marcus hoped, Clement was scanning the faces of his followers to detect flickers of doubt. Nigel had made a fist of persuasion, though Marcus suspected that they remained some distance from talking their way out of the tomb. He didn't understand what had bitten Jane, nor why that must remain hidden. And if Sophie was right, there was a human corpse inside the mound with them too. He hadn't inspected the remains, but no longer doubted her assumption that a human cadaver shared the temple with them.

Sophie changed her tack. Her voice softened, sounding more composed. She spoke to their captor as if she were talking down one of her secondary school pupils who'd become overexcited and done something regrettable that they didn't fully understand. 'Clement, I am a mother. Of a little boy who needs me so much. And whom I love dearly. We are people, in here, with families. Homes. Jobs. Attachments. People who are loved and needed by others. We are not . . . cows. We are not to be mistaken for the cattle that you have disposed of, in your, your . . . religion. I respect your beliefs. It's just a lot for us to take in right now. But we do not share your faith, and we would all like to go back to our boats now and leave your valley with our injured friend who has received no medical attention for her serious wounds. Now, can you please find it in your heart to open the door and let us return to our lives? To the people who are dependent on us. People we are responsible for.'

Outside the walls of the temple, the silence continued.

Marcus moved down the wall, his legs gradually feeling sturdier beneath him as time progressed. Fear appeared to have aided the dispersal of the drug in his blood. He spread his fingers and began exploring the stones. Squinting in poor light, he became more aware and more concerned about whether the time approached when they would be unable to see inside the dome. Where his fingertips found fissures between the stone blocks, they delved inside to assess the width and depth of the gaps.

'Well said, Sophie.' Clement couldn't have been more than a few metres from where Sophie stood, with her hands spread on the wall separating them. 'Rousing, even touching.' But Colman was unable to conceal his condescension, as if he too was talking to someone younger. 'I truly understand how you must be feeling right now. But you're doing no one any favours by persisting with this resistance to inevitability.'

'Please. My son. My little boy.'

'Sophie, we may all believe that we are special, but we are not. Not I. Not you. We're not here for long and we're all destined for dust. But look at it another way. Here, in this valley, in the heart of this very, very special place, one can get close to something that transcends us and all of our concerns, and our brief moments of consciousness in the cosmos. This, surely, is an honour.'

'Are you even human? You wretched, wretched bastard,' Sophie muttered, and there was something forlorn in her accusation, as if she now pitied more than loathed him.

'He's filth!' Her husband screeched with a cry of such desperation that Marcus stopped groping about the walls and turned around. 'Stinking hippy filth!' Nigel added.

'This goes so far beyond all of our species' advancements. AI, nuclear power, space travel, genetic manipulation, anything that you care to name as we endeavour to control creation. Or to be divine ourselves. We've simply missed the point. I did, too, more than most. Because what exists here goes beyond scientific reasoning, biology, mortality and the known fucking universe. Alas, it goes some way beyond my knowledge and control too. What we have found is a completely new form of existence. And at least you have the privilege of witnessing it. Albeit briefly. This is all I can offer you by way of consolation.'

'You arrogant bastard!' Nigel threw himself against the door.

Marcus found himself close to a slot between the blocks that let flow a shaft of sweet meadow air, and an aperture that also allowed him to better hear more of Clement Colman's deranged philosophy.

Seclusion and power and narcissism, he understood, did terrible things to already unpleasant people. And yet, he intuited, it wasn't only their trespass into the valley that had disturbed the man. Clement Colman had a lot of front, but he was unsettled and apprehensive and about to jump ship himself. There may have been a flicker of a conscience inside him, somewhere, before he murdered someone else. This vestige of uncertainty was more likely to be doubt about his own safety, and his ability to manage a terrible situation that he'd caused but struggled to step away from. Though what exactly this situation was about to evolve into still eluded Marcus.

What Colman said next sounded rehearsed. A spiel that other unfortunate wretches inside the temple might have heard in their last hours alive.

'Perspective, folks. Perspective. You can be released from the posturing about one's uniqueness. Only those who enter a temple like this can experience the far greater status of having been in the presence of a god. Only right where you stand can the greatest journey of all be achieved.'

'Fuck off!' Nigel roared.

'Crossing over. Transmigration, if you want. To join with the divine and one of the original deities worshipped by our ancestors. But the animal in you must be destroyed, I'm afraid. That's the only unpleasant part. No other way, Nigel. Always been the case. Never changes. But that part of the process doesn't last for long, fortunately for you. Alas, what we do know only too well is that the end of the animal must be violent. The Little Priests made us aware of this pretty quickly.'

'Oh dear God,' Sophie muttered. 'Jesus Christ. What's he saying? What does it mean?' She bent double and emptied her stomach over her bare, encrusted feet.

'Flesh must be eradicated, my dear Sophie, and the body reduced until it is unrecognisable amidst the detritus of others who have also cast off the animal and become spirit. Whatever we know of consciousness, that is freed. Transmutes. Goes someplace else. Here, that can happen. You'll become part of it. Ask me, I'd say it's a damn sight better than expiring in some hospital bed, after a few more flawed and generally pointless years of your current existences. The great appetite in this rite is for sentience. Yes, the god is a devourer of the body. But the mind and the spirit are what it desires most. Or, quite frankly, things will get out of hand here. We've not much choice these days. But the excited, terrified, frantic mind is like fucking catnip inside there.'

Try as he might, Marcus could find little more than toe and finger holds in the wall; his hands and feet were still too weak and clumsy to support his weight. He stepped back from the unforgiving stones. 'So where is it, Clement?' he called out. 'Where is your god?'

'Far, far away, Marcus. And yet, right beneath your feet.'

'Or do you think it inhabits you, as you rip apart defenceless animals and drugged people who are half-crazed with thirst and hunger. In your temple? It's an abattoir crossed with a urinal. A sewer built by fuckwits. Does it make you feel special, this power and control? Or are you displacing your revenge on us and these poor animals, like some sociopathic teenager, after being proved to be a crook and a fraud? After imbibing your finest piss, my memory isn't what it was, Clement, but I seem to remember that you not only inflated the value of your shitty AI apps but lied about their capabilities. I remember deleting one of your pieces of shit off my phone. Contamination. Slurry. That's all you ever produced. Shite and slop! That's your legacy. And there was all manner of crap in the press about bullying and harassment at your gaff too. You've got form and you left that place under a cloud. So, I wonder, did your staff refuse to serve you as a god, Clement? But here, let me guess, here you've found a way to live out the fantasy.'

'Oh Marcus. Please don't. You're embarrassing yourself!'

'You delude yourself that you're more than a resentful, inadequate, beta twerp. A shoddy little tech bro with a messiah complex. I hope your tattooed mates are listening in and realising just what they've hitched their trailers to. They don't seem that bright, mate. Best you could do, I guess. Because you're all going down hard. And pretty soon too.'

Something of what he'd just said might have stuck a pin in a nerve. Colman tried to cloak the emotion with a detached, ironic tone, though this succeeded in making him sound as if he was trying too hard. 'You might lack the imagination or intelligence to understand what I'm saying, Marcus. Because you're fond of rumours, aren't you? Hearsay. Gossip about people who've achieved more than you'd ever be capable of comprehending. Well, I'm going to share something with you. It's only fair that you know another reason why something terrible but awesome is about to happen to you. What we have in this region, Marcus, is part of an immensely special pantheon. There is no one god or goddess. They're teeming. Here! Concentrated in this region. We have a group of deities in Devon.

'No doubt you will have heard the rumours about Brickburgh, Marcus. And what old Rory Willows and his witch wife worshipped up country? The great Crocuta of Brickburgh. That was no rumour. No folk tale. No story dreamed up by drug dealers. They never found Willows, but consider the bones. How many were found in those caves, old and new? A deity of the pool is also known to exist, one who has long accepted succour through woven vessels. And this was near to where a sow was found beneath a barrow, by cunning folk. There may be scores more gods who sleep close to the surface of this county alone. But none yet rediscovered, to my eye, Marcus, are greater than the Blood Worm of this hallowed valley.'

'Worm, my arse! You hippy twat!' Nigel shrieked.

'I wish it were so, Nigel. But the deity rules a kingdom beneath the earth. The entrances are here. I found two.

Monumental

And I only wish you had the sense to recognise a smidgen of your special role, to consecrate its most enthusiastic return.' His voice dropped, wistful, perhaps exhausted. 'And not least for containing its escape.'

'He's insane. He's clearly insane. They all are. Even now, in this day and age, they believe this crap,' Nigel cried out as he shuffled back across the floor of the temple. When he came to a stop, he kept clear of his wife and Marcus.

'Clem! Clem!' someone called from outside. Vine, Marcus thought. 'Now, mate. They must have left the mine. Better get the cows down.'

Marcus didn't want Clement to leave. He wanted to know where Clement and his cronies were, wanted to goad them some more and to instil doubt and division within their ranks. 'So, what happens now then, oh high priest of the Wyrm Valley? When do we meet your god? Have your companions seen it, I wonder? Or are they beginning to smell the bullshit? I do wonder.'

He cast his voice further, bellowing through a slot between the stone blocks at head height. 'There is no god! No deities in Devon. This is no temple. It's a tomb you've built here. And a shithouse. And the evidence inside it is going to damn you. You're the ones who'll soon be behind walls and bars. You'd best start thinking about how to reduce your sentences!'

Only when Marcus finished shouting did he hear the wind. It wasn't strong but the breeze originating from the west of the valley probed and *hushed-hushed* between the gaps in the stones. One right above his head sighed. Then another higher up. Then two more above that. And so odd were the acoustics inside the stone dome that while the wind that sluiced between the slits didn't exactly make musical notes, it transformed the stone dome into a tuneless organ. The funnelling, piping air through the narrow slits was amplified; the effect inside the rocky mound strange, even eerie.

An edge of concern sharpened the tautness in Clement's tone. It required more effort for him to be heard inside. He'd moved further away from the stinking structure that he'd just tried to hard sell to them as a hallowed temple in which they should embrace the great opportunity of ending their lives. 'You stand in a cathedral, no less – a living church – and you can't even grasp it. A true monument to a living god. And you'll see, soon enough, how wrong you are, Marcus, about, well, everything. But sadly, we must take our leave now. We've preparations to make and you've interrupted us enough for one day. It'll be dark soon and we all need to be safely ensconced behind the henge. For all the good that's done. That needs some fine tuning, to be honest. To contain it. Which is why we don't tend to get too close. It's started to stray, you see, from the temple. But it's supposed to stay close to where *things* are concentrated. It's why we planned on introducing wild pigs. We'd hoped that a herd of swine might placate a predilection for human flesh. And we don't want it roaming any further than it already has done. For obvious reasons. But, alas, we've gone some distance off course in realising our dreams and hopes. That goes for you lot too, I guess.'

'Wait!' Sophie screamed.

'It's time to light the pyres of blood, Sophie! Only the Little Priests can call out its name! I don't want to inflate our role here, beyond being mere adepts. But I believe they're already in the wind. Can you hear them?'

Several pairs of feet scuffed the grass outside. A quad bike grunted awake. Clement's voice faded. 'Shame we can't stick around to see what our dividends as shareholders would have been for our performance this year! For giving so much. A veritable bounty. But it's farewell for now, folks! So, we give thanks for your pilgrimage to a place of such monumental power!'

The second quad bike erupted before both engines growled away, their noise fading as the distance grew between captors and captives.

25

[6–7pm]

*E*ver since they'd entered the estuary, the air had remained still and oddly warm. But an unexpected and sudden breeze now rustled the distant trees on the western slope, brushed over the meadow and tilted the grass towards the campsite. As if exhaled from hidden mouths, hooded by the rocky cowls of unlit caves, the breeze carried the fragrance of stones forbidden the warmth of sunlight. A cold, damp, mineral scent that not only moved Julian and Mary's hair but filled their sinuses, their heads, their thoughts.

The flanks of the erected tent rippled.

Something was about to happen. Something was going to change.

A trace of smoke inside a tall building would have done less to trigger Julian's apprehension. He shivered and his thoughts returned to what lay beyond the estuary basin – the sea.

Daylight was reduced to vestiges. In less than an hour it would be fully dark. Floundering in the creek's mud, without any light save that of a head torch, was still a better option than being here and waiting. Waiting and not knowing; maddening himself with guessing.

'Julian? Julian, are you listening?' Mary asked him again.

Not really. He needed to finish getting his kit ready for departure. He needed to get on the water. There was no more time to waste. *Quite frankly.*

He stared at his boat, the two open hatches. He tried to organise his thoughts into a logical row of tasks that he could follow, step by step. Since returning from the riverbank, he'd forgotten everything he knew about preparing for a paddle. Nor could he still the tremor in his hands. They looked horrible, too white and lumpy. These days, he saw his age in his hands; more so than in the reflection of his sixty-four-year-old face in the bathroom mirror, the glass speckled with toothpaste. The palsy of his fingers made him feel ten years older than that.

'They came out of the stone houses that sit beneath the red sky,' Jane said, her face wet, her eyes wide with a fearful wonder. 'They're coming into the green world to fetch us. So many of them.'

Julian had put on his buoyancy jacket hurriedly. But he should have stepped into his spraydeck first. He unzipped the jacket, undoing what scant progress he'd made. *Where was the radio?* He couldn't see it or remember where he'd placed it on the ground.

Julian hurriedly closed and fastened the two deck hatches, then saw his dry bag, containing emergency food and dry clothes, lying on the grass. He undid the stern hatch. Picked up the dry bag. Stuffed it inside the rear hold.

'Here come the little white children. They're in the trees for milk and blood,' Jane whispered, loud enough for Julian to hear. And, *quite frankly*, he'd heard enough of all that too. If he never heard that creepy gibberish again, he'd be blessed; though he also wondered, now that he had heard these utterances, if he'd ever forget them.

'She's getting cold, Julian,' Mary called to him. 'Can you help me get her inside your tent? My shoulder's gone really stiff.'

No *time!* No time for that. He had to get on the water – the river, the creek, the estuary, the bloody sea. Julian sealed the boat's hatches, then located his VHF radio and stuffed it in a pocket. His water bottle? Where was it? Towline? *By the tent, the tent, the tent. Of course!*

Monumental

The breeze picked up, distantly murmuring through what sounded like an array of pipes. Across the meadow, the grass whispered, the tips of flowers ducking as if avoiding something dangerous in flight overhead.

Julian avoided looking at Mary's concerned yet forlorn face. He'd become tired of seeing that expression. Nor did he look again at Jane's wet head, cradled and often writhing in Mary's lap. Above the top of the sleeping bag that cocooned her, the absorbent pads peeked out, stained crimson. Those he did see, in his peripheral vision, and he felt sick. He hadn't eaten since that morning. Once he was afloat in the estuary, he should eat something like an energy bar. *Where are the bars?* He couldn't remember. *Dry bag, or did you take them out?*

Forget about them.

After locating and retrieving his towline and water bottle, Julian trotted back to his boat. The breeze whipped at the loose folds of his rash vest. He'd put his buoyancy jacket and spraydeck over shorts and a rash vest. *A fleece! A cag!* He'd be getting wet. He needed three layers. And now there was wind.

Bloody wind!

For the second time, he unzipped his jacket with shaky fingers, stepped out of his spraydeck. Ran to his tent and shuffled inside to his rucksack. His dry clothes were inside that bag. As he unclipped the clasps, Mary said, 'Lay out your sleeping bag, so Jane has something to lie on. Then come and help me get her inside. I need you to go through the others' gear and find more water. I think there's a two-litre bottle in Nigel's boat.'

No time for that! Julian backed out of his tent, dragging a fleece behind him. He plucked his winter cagoule from the top of the tent, where it had been airing and was now dry.

Jane's puffy face rose from Mary's lap. 'They're getting closer. They're in the trees and in the wind. Can you hear them?'

Julian's hands appeared to belong to someone else, who'd suffered a stroke. *Right. Get it right. Fleece, cag, spraydeck, buoyancy jacket.*

His hands were shaking too hard to get his cagoule over his head. But at least this time he'd put on the mid-layer first.

'Julian! Can you please help me? I've asked you twice. We need to get Jane inside. Out of the wind.'

Gasping and lathered in fear-sweat, Julian finally tugged his cagoule down his torso to his waist. He stepped into his spraydeck, snatched up his buoyancy jacket, slung his arms through the armholes.

'Julian! You can't just go! I need your help with Jane. I can't bloody well get her inside the tent on my own!'

Julian peered, pointlessly, at his useless radio. Squinting at it, he nodded and said, 'Still no signal.' His white hands fluttered around the zip of his buoyancy vest. As if he was suffering a head trauma and wasn't sure what to do with a zipper, he gaped at his fingers – more delay – until he had a sense of what he was trying to achieve, and ratcheted the zipper pull up to his sternum. That *scrick* of the zipper seemed to underline Mary's fate.

'Julian!'

Julian grabbed his paddle. Then dropped it. Snatched it up again but tripped over one of Sophie's bags and sank to his knees, dropping the paddle. Everything jumped inside his chest, and he couldn't breathe. His mid-layer and cag must be too tight. They squeezed like tourniquets. His breathing was noisy, as if he were trying to draw air through a wet cloth stuck to his face.

Jane tried to sit up. 'Now. Now. Now. We must go. So many are coming from the stone houses. They can hear us.'

'Julian! What's wrong with you?' Mary shrieked.

'Need a bit of kit. Got to have a bit of kit. Obvious, I'd have thought.'

'You're not going anywhere until you've helped me get Jane inside the tent!'

Julian looked at Mary. She was incensed; the black frames of her glasses made her look even more severe. He swallowed. What came out of his mouth was so quiet, she couldn't have heard him. 'I'm going for help.'

She must have read his lips because she said, 'Help! Is that what you call it?'

'Have to,' he whimpered. 'There's . . . something . . .'

'What?'

'Something. Someone was watching me.'

'What do you mean?'

'Down there.' He pointed in the direction of the river. *Was it still there? How will you get on the water, if it is still there? Waiting? For you?*

'Julian! What do you mean?'

'I might get a signal at the end of the estuary.' He could not bring himself to look at Mary as he said that.

He turned his back on her and Jane and skipped to his boat. Then stopped and went back to the campsite for the paddle that he'd left on the grass.

'And from the rows of round houses they're coming. Hopping to us. The pipes were under the ground but now they're the wind. Can you hear? Can someone tell my mummy that I've had an accident? She's a dentist. She's at work. She works on Raddleborough Road . . . They've come from so far away . . . Above the ground, they're children, they're birds. They'll take us away to the stone mounds under the ground. We'll all turn our faces to the giants in the red sky.' Jane began to cry. 'Can someone call my mummy?'

With what resembled a bony claw more than a human hand, Julian retrieved his paddle from the grass. Down one leg of his paddling shorts, a jet of urine flashed hot. He'd not finished on the riverbank before he'd seen *that face! That feathered face!*

He turned again and made for his boat but couldn't swallow and was breathing as if he'd just run across the meadow again, then up and into those appalling trees. One knee cracked, then ached. *Got your kit. It's going to be shallow for a bit. But there should be enough water to drag your boat to the creek. Now that part might be hard going, for a bit.*

'They'll drink us!' Jane screamed. 'They'll crawl all over us and drink us! They get inside you and it's so cold it hurts!'

'Julian!' Mary shouted at him. The force of her voice compelled him to turn around until he faced her and the mess of tents and bags. *Though you managed to get your tent up, mate.* And there again, before him, was Jane's wet head in Mary's lap. And the meadow with the cold-as-stone wind stroking its pelt. But the meadow wasn't only moving because of the wind. Not anymore.

'Julian! What are they?' Mary cried out. She'd seen something in his expression that she'd not liked at all. She'd followed the direction of his gaze to the tumult among the stalks.

Jane was crying. She sounded just like the child that she thought she'd become again. 'Can someone call my mummy! I don't want to. I don't want to go with them. I don't want to see their faces!'

What Julian had seen on the riverbank was but one of many. And even though they were still only midway across the dim floodplain, the probing forward of so many feathered faces was far more alarming than the one that had crept to him at the water's edge.

The cruelty contained within the oval masks was matched by a determination in their grimaces. A uniform expression, frozen on each head. An artisan might have captured the face of a hunting owl at the moment it fell on a mouse.

Before Julian's shock triggered a terrible shaking all over his body, which made his head and arms jerk as if spiked by static, and shivered his skin, and seemed to age his legs by decades, he saw more of what wore the feathered faces.

Pale as grubs, but with a mercury sheen glimmering on their flesh, the host in the meadow resembled a class of primary school children that had been shut underground for years and starved. Against the wintry green of the distant wood from where they'd crawled, some of them rose like hares for a better view of the campsite. Most continued forward without pause. Their pallid knees and elbows jutted as they worked through the grass, knitting a zigzagging course among the bright flowers. Bent over, they came quickly in stooped crouches, moving as fast as albino spiders across a shed's floor once light has fallen through an open door.

'Julian!' Mary screamed.

Jane sat up like a corpse shocked alive. 'Under the hill there are mounds of stone. So many. Houses. The poles grow between the houses. Forever.'

Julian forced feet that he could barely feel to run for his kayak.

26

[6–7pm]

'Are you making any headway?' Sophie called from the other side of the dome. She herself was passing along the wall. Occasionally, she stood on tiptoe to peer through the slits within reach of her craning face. That only intensified Marcus's feeling of enclosure. He didn't know what she might see outside that could help them while trapped inside. 'They've all gone. I think,' Sophie called.

Dusk fell fast. Shadows stained the valley. What was left of the daylight that dropped through the circular flue had faded the porthole of sky to a charcoal smudge. Through random slots in the wall blocks, shards of illumination dimmed to smears. As he'd worked, Marcus had become less aware of where his grubby hands and bone gouger toiled. Once Clement and his coterie had departed, he'd begun hacking at the door with a rib that he'd worked loose from a gristly cow vertebra. A thumb and the palm of one filthy hand were blistered.

Before he'd begun hacking, he'd imagined himself chiselling the rib through the wood at the side of the door. Once he'd gained a purchase between the door and frame, he'd visualised himself levering and splintering the latch and padlock free. All he needed was a gap and some movement. He'd then shoulder and stamp it open.

At one point during his chiselling, he suspected that the door had moved a fraction inside the stone frame. When his trembling fingertips roamed and pushed at the solid wood, near where the padlock hung on the other side, he realised that any play within the frame had been an illusion. The door didn't budge. But his fingertips did detect scratches. Had he made them? Or had another poor wretch in the past futilely toiled here? If these scratches were his own markings, then he'd done nothing more than write the indecipherable signature of the condemned on unforgiving timber.

This was no domestic barrier made of chipboard; this door had not been made to be cracked open with bones. Hard wood was perfectly joined inside a frame of dense stone. So solid was the fitting, the entrance appeared to be airtight.

He'd next tried scraping at the mortar around a stone block. That hadn't worked either. The tip of the rib had chipped and forced him to return to a reeking cattle corpse to find another bone.

Working with the second rib, he quickly felt a sense of hopelessness. By then his aching head was swimming. His arms felt insubstantial; the muscles watery. Gasping and sweating, he'd still dug. Naked and bloodied, with a prehistoric tool, he'd scraped at the dense timber and unyielding stone until he became dizzy.

His thirst burned – was desiccating. He didn't only want to escape the stinking tomb; he was desperate to break away from those he'd been imprisoned with. They concerned him.

From the moment Clement Colman had ridden away on a quad bike, Nigel hadn't spoken. Silent and still, he resembled a statue of a man, ochre-smeared and broken. The meagre light defined his paunch, rounded shoulders, downcast head.

'Door's too thick,' Marcus eventually said, wearily, to answer Sophie's question. He couldn't remember when she'd asked about his progress. Nor did he know how long they'd been inside.

'I'm getting cold. The draughts are going right through me,' she said.

Marcus prodded the soil at the foot of the door. There was a stone sill. Over that the door must swing flush. But the soil before the stone threshold was soft. The sill couldn't descend through the clay forever. Maybe they could tunnel out, under the door. Two or three people working at the earth with bones might dig them out of this premature grave. 'I have an idea. Sophie, can you find a scapula? Shoulder bone. Make it two.'

'I'm not touching dead things,' Sophie said.

Marcus sighed and returned to the open graveyard exhibited around them, in search of another digging implement. Only the very edges seemed free of animal remains. 'While there's still some light, we need to find things that can help us. And quickly.'

At least his brain was beginning to work again. Panic helped. Fear was sobering. The physical exertion refreshed him, pumped his blood and kept him warm, though it made his thirst worse.

So many bones and carcasses were scattered like fallen debris. As he'd laboured against the solid door, he'd tried to pry an answer out of his slow, then often racing, mind: how did the bones come to be arranged in such a manner?

Clement Colman was committed to the insane idea that he had access to a god in this stone tomb. He was a megalomaniac who was surely suffering narcissistic delusions about possessing a hotline to a god. The three of them were to be sacrifices to this ancient deity. Everything that had died inside here before them, reaching back thousands of years, was an offering to it. Or so Colman had crowed from outside the stinking abattoir. This had been the gist of what the derided tech guru had implied.

So what happened to the three of them now? A slow death by thirst and starvation before decomposition? That couldn't be possible; the human corpse between the southern wall and the culvert had not died for lack of sustenance. From as close as he could bear to go to the disorder of ransacked parts, Marcus had inspected the remains. One leg was separated from a crushed pelvis and armless torso that had mostly been rendered to bone. The thigh muscles had been stripped to the knee. The head had retained hair and flesh but had rolled several metres from what was left of the upper body. Sophie had stepped on that. The dead man's face. Marcus thought the corpse was male. A man who'd recently expired inside the *temple*. Within the last week, he guessed.

As he'd dug, scraped and hacked, Marcus had found time to entertain and dismiss several of his own wild theories about the function of the temple. These he'd kept to himself.

He'd considered the disgraced tech billionaire's purchase of a large predatory cat, a tiger or lion. He wondered if the freak show of the Wyrm Valley had been feeding cattle and people to the animal, treating the structure as some kind of Roman amphitheatre. Would that door open soon, like a gate in the Colosseum? And would they see a large feline shape slip into the darkness with them?

The circular culvert in the centre puzzled Marcus. This inspired his giant snake theory; that a Burmese python or anaconda might be housed in a snake pit, something immense, coiled in the void. But then he'd decided that the climate was too cold for a reptile.

What he still imagined was more likely was that Clement and his acolytes would soon show up in fancy dress, wearing their feathered masks. Once they were all hopped out of their skulls, suitably attired and in the zone, they'd go berserk inside the dome with handheld weapons. And they'd not stop hacking until the sacrifices were rent in pieces, like the poor creatures displayed around them. Perhaps the cult even believed that an ancient deity possessed them, instilling prehistoric bloodlust. A Bacchanalian rite. Might Clement and his host even climb out of the well? They had form with hallucinogens. Intoxication was part of the *modus operandi* in the valley; Marcus had experienced this firsthand.

Clement had mentioned the Red Folk of Brickburgh. A few years before, a druggy cult had performed strange pagan rites and inflicted atrocities on its victims in caves and farm buildings. This was only about twenty kilometres north of the Wyrm Valley. There, people had been dismembered, even partially eaten. So, a copycat cult establishing itself in the

Wyrm Valley was not unfeasible. Perhaps this Wyrm Valley operation was an offshoot of Rory Willows's red madness in Brickburgh. Willows was a musician turned cult leader, also a drug baron. The police never found him, or his immediate family. At the end, as they'd murdered each other, many of the cult's members either escaped and were untraceable or were already dead and interned in unmarked graves.

Resentment at the world. Isolation in a valley. Too much acid. Functioning maniacs who'd regressed to a pagan belief system involving animal sacrifice, as a prelude to human sacrifice. In a region with a legacy of pagan madness, he thought all of these notions were more plausible than the captive–predator theory. This very county had set new precedents for human depravity. Willows' and Colman's ideology, however, was more reminiscent of the Aztecs than what he'd read of the ancient Britons. Though how far had Clement Colman gone back in time to seek and source inspiration? Almost as far back as Rory Willows of Brickburgh and the Red Folk, or so it seemed: balls-deep into the Neolithic.

Whatever blood rite was being enacted inside the reeking temple, repeatedly and over a period, Marcus needed a weapon. A bone that might be gripped and wielded like a sword or club. Maybe a femur. He told himself that when the time came, he wouldn't freeze. He told himself that he would go out fighting, tooth and nail.

You've stripped me, drugged me, soiled me, weakened me, and for this I detest you. And I will fuck you up.

Outrage sprinkled gunpowder on his purpose, but anger wasted energy.

And made him feel sick.

With one hand clasped over his mouth and nose, Marcus circled the nearest remnants of the cow from which he'd worked loose the second rib. As he pulled at the neck bones, the moist underside of the spiny heap unleashed a waft of putrefaction that nearly knocked him out. He might have just huffed ether. He dropped the carcass and couldn't bear to bring the hand that had touched the ragged mess, near his face. 'I could use some help over here.'

'What did he mean?' Nigel said.

Marcus sensed that the paddle leader had turned his head towards his wife, who still roamed the inner wall like a condemned queen in a tower. Yes, it was to her that Nigel had addressed the question. 'That bastard lunatic. He said that you'd been indiscreet. What did he mean?'

Sophie stopped moving but stayed quiet.

Marcus cooled to the core. Tension pinched off his breath.

Silence. The disappearing light at the edges of the dome made the stones of the culvert and the wreckage of bones appear starker. Vaulting to the vent in the apex of the dome, the very walls seemed to pause in their inhaling and piping of draughts.

'What! Did! He! Fucking! Mean?' Nigel's roar shook the air.

After he'd finished, he panted like a dog. Marcus thought that he might have been crying, or sobbing. He wasn't. These were bellows of rage that he could hear pumping inside the man. And Nigel, the bloodied statue, finally stepped from his grimy plinth and made his way towards his wife.

She wasn't intimidated in the slightest. 'Not now, Nigel.' Was there sympathy in her voice, or brusque dismissal? No, she was embarrassed for him. Sophie was steel, with sharp edges. Ferocious. Marcus knew that. She'd terrified him, and still did. He'd heard that, in the school where she worked, a place always in special measures, she was one of only two teachers that even the hardest miscreants feared. 'Hardly the right time. Or place.' She laughed drily.

'With him?' Nigel thrust a thick arm in Marcus's direction. Such was the disbelief and derision in the man's reference to him, that Marcus was almost tempted to feel aggrieved. Almost.

'Sort your bloody self out!' Sophie roared back at her husband.

Marcus flinched.

Nigel plodded to the west side of the dome, scowling, hunched, and came to a halt.

Sophie hadn't denied her husband's accusation. Marcus desperately wanted her to.

'I want to get out of here!' she screamed. 'Bloody help us!'

Nigel's voice clawed up his throat and dragged over his teeth, on which each word shredded, before breaking. 'You fucked him.'

Sophie issued no denial. For Marcus, her silence was crucifying. Her blood must have been steaming; Marcus desperately wished that it would cool.

'Of all people. It had to be him,' Nigel ranted. 'That preening peacock wanker!' Again, the stubby arm lashed in Marcus's direction. 'What does anyone see in the prick? I've never understood it.'

'That doesn't surprise me,' Sophie said, and strode towards Nigel. She stopped two steps short of her husband. 'In here? You want to have it out here? You list this as a priority? In here? And why is it such a problem for you now? You've always suspected. I know that. So why did you never say anything before?'

Nigel's shoulders rose and fell. His breathing added a rhythm to the piping between the slits of the southern wall. So profound was the terrible revelation, twinned with the sight of her dim and grimy face, he'd been rendered mute. Grateful for the thin light, Marcus didn't want to watch him suffer.

For a brief, excruciating time in the stinking darkness, Marcus inhabited Nigel and his terrible state and derived a sense of his rival's suffering. He assumed the same suit of ill-fitting flesh that he'd once worn too, in similar circumstances, when flung down the hierarchy: dethroned, demoted, betrayed, embittered. And as he entertained this sense of the man, he understood what Nigel had become. What any man could become.

For Nigel, however, these feelings were more acute. He was married, a father too. And he was an arrogant, disagreeable bastard by nature. Deranged by the fall, and while clawing at the cellar walls of his mind for years, Nigel might even have occasionally deceived himself into believing that nothing had happened between Sophie and Marcus. For a while. But the struggle between acceptance and disbelief must have been immense.

At times, he would have upheld the idea that everything in his marriage was okay and that he would still be regarded as what he'd always projected to the world: a success, a family man – often between jobs, maybe, but his many failures were just a trajectory towards an eventual eye-watering success. *We're fine. Fine. Fine. Never been better!*

But the bitter acid of doubt would always eat away at such frail wishful thinking. Nigel was just too damn clever to be deceived in such a tawdry fashion by a wife who would not fall in line, or see reason – his reason – and by a man that he despised; a rival he loathed enough to blacken his own mind and render him joyless. His idea of himself was too impressive to be eroded *like that*.

By them!

For a while.

So what purpose was left for him but revenge and the slow attrition of the hated enemy?

Spiteful comments: the thrusts. Contradictions: the jabs. Bad-mouthing and undermining offstage: the cuts. The hate. The hate. The hate. The panting, spitting, dizzying, narcotic hate. For Marcus. For his wife. For anyone who had it better than he did. Hate for himself. Hate could become a vocation.

In his working life, Marcus had encountered one or two Nigels. Men who became living embodiments of their grudges. Like them, Nigel was eloquent and put on a good show. Always looked the part. The steaming gears of his mind rarely seized or exploded in public. But the shame and rage of multiple setbacks had melted his fusebox and wiring at a core, fundamental level. New pathways had burned grooves through his mind, his thinking, cindering his thoughts down into hell.

The heat of this grudge had radiated from him in toxic waves, on every paddle for two years. He'd suspected an affair, even known about it, for that long. Marcus had felt the loathing warming his ears and the back of his head. No confrontations had occurred. Nor had Nigel retreated into exhausting acceptance. He'd chosen to hang around Marcus instead, with his chest puffed out. Two reddish eyes had surveyed him from near and far, waiting for the most innocent word from Marcus and immediately challenging it. He'd needed to rip Marcus down, to restore some equivalence, or primacy. He'd not been able to do it with physical prowess, or professional success, so he'd chipped away at his status, his reputation. Something that Marcus was more than capable of doing without Nigel's assistance.

He'd also fought a perpetual nuanced, low-level conflict behind his wife's front lines. Small, surly cuts to Sophie's ligaments; little sullen nips at her heels to irritate her, socially, domestically. Aggrieved and swollen with disappointment and rejection, yet somehow rendered strengthless and without agency, he'd picked at them both, pricked them, while circling the horror of what they'd done to him.

He'd only allowed himself to peer at that adulterous abomination in measured glimpses. Marcus and Sophie had murdered his entire vision of himself.

The slide of the entitled and self-regarding has a more terrible momentum than that of their more self-aware peers. Marcus had seen it happen. To his own father. When Marcus was thirteen, his mother had left his dad for her boss. The gradient of the slope his father had hurtled down had also drawn other mishaps into a descending slipstream: new misfortunes and further rejections, professional, social and romantic, falling upon his dad's head like anvils, anchors, boulders. His old man's rages had drawn rolling waves of marbles underfoot, accelerating his plunge to the bottom.

Nigel's business had recently failed. He was dependent on his wife.

Did they give off a certain smell? Why was everyone against them? Why would nothing go right? There seemed to be no change of direction in Nigel's downhill sprint.

You just weren't ever that special.

But then who is?

Marcus wondered how he'd have coped with this kind of betrayal, from a wife and the mother of his child, at the same time as his gym going bust. Would it be possible for him to shelve that agony and shame and start over? As a wiser man too, carrying only hand luggage? Tall order. The notion winded him. Not easy – not easy for anyone. Certainly no stroll for Nigel, a man as competitive and narcissistic as they came.

The first paddle that Nigel had organised had landed him in an actual pit, from which there was no way out. In such a place, at rock bottom, he must have realised that he could fall still further, lower, into the foetid rot of a sewer. Marcus and Sophie were to blame for that final shove over the edge, into darkness without end.

Marcus felt an urge to offer a hand, to reach out and help him. His desire to make amends was suddenly as desperate as his need to free them all from the sacrificial chamber.

Because Marcus *knew*. Or had a vivid sense of Nigel's writhing agony. He was no stranger to rejection. Of the heart, at least, though few who knew him would guess. But both of the women in his past, whom he'd loved to breathlessness, sleeplessness and near heart failure, had spurned him. Each had taken eighteen months to reject him. Eighteen months: some arbitrary period imposed on him, as if he were cursed. Each woman had made him impotent and desolate for months after the break-up. Each had so blackened him with despair that he'd frightened himself back into the light.

He'd started over more cautiously, guarded, with his ego sanded down each time. He wondered if that's why he'd since become a purposeless knight, committed to endless conquest without commitment to any individual cause. Unmarried, childless, able to flit here and there, addicted to novelty; strung out for those sweet peaks of seduction and the smoked heroin of anticipation. No impulse control. An addict. Take the pleasure. Kick the pain further down the road.

And here was a casualty of his meaningless, selfish addiction: Nigel, this vain man, as brittle and entitled as any martinet he'd ever known. He'd never liked Nigel. But how he dearly wished that he'd never slept with his wife.

Nigel wasn't going to fade away. Not if he'd been crossed, slighted or bettered. He was incapable of forgiveness; he was resentment incarnate. Competition could only be resolved by the opponent's destruction. And Marcus acknowledged that he was the target. Even when stripped naked and covered in cattle blood, amidst the ruined forms of the sacrificed in a putrid dungeon, an intoxicating animal rage committed to his annihilation still burned behind Nigel's pinched eyes. And once he'd dealt with Marcus, he'd grind himself to dust pursuing Clement Colman. The past was never the past; it was dry timber that must stoke the flames until the ashes were too cold to be revived.

We're all terrorists.

Time was something they did not have. Not for this. Not now. And Marcus had conceived an idea of how they might get out. Only it was a job for three people, working shifts. Toiling fast, together, as a team, as if their lives depended on it. Because they did.

'Nigel.'

'Fuck off!' Nigel roared at him before turning to Sophie. 'How many times? How long?'

Marcus cleared his throat. 'I was a bloody idiot. Didn't think. I wish it'd never happened.' And he knew that desperate attempt at contrition had been the wrong thing to say within earshot of Sophie.

'How many times?' Nigel roared again at his wife.

Sophie returned fire at the same volume and with the same calibre of rage and desolation. 'Thirteen times! But does it matter? I needed it and I wanted more. Much more. Far more. If I'd had my way, we'd still be at it now! But a baker's dozen was about *his* limit. He got cold feet. Poor relationship material.But instead of trying to control and manipulate me, every fucking day of my life, with passive-aggressive bullshit, he was only too happy to piss off once he'd had his fun!'

Thirteen wasn't that much, if you think about it, a craven part of Marcus's mind whispered. And it made him want to laugh. He wondered if he'd gone mad.

Inside the sacrificial cairn, Nigel discovered nowhere to place himself that might help contain the blast furnace of his fury. He dragged his feet around in a clumsy circle, studying the floor. He bent over and quickly straightened, holding what looked like a leg bone.

Marcus attempted a suggestion. 'I have an idea—'

'So do I, cunt,' Nigel replied. Gripping the club, he turned to face Marcus.

Sophie laughed, derisively. She was a mess. Nigel was a mess. Marcus knew that he was no better. But Marcus also recognised that he'd made this mess. Shame and loathing immolated him. There are always consequences for bad behaviour. He wondered why he hadn't been sat down and told this at the age of three. And no one got to choose the time and place when repercussions exploded.

Marcus imagined himself selling his house, moving to a new town, quitting the paddles. But he also understood that none of that would be possible unless they got out of Clement Colman's temple. And though they could not be sure how the owner of the valley planned to destroy them, his intentions were clear: they were all perilously close to becoming disarticulated ruins on a soil floor. If they did not get out of the dome, their heads were destined to lie at an obscene distance from their shoulders. Sometime within the next fortnight, their six kayaks would be found upside down and bobbing in the shallows of Dorset.

But how Marcus might recruit Nigel to assist them in an escape eluded him.

'We're going to die!' Sophie screamed. 'In this stinking, filthy, fucking slaughterhouse. We're going to die and I am never going to see my little boy again! And you want to fight with clubs, you pathetic loser. We're through. Over! I fucking hate you! I have done for years, Nigel! And it wasn't just Marcus! There were others! All those holidays with the girls? Every one. On every one I had an affair! I think there were six! I haven't slept with you since Robbie was born. Three fucking years and you still won't let me go!'

'Sophie!' Marcus shouted. 'Stop!'

Nigel's arms quivered and struggled to support the bone. He drifted to one side, as if drunk. Then listed a couple of steps forward.

'And there's more! So why not get it all out now! As it's the fucking end of everything, and us? You're not even Robbie's father! It's about time you knew! I'm sorry. I've done terrible things to you. I'm a terrible person. I don't deny it. But so are you. A bastard. A rotten fucking bastard! We made each other terrible people. We should have written us off years ago. But then *he* came along . . . my little boy.'

'Oh, Sophie. No. No. Please. No,' Marcus said, but knew he hadn't been heard.

Nigel stopped moving. He'd almost disappeared into the growing darkness. But he must have been staring at his wife through the gloom. There seemed less of him physically.

Sophie slumped to her knees and sobbed, chesty expulsions of misery directed at the dirt; animal sounds issued from broken things, moments before they sputter into a final silence.

'His?' Nigel said, sounding like a child. 'Him?'

In what light found her, Marcus saw her nod. 'Yes,' she said. 'The last time. I can't deny it. There's no point now. But that's what I wanted. I chose the right time. I didn't think it would matter . . . who the father was. But it does. It did. It does to me. And it's not you.'

Marcus bent over and gasped for air, his hands on his dirty thighs. *No*, he said to himself. *No*. But hadn't he feared this possibility for years? Of course he had, but he'd also managed to suppress the idea. He'd never allowed himself to wonder whether he was the unwitting father of their child. Such a thought was too monumental, too staggering, too numbing for him to even begin to process now.

But *this* had to stop. *Now.* 'We need to get out of here!' he screamed at the others. 'Listen to me!'

'Listen to this, you fucker!' Nigel loped at him, the bone raised in one hand.

Marcus scanned the murky soil about his feet for something he could use as a weapon. He didn't see a suitable implement and withdrew to the door where he knew there were two ribs, one splintered.

Nigel stalked him, panting, his shoulders hunched forward as if he were preparing to enter a tackle. 'I should have beaten the crap out of you years ago!'

'Oh, please,' Sophie said, sobbing. 'You stupid, stupid twat! How could it have been you? Of course he knocked me up! I barely let you near me back then. But what does it matter now?'

'Coming at me with a bone won't undo what's done,' Marcus said to Nigel, to purchase the time he needed to find one of the discarded ribs.

'No, but it'd make me feel better.'

'I'll give you four free hits once we're on the outside. How's that? I'll get you back into work. I know someone who—'

'Fuck off!' Nigel roared, and came forward, then stumbled over debris. He straightened as Marcus located one of the ribs with his foot. He bent over and came up with the curved bone, gripping it with both hands as if he was at bat at home plate.

Marcus had hoped to let Nigel rant himself empty, but the man's threats had triggered an anger that he hadn't expected to feel as the guilty party. Despite what he'd done, he felt all the provocations that Nigel had launched his way, on and off the water, for years. That hunched, dark form, weaving at him now, had been inexhaustible in his petty persecutions. Just as much as Nigel wanted to kill him, Marcus wanted to beat Nigel to the ground. The intent was mutual. He wasn't going to get hurt by Nigel's dirty bone. He'd had enough. Enough of everything. Enough of hiding and biting his tongue. Of pretending. Sneaking. He wanted to break out and break something. Just smash it the hell apart.

'I'll fucking kill you!' Nigel screamed but did no more than stagger at Marcus, the bone raised above the silhouette of his wild head, poised to strike. Out of the dried blood caking Nigel's scalp, strands of his hair might even have formed horns.

Marcus roared, 'You arrogant fucker!' and he stepped forward, swinging the rib through the air between them. The shaft hissed close to Nigel's head. His opponent hadn't seen it coming and only stepped back after moving air stroked his face. 'You want to do this?' Marcus yelled. 'Then let's do it. I'm fucking done with you. You gaslighting ponce!' Marcus swung again, pushing Nigel back even further.

'Stop!' Sophie screamed. 'Something's happening! Outside!'

Into the temple came the sound of a distant voice; a man outside was shouting with elation. 'Light the pyres of blood!'

It was Clement Colman.

27

[6–7pm]

Carrying kayaks on land can mess up your back. The bow toggles can cut all blood flow from your fingers. In wind, they swing like booms, pulling away from your centre of gravity. They bump and clatter. Sea kayaks need water. On water they can be the epitome of gliding elegance. With one bloodless hand grasping the bow toggle to haul his boat across dry land, Julian was reminded of the craft's dependence on the marine environment. Out of the water, his seventeen feet of composite hull became a cumbersome, unwieldy cross that he must now bear. Alone, with no one holding the other end.

Across the bumpy grass and the scratching shingle, Julian tugged and heaved at his boat, his heart protesting with a salvo of stabbing pains. Angling his body towards the trickle that the tidal river had been reduced to, he fell to his knees twice.

The light had soaked away as quickly as the water, into an indigo-black stain that covered the entire valley. What water trickled over the pebbly river bed he only heard between his gasps for air, pinched by fright. So much adrenaline pumped through his body that his balance was affected. His eyes refused to focus; his vision jumped around the scrub on the banks, his scuffling feet, the expensive paddle that swung here and there and tried to trip him up, the vast canopy of arriving night.

He didn't look back. Not once. Not to where Mary now screamed and screamed amidst the unpacked bags and half-erected tents of the campsite; a place that never had a chance to become home to the six paddlers who'd entered the valley at noon.

Even when he was stamping through the deeper channel in the river, the water was too shallow to cover his knees. But at least there were splashes beneath his feet. At last, he could feel icy water lathering his calves and seeping into his paddling boots – that creep of cold around his toes. And though he heard his hull scraping stones, it would periodically jerk forward in a propelled glide whenever it found deeper water, suggesting the capabilities of a serene and highly manoeuvrable vessel that could be forward paddled at five knots away from this evil valley.

A random image of a Western film came to mind, of men trying to escape an ambush, struggling to mount horses in a river, under gunfire, their mounts rearing in panic. The analogy his memory threw up was not inappropriate: his kayak was his horse and he was being pursued. Only when mounted did he have any chance of getting away.

He had no space in the stampede of his thoughts to fully consider what he'd just seen traversing that meadow. The sheer impossibility of those things had made him feel faint, then half-crazed with terror. Some type of *people* – maybe children – wearing horrid masks. But they had moved like animals, even insects. He told himself that he must not think of them again until his paddle strokes dipped and his hull skimmed across the sea.

Don't, don't, don't, don't think of them.

Run. Keep going. The river widens up ahead. Water looks darker on the left side. Aim for that. Boat might float. Easier going.

If he paused he would vomit. Inside his greenhouse of a cagoule, a pint of sweat must have already pumped itself out of his body. Urine and splashes of water made his shorts itch his inner thighs. Across his scalp and forehead, his hair clung and dripped like a swimmer's cap. Discomforts that he easily overlooked in his haste to flee, until a rash of slippery pebbles shot one of his feet sideways.

Julian came down hard on one knee and released the bow toggle to break his fall. He went hot, then cold. Anger flushed his face warm. Turning sideways in the current, the kayak seemed intent on defying him. *Didn't the damn boat understand that they had to get away from here?*

Scrabbling for the toggle and recovering the rubber handle, he'd been turned about and now faced upstream and the shallows that he'd just been routed through. Where the scrub parted around the little cove of shingle that they'd landed on hours before, he reluctantly found himself faced with the very place where Mary's persistent screams continued to rise. The racket she made had increased his clumsiness, his inability to breathe, or to focus. *How can you even think when someone is screaming and screaming and screaming like that?* It was as if Mary was on fire and there was no one around to put out the flames.

He saw a campsite overrun. Yet somehow Mary remained upright. She was staggering this way and that but getting nowhere. He couldn't see her face. That was covered, as was most of her back. Something pale hung from her front and kicked a pair of toad-like legs in a desperate climb. Looking for a way in, three other small forms skittered sideways in a circular formation, round and round Mary's plodding, aimless feet.

At a glance, an observer in this poor light might suppose that Mary had been covered by a large animal and was grappling with it. But three bloodless ape-things from the meadow clung to her. They had clawed up and over her, like chimps clambering up a zoo keeper's body. Bony extremities clawed for purchase on her clothes. Around her head and face, she wore one of her assailants like an oversized hat, equipped with moving arms and legs. All of the creatures had fastened to her body with their mouths, like leeches.

Julian whimpered, then muttered, 'Oh, Jesus. No. No.'

Elsewhere, an open bag was dragged across the grass. Someone's rucksack. A sound of tearing fabric added accompaniment to Mary's cries. Cries that became groans in a lower register. In turn, these became rhythmic moans, each gradually lessening in volume and suggesting a terrible submission, or acceptance. Mary had stopped sounding like Mary.

Ankle-deep in water, with the bow toggle clutched inside his hot hand, Julian righted the boat's direction. He turned and fled downstream.

He understood that he was crying like a child. Anguish and terror would soon burst, or stop, his heart.

Grateful for a screen of foliage, he managed a spurt of speed. But immediately lost control of his feet and fell sideways. As if clutching a life raft, this time he didn't let go of the boat's bow toggle. He hit the river bed hard, and one half of his body made the shallows erupt. Water gushed inside his clothes, icing his skin. A gasp was punched from his chest. He stopped crying and whimpered instead. After a noisy struggle, he was back on his feet and dragging the kayak. He thought of the cowboys again; this time they pulled laden wagons.

He no longer held his paddle in his free hand. He'd dropped it but couldn't recall doing so.

A spare was broken down and tucked under his bowlines. When Julian saw the split-paddle, he nearly wept again, this time with relief.

Up ahead, the waterway widened. More of what served for light fell onto a black surface and suggested depth. Dead branches, draped in weed, extended into the water from the banks. He remembered paddling this stretch earlier that afternoon. He told himself that he was making progress in the right direction.

The water did become deeper, and he was soon knee-deep, the cold a blessing. He dripped, he panted, he pushed on.

Monumental

He no longer had the breath to cry or whimper. Hoarse and quick, his desperate panting was as audible as his wading, splashing feet.

They stood in a row.

Three of them, in a space between two alders, on a bank veined with black tree roots. Upright, their postures relaxed and unthreatened, indicating patience; they were waiting for him. Thin light glimmered upon their silvery flesh – fish-belly pale, oily-moist. Bandy-legged. Feather-faced. They observed him.

Julian thought of Mary's strange, drunken dance, and of her body festooned with clinging forms. She'd worn a coat and hat of parasites. 'Oh, dear God,' he muttered. When he tried to yank the boat away from their side of the river, he stumbled and indented a shin against where the curved hull became the upper deck. He splashed about some more, then turned to face the three figures.

They'd gone. The bank was empty.

Julian wheeled around. His eyes swept the shadows, before slowing to prod and peer at gaps in the foliage.

Nothing.

The brief pause in his retreat allowed his body to inform him how exhausted it was.

Whipping his head from one murky bank to another, he saw glimmers of branches and dense bushels of leaves that might be fashioned into any shape by a mind as scattered as his now was. He pushed on, dragging a boat that seemed to gain weight every few steps. His left arm and shoulder burned with pain. Each thigh felt like a bruise, purple to the bone.

Ahead, the river narrowed. Tree cover extended onto the water.

As he fought his way through a cross-hatch of bracken and drooping branches, his face was whipped by a thin branch that he hadn't seen. Twigs scraped his cagoule and buoyancy vest. The sticks tried to find his eyes. Below the surface, slippery impediments tripped him. Submerged wood. Dead branches that had banged his hull on the way upstream. But at least the water covered his knees.

He broke through the overgrowth and the river narrowed and turned. Julian wished he wasn't making so much noise. He tried to lessen the sound of his feet in the shallows.

Overhanging trees thickened. The river was darker. Until it widened once more. There was an inlet on the side. A small clearing where trees gave way to a grass bank that sloped into sand and pebbles. It was the kind of place where cattle drank, or forded. Behind the low bank, the trees were thinner and cast the innumerable black arteries and capillaries of their branches against the sky. Or blotted it out completely. This spot had once given them hope that they might find enough bank to camp on, further upstream.

Had *they* gone?

Maybe they were only interested in the meadow. Yes, the camp. That was it. They hadn't liked that. But you're going. Leaving. That's what they wanted, for you to leave. So keep going. Keep going, out of their territory.

Not far beyond the clearing and inlet, he came across another of the wretched things. This one sat on a branch jutting over the water. Thin legs dangled. The sight of the extended claws on the toes seemed to flatten Julian's lungs, then suck them up his throat. The head was a feathery oval mask. The crude mouth hole funnelled a barely audible piping. He imagined white lips pursed. Inside the eyeholes, a sheen.

Julian tried to say, 'I'm going. Please . . .' but he only gargled and sobbed out the word 'please'.

On the bank on his left stood another silhouette, the size of a toddler. The head was bulky with feathered masking. Motionless, the figure also exhaled piping sounds.

If he pushed forward, the thing on the branch might drop onto him. From the bank, the other might leap.

Julian turned his head to the opposite bank, on his right, hoping to see a route out. It was then that he felt a plume of cold air cooling the perspiration on the nape of his neck, on which every hair extended like antennas into a draught. He looked over his shoulder.

Monumental

The moment he saw *it*, standing inside the cockpit of his kayak, he was sure that his bowels were ready to give out.

A rangier specimen – taller. What he interpreted from the rusty eyes, glimpsed at close range through the feathered sockets of the mask, was a sadistic intelligence far from human. A scent of wet stones, soil and blood inflamed his sinuses.

For how long had he towed it downstream?

Julian dropped the bow toggle and pitched himself at the bank, then stumbled and waded back the way he had just come downstream. He looked again at the poised, horribly nonchalant figure standing upright inside his boat, its feet on the padded seat. Like its two companions, it merely watched him thrash and stagger through the shallow water, on his way back up-valley. Three feathered faces, arranged at various heights: he knew he'd always see them if he ever ventured near a river again, supposing he was granted an opportunity to see another river.

As he laboured and sloshed his way to the grassy bank, he could only think of Mary and the moving thicket of clinging passengers that she'd worn. Top-heavy with inhuman ballast, she'd screamed. He'd not heard her cries in a while. He didn't know when she'd stopped. But up the bank he went on his hands and knees and into the thinning trees. Among the willows and scrub, he fell face down. Then pushed himself upright and ran, stooping, through the low branches and bracken and vines and brambles.

Crashing through sideways, he came out onto the river's floodplain. Another meadow, or maybe this was the end of the meadow in which they'd camped.

A few stars glimmered. The forested slopes were inked black and appeared joined to the cold darkness of the night sky.

He didn't pause. Julian raced into the grass and the flowers that had recently closed away their bright beauty until morning. What was left of his wits told him to angle his route across the meadow southwards, parallel to the river. Eventually, the reeds would appear. He must fight his way through those and cross the swamp on foot, then wade through the estuary, then swim. He must not think of how far he still had to go, nor of the obstacles, nor of his punished body, nor that he was dying from exhaustion and terror. He must simply head for the sea.

The sea. The sea. The sea.

He soon suspected that running across the floodplain had been a mistake. And the movement in the grass on either side of him confirmed the hunch.

They cantered to keep level with him. Soundlessly, *they* capered.

He wouldn't be chased. He refused. He'd had enough.

Julian stopped running.

'Please.' The entreaty came out as an exhalation, a gasp.

Around him, the childlike figures stopped moving. They watched him until their feathered faces became too much to withstand. He counted a dozen of them, then broke into a sprint.

Julian had not run so fast since his twenties but hadn't the time to be surprised at the speed he managed, or at what felt like progress.

When the first one landed on his back and shoulders, it planted itself lightly. He thought it no heavier than a domestic cat. That weight seemed to grow over his next few strides. Seeming to enjoy the method of transport, the passenger piped a breezy noise to itself, or even to him.

Julian continued to run, to pump his legs hard, until what felt like two iced needles pierced his head. They pushed in deep, behind the left ear. Before he could thrash to dislodge the biter, his arms were snatched up by two of the rider's confederates. At the bend of his elbows, they too pierced his flesh with pins that coldly scraped inside the joints. He remembered what Jane had mumbled about being drained. Even delirious and injured, she'd had more idea about what existed here than any of them.

In meadow grass, Julian collapsed to his knees.

He thought of needles probing marrow; he imagined the slicing of tubes.

Monumental

Another two sets of teeth broke through the skin on his back. They kept on going through him, deeper and deeper, until he thought the spikes might push his still-beating heart out of his mouth.

The grasping toes of the two pale children that he carried on his back dug into and scored his waist, fastening.

One of his last thoughts was as useless and futile as his hope to reach the sea: from the weight of the things that clung to him, they might have been the unwanted rucksacks of children who had become bored and tired on a hike. From a distance, those that hung from him would resemble children too, as if they'd demanded piggybacks from the adult who'd shepherded them across a field.

Julian looked up and at the wooden poles that extended to a red sky. How had he missed those before? He heard a thousand pipes blowing the same note, from out of the round stone tombs that now lined the valley slopes.

Into a hot darkness he slipped. He was lost in the feverish filth of his own swiftly contaminating blood.

Before his face struck the ground, he was blind.

28

[7–8pm]

From outside the temple came the putter of idling quad bikes. An exhaust coughed.

When Marcus joined Sophie at the western curve of the dome, the agitated lowing of a cow was mixed with the engine sounds. A mournful lament, near human with anguish. The animal's distress lowered Marcus's spirits even further. He shivered, but not from being naked inside the chilled stone dome.

A metal door, or flap, clanged open or was shut. Someone whistled. A cow coughed. Farm sounds: livestock and industriousness, but in the wrong place entirely.

Of equal concern was the emergence of new light. Remnants of the dusk were tinged red, as if a coloured beam or spotlight had been trained on the exterior of the temple. Through fissures, bloody rays lanced the dome and faded into darkness.

Alone with his pain and wheezing heavily, Nigel remained near the door. After launching two warning swings with the rib bone and pushing his opponent back, Marcus had carefully moved sideways and followed the curvature of the cairn, from the bolted entrance to the west wall, which faced the closest valley slope. If the situation had changed outside and they were about to receive company, he wanted to know what to expect. If anyone walked through that door, he would swing and he would not miss.

Sophie paced between four wall slots. Ducking or raising her head, she was determined to see as much of the paddock as was granted her through the apertures. 'People. And cows, I think.'

'Let me see,' Marcus said. As he neared the wall, he felt puffs of cold air against his face. A continuous stream of wind funnelled through the slits, creating the continuous low piping that then inflated inside the structure. 'But watch him. Nigel comes anywhere near me, you have to tell me.'

Sophie looked over her shoulder, in the direction of her husband, and nodded.

Marcus peered out. From the first slot, he saw a crimson mist drifting around three henge poles. Tinted mist. By the time he peered through the next slot, lower down, he heard more clearly the fizz and spitting of a flare, then saw one sputtering in the grass at the foot of a timber pole. A bright emergency flare, from which a torrent of coloured smoke eddied in the breeze. The brightness made his eyes smart. 'Flare,' he said.

'Lots of them,' Sophie muttered, with her face again pressed into stone. 'By the posts. I can see another three. What are they for?'

He didn't answer. He didn't know. He palmed his way across the west side of the cairn, then slipped his fingers into crevices between the large blocks. He pulled himself off his toes to peer through a higher, wider slot. With a big toe, he found a crevice near the ground and pushed up with that foot. Before the pain in his trembling arms and bloodless fingers gave out, he saw a figure stride in and out of view, flicking a cow with a stick. A masked man was encouraging the animal further inside the circular henge, closer to the temple.

This must be one of the cows he'd seen at the top of the valley. Marcus considered the stinking carcasses behind him; cattle in this valley weren't only being used for their milk, and their beef was never destined for high-street butchers.

The drover, he believed, was nasty little Vine; so lithe inside a pale tunic. He'd changed his outfit, or costume, for this next bit. The oat-coloured garment was circled by a belt or plaited rope. The smock's fabric appeared roughly woven. Like an acrobat, his tattooed arms were bare and muscled. A feathered mask concealed his face and topknot; a thick bustle of duck feathers that bounced and swayed as he walked. A whistle pierced the hole from which a beak should have protruded.

Marcus paced further to his left, peering through each slot within reach, tracking Vine the drover.

The man stopped goading the cow and abandoned the large animal in the southern quarter of the paddock. Flares burned at the base of each timber pole in that direction. Curved markings were just visible through the blooded smoke.

'What is this?' Sophie asked. She jabbed her face from one slot to another. 'That lanky bitch is there too and that mean older woman. Two inked bitches. Wearing weird peasant dresses. Smocks. Masks. They're wearing masks. Bird masks. They're dropping flares by the posts,' she said, reporting her impressions in an excitable, anxious stream. 'Hands. Look at their right hands.'

Vine held what looked like a long knife against his far leg. As he turned out of sight, Marcus saw the weapon, as long as a machete with a straight blade. The sight of the dark shaft shut his breathing down for a few seconds. 'Sacrifice,' Marcus muttered. 'The cow.'

Sophie pulled away from the wall and looked behind her. 'Do they . . .'

'What?'

'Cut them up? Throw them in here?' She looked up at the hole in the roof.

'Not unless they have ladders. Or a crane.'

The tall, athletic woman was the next person to stride across the oblong frames that Marcus peered through with one eye. Her tunic rode up her skinny thighs; even in the woollen dress, tied up in the middle like a sack, she crossed the paddock as if she were strutting down a catwalk at a fashion show. She held a flare aloft and was now no more than a few metres from the outer wall. Marcus assumed she was traversing the paddock and returning to the entrance, where the sound of the bikes had come grunting. In her other inked hand, the supermodel carried one of the evil blades. Weapons that now reminded Marcus of the short swords that the Roman legionnaires had carried. He even remembered the name of the weapon: *gladius*.

This was how everything rotting inside the temple came to be in pieces then? Engulfed by a cold, prickling sensation, that usually preceded a race to the toilet, Marcus understood they'd have to fight back with bones. The Neolithic against the Iron Age. To his toes, his muscles went limp. He drew in a shaky breath. 'Sophie. Go get a bone. Big one. Leg bone is best. Heavy as you can find.'

'I'm not—'

'Do it!' He turned his face to her. Cerise light from the nearest flare washed across her smeared features and crusting hair. Tears had cut tracks into the blood drying on her cheeks. She looked like she'd run from a house fire. Two huge white eyes stared at him. 'They have weapons, Sophie. We need to fight like fucking hell when they come through that door. Just imagine that it's me and Nigel you're aiming for.'

She didn't smile but stared at him in horror, with a face that was pure horror.

'If we don't fight, we're dead,' Marcus said. 'Go and tell Nigel. One of us needs to keep an eye on their movements. Track them around the outside until they get near the door. One of us can stand on either side. The lookout can give us a sign when they're right outside. We smash anyone that comes through. Then fight our way out. Go and tell Nigel. Quick! We don't have much time. While they're busy with the cow, we need to get into position. We need to be clear about what we do next. All of us. Together.'

Sophie nodded and padded away across the dome to the door. As she neared the carcasses and bits of devastated animals, she slowed and tiptoed, as if finding herself barefoot amidst broken glass.

Marcus returned his attention to the wall and worked his way northwards, in the direction of the valley's summit. They'd been brought in from that direction, down the pole-lined processional avenue.

In the northern section of the wall, he could only find one slit that offered a view of the entrance they'd been carried through. And, sure enough, there were the quad bikes. Three bikes, not two; something else that Colman had lied about up at the house. And he too was now robed like the peasant that he certainly wasn't. He also wore a mask, but of pheasant feathers, the headgear adding a theatrical but demoniac aspect to his new guise. He stood up in the saddle of the bike.

Beside him was another woman. An older woman, judging by what he could see of her upper arms and the long white hair that drifted around the goose feathers, framing her bulky head. She and Clement appeared to have only small tattoos on their shoulders, which looked at a distance like black smudges. Marcus hadn't seen her outside the house. He wondered if she'd been responsible for the weeping.

Beside the bike that had pulled a second trailer to the temple, another woman protectively draped her arms around the shoulders of the three pale children they'd seen on arrival in the cultivated section of the valley. She, Marcus was almost certain, had been the older woman who'd shouted at them when they'd emerged from the processional avenue near the fields, and who had ushered the children to safety among the crops. The three diminutive figures and their guardian now wore masks. Those of the children were woven from tawny juvenile gull feathers. But their bodies were naked.

So, there was Clement, Vine, the woman he called supermodel and the little mean Nan with the full-sleeve tatts – the very women who had smeared him with blood – plus the kids' nurse and the sullen-looking creature with white hair standing beside Colman. Six adults. And three weird, naked kids. Four of the adults carried blades.

'Holy fuck,' Marcus whispered. He felt sick and overwhelmed at being forced to witness yet more of the deranged micro-culture's antics. A smeared montage flowed through his memory, fragments of documentaries and dim recollections of what he'd read about cults. He thought of rumours of the abuse of minors, and isolated pseudo-religious communities led by predatory sadists. This stream of vague impressions surged and ebbed. Not even his disbelief that he could possibly have encountered such a group could turn back the flood of fear and nausea that now constricted his breathing.

Here? There was one of those cults here. And we're going to be bits of evidence found decomposed in soil, years from now. Grinning skulls. Identities matched to dental records. Us?

How is this happening to me?

Did they make the naked children in their care watch the slaughter of cows? Did the young here witness atrocities even worse than that, inflicted on people, inside this temple? No wonder the children hadn't responded to a greeting when they'd first arrived. They must have been traumatised mute. Where were the parents? What kind of parent would permit such wickedness? And how did a tech entrepreneur sink to such depths?

Why? Why? Why?

Aghast, he wanted to scream into the foetid air and swamp the stinking dome with questions that no one could answer. But curiosity was a distraction that he could ill afford to indulge. Marcus closed his eyes and dipped his head, inhaling the foul air deeply in an attempt to calm himself; to still his racing thoughts and hammering pulse, to enable some reason to whisper again.

Six adults. But only four gladius swords in the hands of the butchers, the berserkers. And they'd be familiar with using the heavy blades too; sharp, weighted weapons with edges that cut through meat and bone.

Oh, fuck.

There were three adult captives inside the temple. All at the point of killing each other. Their blood was up. The drugs were wearing off. They were as ready to fight as they'd ever been in lives that had never known this level of violence. The previous victim had been a lone male. What chance had he against a group wielding swords? But he, Nigel and Sophie, armed with cattle bones, had a better chance. Or, at least, some chance of fighting their way out. Maybe they could get to the quad bikes. If one of them managed to run that far, and if the keys were in the ignition, and the operation was rudimentary, then . . . just maybe, they had a lifeline. Nigel even knew how to ride one.

Marcus thought of Mary and Julian. Where were they? What the hell were they doing? Hours had passed since they'd left the camp. Mary could hardly walk. Jane was out of it. But why hadn't Julian come up the valley looking for them? Maybe he had. If he'd done so, what could Julian do? What *would* Julian do? Physically he was frail, timid. Disagreeable in a group situation, maybe, but only if the numbers were in his favour and he could side with those with whom he curried favour. Marcus didn't imagine Julian being much use in a fight. But if he'd witnessed anything of the lethal insanity that his peers now faced, then he might yet scurry away for outside help, on foot, up the valley.

None of them here were fighters. But if Sophie lost her shit, he imagined she'd be a worthy adversary for a bird-faced hippy killer. Nigel? He wasn't so sure about him, even when cornered. The man was deeply distressed, perhaps even unhinged after his wife's revelations. And in this situation Marcus was not sure where the man would aim his swing.

If they targeted the arms, testicles and feathered faces of their opponents, they might disarm, stun or wound their foes. That might buy sufficient time for one of them to reach the bikes.

Before he could turn to tell Sophie which body parts to target, and to then relay this information to her husband, the state of affairs outside changed again.

'The Little Priests!' someone – a woman – screamed. There followed a thudding of bare feet across the paddock. From south to north, several people raced across the turf, scurrying for the entrance, fleeing the arena.

Marcus stumbled to the slit that offered a view of the entrance and bikes.

He found the gap. Stood on his toes.

Amid tendrils of scarlet smoke, Clement Colman and his adepts genuflected. On all fours as a group, with their feathered faces obscured, they bowed into the turf.

'What's happening? What's going on? What is it?' Sophie asked. She'd drifted back across the temple, clutching a dark bone ragged with black remnants.

Outside, only the three pale children remained upright. They stood in silence beside the servile adults. But they were more alert than Marcus had noticed before. Their little gull-feather faces prodded at the air, as if sniffing. They were looking towards the foot of the henge, towards the other entrance, where he'd first spied the hill of stone that afternoon. The pale, masked children, he was sure, were watching the cow intently.

29

[7–8pm]

'Oh, God, don't look,' he said to Sophie, who stood behind him in the reeking darkness. Between the cow's slowing cries, Marcus heard a noisome, moist suckling. He looked away and swore that he would not look back again.

'I have to see,' Sophie whispered. She joined him at the wall and peered out at what now unfolded within the henge.

After a few seconds, Sophie muttered, 'Oh, no. No, no, no. What are the children doing?'

Night's stony breath, exhaled from the valley side, made them shiver. Deep inside, Marcus felt the very sinews that clung to his joints wilt with a dread that only the condemned can know. In a shaft of misted, scarlet light that pierced the wall, he stared at his begrimed hands and at the rib he clutched. *So many.* What could three frightened people, clutching bones, possibly do against such numbers? Because the impending conflict was no longer a matter of only fighting Clement and his deranged cronies.

As if to shut down his capacity to remember, Marcus closed his eyes. But the image of what he'd just seen would be imprinted into his thoughts for as long as he was able to think. He thought of jackals clustered around a wounded beast on the savannah, before they clumsily dragged its living body to the dusty ground.

Monumental

Marcus suffered the absurd notion that such things as he'd just seen mounted on a cow, clustered like tics, were a species of hairless ape. Primates that inhabited the valley. A tribe that had committed to a feeding frenzy upon the flanks and rump of the tormented cow.

The beast's lowing was hewn from a suffering so acute that he was sure its cries would drive him mad. Behind the struggle, carved poles vaulted into inky oblivion. Flickering flares had bathed the scene infernally crimson. A veneer of smoke mercifully obscured some details. But not all. Beneath the cluster of clinging, pallid forms, each the size of a child, he'd watched the cow stagger sideways. The burden mounted on its back had been terrible. Between the gripping fingers and spiked toes of its tormentors, its hide was streaked black.

And yet, the most horrid feature of all had been the sight of the three children of the valley. Released by their guardian, the trio of little figures had excitedly roamed around the commotion. The blooding of the cow had drawn them in and taken them over. Eager to join a macabre game, in which they'd stood for too long on the sidelines, the three masked figures soon dipped in and out of the feast. Skittish and unsure of their place maybe, but overwhelmed by the sound of an animal's misery, and the sight and scent of its blood, the valley's children had then fastened themselves onto the cow's udders and underbelly and hung there by their teeth. And they too had supped the salty warmth of the sacrifice.

Jane. Marcus thought of Jane. Poor Jane. This is what she had endured. Up inside that dark and silent wood, such opaque horrors had clung to her flesh and pierced her chest. Marcus supposed she'd lost a great deal of blood; he wasn't surprised that she'd been infected by so many dirty teeth. This is why she'd come back to them sweat-drenched, her eyes murky with delirium.

Sophie finally turned away from the slit that she'd been peering through. She'd seen far more than he'd dared to. She bent double and vomited a watery expulsion onto the temple's already corrupted earth.

'Something is in here. There is something in here.' That was Nigel. His words were hesitant at first, then stricken with fear and ascending the scales of panic.

Marcus searched the darkness. He received an impression of Nigel standing close to the culvert or well. He'd moved away from the wooden door. 'It's down there,' he said, his voice low but scratchy.

Nigel scuttled back from the edge and retreated to the bolted door. He threw his weight against the wood, then slapped the panels with open palms. 'Open the door! Open the fucking door!'

Breathing heavily and unsteady on her feet, Sophie straightened her back. She wiped her mouth and looked in the direction of her husband. 'What's he saying?' she asked.

From outside came the dull *whump* of the cow falling onto its side. The animal gave a final groan. The felled beast's ensuing silence indicated its surrender to the wet sounds of so many messy eaters. Through the walls, scarlet light probed.

Only then did Marcus hear what Nigel had tried to draw their attention to. Even above the thumps of the man's hands against the door, and his panicked wheezing and urgent cries for release, Marcus heard an array of new noises. They were emerging from the hole in the floor of the temple.

30

[7–8pm]

At first, Marcus thought a great weight was being dragged across stone, but far below their feet. And then he had an image of a massive, bulky form rotating inside a confined space. The turning and scraping became urgent; a convulsion upwards, through inflexible confines. An enormous thing, trapped in the middle of the well shaft, appeared to be struggling for release. The great surge upwards transmitted vibrations to his bare soles through the cold soil.

As the noises drew closer to the surface, the scratching of claws against stone made him think of a vast rat pulling itself through a drain. To whatever writhed below the ground, the culvert's opening in the temple, or well mouth, must have served as a circular window, a dim but guiding light.

A change in air pressure inside the dome coincided with the noises. The volume of empty air tensed and compressed in anticipation of arrival, the atmosphere altering as if a large group of people were about to enter the hemispherical stone shape. Yet it was something else that would soon spill out and fill the space.

Marcus instinctively huddled against the wall, obeying a compulsion to put distance between himself and the well. Pressed against the cold stone, he was reminded of an exploring mouse clinging to the skirting board of a kitchen.

'Sophie. Get near the wall, and the floor. This way,' he said, but wasn't sure if she'd heard him. She didn't move.

With rock pressed into his back and buttocks, Marcus slid sideways. Feeling his way around the wall, he kept his senses fixated on the indistinct hole in the bone-strewn floor. Each section of wall was equidistant from the dark pit. There was no cover inside the stone prison. Animal instinct alone bade him keep moving, as if he might eventually squeeze himself into a recess or cleft, anywhere that might offer concealment. He wanted to become as small as a vole.

The clatter of claws searching for purchase, and the friction of a dense body rubbing stone, eased. Briefly. Before evolving into a tremendous wet slapping.

Marcus now thought of a huge muscular fish, somewhere beneath their feet, flopping around the stone shaft. Only a thing the size of a single-decker bus, surely, could produce such a frenzy of oily thumps.

A hiss of air, or gas, escaped from the culvert.

Marcus could not think clearly. Not until the stench dispersed somewhat, through the ceiling flue and the holes in the wall. A reek of animal urine. A splashing torrent. Gallons, fermented in barrels and then poured onto red-hot metal plates. His nostrils were scalded, his brain steamed. The acidic pall smoked, then cured, his insides. His hands clawed across his face to stuff a finger up each nostril, to block his mouth. Had there been any significant light in the dome, he was sure that the choking foetor would have been accompanied by a brownish fog.

But what belched out of the sewer next was even fouler: a great mushrooming miasma of rotting flesh, with a sickly floral fragrance.

Marcus tried to spit but his mouth was bone-dry. Noxious fumes stung his eyes shut. Blinded and flogged by the stink, he flattened himself further into the wall, bruising his shoulders. Surely nothing so evil-smelling could be living. Yet only great strength, vitality and intention could have hauled so prodigious a form from out of the void. Through squinting eyes, he glimpsed something of what issued the stench.

Monumental

Faint illumination from the ceiling flue, and a scattering of misted red rays through chinks in the walls, cast glimmers upon a spherical trunk. Nearly as thick as the well shaft that had birthed it, the tubular body continued to emerge. As if it were being squeezed out by contractions in the stone siphon that dropped vertically from the temple floor, most of the visitor slopped and slid free.

Marcus sank to a crouch and smothered his coughing.

Sophie screamed. She still hadn't moved from where he'd left her on the north side of the structure.

Nigel's fists no longer struck the door.

Outside, people began to cry. Clement Colman and his adepts. It was impossible to tell if they wailed from grief or joy.

Through the holes in the walls, stronger air currents rifled and puffed. A choir of mute children hissed a single note. Inside the stone organ, powered by wind, the piping expanded.

Colossal yet sinuous, the immense body slipped away from the culvert. Like a monstrous scarlet anaconda, as thick as a concrete sewer pipe that a man might stand upright inside, the worm rose to the wooden beam.

A scrape of talon on timber.

A sputter of a flare outside. A bright shaft of scarlet light flashed through an aperture in the walls. The flush of crimson illumination dappled reptilian skin; a hide as wet as entrails gloved in blood.

Failing light from the ceiling flue bathed the furthest reach of what had belched from the well and defined an uneven conclusion to a long body. A head, perhaps spiked.

Sliding moistly from the darkness below, the last of the thing thinned and rose from the soil near the hole in the floor of the temple. Marcus heard more than he saw: the tail slapping the ground then wriggling like a purple earthworm in an upturned clod of soil. Bones were disturbed, some flung, rattling, into the air.

As if a powerful wind had inflated a massive mainsail aboard a sailing ship, a sheet of even greater darkness swept the ground.

Wings.

A stinking wind struck Marcus's face. Were his hair not plastered to his skull with flaking blood, it would have swayed like wheat.

Above his head, a wet leather strop might have clashed with the stone wall. A rain pattered the earth about his feet. A squall of rot.

Great wings opening.

As if massive lungs then exhaled, the extended sheets were sucked back into the wet trunk. Though he did not see them fold, he sensed that these extremities, like a pair of huge membranes, had wrapped themselves about the thick body.

Your god.

Marcus wanted to die.

The intensity of the morbid wait for a ghastly fate was unbearable. An image filled his mind of the human torso inside the temple, half-seen but clearly crushed and partially eaten. He begged his heart to stop beating.

If you smash your head against the wall, you might knock yourself out and not be conscious for . . .

The thought was too appalling to finish. His curiosity about the shattered body parts, human and animal, arrayed across the reeking soil floor had been assuaged. Parts of Clement Colman's wild boasts about ancient gods and their Little Priests burst into his mind. Against his inner thighs, precious bodily fluids gushed. Urine spattered his feet.

As it poured out and through the flue in the vaulted roof, the great thing blotted the light that had done little but struggle into the dome since dusk. That was no skylight; it was a door within a valley of doors. Now, only flickering scarlet shafts permitted Marcus to see anything above his head. Until, one by one, on the north side of the dome, these red spots were also doused black, as the thing from the well scraped and slipped down the exterior of the rounded temple.

Clawed appendages used the slots to ease its passage. The apertures were nothing more than steps for large, sharp feet.

Marcus could not move. Nor could his companions. All three of them crouched in the darkness, pressing their unclothed bodies into the walls. All three minds had been shrunk, reduced to animal terror. But, in that darkness, they were forced to listen to the god of the valley worming its heavy body across the paddock to the blooded cow.

A great steel press in a factory would have been no more effective in crunching the carcass flat.

Outside and inside the temple, no one dared breathe.

The distant snapping of bones made Marcus flinch, as if he were being shelled, or fired on. Until he could tolerate being still no longer. He stood up, then stumbled to where he was more familiar with the gaps in the wall. Once there, he tried to climb.

He didn't get far, but further than he believed was possible; about his own height from the ground.

Sophie tried to copy him, but her desperate attempt to climb out never advanced further than raising one foot from the ground. Once she'd given up, she whimpered and said, 'They're going to feed us to it.'

Marcus fell from the wall. Then hugged the stones again.

A hideous silence fell around them, that only ended when Sophie groaned. Marcus knew why. She'd also heard the great worm shift its coils outside, before pushing its bulk back to the lair in which they were trapped.

Up the bumpy curvature of stone the god clambered. Claws and a sliding underbelly worked the surface. Within its jaws, a prize; the first sacrifice, one prepared by the teeth of its wretched priesthood. And back through the hole in the ceiling the thing soon squeezed itself. An immense fleshy cable that swayed and dangled like a gigantic python, drooping from a tree branch, until it found the wooden beam. And onto the perch it settled heavily. Inside what truly had been a temple all along, the god began to feast.

31

[7–8pm]

Smudged from the flares sputtering outside, the perch appeared as a black rod. Upon the spar, the divine bulk squatted and pulled at the remains it clasped to the timber. Strips of wet flesh were extracted, tugged and snapped from the carcass before being gulped by the serpent. Below the beam, the larval tail roamed and swept. Bones scattered and were knocked hollowly against each other. Dropped from above, discarded matter intermittently slapped the soil.

Nothing moved in Marcus's mind. Terror froze and anaesthetised thought into a numb stasis. To preserve itself, at this point of extinction, his spirit abandoned futile considerations. Even a dim comprehension of what coiled above his head and fed, and would soon hunt him through the putrid darkness, was sufficient to mesmerise his limbs into paralysis. Shivering trauma. A fear-struck rodent, aquiver inside a predator's lair.

Sophie might have lost her mind or been driven by a final surge of lunatic courage to act. Perhaps the terrible waiting in the reeking abattoir had become too much to withstand for one moment longer. Out from the wall she came, screaming. Through the air she swished her bone.

And then she was in the air. Plucked from the dirt and lifted to the wooden perch. Marcus tracked her ascent and trajectory by her screams.

As if the entity were idly surveying its prey in better light, she was moved across the pitch of the roof to within touching distance of the flue. Momentarily, she was held there. Her body became a silhouette, screened on a disc of indigo sky. Marcus wasn't sure but suspected that it was the loathsome tail that held her fast.

Her head was thrust back and through the vent she screamed, 'I can see! It's inside me!'

Marcus could not fathom what she meant.

In response, from outside, there was excited laughter and the sort of weeping that is provoked by relief, or happiness. One exultant cry rose above the other voices as Clement Colman finally abandoned his restraint. Perhaps he was overwhelmed by the appearance of what he'd brought forth, what he'd engineered, because this situation was part of the new existence of which he'd bragged. The miracle.

This was the last of the earth's sky that Sophie would ever see. She disappeared from the open crown of the stone sewer and was brought back inside the temple. Her final scream dulled Marcus's hearing.

A moment later, he was reminded of inadvertently stepping on the snails that fell out of his kayaks during the winter months. Beneath his foot, he would feel the implosion of a fragile shell around a soft centre. And he would hear a crunch.

He almost envied his former lover this end to the dread of the wait. But the evidence of her death didn't sound like transmigration to a higher plane of being, as promised by Clement Colman; instead, the sound of Sophie's destruction resembled the noise a reptile might make when closing its jaws on an insect.

Sophie was partially returned to earth. Marcus counted three pieces. He was glad that he didn't see them fall and only heard the discarded scraps slap the soil.

Across the dome, Nigel whimpered and whispered to himself.

Drawn back to the cold air of night, the immense threading of the thick trunk through the flue was repeated. This time the god sat upon the temple mound. Below, in the valley, its adoring congregation fell profoundly silent.

In the Garden of Eden, Satan had reclaimed the throne.

Above their heads, broad sheets of wing extended, then *whump-whumped* at the atmosphere. Down-draughts of beaten air piped between slits in the walls; a stinking breath issued through teeth of stone.

The god took flight and the flue was cleared of the monstrous bulk.

32

[8–9pm]

Marcus pushed himself up the wall and stared at what he could see of his legs. He wondered if they had enough strength and rigidity to get him across the temple to the barred door. They did, but shook enough to make him limp.

He paused by the hole in the earth, the pit from which that hideous thing had so recently slithered. He stooped and picked up a bone, a vertebral joint. Then cast the chunk over the edge. The fragment fell and fell and fell and fell. When Marcus turned away, he heard a distant click, as if a teaspoon had been dropped onto a tiled floor, in a distant room, inside an empty mansion.

The valley was greater in size than anyone in the kayaking group could have imagined. He feared that what they had seen of the woods, river, floodplains and fields were mere parts of a summit above another, vaster place. And what writhed below must always long for the air and earth above.

Thousands of years ago, the temple had been destroyed. The sinus that led up from a region below the pagan site of antiquity had been blocked. For good reason. Anyone aware of what existed beneath the ground, who even considered reopening this door, would be an arrogant, self-deceiving fool. Colman had known something about the evil below. He must have done. Those small abominations that had just bled out a cow had educated him about their god. Or deceived him; one only had to look at the wights to suspect that anything they served would be abhorrent. And yet Colman had still set it free.

Had Colman also suggested, in his most recent oration, that control of what had been brought forth had been lost? And that now the reactor was leaking, he and his fellows were going to make a run from the contamination?

'Nigel,' Marcus whispered, when he reached the door.

Nigel had sat down. The man didn't reply but his hoary, murky face turned to Marcus.

'I'm going to get bones. We'll use them as tools. We dig. Yes? Did you hear me?'

Nigel's hunched and darkened form didn't twitch.

Marcus retraced his steps to the most intact cattle remains he'd yet seen, from which he'd extracted the second rib.

What he then had to do, to extract a jawbone and a rib, made him sick to the marrow. Inside his forearms, for a long time afterwards, he still felt the sensations of the gristly twisting that was required to tug bones free of their sinewy moorings. A task that had required all of his strength with one foot planted on the carcass. A rash of sweat that he could ill afford to lose had bubbled across his scalp and back. He'd been surprised that any moisture remained inside his body. Thirst was now an internal chemical burn.

He dropped the rib beside Nigel. 'Quick. Dig with me. At the base of the threshold. Soil's soft, see?' Marcus dropped to his knees and scraped the earth with the jawbone. 'Help me.'

Nigel didn't. Sitting like a Buddha, he only stared through the darkness at Marcus. 'We're never getting out of here alive, you stupid cock,' he muttered.

'For fuck sake – what happened before doesn't matter. Not now. Only this counts. There's no other way out.'

The round-shouldered figure, slumped over its paunch, returned to its silence and immobility.

On his own, Marcus dug, hacked, scraped.

Monumental

Panting like a dog on a hot day, he chopped at the earth to loosen small clods. Now and again, he dropped the bone and used his hands to scoop the disturbed earth out of the shallow hole he'd made. He'd never done anything as futile as digging at this dirt with a bone and his fingers. But it was the only occupation and distraction that succeeded in pushing from his mind the sound of *her* parts dropping from the perch.

Nigel had heard the same things as Marcus. Perhaps the last vestige of his sentience had succumbed to absolute resignation, or trauma. Marcus didn't blame him but continued to gouge and chop at the floor of the temple. When he reached the bottom of the thick threshold, and was even able to scrape some soil from beneath the deepest edge of the stone block, he turned to his silent companion, as if expecting Nigel to approve of the shallow, uneven bowl that he'd hacked into the floor.

For his efforts, the only acknowledgement that Marcus received was the stinging whack of a cow's rib across his shoulders.

33

[8–9pm]

Strength abandoned his arms and rendered them soft. Unable to think of anything but the brand of agony smarting across his back, Marcus fell sideways, then scrabbled across the damp earth to get clear of his attacker.

A fleshy smack slapped the darkness and one of his thighs was engulfed by a fire of pain. 'Stop!' he cried out.

A breeze swept his face as the rib missed his head by a finger's breadth and bounced from the dirt and out of Nigel's hands. Marcus rolled further from the door but came to a stop against some sharp, shattered debris on the floor.

Feet stamped across the soil and Nigel's excited wheezing filled the air. The sole of the man's foot stamped against the top of Marcus's raised head, ripping encrusted hair from his scalp. Against his calf, the foot stamped again.

Marcus jerked around to stay clear of the blows, but Nigel still succeeded in planting a begrimed sole on Marcus's shoulder, knocking him down and into a scattering of carcass fragments that stabbed into his ribs and hips.

'Bastard. Bastard. Bastard,' Nigel cried out, his words performing percussion to his stamping foot.

Trapped among the shards of skeletal remains, blind with pain and half winded, Marcus could not evade the blows. It was as if Nigel could see in the dark, his vision lit red by psychotic hate. Down came the foot against his knee, a buttock, then a thigh that immediately went dead.

'Bastard. Bastard. Bastard.'

More of his strength dispersed. Panic flared. Marcus struggled to catch his breath or rise any higher than onto his hands and knees. He flopped and dragged himself, here and there, amidst decomposition. He lost the ability to speak as Nigel used the last of himself to stamp a man to death.

'Bastard. Bastard. Bastard.'

Exhausted by pain, Marcus's thoughts veered from terror to a vague notion of what was happening to him. But as soon as he regrouped his awareness into some semblance of an idea of how to evade the attack, the bludgeoning foot descended again and again and knocked the sense out of him.

He wondered if this was how he would die – under a rival's dirty, stamping foot. Strangely, his end seemed inevitable. If there was no protection from social codes or laws, this was where resentment led; angry animals beating to death those they envied and despised. Marcus tried to curl around his groin and protect his throat.

An impression that the air above him had compressed and darkened was supported by the sudden spreading of a filthy smell across the floor where he crawled and flinched. The stench intensified to the reek of open graves exposed to a burning sun. Gassed and choking, Marcus briefly blacked out.

'Bastard. Bastard. Bast—'

Only half aware of his surroundings, Marcus continued to cringe. But the foot did not stamp again. Nor would it, because Nigel was now somewhere high above him. Beneath the vaulted dome, the man screamed and then laughed, madly.

Marcus rolled back towards the threshold and his little hole, as if to a shallow grave. Groaning and whimpering at the pain emanating from his bruised and tender parts, he crawled to sit with his back to the wall, beside the door. There he tried to cough his lungs clear of the miasma. He'd been overcome by the worm's incense. That malodour still lingered heavily, a fresh wave of rot about an already reeking floor. He covered his mouth and nose with a forearm, then looked up at where there was motion in the air above him.

Claws scraped stone.

A leathery flapping.

The god's black form swayed near the flue at the apex of the dome. The muscular trunk of the body slipped through the vent. The thing's passage out of the dome was more efficient this time, though Marcus stopped at considering its departure graceful. But the thing from the pit in the temple was rapidly acclimatising to the world into which it had crawled.

Marcus never caught sight of Nigel again but heard his cries for longer than he wished to. Under the ceiling, then outside the temple, the paddle leader laughed hard before screaming with an equal intensity. His final screams originated from the sky. Only the *whump whump whump* of vast wings and the growing altitude of the god and its sacrifice eventually silenced the strained human voice.

As if confronted by a miracle, a wailing and weeping arose from Clement and his adepts.

34

[8–9pm]

*B*acked against a stone wall, his skin unclothed and stained with animal blood, Marcus waited to go out. Inflamed by his scent, the god of this wretched sewer would soon pluck another grubby morsel from the corrupted soil. When he wondered if he might avoid confronting the idea of his own annihilation, his imagination made him think about his body being torn apart.

For how long will you be aware?

He looked at the terrible black perch that speared the murk above, and he sank his head between his knees, gripped his shins and attempted to steady his breathing. A small, short cry escaped him. Inside the sound he heard a child.

Nothing in this crease of the earth was as it should be; not when he'd paused his ruminations and listened to his instincts. He'd realised this too late. Jane had been affected by the valley, and he'd noticed her disquiet, even before they'd found the carcasses necklacing those skeletal trees. She was one of a few people, he suspected, who remained strongly attuned to the uncanny influences and atmospheres of certain places. But had he not also sensed something awry at the mouth of the estuary; an odd quality in a coastal arcadia bereft of bird flight and song, or any meaningful sound?

The dim, outlying remnants of his animal instincts had indeed reacted to the Wyrm Valley. The reverential caution that his species had once possessed but had repressed over the last few centuries had truly flickered awake here. To have said as much would have provoked derision among the group. But how foolish it now appeared to Marcus to have ever cared about what the others thought of him.

He tortured himself by thinking of what he might have done differently, to prevent his party of six from vanishing here so swiftly and horribly; perhaps without trace too, provided that the wardens of this temple erased the evidence of their annual rite.

Clement Colman and his acolytes had improbably but accurately identified something supernormal here. And then they had blundered, deceiving themselves with their interpretations, wishful thoughts and unwavering self-belief. Curious and confident, they'd enabled the return of ghastly entities that had preyed on Neolithic man. These bones, collected across several millennia, were a territorial marker; a warning and a projection of power.

Discomfort killed his ruminations. Across one thigh and his shoulders, welts branded his skin like burns. Gatherings of hot pain near the bone ebbed to persistent, thumping aches. If he shifted his position, he felt other bruises with spikes of agony that made him gasp. Most of them had been created by a madman's stamping foot.

He didn't think that anything was broken; he could move his fingers and toes freely. But his body had ransacked the medicine cabinet and flooded itself with natural painkillers; he'd only truly know the extent of the damage when he tried to stand and walk, if there was any point now in doing such a thing.

'You're not laughing now, you bastard,' Marcus whispered, unsure to whom he was referring: himself or Nigel.

Outside, the flares were dying. A ruddy smudge was visible in some gaps between the stone blocks. But no scarlet rays flickered on his side of the tomb now. Light had all but abandoned his damnation. The walls had ceased their incessant piping. The breeze had dropped but not vanished. Wisps of cooler air still stroked his flesh.

Monumental

Padding his palms across the soil, close to the door, Marcus located the rib that Nigel had tried to break across his back. Wincing from the pain of even such a slight movement, he picked up the rib and crawled to the threshold. The recess he'd scraped from the soil seemed half as deep as he remembered, and narrower.

He closed his eyes and tried to push away the fear that rose like vomit. 'Come on, come on, come on,' he whispered to himself as he knelt again before the stone step. And once again he scraped and hacked to loosen the dirt, before throwing the pieces behind himself like a dog.

Maybe the god would take him right here, from behind, if that were its whim. He swore he would not look back.

But what if he heard it slithering through the darkness? Then he might be unable to resist turning his head.

The mere notion of such an immensity approaching reduced the strength in his arms and left him panting for breath. 'Stop it,' he said.

With sudden fury, he raised the rib like a pickaxe and speared the dirt.

Again, again, again, he swung the crude tool to dislodge soil, before scraping away the disrupted clods. His back and shoulders screamed and begged him to stop. But again and again and again he tore at the dirt.

When the padlock on the other side of the door rattled, he was simply bewildered. The portal was a mere arm's length before his eyes. He could barely see the wood.

The gritty sliding of the latch startled him so much that he flinched.

Either the door then swung open silently, or the drumming of the pulse inside his ear canals had blotted all sounds from his mind.

As if he knelt in the shallows of a cove, a blessed wave of cool, clean air struck his face.

35

[8–9pm]

From the rectangle of a lesser darkness framed by the open doorway, a female voice muttered, 'Quick. Before it comes back. Quick. Quick.'

Marcus obeyed. He crept from the tomb on his hands and knees. Beneath his palms, the blessed grass might have been the fur of a Persian cat. And as if he was gulping from a glass of iced water, inhalations of cleaner air ached behind his breastbone.

Disbelief and relief flooded body and mind in a veritable torrent. The simple awareness of no longer being inside the hateful, reeking stone receptacle, exposed to its abominations, filled his eyes with hot tears.

Coughing at the pestilence that had saturated his lungs for too long, Marcus turned about on all fours and spotted a pair of small feet in Converse trainers. They paced near his fingertips. The grass seemed to have a faint luminance. Not all of the flares on this side had died. Stars speckled the black canopy. Or maybe he was simply hallucinating after being trapped inside the stinking darkness for so long.

Marcus looked up and at a small, thin woman. He had the random thought that there must be little sugar or saturated fat in the valley diet. Those who lived here were all whittled and wind-burned; they worked for a billionaire but retained, or possessed, something of the street and its depredations.

Or perhaps, out here in isolation, amidst such terrors and inhumanity, they'd turned feral.

This was the woman who'd stood beside Colman earlier: the goose.

An artfully crafted yet grotesque mask of feathers covered her head. Only a wild bush of bone-white hair escaped and fell around her shoulders. Bulky, furred in places with down, the headgear atop her narrow shoulders was another symbol of the monstrous strangeness that infested the Wyrm Valley.

She wore the same woollen smock that had covered Colman's tattooed disciples for their October rite. A powerful scent drifted from the figure. In the odour, Marcus smelled soap but also something unpleasant: a musk tainted with ammonia, as if a cat had pissed on her clothes for weeks.

When she reached down to touch his face, Marcus cringed like an uncertain dog. In her other hand she held one of the short swords that he'd seen her peers carrying as they'd led a cow to slaughter and lit that pyre of blood in the paddock. Trying to understand a situation that utterly confounded him, and how this weapon might now be used, he could hold nothing in his mind but a vague recollection of news pictures of broken, kneeling captives about to be beheaded.

'It's all right, darling,' she said. 'You needn't worry about me. I'm not going to hurt you. But they will. They'll put you back inside.' Breathless with nerves and almost as cowed as he was, she was too agitated to keep still. Her feet padded the grass back and forth. She whipped her head towards the entrance and the quad bikes. From Marcus's position near the temple door, that section of the paddock was obscured by the dome. 'You'll have to leave the valley the same way you came in. We need to get out of the circle and head to the river. Or it'll smell you. It's the blood.'

Marcus stood but swayed. The woman caught his arm. 'Steady. Steady. That's it.' Her bushel of a head prodded closer. Marcus recoiled from the swaying mass of feathers and the suggestion of two shining, mad eyes inside the deep sockets.

The woman pushed the mask up her face, then plucked it off the top of her head, much of her tatty hair rising with it. She tucked the mask under one arm. In the thin light Marcus glimpsed one of the most haggard faces he'd ever seen, shrunken inside the cowl of thick hair and perched on a parchment neck. The eyes, however, were bright and excitable. 'Did you meet anyone inside?' she asked him.

'What?'

Gently tugging his arm, she pulled him away from the door and looked fearfully once more towards the north of the valley. 'A man. Called Briar. Was Briar inside?'

Marcus struggled to understand. Surely, anyone familiar with the temple would know that nothing and no one would ever survive for long inside the dome. He then remembered the scattered remains of the man that Sophie had blundered across in the dark. 'No. There was just three of us. The kayakers.'

Anguish took hold of the woman's eyes. She began to shake, yet still managed to take a few steps to close the door of the temple. The latch slid home. The padlock rattled and emitted a click as it was relocked. Her fist closed around the key. His saviour then drew Marcus further away from the dome and across the shorn grass to the henge. 'I wouldn't come to the temple when it was his turn. I couldn't.' The woman shuddered, then released his arm and scurried across the paddock. 'Quick. Quick. The river.'

Marcus peered around. Silhouettes of the poles reared into the air. To avoid being seen by the others, she was leading him out of the circular paddock in an easterly direction.

Without further hesitation, he matched the rapid pace set by the woman's small, scurrying feet.

His saviour peered over a shoulder to make sure that he was close. 'Clement says it's the start of a great journey,' she said, breathlessly. 'But it's not one we wanted to take. Briar and me. There was no one else this year. No volunteers. So, we were selected. Briar first. I wouldn't watch his transference from here to there. I've heard what happens inside the temple.

I saw it too. Bits. Last year. I know what happens. How can that be a joyous occasion?'

Clean air continued to revive Marcus's mind, though it also made him giddy. His punished feet and legs retained a vestige of the clumsiness that had beset them when drugged. But agility and balance were being restored; his stagger even progressed to an approximation of a jog. And now that he was outside the temple, crossing the paddock and heading for the darkness of the trees that fringed the riverbanks, a new sensation swamped him; Marcus felt unbearably exposed beneath the black sky.

He began to trot at a crouch, as if under gunfire. When the woman noticed his stoop, she peered at the sky. 'It's not come back yet. But it will and it won't find you inside, where it will expect you to be. When you're not brought out to the temple roof, the others will be suspicious. They'll know what I've done soon enough. Clement sent me back to the house in disgrace, because I couldn't get into the spirit of things.'

They darted between two henge posts; ran down the slope of the grassy moat and up the other side. 'Not far now,' his guide whispered.

The river had to be close. 'Thank you,' he said, but acknowledged that those two words hardly expressed the gratitude that he owed this woman. 'Why?'

She paused. 'It was my turn. Tonight. If you and your friends hadn't come into the valley, I'd have already crossed over, like Briar. You saved me. It wasn't right that you should go and not me. This has nothing to do with you.' She ran at a black wall of scrub. 'Quickly now. Through here.' His saviour threw her mask away and into the darkness, then vanished without a sound.

Marcus stretched out both hands, as if blind, and stumbled towards the last place he'd seen her. Beneath the exposed soles of his feet, the turf ended. Broken sticks poked into his arches. Against his arms and one side of his face, unseen leaves and twigs whipped his flesh. When she whispered, 'Quickly,' her voice originated from an alarming distance ahead of him.

'Where is it? That thing. Where does it go?'

'Not far enough,' she said, breathlessly, as if to remind him of her age. 'The blood on you must be washed off, or it'll find you. It lives in darkness. Relies on a sense of smell. No one has seen its eyes. But we don't know much about it. They thought the flares were keeping it inside the circle. Maybe fires used to be lit in the cursus and moat. Before. A long time ago. We never knew. But it roams now. They're all terrified that it'll leave the valley again. This week, it came back with a body. From outside the valley. The Little Priests can't be trusted. They've always lied. Lied and lied about what it will do. Briar warned Clement, repeatedly, but he wouldn't listen. So now . . .'

Though what she'd said confused him, the tone of the information she offered was sufficient incentive for Marcus to rush blindly in the direction of her voice. He made more noise than he thought prudent, but a desire to reach the river and rinse the caking filth from his skin became a greater motivation than caution.

'Your name. I don't know your name,' he whispered. He wanted to hear her voice again, was afraid that he might lose her in the darkness. Other than ambient light from the paler tones of the sky, he could see little under the tree canopy and was forced to feel his way through the scrub. They were deep inside the band of trees that lined the river bank.

Her voice burst from his left side. 'Hedge Pig. That's what they call me here. My name was Rachel.'

'Then I'll call you Rachel. Who was Briar?'

'My partner,' she said, from somewhere behind him. He'd caught her up, then passed her in the darkness. 'We weren't married. We were together forty years.'

Automatically, Marcus said, 'I'm sorry.'

Rachel sniffed. A part of her silhouette moved away. Over the sound of his scuffing feet and laboured breathing, he heard the trickling of the river. The temperature dropped.

'It killed my . . . two of my group. How long has this been going on? How many, Rachel? How many have been murdered here?'

'The river,' she said, from somewhere ahead of him, though he'd not heard her feet cover the ground between him and the water.

Marcus followed the sound of her voice to an outline of her diminutive body, contrasting against the glitter of the water's black surface.

At the sight of the river, Marcus nearly wept. Looming over what was little more than a wide brook, a black facade of tree silhouettes crowded. In the east of the valley, the outline of the wooded slope was just visible. They'd not set foot on that side of the river.

'It'll be cold but wash the blood off. Quick. Quick.' The shape of Rachel's head was angled to the sky. The little sword spiked from a hand.

Marcus didn't hesitate. He stumbled down the bank and fell onto all fours in the stream.

His breath imploded back inside his chest when the icy water ran over his lower legs and wrists. The tide had turned; the estuary and river were slowly refilling again. Around midnight, high water would peak. He'd then have between one and two hours to paddle down the river and creek before crossing the estuary. As much as the chilled water shocked him, the unexpected possibility that he might now leave the valley alive dazed him more.

The burden of such a hope was too heavy to carry, so he concentrated on getting clean. Breathing quickly, near hyperventilating, Marcus sank on to his front and rolled over. Night's cold and the melted moor frosts of the waterway ran through his marrow. With gingerly cupped hands he shovelled cold water into his dry mouth. There would be cattle run-off, fertiliser and other contaminants that had seeped into the flow further upstream. But he didn't care. A bout of cryptosporidium was the last of his concerns. Thirst drove him to gulp and gulp until his gut turned to ice and he thought he might be sick.

He wiped his wet hands over the crusting paste of blood miring his skin, then clawed at it. He couldn't tell if the water running from his arms and chest was dirty or clear.

'I don't know if it was that.' Rachel said, from up on the bank where she paced, and after what appeared to have been a period of tormented contemplation. 'I mean, other than Briar and the man from outside the valley, and those of us who tried to leave, if the others here all wanted to join the god, can that be murder too?'

'What? Who?' Marcus said. His shivering prevented him saying more or thinking clearly about anything but the cold.

'They wanted to go, inside. Last year. Some very unhappy people lived here. They had lots of time to think about it. They did. They really did.'

'Who? Who, Rachel?'

'Our people.'

'The cult.'

'We don't like being called that!'

Marcus suddenly regretted he'd spoken. He thought of being back inside the temple. 'Sorry. Sorry. I didn't mean—'

'Clement brought us all here. He offered sanctuary. We had so many problems. There was drink. Substances. Some of us never had homes. All we had was Green Leaf. The Foundation. And it wasn't always like this. People started over here. They recovered. This was a family. We loved each other. Before . . . before we found the forgotten kingdom.'

She paused and held her head. 'Briar. Briar, Briar.' She walked in a circle at the water's edge. 'We opened doors. The little people came down from the hills. That changed everything. The digging and the building. The rock . . .'

Agitated, breathless and either shaking with cold or twitching, the woman abruptly stopped talking. He heard her sniff back tears.

Marcus crawled to find the channel of the river bed and deeper water. When he found it, he slipped forward, the palms of his hands gliding over slippery, worn pebbles. He gasped and dipped his head beneath the surface. Instantly, his head was encased in ice, his face a mask of needling pain. His lungs clung to his spine. But the chill was a balm to his pain, his wounds.

He pulled his head clear of the surface and dragged in a breath. The whimper that followed was a suppressed scream. But the electric shock of cold water revived yet more of his mind from the druggy lethargy. He realised how long inebriation and the adrenaline of anxiety and terror had consumed him; ever since Jane had screamed, so soon after they'd landed at midday.

The cold's pain faded into a sense of his body being revitalised by warmth. At his core, his blood bloomed hot. A small pleasure, incongruous in the circumstances, but he was grateful for it.

Marcus hauled in a deep breath and slid lengthways in the channel to let the water refreeze him. Slowly, he acclimatised to the cold and rubbed furiously at his arms and shoulders, then each leg, then his feet. His skin was slimy. He felt clots of dross peel away and vanish in the black flow.

'That's it. Good. Get it all off,' Rachel muttered from the bank. 'Be sure. The god and the Little Priests can smell a drop of blood from a great distance. When the girls had periods, we had to put shutters on the windows.'

Marcus returned his attention to Rachel. Desperation to understand what was happening in the valley was a welcome foil to the icy torrent swilling around his body. His teeth chattered. 'The Foundation. Colman's organisation. For the homeless, addicts. The charity. Green Leaf. Everyone here was in its care?'

'That's where he found me and Briar, at the Foundation. We were unhappy in a hostel, in Plymouth, so we came here with him.'

'And people from Green Leaf were being put inside that ... temple?'

'No. Only those who wanted to see the god. Last year. Four of my friends crossed over. We didn't know that it would be like that. We didn't! The Priests lied!'

'Willingly? They must have been bloody drugged. Your friends. We were. Jesus Christ Almighty, we were drugged and locked inside with that thing.'

'Briar said their thoughts were not their own. Because the Little Priests had sipped from them and whispered. Their minds were made up for them. That's the problem now. No one here is in their right mind.'

'How long has this been going on?'

Rachel paused and raised an arm. She began counting, her small fingers writhing around her face like worms. 'Five October Rites since I came here. For five days each year. But it was only cows that went to the kingdom for the first three rites. So many. I never liked that part. Most of us are vegan. The god isn't. And it wasn't satisfied with cows.'

Marcus turned onto his front. His body was now so cold that the chill hardly registered. Had there been a strong wind in the valley, he'd be risking hypothermia. He thought of the campsite; of the warm clean clothes in his rucksack; of his beautiful fifteen-foot kayak. With both hands, with renewed vigour and purpose, he frantically scraped and wiped at the discoloured patches and remaining stains that he could detect in the poor light. He wanted to go downriver.

The woman exhaled wearily, a sound of pure despair. 'Nor were the Priests satisfied with just milk. Milk, milk, milk. So much of it they took. Then blood. Animal blood. Then ours. So much. But then no one could leave, you see, because we'd seen them, and because of those who crossed over last year. Four. No one but us would understand what happened to them! And how it all came to be. That's what Clement says. He had to think of what to do to protect us and the valley.

'Only he was allowed to go out, at the start, with Vine and Swan. His favourites. Only they ever got to go to Morrisons! It wasn't fair. But then that wasn't allowed either. The Priests forbade anyone from leaving. Ever since last October, we've all been here together. Stuck. Trapped.'

'You can just walk out of here. The top of the valley. The road up there. I've seen it on a map. Why didn't you just go?' Marcus's voice fell apart; his entire body shook and pimpled with cold.

'No, no, no. The Priests won't allow it. They decide everything for us.'

Marcus thought of the childlike figures amassing on the cow. They'd been joined by what had resembled three actual children. He thought Rachel unhinged. She didn't appear to grasp the full gravity and consequences of what she and her associates had been doing in this awful place. Her thoughts appeared scattered between grief at losing this Briar, a suspicion that she'd been duped by Colman, remorse at her collaboration, or silence, and these banalities about who, in some cultish hierarchy, had been permitted to go shopping.

Nonchalantly, yet defensively, she added, 'You'd be surprised how many wanted to cross over. They had terrible problems. They wanted release, you see. In the kingdom, you start again. That's what we were told. By the Priests. We saw the other side in the dreams they gave us. Some people wanted to take that opportunity. There was nothing for them here, on this side, not compared to the kingdom.'

'These Priests, they asked for people?'

Like a child, Rachel nodded her head enthusiastically. 'Last year, when the cows weren't enough, the Priests asked for some of us to enter the kingdom.'

Marcus stood up and scythed as much surface water from his face, arms and chest as he could. His joints had stiffened but his flesh glowed, and his mind had not felt so clear in hours. 'An assisted suicide scam. Clement convinced mentally ill people and addicts to die in that stone abattoir. People who were groomed in his Foundation. That's how it will look. And he knows it. To you, he sells being torn apart in a sewer as something else. Crossing over? I think I'm beginning to understand, Rachel. So, correct me if I am wrong, but when the homeless addicts who had *chosen* to cross over to the kingdom ran out last year, Clement asked for more volunteers this year? And the pickings were slim?'

'They asked to go during the last rite! It was considered an honour then! We'd never seen it, the god, before last year's rite. Only heard it. But last year, we saw the god. For the first time, *we saw*.' As if suddenly sapped of strength or balance at the mere memory, Rachel sat down. 'It came out. Like a worm. Up, up. Onto the roof.' She dropped her face into her hands. 'This year, the wings. It flew . . .'

'But you and Briar had more sense.'

'We had doubts.'

'You can't climb out at the top of the bloody valley? Clement told you this, did he? These Priests told him, I bet?'

'We can't. No one can. The Priests guard it. There was a lady here called Karla and she gave a note to the food delivery men. The police came. They thought we were mad and left. And by then Karla had run away.' She looked at Marcus and her face trembled with emotion; fear, he thought. 'The Priests brought some of her back.'

'What are they? Those things. In the masks. They look like children. Are they the Priests? They must be children. What the fuck?'

Rachel visibly recoiled when forced to remember something else that clearly horrified her. She clutched her hands over her stomach and knitted her fingers together before unpicking them again. 'They caught Karla before she reached the gate.'

Before Rachel finished recalling the episode, they both heard the flap of vast wings in the middle of the valley, in the direction of the temple. A murmur of raised voices flowed from the same place. 'It's come back,' she whispered. 'Quick. We have to go to where you came in. Right now.'

Marcus needed no further encouragement to begin wading and splashing downstream. In early afternoon, it had taken him between thirty and forty minutes to jog and walk from the campsite to the temple. They had a lot of ground to cover in freezing, shallow water. He had to keep warm now too, keep moving.

Between encroaching tree branches and impenetrable shadows, he thrashed through the channel, until he came across submerged, cross-hatched strainers of fallen wood.

The obstructions forced him to alter course, picking about in the water for another place to get through, or to even climb over the fallen debris, and then he'd often divert again if hanging vines attempted to string him up like a puppet. His fear of cutting a leg, and of the scent of his blood being exposed to the air, reduced his speed. But wading through the glimmer of trickling water became his sole motivation and focus. Downstream led to the sea. He began to imagine that he could smell the brine.

Rachel came and went on the bank, cutting inland when meeting obstructions, before disappearing again. Even if she vanished and never returned, all he had to do was follow the river until he arrived at their camp. Once there, he'd get dry and dressed quickly. He'd stop for nothing else.

He hadn't thought of Jane, Mary and Julian in some time. He wanted to believe that all three of them remained at the campsite. But the scant and enigmatic details that had been offered by Rachel, about the colonising and controlling behaviour of these 'Priests', tempered the temptation to indulge in wishful thinking.

After Marcus had failed to see or hear his saviour and guide, up on the riverbank, for some time, she finally reappeared by a stretch of rocky shallows. She'd been waiting for him to catch up. 'How are you getting on down there?' she asked.

'I can't feel my feet. Is there a towpath?'

'No.'

Marcus stopped to catch his breath. He bent over and looked east. 'The other side of the valley. Might it be easier for me to cut through the woods. There must be farmland over there and buildings outside the valley.'

'There is a fence. It'll give you a terrible shock. And the Little Priests live on both sides of the valley. In the old mines. You won't make it. There was a couple here once. They'd been with Clement from the start. Moon and Dawn. They all worked together before Clement bought the valley. They tried to leave after last year's rite, through the trees, but they never came back. I heard some talk about them later. They'd been used like the cows. The Priests lit them as pyres of blood. And once we're marked by them' – the woman tapped the tattoo on her shoulder – 'Clement said they'll find us anywhere.'

Marcus gaped at the rumpled figure, though he no longer struggled to believe much of what she said. 'He condemned you all.' He dragged his feet through the water to the bank. 'We're clear of the temple. I'm clean. I'll be faster on land. And I need to warm up. Will you help me find a path, or some clear ground?'

Rachel nodded. 'Let's see how far we can get.' This she said quietly and with a morbid resignation that made Marcus pause.

'What do you mean?'

'A pyre was lit. The Little Priests are out now.'

Marcus joined her on the riverbank. 'I asked you before, what are those things?'

She offered him her sword. 'This is for you. They don't like iron.'

Marcus stared at the dark blade.

'Take it. We're entering their part of the valley now. They only go higher to feed or catch runaways. And only Vine goes below the temple now, with their milk. That's how we do things here.' She rummaged inside her smock and withdrew a hand holding a plastic bottle. 'And rub this all over. They don't like the smell.' She handed the bottle to him.

Marcus took it from her but merely stared at it. 'I just cleaned off the blood. What's in here?'

'Fox urine, garlic and dishwasher soap. Briar made it. Clement banned it. But I kept a bottle.'

'No way.' Marcus attempted to return the bottle. The curious astringent scent that wafted off her body was no longer a mystery.

'You must or they'll snatch you. The smell can make them hesitate, long enough for you to use the pacifier. We must keep moving. Put it on now. All over.'

Monumental

Unable to bring himself to unscrew the cap, Marcus stood dumbfounded while trying to make sense of the repellent and the use of iron to ward off what Rachel called Little Priests.

His mystification served as a prompt, though nothing of what Rachel shared brought him any comfort. 'They're not children. You must never think that. Never. We used to call them the little people. But they're not people. Some of us thought they were goblins and fairies. Elves. Jessica said they were wights. She knew lots about legends and history, drugs too. Clement said they were the original Priests who taught the druids. But the Romans destroyed all the knowledge and the rites, the whole religion. Clement wanted to bring it all back. He encouraged the Priests to come out of the mines that were abandoned. We never saw them at first, but they had returned because they ate all the birds. Eggs and everything, like rats. No birds fly here. Did you notice?'

Marcus nodded.

'We once had thousands of birds here. Egrets, herons, waterfowl. A bird sanctuary. Every time the birds returned and tried to resettle, they would vanish again. We think the Priests go outside the valley now for feathers. To restock. It's all getting out of hand. But no matter how deep you go inside the mines, you will never see one of the Priests. We don't know how they come and go, but Clement says old doors are opened with blood. Offering the milk and blood at the right time brought them back out. The old family did it here too, the people who built the house. Clement learned about their books. He bought them from a collector for a lot of money. He used their knowledge. And after the dig and the first rites, the Priests told us how to build the temple for the giant. But we didn't know we would get that kind of giant.

'The valley is an old gate. To the underworld. It was the centre of something, you know, for the people who lived here before the Romans. The druids kept it secret. It was sacred. But that was the problem, you know? Us trying to be the druids. We've made a terrible mess.'

Marcus thought of Jane's bites and of a large cow smothered in white leeches. He unscrewed the bottle, then winced at the stench that greeted him.

'It helps. Not foolproof, though, I'm afraid. But it can help. For a while. The Priests are very fast. This can slow them. The recipe was in one of Clement's books. Briar read them and he was a herbalist before we came here. But Clement stopped us making the protection. He didn't want to make the Little Priests any angrier. They're always furious now. And hungry.'

Marcus poured some of the noxious liquid into the palm of one hand, then lathered his shoulders and chest. Within the chemical reek of detergent and piercing spice of something that he tried not to dwell on, the garlic was hardly noticeable.

'Legs too. But don't swallow it.'

'I didn't intend to.'

'Let's go. Quick. Quick.'

Marcus followed Rachel into the scrub. 'We should run, when we get to the level ground, the floodplain. Can you run?' he asked.

'I'll try.'

'We have kayaks at the campsite in a meadow, not far from the reed beds.'

'I've not been down that far in years. But you chose the wrong spot to make a camp. The Little Priests live right above there. They bite. What they don't take underground, they hang in trees.'

Marcus's breath shortened, and he needed to concentrate on regaining his balance in the darkness. 'If the boats are still there, I'll tow you out. The estuary's shallow and we'll only have enough water for an hour or so before it empties again.'

'Oh, I won't be going with you. It is forbidden for those who are marked. But you must tell people about what is here. What Clement brought into the valley. The stone has to go back over the hole in the temple. The mines need to be filled in and blocked again. They should never have been opened. Clement paid people to do it with explosives. That's how we started. Then the milk and blood went in. After that, the Priests appeared. They got out.'

'Rachel, if you stay, you won't survive. Clement will feed you to that thing in the temple.'

'This is the last night of the rite before the god goes back to the kingdom for another year. If I can hide until morning – and I know places – I have a chance. You'll come back tomorrow, with help?'

'Of course, but I can't just leave you.'

'They'll find me, and you with me. The marks.' She tapped her shoulder again. 'They were in the books. Vine inked all of us. We weren't told what it'd mean until later.' She looked about the scrub. 'There are a lot of Little Priests. Those above ground will be sleepier now they've eaten, but they'll still be around. The valley is theirs now and they're with us all year.'

Marcus offered her the bottle of ointment. 'More?'

She shook her head. 'They'll beat and drive us into the water to get it washed off our skin. If I run and they catch me, they'll hang me. Like Moon and Dawn. They ran Cynthia down too. But they took Cynthia underground because she was young. She was a paranoid schizophrenic who tried to run away, a few summers ago, after it all started here. She wore the ointment, but the Priests herded her like a sheep into the water. Vine was chasing her. He saw it happen. But no one ever saw Cynthia again. We only heard her, up in the trees, shouting about stone houses and poles under a red sky.' Rachel paused. When she spoke again, her voice dropped. 'Later they gave us her children. Cynthia's three children. Triplets.'

In horror, Marcus stared at the diminutive, odd-smelling figure that scampered alongside him and who spoke so candidly and earnestly about such mad, vile things. 'The children who . . .' He couldn't finish.

Rachel nodded. 'They can't speak. We don't know what they are. Half this and half that. Huntress looks after them in the house. They live in the cellar. Sometimes they bleed her when she sleeps. They want the milk and blood, you see. That's mainly who Briar made the ointment for. Huntress. Their carer. Swan is the wet nurse. She's the only one left who's young enough to produce milk.'

36

[9–10pm]

Their hasty overland hike eventually brought them into the lower valley. Light trapped between the open floodplain and clear night sky marginally increased visibility. Back among the scrub and tree-encrusted riverbanks, Marcus had been near blind.

Facing downriver, he now perceived an impression of the flat land: the grassy floodplain extending to the reed beds; the belly of the valley, a vast intestinal tract.

At the edge of the broad meadow, he rediscovered the crescent of pebbly beach, fringed by wildflowers, where the group first landed.

The long shafts of five boats emerged from oblivion. Five boats, not six.

Marcus trotted to the kayaks and inspected them. Julian's boat was missing.

He must have cleared off, alone; he couldn't possibly have taken a passenger across the deck, let alone two. After an air ambulance had failed to materialise, and once he, Sophie and Nigel had not reappeared, a decision to break out must have burned a hole in Julian's skittish brain. For hours, the waterways had been too shallow to paddle; he would have been forced to struggle down the valley, dragging his boat across the stony river bed before labouring through creek mud. Only the desperate would have attempted such a journey; those whose survival depended on traversing such unforgiving terrain.

Particular situations and inducements always revealed the strongest, most abiding impulses that preoccupied people and drove them. Marcus had long suspected as much, but he fully grasped the truism now. He'd become accustomed to observing the fixed self-interest of those aroused by greed or romantic infatuation, or seeking attention and status, or displacing their resentments, or simply avoiding discomfort and inconvenience. Had he too not indulged such an array of human weakness? Self-preservation, however, trumped everything. There was no greater discloser of character than danger.

This beautiful, sinister valley possessed the power to unravel and strip any entrant down to their core compulsions. How swiftly Sophie had been prepared to end her marriage and reveal the paternity of her child. Nigel had tried to club him to death with a bone. And how rapidly the Wyrm had tempted, then converted, Colman and his cronies into sacrificing the vulnerable among themselves to something blind and foul that waited, coiled in a stinking abyss.

Marcus had no trouble believing that Julian had run to save himself. But he stopped short of judging the man. After what he'd seen today, inside and outside of the stinking stone dome, any energy he had not expended on escaping simply increased his own panic. But if Julian had escaped to the sea, two questions remained unanswered: where was Jane? Where was Mary?

The Little Priests.

A cold nausea beset Marcus's gut; feebleness his legs. 'Dear God,' he whispered, and wondered if, from somewhere up on the slopes, right now, small eyes were piercing the night and observing him.

Confining walls of mute darkness concealed the forested valley sides. Not a whisper or rustle of leaves came from the woods. The curious piping wind, wafting from the south and west, had long ceased. Instead, an uneasy stillness had descended. But silence did not indicate inactivity. Not here. Terrible, impossible things lived in the lightless enclaves and even the very air of the Wyrm.

Rachel had suggested that the wights above ground would be sluggish and distracted after gathering like vermin at the sacrifice and feeding, satiating themselves on the blood of the cow that they'd made ready for their god. They'd bitten Jane too, up on the slopes. Perhaps they'd since supped from others as well. But the parasitic clergy appeared numerous and widespread, and no one in Colman's sect had yet escaped it. Might others rise from where they languished below?

Colman and his team would definitely be in pursuit of him, and soon, if they weren't already. They rarely ventured south of the temple because of the Priests. But the cult would surely make an exception to that aversion, once they'd discovered that he'd been freed from the temple. Under no circumstances could he be allowed to leave the valley. Though how long it would take for Clement to realise that the final captive was in flight was uncertain. Marcus didn't know how much time his surreptitious release from the temple had bought him, to get further downstream. He didn't imagine the hippy killers venturing inside the dome to see if Marcus had found a niche in which to hide.

Something far worse than men and wights might also be hunting him. When Marcus considered the thing that had slithered out of the hole in the ground, his breath caught. On return from its most recent sortie, the expectant god would have found nothing but old bones and scraps inside its lair. Yet the creature would be aware that he'd been inside the temple; of the three morsels daubed in blood and reeking of filth that it would have smelled, one was now missing. Surely it would seek what was absent.

He had to assume that all three threats were at large – the god, its priesthood, and the useful idiots of Colman's cult – and that all three entities wanted to find and destroy him.

Marcus directed his attention to the indistinct ground of the campsite, a smattering of murky lumps huddled in shadow. He picked out Julian's erect tent. Nigel and Sophie's slouched beside that. Further along the paddock, his wild camping tent protruded; an inky coffin shape. And there was Jane's pup tent that Julian had almost finished assembling for her; it was hunched by Mary's half-collapsed ruin, still awaiting guy ropes and a flysheet.

But even in the dark, it was clear that the condition of the site had worsened in his absence. The camp had been ransacked, as if by an animal. A curious or hungry animal. Around the tents, articles of camping equipment were strewn around the ground. At least four rucksacks were turned inside out, emptied of their contents. Only the paddling gear they'd left to dry on the decks of their boats appeared to have escaped disruption.

'Mary? Jane?' Marcus called, softly, as he stalked among the detritus.

No one answered.

At the sound of his faint and circumspect voice, Rachel retreated to the riverbank and stepped into the cover of a willow tree. If Marcus didn't know that she'd hidden herself there, he wouldn't have seen her.

He made his way to where Jane had been laid out on the ground. Nothing remained of her stay but a ruffled three-season sleeping bag. Empty water bottles and the disgorged contents of a first-aid kit littered flattened grass. A disorderly circle had formed, as if the articles had been kicked or cast aside.

'Quick. Quick,' Rachel muttered. 'The boat. You don't have much time. Go now.'

Marcus looked to the willow tree beside the kayaks and his entire being warmed with gratitude for poor, wretched Rachel, who'd unlocked that terrible door. She'd reminded him of his intention to get dressed and collect his gear. And yet he still hesitated. He thought of his friends instead, poor Mary and Jane. He remembered Jane's laugh and Mary's smile.

'I'm sorry, girls,' he eventually whispered, as he stared into the silent, empty darkness surrounding the tents. He had to go. He could not waste time searching the vast valley for missing peers. They could be anywhere. Anything might have befallen them, none of it good. As if a force seven gale had just squalled over a group of kayakers, one mile out at sea, it was every man for himself now.

Go, go, go, go. Bloody go.

Marcus made his way to his tent.

Mary. Jane.

Desperation to be relieved of the dread and terror that he'd endured since midday competed with a stubborn, cold guilt.

Again, he pushed their names and their faces from his mind.

On his patch, he placed the ointment bottle and iron sword on the ground, then located his spare clothes, close to his emptied rucksack. He dragged shorts up his legs, the immediate warmth so welcome that he shivered from the pleasure. A dry thermal vest followed. He zipped a fleece up to his throat.

Tears filled his eyes. The clothes knew the shape of his body. They smelled clean. His paddling boots were up at the manor, but he found the trainers he'd packed for when they were ashore. Marcus tugged a beanie hat over his frozen crown. He fitted the band of a head torch to the cap.

He jogged to the riverbank. Once he'd arranged his buoyancy jacket, towline, cagoule and spraydeck on the rear deck, he assembled his split-paddle.

My God, you're nearly on the water.

'Water. There's no water among the stones,' a woman cried out from the darkness, from somewhere behind him.

That wasn't Rachel. That was Mary.

Marcus stopped.

Mary.

He dropped his paddle and set off through the tents and into the meadow, towards the voice.

37

[9–10pm]

*I*mpossibly, she was still alive.

Mary's hair was plastered to a burning forehead. Same symptoms as Jane, but unlike her, she had been stripped naked. Her body was exposed to the elements, but her flesh was afire with fever.

Marcus had always known that Mary was thin, but not that she was skeletal. The cancer treatment had withered her figure so that it looked like something found behind the fence of a gulag. She should never have attempted the paddle. That was painfully clear.

Marcus picked up her cold fingers and held them. He swept the beam of his head torch across her scrawny chest and neck, the white flesh marbled by spilled blood dried black. Like the cow at the temple, she'd been bled out. Suckled from the abdomen too. Couplets of punctures amassed over what remained of her throat, breasts and stomach. Around her, the grass was flat. She'd writhed on the ground until her strength had drained.

He wondered if Mary had crawled to this spot, away from the tents and gear. Or maybe she'd only hobbled so far in a desperate, misdirected attempt at escape, before being brought down by a swarm of pallid forms; the very things he'd watched leech onto the cow and fell it.

The Little Priests.

'Oh, Mary,' he said.

Weak fingers curled around the warmth of his hand.

A sudden convulsion of rage at Clement Colman overcame Marcus, blinding him. His teeth clenched so hard that they threatened to break the enamel. He wanted to kill the man.

Mary's murky blue eyes discovered the light of his torch, then squinted.

Marcus flicked the bulb up, out of her eyes. 'Mary. It's Marcus.' He thought of how he must now dress her and struggled to remember the correct technique for towing injured or unconscious paddlers. They'd need to raft up, so that he could regularly check on her during the return trip. A short towline would be needed. He had one on the bow deck.

He'd progressed no further in developing his escape plan into a rescue plan, when Mary's frail voice muttered, 'Can you see them?'

'Mary, it's Marcus. I'm right here.'

'Don't waste time,' Rachel said. She'd crept from the willows and was now among the tents behind him.

Marcus turned his head. 'Help me! Grab that first-aid kit over there. And water.'

Rachel didn't move from where she crouched. 'The Priests have lit her up. It's too late. She's lit up.'

'What?' Marcus barked over his shoulder.

'I told you. For the god. She's a pyre. A pyre of blood to guide the god. It will smell her.' Rachel peered fearfully at the black sky. 'Even from way up there.'

'I can't leave her!' He turned to Mary and leaned over her face. 'Jane. Julian. Where are they?'

'Among the houses of stone . . . a forest of poles . . . pointing at the red sky. See them? How do we leave here? How do we go back? Does anyone know?'

'It's not real. You're hallucinating. I'm going to get you help. But where is Jane? Can you remember? Was she taken?'

'The children came down from the stone houses. They bite. They bite so deeply.'

'These children, where did they go?'

'With birds' faces.'

'Yes. That's them. Where did they take Jane?'

Mary wept. 'Inside the stones with the holes. They're doors. They're houses. But which one is she inside? I can't hear her anymore. That's where we're all going. Inside them. Geoff is inside one of them. I don't know which one, but he was crying. I heard him. Help me look.'

Geoff was her husband's name.

'She's claimed!' Rachel insisted.

Tears burned Marcus's eyes and his throat clotted. 'She's not! She's my friend!'

'Come away!'

'What did we do? What did we fucking do to deserve this?' Marcus shouted at the darkness.

Rachel answered him, but as if she were speaking to someone no older than four. 'I know, dear. I know. But we all lose our friends in the valley. Nothing lasts here, only the god and the Priests. You have to go. Now.'

'I won't leave her. The first-aid—'

'Run!' Rachel cried.

And Marcus felt the thing's presence before he saw anything of it.

A vast form arrowed at the earth.

Wind rushed across the contours of outstretched wings.

Marcus dropped Mary's hand and fled as a fieldmouse might flee a hawk. Unable to think, he was driven solely by the fire of terror that spread wild through his mind, limbs, fingers, toes, and each individual hair on a body electrocuted alert.

Something heavy thumped the earth nearby and shook the very ground.

Behind his heels, a fleshy cable lashed out. A hasty roping of serpent, hissing across dry grass; a combing that rendered the stalks flat. Gusts of carrion poisoned the meadow's sweet breath.

Marcus dropped and rolled into longer grass. Then dragged himself along the earth, face down, trying to bury his awareness among the field's chilled roots. Toes propelled him into a crawl. Then he was up and running before he realised it. He sprinted further into uncut pasture, dropped and turned onto his back.

He glimpsed a great darkness; one far deeper than the cloak of night covering the world. A rearing column, as tall as a three-storey house and as thick as a great oak. A vile black maggot with a head that faced the sky. Bat-like, membranous wings were sucked back into the larval pillar to wetly wrap about the bulk. Around what must have been a busy mouth, a frail human body and its dangling limbs resembled whiskers.

Mary.

Her shriek became a croak, became silence. As if a giant fist was raised into the night air, a handful of sticks snapped within that grip.

What was held fast by the indistinct mouth was then walloped against the ground. The saurian column formed a grub's arch. Infantile limbs probed from below the worm's head. They worked as fast as machines on what they held against the grass. Mary's arms were snapped away from her lifeless torso. Split asunder, her trunk was rinsed empty by the rummaging of a large, moist face. Even with his ears covered, a soupy noise of clots inhaled through narrow confines turned Marcus's stomach inside out.

Whump, whump, whump. A god thrust itself at the heavens. The thinnest extremity of its form bull-whipped the grass before the devil was aloft and swallowed by an unlit ocean of cold air.

38

[9–10pm]

'You said these things, the wights, or Priests, come from mines. That bullshit artist Colman excavated them?'

Rachel eyed Marcus. When subjected to his interrogation, a fearful wariness crept into her eyes. She guessed at what he was thinking, and the wights terrified her. He intuited a deep and abiding shame for what she'd enabled in this sanctuary. Her sect and its rites were responsible for the death of her partner of forty years. His end had not been easy. Marcus could attest to that. But unlike her glorious leader, at least she had retained a conscience. Her saving Marcus from the temple had not been for self-preservation alone. And now, as much as when she'd unlocked that door, he needed her help. This time, it wasn't about him; this was about Jane.

'The old tunnels, yes.' Her words were faint and they shook. 'They were sealed when we came here.'

'With good reason.'

She sighed, nodded.

Marcus stared at her face, a haggard mask of regret and despair that had been forming for a long time.

After the god had sated its appetite and taken flight from the meadow, neither he nor Rachel had felt able to emerge from where they'd hidden. Each of them had been so shaken with shock and fear, they'd been incapable of speech. Eventually, Marcus had stirred and crept to the boats at the river's edge.

Remaining in the shadows and intermittently peering at the sky, Rachel had delayed breaking cover until Marcus had prepared a second boat: Jane's. Even without help from the head torch, he could see how she'd shivered. 'You never get used to seeing it,' was all she'd said; an observation compelled by terror, disgust and awe. She was not talking to him; she simply couldn't keep that thought inside herself.

Marcus peered at the western slope, from where Jane's scream had electrified the valley after midday. She'd encountered the wights up there and barely escaped. She was young, strong, undemonstrative but wilful. She'd survived. Sort of. The bites must carry a toxin. An immobiliser. Perhaps they'd even let her go to create chaos among her fellow travellers. Had they not since split up? One half of the group was captured upriver, the second had been reduced to sitting ducks down here. Were he told that the wights intended to handicap the group with the burden of an injured person, he'd not be surprised.

'Jane, Jane, Jane,' Marcus muttered to himself. He saw past her injuries and remembered her lovely eyes. He'd always felt the tug of her undertow and resisted it, briefly succumbing at times, before pulling himself away from the deeper water she represented. Patient and quietly confident, she'd been puzzled by his reluctance to take things further between them. She hadn't known much about his past, only rumours about his reputation. She hadn't known about Sophie. Even so, Jane had never gone cold on him, never lost respect for him. She saw sufficient value in him to gently persist.

If nothing else, they would have been friends who lasted. He'd been determined not to disappoint her. He'd have hated that. She was a good person. Kind. Thoughtful. Considerate. Sweet. Clever. And the idea of her up there in the dark, among those pale abominations, not only caused him distress but was so excruciating that it was unbearable. He felt an actual burn behind his breastbone. 'Might she still be alive? My friend, who was taken by the Priests? Is there, at least, a chance?'

Rachel shrugged, as if to indicate that such an inquiry was irrelevant. 'No one comes back. She was a young woman? I don't think they kill them. Not at first, anyway. Cynthia . . .' Rachel didn't finish the sentence. To spare him, he presumed, about what had befallen some poor wretch – this Cynthia – who'd tried to run for her life. According to Rachel, she'd been captured and bred. Earlier, he'd seen this brood of Cynthia's feeding on the underbelly of a cow. Rachel must have witnessed the wights' grotesque behaviour in ways that he'd merely glimpsed. He was amazed that a woman who'd lived with such horrors for so long was still able to function.

'You said the rite lasts for a week and is nearly over. What then? After it's over?'

'The god returns to the kingdom. The Priests will be away in the morning too, for another day, to avoid the sun. They prefer the dark and appear less in the colder months but can still appear at any time. Here they prolong summer. Briar believed it was to encourage life and fecundity, in order to attract prey. They may even hibernate for a few months but sometimes wake, hungry. A few of them always stay alert to spy on us. Your friend will be taken by them to the kingdom.

'But Clement never found the place they were coming through. They can flatten themselves like mice, squeeze through crevices. That's how they were getting into the house, through chimneys, a coal chute, windows left ajar. Their magic is too old to be comprehensible to us. I'm sorry.'

'This?' Marcus held up the long iron knife. 'They fear it?'

Rachel nodded. 'It was in the books. Iron. The family who built the house, a long time ago, lost their livestock. A blight, they thought. Rats were blamed. Until they saw the Little Priests. There were always stories down this way about little folk, and that the valley was cursed and bewitched. Hell mouth, some said. The devil himself appeared here. But what lives in the Wyrm is so much older than the devil.

'Rumours, folk tales, you see. That's how the old family learned about iron as protection. They built the house.

They made a fortune from a china clay quarry and bought the valley. Iron helped them but never saved their children. They lost all of the girls. Nor did it save the young women whose families worked the land here.' The old woman paused and peered into the darkness, as if trying to locate something in the distance. 'To think how excited we were. We thought we were privileged to be close to such ancient wonders.'

'Some of you still do.' Marcus unscrewed the cap of the bottle and sprinkled liquid on one arm. He rubbed the acrid smelling ointment up and down his clean jacket. Then proceeded to stain the sleeves.

'We thought it would be different for us,' Rachel whispered.

'Clement. The others. Surely they could have left. Or sealed that mine.'

'Yes. Maybe. In the beginning, not later. You see, he got it all wrong. He believed that he had a special relationship with a god, with its priesthood. He thought he was a prophet passing between worlds. But it was the bites that brought the visions, the enchantment. Briar told us this. We all kept seeing another place. All of us. Another world behind this one here. Once we were nipped. Briar said they were making us docile, like cattle. I think the only thing we ever saw was hell.'

Rachel clasped her hands together and began padding around in the grass. 'If you go up there, you'll be blooded for the god. Then who will know about what has happened here? You'll be lit up and left for the god to feed on. Your friend will vanish. Forever. Neither of you will leave the valley. Clement and Vine will get away with it. Again! You can't. You can't!'

As if it were insect repellent, Marcus continued to rub the concoction of fox piss, detergent and garlic up and down each calf and shin. 'Clement thinks he's found a way to get out. He's going to cover this up and flee. Feeding six of us to that disgusting slug has provided him with a distraction, he thinks, and an opportunity to slip away.'

'It won't work. He'll never get clear. The Priests take turns feeding. They won't all be full and sleepy. They make sure.

They're clever. They'll know what he's thinking. Others will come up from down there, to keep their food in the valley.' Rachel continued her anxious pacing. 'Next year, it'll be my turn. Again! Unless they find someone else. It'll want more next time. The Priests always ask for more. The more we gave, the more they took. That's how it happened. Every rite became more demanding than the last. Every year they bleed the herd white. Briar told Clement! Told him that we were just livestock too. We were the new herd!' When she stopped talking and fidgeting, they looked at each other. 'My Briar.' Her voice broke.

Unsteady on his feet, Marcus bent over and placed his hands on his knees. He inhaled deeply before whispering, 'I have to know if Jane's alive. I can't leave her. You've seen . . . what happens. But I don't have long to find her and get us out.' He shook his head, as if to knock out the irrational notion of mounting a rescue. 'We go at the pace of the slowest paddler, Rachel. She's not been on the water long. I've been looking out for her.'

What he could see of Rachel's face regarded him with a quizzical sadness. Finally, she reached for the bottle of ointment. She took it from him and began to reapply the salve to a forearm. 'I know where they come out.'

39

[10–11pm]

They crept up the slope, moving noisily while the woodland held its breath. Between silent trees they passed themselves. From one gnarled trunk to another moss-furred pillar, low branches served as rungs. A narrow band of illumination, cast from Marcus's head torch, adjusted to low-beam, found spaces for their feet between the bracken and dead wood. Inside these fissures, the ground resembled a lightless ocean bed, cold, silted, vast and deep.

'I found her somewhere near here,' Marcus whispered, once he was sure that he'd covered a distance similar to his earlier ascent. 'We must have missed the mine. We're near the top of the slope.'

'The entrance is closer to the top than the bottom. We entered by the tree that looks like an old man, falling sideways. So that was the right tree where we came in. It's straight up from there. Have we been going straight? I can't tell.' Rachel was breathless but hadn't slowed him down. Before they'd ventured far inside the wood, after finding the tree at a tilt, with its branches thrust out as if to break a fall, he was the one winded. Rachel had needed to wait for him to gather himself.

This gave Marcus cause to examine his impression of the strange woman beside him; an outcast and eccentric, for sure. Yet seemingly preserved by home-grown food and an ascetic existence. There wasn't an ounce of extra weight on her wiry body. Her life was close to nature. She was a member of a community, isolated from the outside world and the old temptations. That must have drawn her here: the promise of enclosure within a sanctuary. A place that fostered an emphasis on the soul, on its wellbeing. Such things must have nourished her and once provided strength and purpose. Yet in stature and demeanour, he found her childlike.

And then the idyll had imploded so wretchedly, into delusions, madness, death. The woman had seen everything that she loved and believed destroyed. What she understood about the world had been turned upside down and shaken hard. They had that in common. The Wyrm Valley had brought him up to speed, and quickly. As if acknowledging this brief, silent moment of empathy, Rachel placed a hand on Marcus's shoulder. 'Around the old mine, the ground is clear. Look for the break in the trees. That's all I remember.'

'There is no straight route. Too much of this shit in the way.' Marcus trampled down a cross-hatch of dead twigs, cloaked in ivy. His trainers were already full of burrs. The welts and bruises marking his body from Nigel's frenzy thumped and stung every time he took a step or moved his arms.

He fantasised about a bath filled with ice, followed by immersion to his chin in his bubbling hot tub. If he lived through the next few hours, an X-ray on his left shoulder would be required. Might such an eventuality even be possible? He doused the spark of hope, because any thought of the future made him want to run for the river.

More than anything, he wanted to believe that he retained enough mobility in his arms to swing the sword at any small, pale form that came within range. And he had good reason for such a compulsive thought, because during each tortuous step upwards, no matter how hard he tried to suppress the memory, he could not remove the image of a tormented cow's punctured flanks, festooned with the spidery Priests.

Barely enough of Briar's stinking concoction remained in the bottle for Jane. In the unlikely event that they found her, his priority was to wipe all blood from her skin, using disinfectant from the medical kit, so that the dreadful thing in the clouds would not detect her scent below. He'd stashed the first-aid materials and the ointment in his rucksack. He'd then coat Jane with the remainder of Briar's mixture.

Before they left the campsite, he'd also packed some of Jane's spare clothes and water. He'd got their two boats ready, placing their paddles, spraydecks and buoyancy vests on each seat. Then, on the screen of Jane's recovered phone, he'd seen the time and the swift approach of high water had registered.

The tide would soon turn again. Inexorably, the levels would drop, the waterways drain shallow. They had between two and three hours in which to leave this valley on the new outgoing tide. If that window closed, they would be trapped in the Wyrm for another twelve hours.

To Marcus, that felt like a year. And he didn't allow himself to think about carrying Jane through this woodland again. The mere thought would break what fragile impulse had dragged his feet this far up a slope, in the dark.

Marcus groaned but forced the pace. Speed was now as important as caution. And as they headed to what was likely to be their end, his thoughts turned to the spaces through which the wights slunk to enter this region above ground. When he pondered how deep he might need to go into the mine to find Jane, his chest tightened and panic flickered awake. Fear was as exhausting as climbing the hill.

To distract himself, he spoke to the woman behind him. 'What was Colman's theory about where these tunnels go? The doors?'

'They lead to the kingdom. But the doors in the mines can't be opened from our side. Only the Priests can open the way in and way out. The Priests said that no one ages over there.'

'That what Clement was after?'

'Promises were made, of benefits, in return for worshipping their god.'

After another ten steps into oblivion, Marcus stopped to catch his breath. He leaned against a crooked tree but never removed his eyes, or the light, from what lay above and ahead of them. 'Eternal life, with those devils? I can think of better versions of salvation. All that money and his own valley, his own fiefdom, wasn't enough, eh? But they tricked him into building a temple and resuming this blood rite, to coax that evil thing out? Jesus wept, what were you all thinking?'

'Clement never saw it like that. You can only *see the way* with sacrifice. What's a bit of blood, he told us, in return for a new world? It was only the cows back then. But so much has happened since. None of it was expected. You can't understand.'

Marcus shook his head. 'You all still went along with it until it was too late. Sounds as if only your Briar had his head screwed on.'

'It was never simple! At the start, at the first rites, we were all thrilled. It was incredible. You wouldn't believe what we experienced. What we saw. We'd created a miracle. To find something like this? To discover that there is more, much more than our world? How small and shy they were, the little masked children from the hills. They even brought us flowers.'

'You're starting to sound like him.'

Rachel bent over and placed her hands on her knees. Her voice deepened, coarsened. 'We were tricked. Deceived. And now we betray each other and everything this community stood for. I know it. But Clement's not been so sure of the situation for a long time. We could tell. Me and Briar. The Priests, they deranged him. They started to control him. Everybody here is terrified. But sometimes I think Clement realises what he's done. Then he shuts himself away. Though he can't hide from the Priests, or the visions. He can't stop seeing what they show him, or hearing what they tell him. Not anymore.' Rachel sighed and Marcus suspected that in that sound he heard a lifetime's worth of regret and despair.

'When he suspected that some of us had doubts, he became a bully. He changed. Turned on us. And made the others treat us differently. Briar knew where we were headed. Briar knew too much. He guessed that Clement had an arrangement with the Priests or was being extorted. Briar doubted that this bargain Clement had made included the rest of us. And there aren't many left now, as you have seen. Last year was costly. And those that ran never escaped or returned alive.'

Marcus shook his head. Disbelief competed with disgust. 'This *thing*, his god, took three of you. Last year?'

'Four. Plus a dozen cows. Then the Little Priests weakened and sickened half of the herd this spring. We'd already spent most of the year to provision for this rite. So many cattle coming in, nothing going out. The suppliers suspected foot and mouth. But Briar always believed that Clement would do anything to save himself. And he was right. That's why Clement offered me and Briar to the rite this year.' Rachel paused. When she resumed talking, her voice shook. 'They forced Briar inside. Because the god had left the valley. The night before Briar crossed over, the god left. And it returned with someone. A man from outside the Wyrm.'

Marcus briefly closed his eyes.

'We don't know who it was, this person who was fetched. We only found the man's hand. But somebody local going missing would make more trouble. I've never seen Clement as desperate as he was this year. And Briar was a thorn in his side. He wanted rid of him. Tonight, it was my turn. An easy choice, I suppose. Clement couldn't risk another stranger from outside the valley being taken. Then you came. Like a gift.'

Marcus scanned Rachel's face to see if she was smiling at such a cruel joke. She wasn't. He doubted that her existence in the valley had allowed much capacity for humour. 'You've all been hanging on Clement Colman's every word, while being whittled down. His supply of addicts and the mentally ill dried up last year. The *volunteers*. That it? All of you guided by his interpretations of what these devils want? How would he really know? You said that even the children don't speak.'

'But Huntress understands their silence. She mothers them, cares for them. Your arrival upset her greatly.'

'A bloody shame.'

'The children show her things. Pictures. In the mind. Clement calls her a seer. And he's been infected too. His will is not his own. He lives in fear now. Is tormented by visions. It's all a terrible mess.'

'These *children* and the Priests tell you what to do, through Colman and his seer? This childminder for the things that drain blood from cows? She's the oracle? And Clement. False prophets. And in order to *see* too, you let those bleached rats bite you? With your skin marked with the tatts, they own you? Am I right?'

Rachel nodded. 'More or less.'

'This just gets better and better. For God's sake, did you never think of dethroning your pretend king and letting him cross over? If he wants this new world, let him go to it.'

'You don't understand. It must be easy to judge us, after having been here for one day.'

'I find it effortless. Remarkably so.'

Rachel scratched her scalp with both hands. He'd upset her, made her angry, and immediately regretted doing so. 'How can you understand that Vine loves power and worships Clement? Only Clement has any control over that man's need to hurt people. If Vine left the valley, he'd go straight back to prison. Swan is Clement's lover. A heroin addict. You've seen her. The tall, beautiful woman. Her depression is terrible. Clement saved her life. She tried suicide twice. She'd die for him. And Huntress will never leave the children, even though they bite her. Thorny would rather cross over than leave the valley.'

'That the old, mean-looking bitch with tatts?'

Rachel, nodded, though even in the dark he could see how uncomfortable she was with his description of this 'Thorny'. 'She and Huntress have nothing left outside of here, this life. They spent years in prison. Huntress had her children taken by social services, when she was young. Thorny died twice, from overdoses. They would never betray Clement. We all depended on him. We all came here with nothing but the clothes on our backs. When Briar needed an operation to save his life, Clement flew him to Switzerland. Before we were housed by the Foundation, Briar and I were homeless.'

'You don't owe him a horrible death in that stinking stone sewer. And neither did Briar.'

Rachel knitted and knotted her lumpy fingers, long enough for Marcus to feel anxious about his saviour's stability. She'd even volunteered to become his guide to almost certain death. He began to feel his own strength draining as quickly as his will to continue looking for Jane.

'This isn't what anyone wanted, or expected,' Rachel whispered. 'Nor Clement. This is not what was promised. But it can't continue. Things are desperate. There are messages.' She wafted a hand in the air as she struggled to recall a word. 'Emails. Emails coming from relatives. The people who suspect that their family members in the Foundation aren't here anymore. Then there was the stranger, taken from outside the valley. And—'

As Marcus turned to see why Rachel had sucked in her breath as if she'd trodden on something sharp, the sweep of his torchlight revealed a masked face. Near enough to touch, and no higher than his waistband, a ghastly apelike figure stood erect. A mass of gull feathers, fashioned into a frightful grimace, regarded them.

40

[10–11pm]

*M*arcus flinched, lost his balance. The head torch's beam flashed away, across uneven ground.
Regaining his footing, he returned the light to where he'd seen the face.

Holly and ivy chokeholds, wreathed around roots and trunks, were the only things the light found now. Trees as pallid and greenish as the masts of sunken wrecks, loomed within varieties of darkness and extended into oblivion. It was as if that feathered bushel had never existed.

Terror accelerated his breathing. Adjusting the torch to full beam, he turned full circle.

Rachel crowded into his back. 'They are fast. But, remember, the pyres of blood, the feeding slows them. There was the cow. And your missing friends. The Little Priests will be sluggish. This might help us. A little.'

'An advantage that makes me want to puke. But our only one, because surprise is now off the agenda.'

'But we must be close. What do we do?'

'Keep looking for Jane. Quietly.' Marcus raised the old blade, his grip tight enough to hurt his hand. 'This better work.'

'I've never used one. Huntress uses a pacifier in the nursery, when milk is not enough for the children. And when the priesthood tried to take Swan, Vine chased them away with iron, a pacifier. The Priests hate the touch of iron.

This was written in the journal of the family who built the house. It was one of the parts we could understand. Briar transcribed what he could.'

'Could you not have invested in something more powerful?'

'Vine asked for shotguns. But Clement has forbidden firearms in the valley.' Rachel peered at the canopy. Between dense foliage inked black, the lighter portions of the night sky might have allowed them to see their hands before their faces, not much else. Without Marcus's torch, entering the woods would have amounted to a suicide pact.

'Just don't let them light your pyre.' Rachel didn't elaborate. Nor did she need to. Marcus knew what existed above their heads. *Somewhere.*

Hunting.

The pair pushed on, their movements slowing and not only on account of the steep ascent. Caution and fear bowed them as if they carried rucksacks filled with house bricks. Every few steps, Marcus paused to sweep the surrounding undergrowth with the torch beam. 'Keep watching behind us,' he whispered. 'I'll cover the front.'

Once they'd neared the summit, with the peak's treeline coming into view, he stopped. He'd not seen anything move again. 'We must have walked past the mine.'

'No. It's around here. The hole. It is.'

'What's on the other side of these trees? Over the top?'

'The fence.'

He detested himself for asking, and even more the sound of the quiver in his voice. 'Can it be climbed?'

Rachel shook her head. 'Anti-climb paint. Razor wire. Electric shock. You have to get out in the canoes.'

'Kayaks.'

'What?'

'Never mind.'

'I don't . . . I don't understand,' Rachel whispered and so anxiously that her frail voice cracked. 'It should be here.'

Peering at the furthest extent of their light, in a horizontal direction, Marcus sensed as much as saw a break in the trees, some distance below their position. 'Follow me.'

Walking side-step to prevent a turned ankle, and clinging to branches, Marcus led them on an angled descent to where he suspected the trees thinned. And as they drew closer, he realised that his hunch was right; as if a giant step had been cut into the valley side, a plateau gradually became visible.

They'd taken only a few more steps towards the open area, when a sound of distress grumbled from out of the void. The groan seemed to issue from the tree canopy, not from near the ground.

Marcus switched the torch to the lowest setting, then cupped a hand over the lens. Crouching, he bade Rachel come closer and whispered, 'You hear that?'

She nodded. 'A man, I think.'

'Wait a moment. Let your eyes adjust to the darkness.'

'We won't see them!'

'I'll turn it back on when we're closer. Listen.'

In the silence that followed their sibilant whispering, only a woody creak issued. A tree branch might have adjusted in the wind. The air was still.

'Closer,' Marcus whispered. 'Come on.' He turned off the head torch. Blindly, they inched closer to where the sound of distress had originated.

A few more steps and a faint ambient illumination, seeping from above, offered a better sense of what lay before them: an impression of a space open to the sky. Only one object was visible in the middle of the glade; a solitary trunk, or pole, appeared to splice the air.

'I'm turning the light back on.'

Rachel tensed and her hand gripped his arm. Marcus held the iron blade before his face. With his other hand, he fingered the torch and flicked the switch.

Light washed away the darkness.

41

[11–Midnight]

The sight of what hung in the clearing forced a whimper from Rachel.

Before Marcus's crouch stiffened to stone, his shock registered as a sickening disorientation. Not a breath escaped his mouth.

Together, they could do little but stare at the tortured article of humanity confronting them. Suspended from a branch that arched over the cleared ground, the stripped and strung consequences of Julian's attempt to paddle out of the valley were presented to them as either a terrible warning or a dreadful inevitability.

A similar twine to that which bound the cattle remains to the dead trees of the marsh secured his thin ankles. Between two scrawny feet, strapped together, the leash ascended to a tree branch. From calves to bearded face, the flesh was puckered with bites and grubby with blood. Trailing fingertips and a wispy ponytail brushed bare earth.

Pressed against Marcus's spine, Rachel shook so violently that he wondered if she was having a seizure. What remained of her voice muttered, 'Priests.' More accustomed to bloodshed than him, she'd been the first to look beyond the hanged man and the first to see the clergy of the mine encircling Julian's ghastly demise.

A moment later, Marcus too noticed the messy ring of supine forms, sprawled in the undergrowth that bordered the clearing. Pallid as grubs or the emaciated corpses of abandoned children, the wights lay on the damp woodland floor. At one side of the clearing, an evil-looking tub squatted, a cattle trough or sarcophagus.

The gathering in the clearing did not remain still for long. The intrusion of light prompted two of the figures to struggle into sitting positions. Like unstrung puppets becoming familiar with a clumsy, unnatural mobility, other small bodies soon stirred, then rose.

Across the entire area, the torch's illumination followed the sweep of Marcus's head, until the beam was swallowed by the black mouth of a cave, at the rear of the plateau. There was no sign of Jane. Instead of what they sought, a small wight crept from inside the entrance and presented its feathered face to them. They'd seen this one on their way up. It had withdrawn here, to the mine. Had it been afraid, or had it rushed up here to summon reinforcements?

Marcus returned the light to the glade and the hideous centrepiece of Julian's streaked torso. In the foreground of the nightmarish tableau, a second hairless form now stood upright, no more than three steps from where he and Rachel huddled. Its approach had made no sound. The mercury tint of the thing's flesh cast back the light. And this wight was unmasked.

Inside a face so wrinkled that it appeared mummified, or as desiccated as dried fruit, two rusty pips peered at them. Marcus saw no nose or ears. But the mouth was disproportionately large for the wizened head. That was open. The interior of the cavity was fish-belly white and possessed two teeth; wet spikes akin to what might be glimpsed inside a viper's yawn. From the aperture came the sound of a child blowing air through a pipe.

Deafened by his own exhalations and the stuttering bumps of his pulse, Marcus wanted everything to end. Right then. He'd had enough.

Then his body shook with an impulse to run, down through the trees, before throwing himself into the river.

When the wight staggered at them, Rachel screamed.

42

[11–Midnight]

*I*nstinct thawed Marcus's terror. He stepped into a lunge and thrust the black blade at the toddling form.

His ungainly jab of the sword came to a stop; the diminutive creature's momentum had carried the rushing body onto the stabbing tip. The sensation inside Marcus's wrist was like sinking the blade into soft sand. The wight made no other sound beyond a change in the frequency of the piping. But, like a gull winged by a stone, it struggled, then flapped to one side in agony, or panic, perhaps both.

Under the tree branch, Julian's eyes opened inside his purple, disfigured face. He rasped, 'Do you have water?' Then began to weep. 'Have you seen it? How many must live in a city of that size . . . My head hurts.'

Competing with his fear, a sadness welled inside Marcus, so great and cold that his eyes seared with tears. Feelings of fondness for the man that he'd previously been unaware of forced a sob. Thoughts of Mary, of Sophie and even Nigel flitted through the chaos of his mind. He saw them all again, disrobed of their dignity, their liberty, his companions yanked upwards and into the dark.

Captivity within the temple had broken something inside him. He understood this, though he couldn't even guess at what faculty was now forever ruined.

Driven by a squall of emotion and a blind loathing for the things that had done this to a man, Marcus's revulsion boiled into fury. Rage swamped him. Only a desperation for revenge could carry him now. Until he was spent. Or until he fell in this glade.

His legs didn't feel good and one of his arms shook, yet Marcus still stamped and smashed his way into the clearing.

A pack of three ungainly wights swayed at him like the drunks of his youth, intent on inflicting casual violence upon strangers. He met them with a wild sweep of the blade. The flat of the sword that he all but dropped clipped one vile head. As if suddenly finding itself on fire, the creature patted then clutched its skull. Two other pairs of frog-like arms stretched for him. Adjusting his grip on the sword handle, he set about them. This time he used the edge to hack.

A flash of dirty claw whipped past his nose, before his weapon sliced into a spindly body. A *chocking* sound, as of a spade striking clay, sickened him. He shook what resembled twitching sticks from the blade. The third assailant clutched his thigh: a bleached devil and a mockery of a primate with a serpent's teeth. They were a moment away from breaking his skin.

Marcus cut down at it. Once he'd buried sharp iron in its side, the thing released his leg.

Marcus strode deeper into the glade. He'd never recall the correct sequence of what happened next.

Clawed feet scampered about his lurching and swivelling body.

He wielded a flurry of blows on one side.

Twisting around, his blade swept at anything white that flickered or darted within the flash of his torch beam. With each swing, he tossed sluggish forms out of his way or set them tumbling and broken across the soil.

One of them flopped, more than leapt, onto his back. Four sets of pins scraped the tough fabric of his cagoule, snagged, then threatened to pierce cloth and flesh alike. If those were claws, then the Priest's teeth were millimetres from his nape.

He reached under one arm and gripped a cold limb, no thicker than a hosepipe; an upper arm, as wet and muscular as a mackerel. From his back he tugged a form, no heavier than a tabby cat, around his body and onto the ground. When he released the little arm, a silvery powder, as if from a handful of moth's wings, stained the palm that had clutched the horrible limb. The thing that writhed on the floor before his feet he broke with one stroke on its lower back. Barely moving arms and elderly hands clawed at the earth and pulled the dipped head and smooth upper body across the ground. As the crippled wight slid into the nettles, he saw that he'd turned its legs into a useless tail.

A creased face leapt for his eyes. He stabbed deep into the moist maw, with force. That sensation he'd never forget, the splitting of something unripe.

Three others he pursued from the glade. They scattered like hens. As he ran, he hacked at the soft skulls bobbing before him. Two broke like juvenile coconuts; the spilled blood was as yellow as what bursts from crushed maggots.

Thousands of years of a vile, parasitical existence beneath the world; that was what he wished to end. As desperate as a man who discovers poisonous serpents within his home, where unaware children sleep, he kicked, punched and stamped the middle of the glade clear.

Around the borders of this pagan altar, as if swatting rats from the swaying, hung meat of a full-grown man, he cut down the Priests that milled, dazed. Those that attempted a stumbling return to the fray, he staggered to meet, clubbing as much as cutting them.

Soon, he only had to rush the figures in the undergrowth to watch them careen, fall over each other or crawl away. Off into the darkness that lay beyond the flare and sweep of his torch, they scurried or loped on all fours.

Until the glade was clear of the dazed wights, his beam swept to and fro, searching for new assailants. When none of the clergy were within reach, he paced the perimeter of the clearing. He pierced the surrounding darkness and stroked the seething undergrowth with warning beams. When he sighted the silvery litheness of their bodies, creeping like larvae through the scrub, he waded up to his knees in ferns and, as if wielding a machete in a jungle, hacked at anything that moved along the ground.

When he'd stopped thrashing the gladius at those that piped and slunk among the roots, his heavy arm ached. He could only snatch at the air to catch his breath. Sweat slicked his entire body. Spores from their flesh glittered on his hands and arms.

'Are you bitten?' Rachel asked. She was reluctant to approach him and hadn't moved from where he'd left her.

Marcus shook his head. 'Don't think so.'

She didn't appear convinced.

'I'm pretty sure.'

As if needing further confirmation, she drew a little closer and studied his limbs. Eventually, the old woman turned her head to the tunnel and carefully padded across the glade.

Marcus watched the surrounding verdure and slowly walked backwards to the unlit mouth of the abandoned tin mine. Swivelling his head from left to right, he shone a light on the undergrowth and boughs of forlorn, sleeping trees, to make sure that nothing had crawled back into the glade.

He checked Jane's phone, now useless save for the clock on a locked screen. Near midnight. High water waited, glimmering in the waterway below. Until dawn broke, the god would hunt through darkness for the remainder of its tithe. Once sobered from their ghastly repast, the able Priests that he hadn't killed or injured would regroup. More of their brethren might emerge from the dark below. Clement and his fanatics were loose in the valley. There was no time to think of anything but the next step.

Rachel never removed her attention from the dark entrance of the mine. 'If they've taken her through the doorway, she is gone.'

'I'm going in,' Marcus said.

43

[11–Midnight]

As soon as he was inside the tunnel, Marcus fought a tremendous compulsion to leave it.

After taking only a few cautious steps, he had to stoop while struggling for balance on the weathered rubble beneath his feet. Ahead of him, a tongue of debris extended down the narrowing gullet of the cave, before being consumed by complete darkness. He imagined the explosion that reopened the blocked entrance had been responsible for the wreckage, not a cave-in. Small comfort, because the most recent excavation had extracted a far grimmer resource than tin from the earth.

His clumsy progress cast haphazard illumination over a moist spectrum of black, grey and near-bluish stone. And once deeper inside the sinus that enclosed him, part of the original mine shaft became visible. It had been so roughly chiselled, the narrowing chute appeared no less natural than a coastal fissure eroded by the sea. He'd paddled through countless caves along the county's coastline, and a familiar claustrophobia and terror of entrapment within the suffocating stone and darkness gripped his thoughts. His chest tightened until his breathing was rendered shallow and hurried. A notion that the priesthood might soon swarm around his legs and feet brought him to a stop.

'Jane! Jane! Jane!' he called, recklessly, into the black throat of the mine.

Behind him, Rachel's silhouette outlined itself at the tunnel's entrance. He couldn't tell which way she was facing. He'd asked her to stay outside and warn him if the priesthood returned to their chapel.

After a mighty inhalation, Marcus pushed on, stooping further and into a gathering miasma. A reek of rot, not as fearfully potent as that of the temple, yet clear evidence that this was another place filled with animal decomposition.

At the furthest reach of his beam, rocky lumps glimmered pale and necrotic. Stone walls ran wet. He began to fancy that the unrevealed spaces at the edge of the light were animate with the antics and motion of small limbs. He hesitated until he was sure that these flickers were shadows of his own making.

Another few dozen metres of struggling while bent double, and his light reflected from what he mistook for a collapsed ceiling. At first sight, the lower portion of the tunnel appeared to be completely blocked but as he shuffled closer, his shoulders and head bumping and scraping the uneven roof, he realised the obstruction he'd seen was not made of stone. None of it. It took him several seconds to ascertain what it was – this grey-white mass piled on the ground.

Several beaks and fanned wings added the gruesome details that finally enabled him to comprehend what he was looking at: a cull, a veritable massacre of birds.

He'd never seen so many dead birds piled in one place. Mostly gulls, mingled here and there with other varieties of seabird, shags and herons. A cluster of pheasants and ducks and several bright white egrets had also been heaped here, as if awaiting collection. Sinewy necks flopped at odd angles. Wings were splayed. He estimated that more than a hundred birds were amassed – which is why it took him several seconds to identify the naked human leg that also stuck out from the mound.

Monumental

The sight of the slender, dirt-smeared foot led his frantic eyes to a delicate arm, protruding towards the back of the reeking pile.

Marcus bumped and tripped his way to the feathered mound. As he dropped to his hands and knees, he spotted the side of Jane's head, wrapped in dark hair. She'd turned her face into the mass of dead fowl, as if to hide her sight from what had dragged her inside here.

Among the birds, odd trinkets glimmered: several empty bottles; articles of human clothing, stripped from a washing line and deposited with the plastic pegs still attached. Either they belonged to Clement Colman's crowd or from the wight's sorties beyond the valley. Julian's helmet and cagoule, and his paddling shoes, also lay tangled amid his expensive sleeping bag, from which the goosedown had burst.

The stench was near intolerable. Marcus breathed through his mouth as he picked the birds up, one by one, and either dumped them at the sides of the chute or threw their broken bodies into the darkness ahead. Gradually, more of Jane's grimy, blood-smeared body became visible. When her nearest arm was within reach, he grasped her wrist and checked for a pulse. The flesh was cool, but pressing a thumb hard into her wrist found a regular beat.

Jane whimpered. Her crusted eyelids parted.

Marcus crawled into the heap and gathered her legs together. Then clasped her ankles and staggered backwards to haul her from among the heaped bodies. Under the glow of his torch, bites tracked her blanched skin. Old incisions finally scabbed. Beyond the litter of punctures, bright scratches scored her arms and legs, where the marks of claws had held her limbs to carry her.

Once free of the stinking avian carcasses, Marcus slipped his weapon inside his cagoule, bent low and slipped one arm under the girl's back, the other behind her knees. With a groan, as every tired and punished muscle strained and quivered, he raised her limp body from the ground.

Hunched and struggling sideways, so as not to bang her head against lumps of stone protruding from the walls, he stumbled along the tunnel to the entrance.

44

[11–Midnight]

*O*utside the cave mouth, Rachel helped him settle Jane on the ground.

When they tried to get her to sit up, her head lolled. Supporting her neck with their hands, they slipped water between her dry lips. She coughed before desperately sucking at the nozzle. Her eyes opened in slits, but she didn't speak, or couldn't. Her pulse was regular, but she remained insensible, her skin unpleasantly clammy, her complexion cadaverous and silvered in places with the Priests' dust. Marcus wondered if he was seeing an accumulation of microscopic scales, similar to those that powdered a moth's wings.

Rachel needed no prompt to open the first-aid kit and to splash liquid antiseptic onto a cotton pad. She wiped and flannelled Jane's limbs, belly and chest, removing as much of the dried blood as possible. She then used a roll of bandages to sponge and mop the moisture. Marcus hurriedly fished her clothing out of his rucksack.

They worked fast, in silence. Together they laboured, in the splashes of light from the head torch, to pull shorts up the girl's inert legs. A struggle ensued with Jane's unresponsive limbs before a dry vest, fleece top and cagoule followed the shorts. As they tugged her body around, she became marginally more alert – but she was convinced that it was her mother who was dressing her, before forcing her to go to school. 'Not to that place.' She wanted to be in the other school. 'Not in the stone school'.

'You can manage from here?' Marcus asked Rachel.

When she nodded, he picked up the sword and crossed the glade to Julian. Averting his eyes from the wounds scarring the man's flesh, he gripped the hanged figure around the waist with one arm.

Julian was slim yet still heavy and it was hard for Marcus to grip his slippery, cold flesh. With his other arm, he hacked at the binding extending from between the man's ankles. Failing to sever the bond, he tried sawing the twine with the blade's edge. Eventually, a nick in the binding, combined with Julian's weight, released his body from the gibbet, and clumsily Marcus lowered his unconscious paddling companion to the ground. He raised Julian's head and offered the water bottle's nozzle to his parched lips. When a trickle wet the man's tongue, he began to gulp, his scrawny neck working hard. Marcus fed him like a lamb, Julian's head in his lap. Despite the refreshment, not a finger or toe twitched. He appeared to be paralysed.

One eye partially opened. It looked beyond Marcus and into the distance. 'I know you,' Julian muttered. 'Don't know from where. Have you seen it? How many must live in a city of this size?' The rest of what he said, Marcus didn't catch.

He eased the man's head to the soil. 'I'm sorry, Julian. I can't take you. I can't carry both of you. So, you rest here, mate, while I go for help.' He picked up one of Julian's cold, limp hands and squeezed it.

Then he struggled to his feet and circled the glade, his weapon poised to thrust or hack. Among the black boughs, trunks and the entanglements of scrub, he never saw a single Priest. But he heard them.

What he'd mistaken, earlier that day, for a breeze passing between leaves, and through holes in the stone walls of the abhorrent temple, was no natural air current. Beyond the reach of his light, the priesthood were gathering again. Somewhere up-valley, crouched inside the still woodland, they'd formed a chorus and now issued once more their peculiar, persistent, breathy utterance.

'We need to go,' Marcus said.

Rachel helped to lay Jane across his cupped arms. He didn't believe he had the strength, or technique, to get her over a shoulder. He'd have to carry her down the slope draped over his weakened arms. But as soon as he tried to carry her in this position, his lower back screamed.

'No good. No good,' he muttered. 'I won't get far. Try and hold her upright. Just for a moment.' He crouched and dipped his shoulder into Jane's midriff, and, following the technique he used for squats in his gym, with a barbell straddling his shoulders, he thrust upwards with his legs, keeping his tormented back straight.

That was better; Jane's legs dangled down his front, her upper body hung over his back. He'd carry her like a carpet.

With Rachel holding the sword, they set off down the valley side. Desperation to flee the wretched glade might have been all that powered their tortured legs.

They hadn't stumbled far – no more than twenty paces – when the woodland canopy, on the slope behind them, thrashed.

In moments, the din progressed to whole branches being snapped clean from trunks. As if a bolt of lightning had impacted mere metres from their heels, Marcus and Rachel flinched then ducked, Marcus barely managing to keep his footing.

Behind them, the heavy but supple weight that had just flopped from the sky crashed through the lower limbs of the trees encircling the glade, before slamming the earth.

Even though its powerful body filled the clearing and continued to create a cacophony of splintering and snapping among the trees, this time they saw nothing of the god of the valley. Not even as it settled the thick but sinewy coils, no more than ten metres from where they crouched, did they catch a glimpse of it; not even the whipcord tail that slapped the earth and raked the scrub.

Just in case the thing could see, Marcus had turned off the torch, not only to hide their position but because he believed that if he caught so much as a glimpse of the thing engulfing its prey again, his mind would go out like an exhausted lightbulb. But they still heard the eagerness with which the fiend seized the offering in the wights' glade, and they were forced to listen to the hasty, violent feeding. A terrible commotion, producing a sickening noise that travelled far along the valley. Each of them stopped breathing as human bones were cracked like kindling, and flesh was torn like linen.

Until this acceptance and collection of another sacrifice had concluded, and the beast had departed once more for the sky, Marcus and Rachel did not twitch. Jane never spoke either, but in case the thing could hear, Rachel had taken no chances and had placed a hand over the girl's mouth.

45

[Midnight–1am]

*B*efore them, an expanse of preternaturally motionless grass stretched to the distant river; a meadow sodden with night and frozen by silence. What had swayed and rustled beneath the sun was fixed into stillness, yet also tense with a strange expectancy; an anticipation of an imminent event or arrival.

To catch his breath and relieve the pain crippling his back, neck and shoulders, Marcus stopped struggling at the foot of the slope. Sinking to his knees, he eased the burden of a full-grown woman's body onto the grass. Panting as if for his life, he stared at the broad, indistinct meadow that he must now cross.

To his weary eyes, straining in the dim light, the plain appeared to be bigger than he recalled; a football pitch pocked with concealed holes, every metre of turf uneven. Marcus wondered if he would ever reach the distant river, and, if he did, if the accomplishment would only result in him meeting his overdue end in shallow water.

To even have a chance of launching the kayaks, they needed to reach the far side of this infernal field. They could not work around the scrubby edges before making their way to the tents and boats. That route would take too long to complete. Within the hour, the slack water of a turning tide would end; the river and creek would begin to empty.

Nor could he carry Jane around the meadow. His heart would fail.

To reach the kayaks, they had no choice but to pursue the most direct route to the ravaged campsite. Straight across the floodplain. Under an open sky.

From his scrutiny of what could be seen of the eerily stiff flora, Marcus switched his attention to the heavens. And, as if the sun was blazing, he struggled to look up for long. Only the anticipated exertion of getting Jane across the floodplain would distract him from unwelcome yet inevitable notions of what might fall on them from the air. At any time. The sound of Julian's dismemberment was trapped inside his ears; deeply too, where the noise seemed to echo as if within a well.

To think they'd intended to camp here.

Marcus counted their blessings, with one finger. Only blood appeared to mark the beast's tithe and stimulated whatever super-senses it employed. Neither he nor Rachel were cut, and Jane's marred skin had been cleaned as much as time and their resources allowed. Her skin was also mostly covered.

Rachel nudged Marcus. 'Why have we stopped?' She peered behind herself at the night-blackened wood. 'The Priests will follow us.'

'Just taking a breather. I'll have to drag her backwards. I can't carry her anymore. Not that far. I'm fucked. In fact, I was fucked at midday. A lot's happened since. Take the head torch. But keep it turned off. We don't want to be seen from a distance by your mates the Manson Family.'

Marcus slipped his arms under Jane's armpits and, with a tormented groan, raised her upper body from the ground so that only her heels touched the grass. He'd have to walk backwards and pull her body. Once his vision better adjusted to the lightless plain, in this position at least he'd spot any wights that stalked after them.

'Let's go.'

Rachel nodded. She slipped among the wildflowers that had closed their faces to what ruled this night.

Close to halfway across the meadow, Marcus dared to believe they might reach the boats. An urge to salvage Jane's life, and to survive, had driven him so far. Faith that he might escape the valley with one of his companions had been thin since he'd made the decision to search for Jane. But hope, albeit with such slender prospects, rekindled itself at the midway point. Hope would not give up.

No great crack of wings had been heard, nor monstrous shape glimpsed crossing the canopy of sky. Nothing had dropped to the earth over which they staggered. No pale horrors had scampered from the treeline in eager pursuit. Marcus had even conjured a spurt of speed, as he manhandled Jane's flopping body across the tufts and rabbit holes. He only paused in the middle of what so quickly became no-man's-land when the horrible grunt of the quad bikes polluted the silence.

'Clement!' Rachel cried. 'They're coming!'

46

[Midnight–1am]

*I*nland, to the north, the noise of the approaching engines erupted from a distance hard to gauge but Marcus didn't waste a second and resumed stumbling in the direction of the river, dragging Jane at a speed beyond the endurance of his thighs.

He'd not taken more than five steps before he saw headlights. Two white spots upriver, appearing and disappearing within the hedgerow that bordered the north side of the meadow. Above the lights, twin sparks pierced the darkness. Around these, scarlet and pink clouds of smoke soon flooded the air. Flares.

A third headlight then peered through the night to create a trio of bikes, shaking and bumping over rough ground. Within seconds, from where the track broke the scrubby hedgerow and entered the meadow, the bikes roared into the open, the riders' flares fizzing and dripping light.

When the vehicles rode between the campsite and where Marcus and Rachel now crouched in the field, they caught sight of the riders. Each extended one arm to support a flare. Headlights probed, washing the grass white.

Marcus whispered, 'Down!'

Together they sank into the meadow and lay flat on either side of Jane.

Marcus asked for the sword.

Rachel passed the weapon to him.

Monumental

The engine sounds slowed when the group of vehicles reached the outskirts of the camp. A pinkish illumination extended far enough to discolour the tips of the grass that surrounded Marcus's face. He immediately feared for the boats, that they would be holed and rendered useless. One was already missing and, surely, that would be noticed.

The whine of engines in higher gears soon increased but separated into three separate entities. One patrolled the riverbank. The other two scored parallel lines of crushed verdure across the field, straight grooves that furrowed towards where Marcus and the women lay; the straightest route to the middle of the plain. The air and their faces soon tinted pink. Smoke misted like low cloud.

As the closest bike appeared to stop no more than a few paces before their lowered faces, Marcus feared they'd been seen. Their passage from the woods and through the grasses to where they now lay must be visible and would be until the squashed stalks eventually righted themselves. A crazed impulse urged him to stand up and scream and sprint in any direction, to alleviate the agony of waiting to be discovered.

From the river, the third bike turned and accelerated across the plain to join the others. As this vehicle closed on the others, Vine called out, 'One's missing! A kayak. There's only five on the bank.'

'Shite!' Clement yelled in the darkness. 'Fuck, fuck, fuck!'

'They can't get far,' Vine replied. 'Priests will have who took that boat.'

'You better be right!' Colman again, rattled, near frantic.

Vine tried to reassure his leader. 'Priests and the worm would definitely have had the two they left behind in the camp as well. No doubt in my mind. They would have been sorted out hours ago. There's even bits. Blood Worm's had someone. Must be one of them they left at the tents.'

'Male?' Clement asked, his hope desperate.

'Nah. It's the head of some old bird.'

Colman remained incandescent with fury. 'Fuck! Hedge Pig bitch! That mouthy prick Marcus! She let him out. He's run down here and paddled off.'

'He won't get far, swear on my life.'

One of the bikes left the encirclement and grunted away towards the valley side, passing on their left. Marcus could not believe that they had not been spotted. He suspected they were being toyed with.

The quad bike soon arced to appear directly behind them, before slowing to an idle. The other two engines dropped from a rumble to a purr.

No one spoke.

With his head now pressed into the earth, Marcus was unable to see beyond an arm's length in any direction. He exchanged glances with Rachel, whose enlarged, frantic eyes revolved around her sockets. Her panic was contagious. He felt it flood his body, but he clung onto the last few tendrils of reason. He thought of reaching out to grab her shoulder and hold her still; or to at least indicate for her to remain silent, by raising a finger to his lips. He feared she was about to run and expose their position, but couldn't bring himself to budge lest his movement in the grass was spotted.

Quick footsteps rustled and scuffed through the grass, somewhere behind them. Vine must have dismounted. 'Hang on. Something's here.'

Right now, the furrow they'd made was probably being inspected. As soon as Marcus entertained this thought, and had grown cold at the realisation that this is how they must be discovered, Rachel stood up.

'No!' Marcus whispered.

Above him, the old woman twitched and tottered, her smock and tatty head bathed in pink and white light. She appeared too dazed and too wretched with despair to move her feet. But only for a moment before flitting away and out of his sight, setting off in the direction of the southern edge of the meadow.

'Here!' Vine cried out, excitedly. He followed this with 'Bitch!' He returned to his bike and opened the throttle.

Marcus swivelled onto his back but didn't rise. He knew what Rachel had done: she'd run to divert attention from where he lay with Jane.

Monumental

Penetrating the noise of Vine's bike, her scream followed not long after.

Winded with fear, Marcus rose to his knees. The first of their pursuers that he saw was their leader, Clement, standing astride his bike, but looking back towards the river. He wasn't as close as Marcus had imagined; he'd misjudged the proximity of the engine noise.

Thorny was even further away, standing in the grass beside her idling vehicle, with one inked arm thrust overhead. At the end of her thin arm, a sparking torrent threw a beam of scarlet light across the night-charred grass.

Neither Clement nor Thorny had seen his protruding head and shoulders. Marcus looked in the direction that Rachel had taken: towards the reeds and sea; a region that he would assuredly never lay eyes on again.

Vine had already run the old woman down. He loomed over her, one inked fist gripping her hair close to the scalp. Rachel's face was obscured by the long grass. Her assailant's ferrety features had recast themselves from a sullen wariness to a humourless smirk, radiating a savage eagerness. 'Fucking rat!' He dragged Rachel back towards his bike, as if he were manhandling livestock; a sheep about to have its fleece sheared, or throat cut.

The bedraggled state of Rachel and the way in which her garment had twisted up her scrawny legs – the dehumanising display and abuse of the elderly woman who'd saved his life – brought a roar into Marcus's throat. Even Vine seemed momentarily baffled as Marcus rose to his feet. When he ran at Vine, holding the iron blade low, the man's surprise switched to alarm.

'Quick. Help him!' Clement roared at Thorny, though made no attempt to move himself.

'Vine!' Thorny shrieked from somewhere behind Marcus's head.

Grass whipped Marcus's shins. The night's chill broke against his grimace, dispersed by the heat of his fury. After having fought the Priests into a rout, the sight of this small man in the long grass presented no deterrent. And as a snapshot of Julian hanging from a tree slid into his mind, Marcus bellowed, 'Bastard!'

He wanted Vine dead.

Into his burning thoughts came a memory of Sophie being yanked aloft by the vermin that these people worshipped. Up and into the unlit dome of the temple she'd been hoisted. A trace of the stone dome's mephitic stench contaminated his sinuses all over again.

He wanted to smash them all apart.

Vine released Rachel's ankles and stepped away from her. His blade rose level with his ratty eyes that closed to slits, the sharp iron moving with the easy, graceful movement of an arm familiar with handheld weapons. A nasty bearded grin below the malicious eyes presented a portrait of brutish ugliness; the pitiless face of a man who was no stranger to violence.

Or murder.

Marcus swung as Vine lunged at his chest.

Iron clanged and rang out across the floodplain. Painful vibrations racked Marcus's palms, then juddered up his forearms and settled within his teeth. The tip of Vine's blade had swiped close enough to rip the front of his cagoule.

Another quad bike engine roared through the darkness behind Marcus, rapid in its approach.

Grinning and assured, Vine feinted, twice, then darted at Marcus again, this time stabbing for his gut.

Marcus leapt back, losing his footing. As if trying to keep his feet on ice, his arms weaved desperate circles in the air.

Grinning even more blackly, Vine pressed his advantage and rushed Marcus's back-peddling retreat. As if to punch the weapon into his stomach, Vine grabbed the collar of Marcus's cagoule and pulled him forward, to press his bulk onto the point of the gladius.

In that moment, as the little man drew his sword arm back, Marcus imagined the evil pacifier in Vine's inked hand thrusting inside his torso. He imagined the blade working at the incision, from side to side, and every muscle in Marcus's core and abdomen tensed for the insertion of that horrible shaft into his entrails. Pure panic jerked his own weapon between their closing bodies.

His sword slipped under the skinny arm of his attacker that held his collar, deflecting the gut-jab away from his navel, though only by millimetres.

Instead of skewering him, Vine's blade tore into the cagoule that lay slack at Marcus's waist. And so sure was the stabbing motion, the blade ripped out the back of his jacket.

Clement roared his approval. 'Fuck! Him! Up!'

Within the weasel's eyes, Marcus detected a flicker of alarm. Vine knew he'd impaled cloth, not flesh. Marcus had gasped; not from pain but from relief. Vine's blade was now caught, entangled.

'Right through the fucker and out the back!' Clement shrieked. 'You're one sick mother—'

The tip of Marcus's blade was still angled up.

Vine released the collar of his jacket and at the same time attempted to extract his blade from the cagoule. But he wasn't quick enough.

Marcus fisted his hand in Vine's beard and held the little snarling head still. The man jerked about but could not tug his beard free.

With a calm concentration that would have alarmed him, had he had the time to think of what he was about to do, Marcus placed the tip of his blade under Vine's hairy jaw. And he punched that tip up, with every Newton of muscular strength that a desperate man can summon at the moment of his own extinction.

Vine didn't die. But he probably wished that he had done.

Marcus released the fistful of facial hair.

Vine staggered back. Both of his hands tugged at the iron shaft that hung below his jaw. The tip of the blade must have lodged in the roof of his mouth, because not even his lips moved. Nor could he cough out the wave of his own blood that poured into his throat and pumped like syrup into his sopping beard.

'The fuck! The fuck did you do?' Clement yelled.

'Marcus!' Rachel's voice was just audible because of the oncoming roar of a quad bike.

Marcus flinched, then half turned, before he was blinded by the oncoming headlight and deafened by the scream of a quad bike's engine.

He fell more than he leapt sideways and hit the grass with a shoulder.

Thorny and her bike jolted past him, a hand's breadth away from his face. A hot oily smoke seared his eyes; diesel steam stung his throat. Marcus thrust himself up and to his knees. With a desperate yank, he withdrew Vine's blade from his waterproof.

Back on his feet, his new blade pointing up, Marcus turned to face the rider's next pass.

As Thorny arced the bike around, Marcus could see the determination and emotion twisting her narrow features into a snarl.

Vine staggered between them, still tugging at his new iron beard. When her headlight projected the full horror of the man's plight and injury back at her, Thorny's bike slowed. She screamed.

'Take him out!' Clement roared, from a safe distance.

Marcus turned now to the leader, who stood upright astride the bike. He still held a flare aloft, to illumine the area in which his butchers needed to work.

Taking advantage of Thorny's shock at the dripping obstacle that her comrade now presented to her, Marcus switched his focus and charged at Colman.

Clement caught the oncoming charge and sat down. He tossed the flare, turned the throttle and tugged the handlebars, urging his bike to move. It wheeled around in a half circle.

The ground boomed from the tremendous thud of an impact from above.

Vine tried to shriek but only gurgled.

Then he was above them, above the grass and the valley and the world.

Monumental

Clement made the mistake of looking back, instinctively, at the sky. Even though Marcus was four long sprinting strides away, he witnessed how Colman's face transformed and became bloodless and stricken with terror. By the time the landowner returned his attention to the operation of the vehicle, Marcus had reached him.

And was on him.

He hacked at the man's right arm. That was bare, exposed.

His blade came to a standstill in Clement Colman's upper arm bone.

Marcus ripped his blade free, then darted away, at a ninety-degree angle, running at a crouch with his head down.

Clement's cries chased him through the grass.

Above the world a great wind roared, the air slapped by vast wings.

The third quad bike adjusted its course and circled towards Marcus. Only Thorny remained mounted.

Marcus turned to meet the last rider, now but a dim outline behind the headlight. Her full beam caught an object that fell from the air like a heavy, wet tree branch. One of Vine's inked legs. The limb landed, then bounced, then settled in the grass.

Thorny saw the limb and peered up fearfully. At the final moment, she decided to change direction, to alter her course and to abandon her pursuit of Marcus, because of what was in the air: their god. A deity that bestowed no favours on those who'd summoned it from the void and given succour to its loathsome appetite. She turned her quad in a tight semicircle, to steer clear of Clement, who knelt in the grass beside his stalled bike, gripping his arm, his hand dark and shiny as if dipped in fresh tar. He screamed, 'Help me! Oh, God, help me!'

At its slowest and most unwieldy, during an abrupt turn in long grass, Thorny's swerving quad bike reduced the gap between herself and Marcus. Head down, exploding into a sprint, he closed on her just as she opened the throttle. He invested what remained of his upper body strength into a wild blow, directed at the bike's rider.

And so hard did he strike her head, as she'd unwittingly accelerated in his direction, that the blade was knocked clean out of his hand.

The small woman was lifted from her seat.

She tumbled into the grass like a jockey tossed from a horse. She never made a sound. But the noise of his sword meeting the side of her head made Marcus shudder.

Again, he bolted into the dark, away from the headlights, away from the screams, away from the spitting scarlet flares in the grass; he dashed as far away as he could from those who bled in open air.

'Marcus! Marcus! Here!' Rachel cried out, on his left.

He turned and stumbled towards her voice, dropping to a crouch when a terrible *whump whump whump* announced itself from directly overhead.

A great downdraft of foetid air near flattened him. He swung an arm backwards, as if to fend the winged predator away, but it was no longer above him. Its interest lay elsewhere.

Unperturbed by the bikes, their lights or the three burning flares, the god of the pit fell onto Thorny.

With one backward glance into a halo of sputtering scarlet light, Marcus was appalled but also surprised to discover that the Blood Worm of the valley possessed a feathered head, a giant loathsome bonnet or headdress of feathers. They were the colour of scorched copper.

Infantile, skeletal arms raked out from the larval flanks, patterned by scales. Their three-fingered extremities clawed Thorny's arms and head, swiftly separating arms and skull from the torso. It was as if the beast were stripping dry twigs from a dead branch and making as much noise as if it were strong, fresh wood. Mercifully for her, after Marcus's blow, the morsel did not regain consciousness.

What fastened the remnants of Thorny into its worming mouth was soon no longer on the ground. A tremendous, propelling spring of coiled muscle fired the great serpent heavenward. A final slap of its tail rang against the earth until that appendage straightened to assist the ascent.

Marcus stumbled and slipped about until he found Rachel. She was crouched beside Jane. The girl's eyes were wide open. 'They cross the red sky. They cross the sky above the city of stone. The gods. Can you hear the pipes?' she said.

'She's not here,' Rachel said. 'I think her soul has already crossed over.'

Marcus dismissed the suggestion and squatted beside Jane. 'Down,' he said to Rachel. She quickly nestled on the other side of the girl. 'And don't move. At all.'

Clement whimpered. The valley owner's ragged, bowed head was visible above the stalks of the long grass in which he knelt. The disgraced tech billionaire remained on his knees, paralysed equally by agony and the awful sight of his own blood loss. For Marcus, he wasn't far enough away from where he and Rachel lay.

Above Colman, his god fed. From where the rain of blood and matter dropped to patter on the river meadow, Marcus spotted the outline of the great wingspan, gliding like some impossible kite, its pattern a shade darker than the night sky. Like a snake newly disturbed from rotten wood, a thick core writhed between the vast sheets of the wings. From that sinewy trunk came the sounds of the messy suckling of what was held within efficient jaws.

Even when consumed by a delirium of agony and shock, Clement's instinct for self-preservation fired. He stumbled to reach his stalled, motionless bike, but took no more than four steps before he was slammed into the very soil for which he had the deeds of ownership. He was covered by a roping mass that stank like a large septic tank convulsing with offal and maggots.

'Quiet,' Marcus whispered, and he shuffled sideways and clambered over Jane's body. Then he drew little Rachel under his arm. Together, under a black canopy of cold air, the three motionless bodies warmed each other. Two of them waited with their eyes closed, not breathing, and they prayed to another god that they would not be taken in this year's most generous stipend of human flesh and screams.

47

[Midnight–1am]

Under the flitting beam of the torch that followed the movements of Marcus's head, he and Rachel struggled to fit Jane's unresponsive body inside her kayak. As they toiled, they each took turns to peer fearfully at the sky. Standing beneath rickety scaffolding in a high wind, or at the base of an incline that had just unleashed a deafening avalanche, would have been preferable to crouching beneath the enormous canopy of night that had swallowed the Wyrm Valley.

The god of this valley, the Blood Worm, was close. Before the hideous thing tore Vine apart, that's what he'd called it: the *Blood Worm*. Right now, it was either perched out of sight, or aloft and circling for the scent of more blood. The thing dropped on prey within the space of two heartbeats. Marcus had now seen, or heard, the creature demolish seven human beings since late afternoon. None of them had died easily.

When his wayward memory erupted with these grisly recollections, his mind was ready for a white-out, a temporary shutdown. Tremors frequently wracked his hands. Since reaching full awareness inside the temple that afternoon, he had fought an urge to sit and not move, to become unthinking and unfeeling. He'd become so frightened, over and over again since then, that he was surprised not to have suffered some kind of seizure, or become catatonic and unresponsive.

Had he done so he would not have blamed himself. But here he was, continuing. Holding a blade and using it. Unburdening himself, perhaps, of himself.

Two more of Clement Colman's followers were still at large. As were the Little Priests of the tin mine. And he knew that he was close to broken. From Nigel's furious assault in the temple, the very bones of his back, shoulders and one arm continually throbbed with pain. Perhaps there was a hairline fracture inside this rhythm of hurting, this second heartbeat. Each thigh groaned with pain and felt as heavy as a lump of cement, from carrying or dragging an adult body twice since noon. Years of sea kayaking, teaching circuit training classes, lifting weights, five-a-side football, hiking and mountain biking had provided enough stamina to endure a day in this valley, with little left over.

He'd become clumsier since getting Jane out of the woods and across the meadow. He was repeatedly dropping what he picked up, was listing when he tried to walk in a straight line. He was aware of this and struggled to correct it. He was upright but not sure how he remained so. Repetitive thoughts circled. Unwelcome thoughts intruded.

An awareness of the miracle of his continuing existence – of his breathing and the sluggish bumps of his heart – must suffice for now. Any musing on the future he must restrict to considering his next step and extend hope no further than that. He daren't even think as far as the next few minutes. *Because that's where I am*, he said to himself. *This is where I am and nowhere else. I'm only here.* Fear, caution, flight, violence: that was his existence. He recognised that he was now solely reliant on what a few million years of evolution had done for his species' animal brain.

Other useful articles and implements were buried inside the bags of his dead companions. Lights, rations, water. But he'd leave all of it behind. His need to feel the swollen river flowing beneath his hull, on his way out of the valley, was too desperate. Searching through bags would delay their departure.

High water had peaked, and the tide was slack but would soon ebb. Earlier, at noon, the paddle up the valley to the meadow, at the leisurely pace of kayakers exploring territory for the first time, had consumed around forty minutes. Towing an injured paddler, his paddling speed might even be slower than that. He'd also have to make regular stops to catch his breath and check on Jane. But the river and creek should remain full enough to enable them to reach the estuary. After that, enough water should cover the basin to carry them to the sea. If he suffered no more delays.

As they attempted again to slide Jane's recalcitrant legs inside the cockpit, while her upper body was sprawled on the rear deck, Marcus was forced to his knees, panting for breath. Fresh sweat washed salt from his brows and into stinging eyes. Though old, Rachel was strong, and it was she who eventually managed to straighten and slide Jane's feet inside the hull and towards the foot rests.

Once Marcus had zipped the girl into her buoyancy jacket, her head and shoulders flopped back over the rear deck. He stretched and fitted her tight spraydeck over the cockpit. That took four attempts. By the time the neoprene was fastened, he was on the verge of tears. He stood up but staggered sideways.

Rachel grabbed at his elbow. 'Tell them. If you can.'

Marcus nodded. 'We're not out of it yet. There are two more of your lot. That tall bitch.'

'Swan.'

'And the one who looks after the children, or whatever those things are.'

'Huntress.'

'Unaccounted for.'

'Huntress will never let the children out of her sight. Swan was Clement's lover. He'd not let her roam while the Priests were overtaken by bloodlust. He must have bidden her remain at the house.'

'Good. But the Priests, they want Jane.'

Rachel nodded. 'They'll come for her.' She tapped her wild head. 'She's still with them up here. And they are still with her too.' This was said with such a melancholy conviction that Marcus felt the gravity of despair add weight to his fatigue. He refused to consider the damage they'd already inflicted on Jane. There would be time enough to think about that, if he could get her out and then seek a way of freeing her from their contamination. 'She'll get better,' he muttered. 'Once we're out of here. She will.'

The old woman didn't answer or look at him.

Marcus slid spare split-paddles under the bowlines of each boat, then bilge pumps. He crowned himself with the head torch. 'Come with us. I can prep one more boat. You'll have to paddle but I can show you how.'

Rachel shook her head. Then clasped one hand over the tattoo on her shoulder. 'Two that they have claimed leaving? Don't tempt the wights any more than you're doing. Better I stay until morning.'

The idea that the people here were livestock, branded slaves at best, triggered a fresh wave of horror and revulsion in Marcus that left him feeling sick. He thought he was long past reacting in such a way, but he was wrong. 'I'd better get going.' As he turned to the river, he looked at the black sky. 'Will that thing come again?'

'As long as you're not bleeding, you've a chance.'

Marcus nervously inspected his torn cagoule. There had been a hair's breadth between Vine's blade and his skin. Had the sharp edge nicked his flesh, then, like a hare beneath an eagle, he'd have been destroyed in the meadow with the others. Marcus gripped his left wrist to stop the shaking of that hand.

'I think we scrubbed all of the blood off your friend,' Rachel said. 'But it was dark.'

Marcus picked up his paddle. 'I'll come back for you. With help.'

She briefly covered his hands with her cold, thin fingers. 'Bless you.'

He held her bony shoulders and pressed his forehead to hers. 'Thank you.'

Marcus picked up the bow toggles of the two kayaks and tugged them towards the water. Rachel pushed at the sterns.

Earlier, as he'd waded downstream to reach the campsite, the river level had barely covered his knees. Now, the dark surface rose to his groin. Frigid water punched the breath from his lungs. But it also helped him focus and he was grateful for that.

Marcus swung his legs astride the rear deck of his kayak, then slipped his feet inside. His wet buttocks followed, dropping into the cockpit and onto a familiar seat. He fitted his legs beneath the upper deck, and his feet found the foot rests. Once his knees nestled against the inner hull, he snapped his spraydeck over the cockpit rim, then sculled to the bank and grabbed the bow of Jane's boat.

He clipped the large karabiner that hung from his belted waist through her deck lines. Her boat would now be strapped parallel to his own, her cockpit settled behind his back. The river was wide enough to allow for such an arrangement of two boats, side by side. In the narrower creek, he'd tow her behind his boat on a short line. A stage he'd confront when, or if, they reached the reeds and marsh.

Behind Jane's boat, Rachel waded up to her knees in the river. She pushed the second kayak through the shallows. 'God speed,' she whispered across the black water.

Marcus slipped his paddle blade through the inky surface and drew the first forward stroke.

48

[1–2am]

Cold, clean smells from running water mingled with a taint of mulch, from where the riverbanks received little of the sun's heat. The slowly shifting surface made no sound. Nothing was audible but the hollow clunk of two boats knocking together, and the splash and drip from Marcus's ever-moving paddle blades.

What he remembered of the river from early afternoon was now concealed. Trees, fallen branches, clumps of rhododendron and witch hazel, sprays of flowers and the tumble of boulders swelling from the shallows, all were cloaked by darkness.

He kept the head torch turned off and paddled near blind, following the course of the channel. Often, he clashed with overhanging branches, unseen until they raked his face and tangled with his paddle. He'd unknot himself, clumsily right the boats, then push off again by poling a paddle blade against the pebbly river bed.

The odd collision with a tree limb produced regrettable noise but was preferable to being exposed to the valley slopes. The overhanging canopy he counted as one slender blessing; as a barrier, it would do nothing to hinder what haunted the skies, but the sense of concealment encouraged his attempts to steer the two kayaks downriver and at a quicker pace as the journey out progressed.

As they glided, Jane drifted in and out of consciousness but never moved. He'd been paddling for some time before he realised that her eyes were open, though she was unaware of him or where she was. She remained slumped against her seat rest. 'No sun, moon. No stars . . . Who built the round houses . . . the silver children. Mummy, they bite . . .' Much of her garbled, childish monologue he failed to hear. And he was glad of that, because anything that Jane muttered did nothing good for his nerves.

The air lightened once they'd glided out from the funnel of arching trees. The channel narrowed and the reed beds began their dominance of the valley; thin, motionless stalks gathered in vast crowds, dry and brown and starving, on either side of the creek. It was here that a new fear appeared in Marcus's thoughts and persisted: an anxiety that small, horrible arms might dart from the unlit canyon of vegetation; and clawed, infantile hands would clutch his face. And draw his blood.

As a precaution, he moved Vine's gladius, placing the old blade on the upper deck. Should he need to snatch at the weapon in a hurry, he wanted the pommel close to his stomach, so that he could drop a hand from the paddle shaft directly onto the sword's hilt.

This acute feeling of vulnerability was made worse by his being in a sitting position, trapped inside the hull from the waist down. He'd have preferred pulling the kayaks with one hand, leaving his other arm free to wield the blade; but uncertainty about the depth of the water, and the sinking mud on the creek bed, kept him inside his kayak.

Cooling currents of air threaded the reeds. Occasionally, the stalks softly rattled. But he saw nothing move.

When they passed out of the reeds, a low wind from the south brushed his face. Carried within it was a briny message from the sea and a promise of a watery expanse in which to hide. He could feel the outgoing tide beneath the hull, and guessed the flow would add at least one knot to their progress out of the valley.

Against the horizon, vestiges of light soon defined the skeletal silhouettes of the dead wood. They'd reached the wetland.

Beyond the mud and lifeless timber, the valley's leafy arms spread wide to make room for the broad estuary. That water remained black, and he couldn't yet see the surface beyond the marsh. But the fragrance of the sea strengthened sufficiently for Marcus to indulge a glimmer of belief that they might actually leave the valley by water. An idea that had seemed impossible less than an hour before.

Jane didn't share the change in his morale or spirits. At this point, her whimpers increased. She tried to sit up and made her boat unstable. Had Marcus not pressed on her front deck with all of his strength and added his weight to her boat with his own kayak edged over, she would have capsized.

When he tried to calm her with whispered reassurances, she remained insensible. He raised his voice but her distress only increased. She clawed at the impediment that held her fast: her spraydeck. 'I don't want to go back,' she cried out.

'Jane! Stop. Jane!' Marcus swiped a hand to grasp one of her wrists, but clutched only two fingers, his very touch turning her whimpers to tears. 'You'll pitch us over, Jane! I have to get us out of here. Help me,' Marcus begged but quickly understood what his companion had been referring to – what it was that she did not want to be returned to. She'd not been referring to the world beyond the valley.

On their right, to the west, the Little Priests had come down from the hills to retrieve what had been stolen from the mine. As if they were crabs with exceptionally thin legs, a cluster of wights was now picking its way across the mudflats towards them.

49

[1–2am]

*M*arcus didn't pause to count the horrors advancing towards the creek bank. At a hasty estimate, the congregation of Little Priests must number close to ten. All of them were masked.

After a moment of bewilderment, haloed by sickening panic, he threw himself into a forward stroke. Coordination under duress became clumsiness. His paddle blade clashed against Jane's boat, then hit the bank that he could barely see in such poor light. Changing the position of his arms, he was forced to hold the shaft vertical to drag the blades through the water on one side, while trying a sweep stroke on the far side of Jane's boat. But he didn't feel as if they were moving – merely rocking about. The two boats were too heavy, too cumbersome in the narrow channel.

The patter of the wights' feet on the mud became audible, faint at first but growing louder.

Marcus abandoned his attempt to outrun them. He righted his boat, then unclipped the karabiner at his waist from Jane's bowlines. He pulled the cord of his spraydeck and the neoprene skirt pinged free of the cockpit. He pulled his legs from inside the hull, straddled his cockpit, then slipped into the water.

To his shins, his legs sank into a cold ooze of mud that immediately tried to set like mortar. Creek water sloshed against his waist. The kayaks bumped together. Around his clumsy movements, bubbles unleashed sulphurs of rot.

He tugged the iron blade from under the deck's bowlines, then worked both boats behind his buttocks, to position himself between the kayaks and the bank that now teemed with small figures.

Attempting to balance by wrenching one foot from the mud dipped him sideways. One foot remained stuck, the second gave. His hands sank into cold water, the murky surface rising to slap his face and swallow his shoulders. He nearly let go of the short sword, only just gripping the handle before it sank, irretrievably, into the silt and sucking mud.

The unwelcome notion of being immobilised by creek mud, as the wights clung and fed, propelled him back upright, swearing, dripping and furious at his ungainliness.

With a grunt more of desperation than of determination, he freed his sopping arms from the creek. He grabbed the pointed stern of Jane's drifting boat and dragged the kayak so that it was positioned behind his back once more. If he didn't stand between her and what skittered ever closer, she was gone.

Now behind him, the girl whimpered from the terror of what she must have sensed nearby; the presence she perceived within the perpetual nightmare of her delirium. Like Julian, her eyes were open but she wasn't seeing the same world as Marcus. And even though he was looking at a cluster of wights, Marcus still did not envy her the sights that fever had forced her to behold.

'I don't want to go with them, Mum. I don't want to!'

The first Priest to leap onto the front deck of Jane's boat Marcus saw little of, but he heard its weight softly thump the plastic deck. Fury and frustration at his inability to move his feet provoked a roar. All of his mobility was from the waist up. His feet had set again in the creek bed. But he swivelled at the hips and cut into the thing with a mighty backhanded swipe, his follow-through nearly striking one of Jane's limp arms. The sharp edge of his blade met resistance, and he sensed a pulpous lump folding around the blade. Several firmer appendages slapped and thrashed against the hollow plastic hull.

The wight leapt onto the mudflats on the other side of the creek, and fled as fast as a frightened cat, before slowing to a trembling crouch. Then the thing fell onto its side and became still. Lifeless, he hoped. He couldn't let them get behind him. The first one to attack had nearly achieved exactly that.

Four wights nearest to the raised bank drew level with his eyes. After poking their feathered heads at him, they hesitated, then stalked away from the blade's reach. He wondered if they could smell the iron that they detested. They had seen it smite their brethren too, among the trees of their dreadful chapel. And he'd just reminded them of how much power he could invest in a blow, particularly when cornered. They had numbers; he had desperate wrath.

Behind the first row of agitated wights, a second group milled. Another four, weaving around each other, their small feet pattering mud. Small, feathered heads rose and fell as each creature looked for a way to get around their comrades and through to Jane.

Marcus turned on the head torch.

It illuminated what resembled an unlit battlefield. Stunted, blasted, bone-white trees. Mudflats glimmered greyly. A plain in hell on which pale devils pranced in expectation of claiming the damned.

Marcus seized a moment to yank one leg free of the sucking mud. His shiny leg, begrimed with a glossy second skin of mud, pulled free, but there was no paddling boot on the retracted foot. He lurched forward and at the nearest bank, now busy with the first quartet of scuttling Priests. Brackish water swilled about his waist. The ambushers tensed.

The flash of a sleek form darted through the air.

Marcus punched up with his free hand and struck it airborne. As if it were an ape that had fallen onto a lower tree limb, it quickly wrapped itself around his arm. Feathers whisked his sleeve. A half-hidden, appalling face sought out his soft wrist.

The hideous wriggling weight on his forearm made him flinch with revulsion. Trying to shake the thing loose, he dunked his arm into the water. Plunging it under the surface ignited an explosion of scrabbling limbs that churned the creek white. It detached itself from his cagoule sleeve, slunk away from him and back up the bank. He swung at its retreat and caught one extended leg with the blade. As if punctured, the stunted creature expelled air like wind rushing through a keyhole. His second swipe missed and carved mud.

Provoked, the creature's spidery brethren surged to press their superior numbers. Marcus swung at them, blindly directing a blow into the thicket, but the gladius found nothing on its arcing journey but thin air. The group had hastily withdrawn, in unison, out of range of the blade's tip, jerking backwards and slipping about in the slime in their desperation to escape. It was as if the weapon reeked of some foul toxin. Again, Marcus cut the air before their shrivelled eyes.

'Bastards!' he screamed at them. His torch beam swept across their mercury flesh, the nests of feathers that formed their false faces, a larval ribcage here, a frog-like leg there, the extremity horribly clawed. Within the mouth-holes, nasty barbs of wet cartilage glimmered in the electric light he cast into their faces. He imagined such a feathery orifice pressing his flesh, before venomous needles broke the skin. How could something so unholy ever earn the name of Priest? He thought them more reptile than primate.

There was another joint thrust from the clergy of the mine, which he repelled with two arcing swings of the blade that met nothing again but hissing air. Like a bat, another wight flung itself onto Jane's kayak. Marcus slipped, losing his balance.

Landing hard on the stern hatch, the loathsome thing tipped the boat and missed its footing. Grasping an opportunity that had to be taken in a split second, Marcus righted himself and swept the blade backhanded, twisting at the waist as far as his body would allow.

As if a metal bar had struck drying, hollow pottery, something crumpled at the end of his blade. Tremors of a soft implosion ran along the sword and into the fine bones of his hand. He'd caught the back of the thing's skull, behind the mask. On the other side of Jane's boat, the lifeless figure pitched near soundlessly into the murk of the creek.

Marcus lurched in the opposite direction and desperately swung at the slick but faint whisk of a small foot on soft ground. At the end of his arm's arc, the blade struck another wight's head. This one had slunk forward, low to the ground. The mask was torn from the rotten apple of its fanged face. The sleek creature flopped sideways, either stunned or dead.

Arms wilting, as if even such a short weapon weighed as much as a heavy dumbbell, Marcus wheezed. He hadn't the strength to tug another foot from the mud in which he'd planted himself like a tree, nor would he risk losing his balance again. If the wights rushed him now, he'd one thrust left.

Make it count. Then squeeze their throats flat.

It was not long before what he believed was his last stand commenced.

50

[1–2am]

Drawing back his sword arm, Marcus screamed at the hoard.

In response, the mob at the edge of the creek bank rushed forward.

The horizontal swing of his blade forced three wights to rear backwards at the water's edge, but a fourth leapt over the iron and latched onto his chest. As if suspended within a papoose, the parasite hung onto his front. Claws at the culmination of flute-thin arms spiked through his cagoule and under-layers like syringe needles. Around his waist, the attacker's bony legs belted him. Toenails pierced his shorts and the skin of his buttocks.

Punctured.

Marcus bellowed from the pain.

Rummaging inwards came a feathered face. A whiff of damp amidst a stench of carrion filled and infected his sinuses. He heard the moist click of a small mouth opening. The rustling head dipped to fasten on the side of his throat. He thought of the lowing cow, festooned with these feeding grubs.

Marcus thrust a forearm between the creature's neck and his chest, but not soon enough to evade the nick that became a rip in his throat. Blood trickled warmly inside his collar. He pushed the wight's head away from his throat and peered into the feathered face, one hand's breadth from his nose.

Terrible opaque teeth extended from the mouthpiece of the mask. Above the maw, two tiny eyes glinted like shards of black glass.

Besotted by the taste of his blood, the thing thrashed its furiously eager head, rustling and worrying at his face. Marcus locked his forearm harder under the thing's mask and yanked his face further away. Claws sank deeper into his shoulders and buttocks, the wight embedding itself into the prey that it was determined to drain.

Marcus straightened his sword arm. Angled the tip down.

He growled, tightened his core and clenched every muscle along his back, his arms, his shoulder and neck. To end the agony of having his skin punctured by the small, tightening claws, he thrust the sword down and into a feathery eye socket.

A hiss escaped from the mask.

The wight's grip loosened.

Marcus pressed down hard. And as if he'd plunged a carving knife into a white cabbage, the resistance in the wight's skull soon gave way. The iron blade slicked through the small head, squelching as the shaft slid through the mask and divided what served as the thing's brain.

The near weightless body slumped then withered against his chest. Marcus gripped the thin neck, tore the pale ruin from his body and then slapped the spindly mess into the creek.

He roared a challenge at the others on the bank; all were poised for their turn to leap, clamber, fix and feed.

One he'd injured and was lame, others he'd knocked dead from out of the fray, two more skewered and sunk. The remaining wights hesitated.

They knew they could defeat him. But at what cost?

What Marcus interpreted as an innate wariness and a contagion of fear turned into retreat, as the remaining congregation scampered out of his reach. As they went, their feathered heads still reared and bobbed like serpents. As if their intention had been to shriek with outrage, Marcus could just detect a higher-pitched piping. No other sound seemed able to take form inside the horrid, bloodless mouths.

Slowly, with their feathered visages still confronting him, the childlike figures withdrew across the mudflats, until their vague shapes faded and merged with the ruins of the trees from which the bones of their previous feasts hung like thieves from gallows.

Marcus clamped one hand to his wet and stinging throat. The scratch, or slit, that the wight had made ran freely with blood. When he lit the hand that had touched the wound, his fingers shone, gloved with crimson. He looked away. Even he could smell his own blood.

Marcus raised his face to the sky. 'Dear God,' he whispered.

51

[2–3am]

'They crawled. Bit me. It's inside. Inside me. They left it. They want . . . what they left in me . . . we can't leave the stones . . .' In the darkness engulfing Marcus, Jane's face was a pale smudge behind his shoulder. Sometimes, her mouth moved.

She'd revived sufficiently to perceive that she was leaving the valley. This vague awareness caused her distress. While Marcus weakly dug his paddle blades deep, slowly pushing the two attached kayaks out of the wetland creek and into the marshy beginnings of the estuary, she'd been voicing more or less the same delirious preoccupations. The greater the distance they traversed, the more noticeable her agitation became.

Marcus attempted to ignore her raving and to concentrate on paddling, while always scanning the sky for movement. Incessantly, he checked the wound in his neck. Every few metres, he scooped up a handful of water and splashed the slit. The wound would sting and bring tears to his eyes. Each time he bathed the punctures, cold, salty water ran inside his cagoule. Electric rivulets shocking him from a growing stupor.

Out here in the gullet of the estuary, the darkness was thicker, the air too. This lightless flood of nothing seeped inside his skull, oppressing his thoughts then dispersing them to make room for nothing. He had expected the world to be lighter here, the sky clearing as the estuary basin broadened and valley slopes retreated. Yet the opposite was true.

He was bleeding in three places. Beneath his shorts and cagoule, fabric stuck to his tacky flesh where the Priest's claws had broken the skin. The bleeding would not stop. But might his layers prevent the scent of blood dispersing into the air? He told himself that they would. Then he doubted what he'd told himself.

Washing his throat must have diluted, or even cleansed away, the odour of the fresh wound there. He tried to believe this too. He didn't have much success, and thought instead of a hideous, sinewy weight flopping from the sky.

From the wetland and the bony timbers of the salt-burned wood, he was soon sluggishly clawing their boats across the shallow first third of the estuary. Outgoing flow and currents were meagre but would build; the ebbing tidal cycle would soon push harder at their hulls. Since their arrival, twelve hours before, it would be the only favour that the valley's waters had bestowed on them.

Of the obsidian surface he saw no detail save a few glittering splashes around his paddle blades. A lake of ink. Expanding on either side of their boats, a vast plane of oblivion stretched towards a horizon that was lost in the infinity of night. Gusts from the south-east had moved a shelf of cloud between them and the stars. That must be why it was so dark. The valley sides were no longer verdant and near overpoweringly green; they were the colour of pitch and smothered any sense of what bordered this cleft in a once familiar county.

They'd crossed a border to get here; they were now crossing back over this border to enter somewhere else. But where they were heading did not feel like the intended destination; that's what the impenetrable darkness made Marcus suspect. Panic flared, thickened and tried to choke him.

Only when they entered the second third of the estuary did he notice smudges of scarlet light at the edges of his vision. Ruddy smears that appeared above the valley's slopes.

There was no chance of this phenomenon suggesting sunrise. Dawn was hours away. And when he looked to the wooded peaks, his vision swam and the crimson stain had either disappeared or never been present.

Heavy arms, clumsy hands. The collar of his jacket was itching, irritating his throat. Blinking sweat from his eyes, he wiped a hand down his face. His hair was sopping, his cheeks slick. Marcus unzipped his cagoule to his breastbone.

Increasingly, he felt woozy, dizzy. He thought vaguely about the possibility of exposure, the effects of hypothermia. Might he have that? He'd been naked in the cold river to remove a hide of cattle blood, then become wet again to his waist after alighting from his boat in the creek to repel the wights. His skin was too hot; his thoughts began to bubble as if a flame licked their undersides.

As if he could no longer find water, three times he struck the side of his boat with a paddle blade. He hadn't eaten in hours. He'd been drugged. The way he felt might have been caused by anything, or might be the culmination of everything he'd suffered.

'Snap out of it!' he said to nothing. He squinted forward. And saw nothing. He felt that they were paddling inside an abyss, suspended, removed from light and from nature as he'd always known it.

Where was the sea? Or was this now some other body of water? Another place, another ocean, where terrible blood worms flung themselves through unlit skies; where the land was marshalled by pale, rapacious horrors, that squirmed from holes in the ground? The horizon blended with the valley sides, with the surface of the water. All of the world he thought he'd returned to had disappeared.

Marcus closed his eyes then opened them. As if to wake from a dream, he shook his head. But this glimmer of wakefulness only served to remind him of when he'd found Jane, the first time, just after midday; exhausted, drained, delirious, thoroughly bitten.

Monumental

Bitten.
Venom.

The very idea of those shards of moist cartilage – the protruding pins of the wight's mouths, concealed inside feathers – turned his stomach. He burped. He imagined his heart pumping a liquid smoke of black poison through his slowing limbs.

Even with his eyelids pulled back, the swamping tiredness squeezed darkness from the back of his skull, threatening to put him to sleep at the paddle.

He doused his face with cold seawater but could not shake the fatigue.

He thought he had been asleep.

Just then.

For a few moments.

If he succumbed, he would sleep as if in a coma. If he slipped away and passed out, they'd drift to the nearest bank. And run aground, only to be picked up by the incoming tide, in six hours. Their boats would be washed back to the marshes.

For some relief from the parts of him that burned with pain, he even wondered if he should pull ashore. Maybe on the other side of the southern headland that gated the Wyrm Valley. That is, if he could find dry land at the base of the cliffs. But even in a cove, or marooned on a rocky promontory, they would still be close to what haunted the woods and skies.

He was bleeding, softly bleeding a thin, silky blood. His wounds would not scab and seal.

Sleep washed smothering waves over the bobbing of his thoughts. Fever smouldered on the flesh encasing his body. He wanted to strip naked. He was struggling to sit up straight, was leaning. If he capsized, he'd never get back inside his boat. He did not have the strength for a self-rescue over the rear deck. If Jane was to swim, he'd have to tow her through cold water. Exposure would finish her. She was weaker than him and he hadn't much gas left in his tank.

Marcus laid his paddle across the cockpit. Dunked a hand over the side and cupped seawater. He threw it into his face. Then repeated the action.

His boat lurched.

He turned his head and saw that Jane had tried to sit up again, her boat rocking onto an edge. 'Don't move, Jane! Stop!' he shouted at her.

From some far recess of her inebriated mind, she summoned an instinctive hip-flick that righted her boat beneath her; enough for him to raft up again and steady her kayak. She was trying to turn around, to peer back into the darkness from which they had just paddled.

'I'm here, Jane. You have to stay still. You rock the boat, you'll go over. You hear me? I can't help you then. Please. I'm not in great shape.'

She must have heard some of his desperate entreaty; she settled into her seat, less slumped but with her hands uselessly trailing in the water. She turned again to stare into the murk behind their sterns, as if to watch whatever was following them. She raised a hand and held it before her eyes. 'Can't you see? Look through my fingers. The stone city that goes on for ever, under the red sky. I don't think . . . I can't go. Too late for me. I'm there, I think. Still there. I can't go anywhere else. Not now . . . Mary. Julian. I can hear them. Can you? Sophie . . .'

As she repeated her forlorn and despairing mantra, Marcus clenched his jaw and resumed paddling. He timed his laboured forward strokes to the beat and rhythm of his own silent words. *Left. Right. Left. Right.* No matter how much his back and shoulders screamed in protest, or how much his vision swum as if he were being tossed in swell, he continued, pushing the soles of one bare foot and one booted foot against the hard plastic rests in the bow, grateful for that discomfort.

Eddies inside his head surfaced with fragments of recollection, half thoughts and images that immediately sank again. Resolve stumbled and dropped to its knees, then onto its drunken face.

Monumental

Sophie's son, Bobby.
My God. My God. That boy. Yours. She said...
Like a demented clown, Nigel laughed and screamed as he came apart beneath strange stars.

The wet noise inside Mary's cavities. Wormed out, rinsed empty.

Sophie ran through the darkness, clutching a bone.

Julian gulped at water. A whiskered old-man throat. Adam's apple. Exhausted eyes. Going. Going. Gone.

The devil's eyes inside feathered sockets, no bigger than almonds. A glimpse of hell.

Marcus burped again and wiped sweat from his face.

He believed he could feel the outgoing tide, tugging at their hulls. From out of oblivion, he sensed that the headlands loomed and would soon become visible – great black claws at the end of long stone toes. Beyond them, the open water.

We can make it.

There was colour in the sky again. He hadn't been mistaken. The night was definitely blushing crimson, as if aglow from the reflections of distant fires in the plains beyond the valley. Above the summits of the slopes that were hidden in darkness, a red smear bled upwards. Light, red light. Unless he too was hallucinating, there could be no mistake.

'It goes forever,' Jane said. 'It never ends.'

A light swell buffeted them, lazily moving their boats up and down. Marcus took the motion as a good sign, of their approach to less enclosed water. The tidal stream must be guiding them to the horizon that he couldn't see. Ahead, the English Channel would broaden into the Atlantic. It must do. Must do. Must do. Must do.

Left, right, left, right.

But where did the sky touch the water? It was terribly dark.

Far above them, a sound similar to that of great sails snapping in the wind ended the stillness.

Marcus stopped paddling. He looked up. He did not see the Blood Worm, but he heard its downward velocity, parting the air, and he heard the slipstream that curled around a pair of vast leathery wings.

Without hesitation, he reached for Jane's boat and unclipped the short leash. He clutched the bowlines and turned her kayak upside down. Without making a sound, she was flopped over and into the water, her pale face vanishing below the surface.

Marcus rolled left and plunged his hot head into a black freeze.

52

[2–3am]

The explosive immersion in cold water pressed all of the air from his chest.

Marcus could see nothing around him.

Within seconds, his mind was overrun by carbon dioxide.

Being upside down, with his legs enveloped by the cylinder of the hull, left no room in what there was of his mind for any consideration but the urge to extricate himself from the cockpit, to seek air above.

Instinct, honed by rescue training, enabled his fingers. They snagged the canvas loop of the spraydeck, then ripped the neoprene cover free of the cockpit. Seawater gushed inside the hull, pushing his legs out of the hollow cavity.

Before he turned to deal with Jane, her frantic hands found him inside the bubble-streaming darkness beneath their boats. Animal fear had engulfed her. Her fingers raked his face, then clawed his cagoule before seizing the tough fabric at his shoulder. The clenched hand refused to release his jacket.

Pain from depleted lungs expanded through Marcus's chest. Unless she kicked her legs from her boat, she'd remain trapped, inverted and unable to breathe, while keeping his head submerged too.

Above the underside of their now exposed hulls, the water thrashed and churned as it was pushed outwards and away from the boats. A helicopter might have been hovering above the sea to produce such a downdraft. A maelstrom caused by the beating of great wings.

Their boats rocked and spun from the blasts of air. Nor far from their submerged faces, a great repulsive head, crowned with feathers, sought the molecules of haemoglobin, the very salt of red blood and tang of plasma, that it had detected from so far above. As if it were a predatory bird with a snaking neck that sought flashes of silvery nourishment in a watery darkness, the god's thrashing power continued to rake and smash the surface. They couldn't come up for air.

His eyes were wide open and stung in the salt, but Marcus still saw little but the vague curvature of one plastic hull, the sleeve of Jane's jacket, the expulsions of bubbles. Only moments from inhaling seawater, they simply had to break the turbulent surface and breathe. Half a pint in the lungs and they were dead.

Marcus snatched through the darkness until his desperate fingers found Jane's cockpit rim. While kicking his legs to sink no deeper, he found the loop designed to pull her spraydeck from the cockpit. When her boat lurched, his fingers lost the loop.

A black pressure encased Marcus's skull; it squeezed and passed through bone and stampeded his entire consciousness into a higher pitch of panic. His chest might have just been flattened by the rear wheel of a bus.

Air. They had to come up.

Marcus scraped his fingers across Jane's spraydeck again, recovered the loop, then yanked it.

As if rolling forward, her body spilled from the inverted kayak and plunged down and into the water alongside him.

At the point of hauling in a frantic breath, the pain in his chest now unbearable, Marcus kicked himself out from under Jane's boat. And as he thrashed towards the roiling surface, he seized a handful of Jane's buoyancy jacket and dragged the awkward bulk of her body upwards, through the water behind him.

Monumental

They broke into the night air at the same time.

Gasping, with his sopping head tilted back, Marcus drank blessed oxygen. Jane coughed, or vomited. Alongside them, as if it had a mind of its own, a paddle bobbed and drifted. Their boats slipped over ripples, inching away as if their former hosts were contagious.

Marcus blinked water from his eyes and waited for the hot, cankerous mouth of the Blood Worm to close, to fasten and hoist him into the air. He waited to be limb-stripped into the barrel of a fleshy torso, and to have that shell hollowed out, like a mussel ransacked by the beak of a gull.

53

[2–3am]

Though filled with more light and stained by a curious ruddy tinge, the air above his wet face was empty.

Whatever had swooped at their boats had now risen. From the east, already at an impossible distance, drifted the *whump whump whump* of the creature's wings.

Jane's eyes were open and as wide and white as eggs. Choking out seawater from her airways and thrashing her arms, she turned water to foam. But in seconds, he heard her gasps lessen to rasping inhalations of air. Her body calmed.

Paddles, both kayaks, a drink bottle and one yellow bilge pump moved on the surface. Everything was trying to float away. Marcus let go of Jane's buoyancy jacket and reached for the nearest boat.

He slowly became aware of his wounds. The cold had mostly anaesthetised the punctures in his buttocks and back. The slit in his throat was now a faint line of stinging fire. But to keep the wound submerged, to prevent one molecule of scent wafting into the atmosphere, he sank until the surface lapped his chin.

The cold water's shock had mercifully cleared his head, slapping him awake from the dreamy stupor that had tried to put him to sleep mere seconds before they'd entered the water. Or so he thought, until he peered at a lightening sky, rippled with crimson and the yellow of sulphur. He could not fathom such colours. And so soon after regaining his breath, the evidence of what now surrounded the estuary stole it away again. What remained of his reason derailed.

'Where are we?' he asked Jane.

Behind their sterns, in the direction of the wetland and river, the earth was bathed red as if from a crimson sun that hadn't revealed itself as an orb, or even a smudge in the sky. Thin, ashy clouds, resembling the smoke from scrub fires, drifted below the discoloured firmament. In the other direction, a sickly turmeric stain stippled an unfamiliar horizon.

When he noticed what extended upwards on either side of the valley, Marcus stopped examining the discolouration above their heads.

This was the Wyrm Valley. *Surely?* The same coastal crease they'd entered the previous day? The topography was identical. But what trees remained on the slopes had been rendered skeletal and leafless as if petrified. Between them, at irregular intervals, ranging from the rocky headlands to deep inside the valley interior, black poles extended to the sky. As if a great fire had recently burned a forest into these charred pillars, the discoloured stanchions haphazardly marked the sloping landscape into the far distance, on both sides of the valley. A chaotic henge pinned into the earth.

At the base of the ghostly trees and the ebony stanchions, the ground undulated with stone domes. Perfectly rounded, like a rash of eggs, each was perforated by a single black hole, or pore. A window or door.

Dead trees. Blackened totems. A host of tombs, or crude cement-coloured mounds: this was the Wyrm Valley but changed, and as it must be in another place.

Struck dumb, Marcus peered back into the valley and as far inland as his eyesight permitted and he saw a mountain range. The summits were aglow with blooded light. Above the infernal peaks, a terrible host flapped and flitted in the unearthly ruby light. Tiny silhouettes, reduced to the size of flies, flocked in hell's light.

To either side of where they floated, water as black as oil lapped and slopped. But it was towards the sickly yellow luminance of the horizon that the slender currents inched them and their upturned boats.

Marcus seized hold of Jane's hand. He drew her through the water and closer to him. He turned her around, so that the back of her sopping head rested on his shoulder. He pressed his cheek against her cold face. 'Hold on, kid.' With his other hand, he scraped for purchase on the bowlines of the upturned boat and held onto those too. He hadn't the strength to turn the boat over, to empty it and get back inside. That time had gone. He was but an effigy of dull pain now; a broken stickman chilled by black water, through which his blood sluggishly moved in polluted streams.

Instead, he pushed his feet at the water. With the last of his strength, he pushed his one bare foot and his one shod foot at the water, to move them further away from the terrible black mountains bathed in blood.

'Can you see them?' Jane muttered. 'Stone houses?'

'I can,' Marcus replied.

'Can you hear them, the pale children? Is it music?'

Across the thick water drifted the reedy expulsions of air, funnelled from so many small, hideous mouths.

'Yes,' Marcus said, and he kicked hard with his right foot to correct their drift towards one of the stony shorelines.

They had floated, carried by the currents. When Marcus finally snapped from a delirious half-sleep, he didn't know for how long.

He also broke from a fractious exchange with Julian and Nigel, each of whom had been reduced to a speaking head. Their faces were waxy-skinned, bloodless and artificial in appearance, and mounted on blackened totems, the timber etched with snakelike runes.

Monumental

Shivering had snapped him from the nightmarish discourse that he'd conducted with what was left of his dead companions. When he came to and their angry faces retreated, the sea remained as black as tar. But the firmament had darkened to indigo. A silvery band etched the horizon. Gone was the sickly, spoiled verdigris and vanilla glow, nor was there any trace of crimson above them.

Jane was breathing, but only just. He could hear a slight whistle in her sinuses. Her eyes were shut. One of his white hands remained frozen around the bowlines of her boat. He could not unclench those fingers.

Behind them, he could see that they had passed out from between the headlands of the Wyrm Valley. The slopes remained dark. Whether they were coated with living timber or the stone tombs, he could not tell. But where there had been a mountain range that had stolen his breath with dread, there was now only empty sky above the pale glimmer of the marsh.

It took several seconds for his addled mind to make sense of what he heard next: a crackle of static.

Beside his face, he heard a voice. A woman's voice, calmly intoning a test, on behalf of the Falmouth Coastguard, on Channel Sixteen. 'Argo, you are loud and clear.' The voice issued from the VHF radio clipped to the shoulder strap of his buoyancy vest. A radio that had been dead from the moment they'd entered the valley at midday. But now they'd left the Wyrm behind, the little radio spoke again. And so pristine was the woman's voice, the coastguard might have been in the water, bobbing beside him and Jane.

Marcus fumbled for the radio.

One of his stiff fingers found the press-to-activate button. And pushed down hard.

He cleared his throat, then whispered, 'Mayday. Mayday. Mayday.'

54

[2–3am]

Milk had not been enough for the children. Not that day. Nor had milk been sufficient sustenance for a while.

These last three years, Huntress had done her best to contain the triplets and to appease them. Her three angels. As a young addict in Edinburgh in the eighties, Huntress had given up her own child for adoption. But here, in this valley, she'd found the motherhood that heroin had stolen from her many years before. She'd have followed Clement into hell for providing her with that maternal privilege again, and it appeared that she had done so today.

The triplets had set about their guardian in the nursery.

The lights were still on in the old cellar, where the children were kept and slept in three small beds. And across the polished sand-coloured flagstones, Rachel found Huntress's blood. Red petals had dripped and spattered to pattern a macabre track around the nursery floor; the splashes marked the carer's struggles as she'd attempted to escape from her three beloved wards.

No one could have been present to assist poor Huntress. Swan usually piled in, so it was odd that she had not done so today. Where was Swan?

Down at the temple, when the children fed on live animals, two people always accompanied their drowsy, sated forms back to the house. Even when sluggish after an intense

Monumental

feed, the children could not be trusted; like violent drunks combined with wild animals, the little silvery creatures needed watching. The state of the nursery floor was all the proof Rachel needed of that.

Swan had not been on a bike and in the meadow either, so she must have come back to the house with Huntress and the triplets. But then Swan had not been present for Huntress's darkest hour of need down here. This perturbed Rachel.

Vine had often employed the flat of his blade to lever and press away the over-eager, hungry children from Huntress's bosom, even though it could provide no milk. But Vine had not walked away from the floodplain. He'd been accounted for. He'd passed over.

Freeing Marcus had disrupted the October rite.

Sometime after the Blood Worm had appeared on the pinnacle of the crude cathedral to display its torn bounty, though only twice, Clement, Thorny and Vine must have begun their search for the third sacrifice: Marcus, who'd escaped. This quest had eventually led them to the campsite and to their own brutal demise in the meadow. But where was long, graceful Swan?

Rachel paused, closed her eyes and supported herself with a hand against the wall. Though it was hard to begin, she performed the mindfulness exercise that had helped her and Briar daily, during all their years of strife and disappointment. She cleared her thoughts of that unholy lump, slamming the earth and tearing apart what it found in the grass.

Since she'd left them at the riverside, Rachel could only hope and pray that the god's mouth had remained empty of Marcus and Jane.

Rachel opened her eyes and wondered anew what had become of Swan.

After their participation in the rite, and after they'd lit the cow's pyre, if the children had appeared to be soporific they were pretending. The blood on the floor made that clear.

The piping noises they made were as mysterious as the songs of birds. If Huntress had never managed to decipher much of them, then no one could.

Down here.
The children.

Swarming like pretty white spiders, they must have overwhelmed Huntress. Filling their small bellies and lighting her pyre at the same time. Alone, Huntress had run willy-nilly around the nursery. From where Rachel stood, near the three small beds, to the scattered bones that the children played with – because they showed no interest in normal toys – poor Huntress's strength had bled out and marked her dreadful passage across these flagstones. She must have carried her adopted brood, who would have clung to her back and wound between her legs; all of them would have been attached to her by their mouths, like serpents. Greater numbers. Teeth. They'd learned from their pale fathers that crept out of the mines.

Blood was smudged in whirls and swipes, before pooling in the spot where Huntress had sunk to her knees beneath the clinging weight of three lithe, determined bodies. Two boys and a girl, whose eyes were always hidden behind dark glasses. Children who knew to keep their mouths shut too. Not that they spoke – but no one had wanted to see those teeth.

On the big padded mat in the middle of the cellar, where Huntress had once changed the triplets, and where Swan had suckled them, Huntress must have finally given up the fight. Three pairs of small, unshod feet had traipsed through what seeped from their carer; the portion of liquid that their pale mouths hadn't collected. And some juice would have been left within her flesh for their god. Like their masters, the Little Priests of the mine, the children were only loyal to the thing under the temple: the Blood Worm that ruled below the ground and flew across crimsoned skies, under which the children had been born.

Clement and Vine had told Huntress to keep her iron at her side, at all times. Vine had even made a sheath out of leather for Huntress's pacifier; a scabbard that could be worn around the middle, so that its iron could be drawn at any time. But Huntress had always struggled to strike the children.

When the litter became agitated, it was generally Swan or Vine who had performed that task. Vine, perhaps too enthusiastically.

Rachel could see Huntress's black blade, discarded by her bed, still sheathed.

Like the others, Huntress had her own caravan. But, most nights, she chose to sleep down here in the dark, with the triplets. They'd never said a word to her in three years, but they dutifully took her hand each morning and she'd loved them. Their lives had been of greater value than hers. Tonight she'd proven that too. Feeding from the cows had not been enough for the kiddies. They'd become restless, then unruly, weeks before the rite. An early warning system, Briar had once remarked, that the Priests would conduct their rite again this year.

By the time they were two, but as big as ten-year-olds and as strong as teenagers, the litter had become too wilful for even the most ardent foster parent. Briar had called the triplets that: the litter. *Human only in appearance,* or so he'd confided to Rachel, *but pure wight under the skin.* Their characteristics and intentions they'd inherited from their opaque parents in the kingdom below.

Spies for the priesthood too, Briar had claimed. According to him, the presence of the young in the community had a dual purpose. Bred in the underworld but displaying the physical charms of their pretty mothers, they were placed among the people of the valley to establish the priesthood's presence and influence on Clement. They'd helped prepare the ground for the arrival of the deity and its rites. The Blood Worm.

A similar pattern had destroyed the old family who'd built the house and farmed the valley. The Waddetons. Briar had painstakingly transcribed that story for Clement; a grim tale that had been written by a frail, spidery hand in French, Greek and Latin, as if to protect the terrible contents from all but the most educated eyes. The children of the Waddeton family had been taken, then replaced with others. Clement had purchased the journals from a collector.

When the house was adapted into a military hospital, the evidence altered but the legacy continued. There had been two incentives to lure out the wights: herds of cattle for the war effort had offered an abundance of blood, as had the frailty of the human wounded. Not every burrow had been blocked by early man. Land eroded, chinks appeared.

Briar would return to their caravan, amazed yet shaken by what he'd learned from the documents that Clement had procured. Briar had wanted them both to leave the valley around that time. But to go where? Even if they'd slunk past Vine and Thorny, they wouldn't have cleared the main gate. By then, each of them had already been branded with ink. The knowledge concerning the valley's original occupants had come too late for them. And always had done so, for those that had made homes in the Wyrm Valley.

In time, Clement and Briar had learned even more of the place's history. None of it good. Residents in the care home had been bitten at night. Their senility had evolved into behaviours disturbing enough to require sedation and round-the-clock supervision. Some had disappeared completely and were believed lost in the sea. But even the staff, before leaving their employment, had seen horrid faces at windows. Inquiries had mounted.

Even in such a beautiful setting, guests of the hotel had thinned over time as well, until too few visited to maintain the business. Clement had paid people to find all of this out, and more, and he'd shared his findings with Briar. And yet he'd persisted. Old fairytales, myths and folk stories merely amused him. Others in the past had succumbed to what crept into this valley because they were simpler folk; that's what Clem had claimed. They'd failed to understand and manage the miracle that had appeared here throughout history. But only on its terms, or so Briar had long warned. And Briar had been as afraid of Clement's arrogance, his narcissism and ability to deceive himself as he'd been frightened of the Little Priests.

Monumental

Rachel turned and looked up the stone steps. They led to the ground floor of the house. The spatters she'd noticed on her way down to the cellar did not mark the trail of a wounded Huntress descending the stairs. Nor, as she'd first assumed, did the stains mark the return of the sticky, mucky children after they'd drained the cow. No, the children had felled Huntress in the cellar, then guided her outside, directing her, blind with pain and weakened by blood loss, like a heifer to a slaughterhouse. These spatters and trickles marked the passage of a weakened, delirious Huntress, as she was led up the stairs by her little wards, then coerced into the open.

Those were definitely Huntress's tattoos that Rachel had seen on the arm that had been discarded on the lawn. The evidence in the nursery had only suggested the missing scenes from a story that she had been forced to complete for herself.

A little further along, when the security lights pinged on and turned the front lawn white, she'd glanced at the stump with a female foot attached. That had been near a black, moist patch on the grass. Like a big oil stain, the dark, wet grass suggested that an engine had leaked all over Clement's perfect lawn. But no vehicles were ever parked here. Something else had been emptied.

Rachel decided not to touch anything in the cellar, nor what remained on the front lawn. When people came here – the police, she hoped – she wanted them to find the bits and pieces. The god wouldn't return for another year, but people were clever these days and would have ways of testing things and finding out how that foot and the arm were no longer joined to a body. The police would have Huntress's fingerprints, so they would establish to whom those appendages had once been connected. Before she'd found sanctuary at the Foundation, Huntress had been in prison. A few times.

And Vine. And Swan. And Thorny. All of them.

I don't know that this is for us, dear. Briar had said that towards the end. *We're living with criminals, addicts and broken people, who've been manipulated, just like us, by a liar and a fraud. A charlatan.* But even in better days, where could they have gone? Their mediaeval tapestry weaving business had failed, as had their attempts to farm organic pulses, as had Briar's wild-camping-with-mindfulness project. They were bankrupt.

The valley is a nicer version of a poorhouse, Briar had once remarked to her, while working as a volunteer for the Foundation in Plymouth. That's where he'd heard of the plans for a valley that Clement had bought. *We can contribute a great deal to the sanctuary*, he'd decided, for both of them. Briar had a fine mind that had never found a place to shine, and Rachel had loved him dearly. But he'd always made terrible decisions. For both of them.

Though where was Swan?

Swan must have helped Huntress return the children to the manor house, transporting them up-valley in the trailer. Both women would have planned, as usual, to flannel the children clean, then put them to bed. The brood would have been filthy with blood. Yes, Swan must have returned with Huntress. That was a two-person job.

Swan was no pushover and, when she was anywhere near the little ones, carried her pacifier. She knew too well how the triplets had once tugged at her breasts, when they were infants, fighting like puppies for her milk. And they'd never stopped craving it, though Swan refused to let them near her again, once they'd turned fifteen months and were racing across the floor like little crabs with ghost-white hair.

Perhaps this year was their coming out. The triplets had grown too wild and strong for two adult women. In the spring, Briar had suspected that such a time had been close; that the triplets' true nature would soon take control of what served for their tiny minds.

For everyone's sake, Clement had them fitted with dark glasses, at age two. No one liked being watched by the tiny ferret eyes. But the glasses were a mistake, according to Briar, because once the rusty pips were concealed, no one could guess their intentions.

So had Swan hidden, somewhere in the house, while the litter was busy with Huntress?

Rachel wandered through the building. She wanted to find Swan and tell her that it was over and that her lover, Clement, was no more; that he'd been destroyed by the abhorrence that he called a god. Just like her Briar had been in the temple. She sometimes thought of the valley as one of those carnivorous flowers with bright colours and heady perfumes that lured insects to settle among its petals.

Downstairs, Clement's huge living room and dining room were both empty and as spotless as ever, after Huntress had cleaned them for him. His cinema room lay in darkness. Flagstones, marble counters, timber beams, steel implements and chromed appliances glimmered in the enormous kitchen – chic dereliction. The covered hot tub in the empty wet-room hummed. His gaming room, gym, office, wine room and larder waited in silence for activities and uses they'd never know again.

From the office, Rachel took keys.

Eleven of the twelve ensuite bedrooms on the next two floors had been locked since Clement stopped receiving guests, more than three years before.

His master bedroom remained as undisturbed as it had been after Huntress had changed his sheets that morning. Swan's red high-heeled shoes had been tidied away and stood together in one corner. She would never wear them for him again. That was the only part of her that he'd ever permitted to remain inside his magisterial bedchamber.

With the keys Rachel had taken from his office, she let herself into the attic.

No one but Clement was permitted to go inside; not even Thorny, Swan or Vine, his closest confederates. Briar took care of his and Rachel's correspondence in the office downstairs, on a laptop that Clement let him use. Sometimes he would set everything up for Rachel and she would write an email to her estranged sister, who lived in Canada, though not very often. She'd come to the valley to build a new world, not linger in the old one.

This cool, low-lit attic didn't seem to belong in the valley at all. Nothing inside it appeared to have any relationship with the vineyard, pastures, cattle, the temple or woods.

Grey carpet tiles and a curved desk. Three vast flat monitors displayed split screens. They mirrored the images and data on the broad wall of larger screens that curved around the rear of the converted attic. The two flat screens on the right were filled with streams of data and graphs in bright colours. One showed satellite pictures of what looked like clouds drifting across land, or maybe the sea.

Rachel squinted at the bars and green curves, the orange numbers, but would never understand any of it.

The screen on the left, however, was split into dozens of smaller squares, each a section of the estate. Some screens showed images in colour, some were in black and white. Others displayed a greenish night vision. Rachel drew closer.

The main gates at the top of the valley.

The caravans.

Sections of the vineyard divided between four screens.

Inside the cattle barn and pens, revealing what was left of the herd. Had Marcus and his friends not paddled into the valley, the poor animals would have soon been consumed and replaced in the winter months.

Parts of the river she didn't recognise that must have been further downstream.

Monumental

The rooms of this house that she'd just wandered through.
The exterior of the manor house.
Two perspectives of the horrid temple's interior.

Her eyes took no more than a moment to glance across the images, within these small square screens, before settling on the only black square that revealed any motion. A red border around this screen flashed rhythmically.

Clement must have placed one of his cameras inside the mouth of the mine. He'd obsessed over where the Priests emerged. He'd tried many times to survey the old tin mine, but the wights had chewed his appliances dead. Except for this one.

Rachel finally understood where Swan had gone.

Rachel covered her mouth with her hands and closed her eyes. In the time that elapsed before she reopened them, she guessed that after she and Marcus had removed Jane from the mine shaft, the Priests had collected Jane's replacement.

Rachel was reminded of ants, removing dead matter from a garden path.

It was impossible to see Swan's face. Not with so much hair wrapped around it. Not with so many grub-like bodies moving across her.

She lay on corpses of birds; dead fowl that formed a ruptured mattress intended for a princess. And from her ghastly resting place, her long body was being shifted away from the tunnel entrance and deeper into a darkness where Clement's camera could not see.

Swan was young enough to bear children and produce a yield of milk. Huntress had been too old, so had been retired as fodder for the god. And as if the brood was a living augur of Swan's fate, the triplets that Huntress had loved as her own mingled and hopped among their true family. They were finally going home, and they were taking poor Swan with them.

Rachel left the control room on unsteady feet. As she listed and hobbled, she wiped at her eyes. They'd all been friends once. Boyish, sly Clement. Beautiful, imperious Swan. Sullen Vine and bitter Thorny. Tearful, loving Huntress. Dear Briar, and the others who'd crossed over.

Once Rachel had gathered herself, she looked for a bag. She would fill a big sack with as many of the journals and hospital and care home files as she could carry; she'd remove what she could of the library that Clement had spent years collecting. These materials were stored behind glass in the living room. And if Marcus came back for her, she would ask him to find someone who could understand all of what was written in these records. And she would beg him to find someone who might move that carven rock from the front lawn, and take it into the temple, to block the mouth of the vile duct from which the Blood Worm was so fond of crawling.

Every year now.

Story Notes: About This Horror

I've been kayaking on the sea, but also on estuaries and summer rivers, for seven years as a club paddler. I've now paddled all of South Devon's coastline (save a couple of kilometres that fall between where paddles start and finish), the estuaries and rivers, as well as parts of East Devon and Cornwall. It's been a fabulous privilege to experience the natural world in this way, to see the land from the water and stretches of coastline inaccessible from up on the cliffs. Further out at sea, I don't think there is a better way of navigating and exploring the plethora of impressive offshore rocks than by sea kayak. I've also made a lot of friends and met a good many interesting people through the sport.

And the first thing I will say about kayakers is that they are nothing like the characters in this story. Which is just as well, if you think about it.

All individuals are complicated; groups more so. But out of all of the organised gatherings of people that I've experienced socially and professionally, few groups are as affable and inclusive in nature as kayakers; few endeavours are as amicable as organised paddles.

Much contributes to this social cohesion and harmony on the water, as well as the camaraderie. There is the binding common interest in exploring water, waterways and coastline by kayak; an embedded sense of responsibility in staying safe on the water, as well as getting heavy boats in and out of the water. The inexperienced are guided by the experienced. Careful planning is conducted before a paddle. Strengths and directions of wind, tides, tidal flow and local knowledge about conditions pretty much determine where you can go, and at what time you need to be on the water and then off it. In our club, you can't even go on a paddle without taking the training course, one evening a week for about three months.

It's a sport that requires commitment and it is expensive. Sea kayaking is, therefore, a team sport – fewer than three there should never be – and you all need to look out for each other, while assuming a high level of individual responsibility. It's a good dynamic for a horror story but only an atypical group of paddlers could make this kind of story. And so: artistic licence. Most of this group were carrying too much baggage and they took it with them on the trip.

Would a mixed group of paddlers attempt a paddle of this complexity and scope in the forecast conditions within the story? Probably not, though I wouldn't put the challenge beyond very experienced kayakers and five-star coaches. Or wishful thinkers. And despite any amount of navigation and trip planning, there is always an element of uncertainty: the weather can change, even after you've checked the forecasts before launching, and even known conditions may create dynamic water off headlands, or over hidden reefs. Water is incredibly hard to read, and I've seen it do things that turned me white with terror. But this is not a story about typical kayakers, or kayaking. Not really. The kayaks are vehicles to get the characters to a particular place, and then strand them there.

You might also ask: is a private valley, in which even the water is privately owned, and dependent on tidal cycles, credible? The answer is yes. I've paddled one. And that valley may have given me the setting for *Monumental* – right down to the specific details of the dead wood, the wetland, the river leading to a weir, as well as the remains hanging from trees.

Story Notes: About This Horror

So the Wyrm Valley exists, though is known by another name and it is one of the most beautiful spots in the county, maybe even the country. In this very real location, I have come across bones hanging from tree branches that fringe a wetland; though in that case a member of the group researched the remains, from photographs taken on the paddle, and worked out that we had seen the skeleton of a dolphin (and not the large carnivorous bird, like the rhea or ostrich, that I might have offered by way of explanation when we discovered the hanging remains). So, after so many adventures on the water, and explorations of secluded places, how could my horror brain not invest itself into kayaking and begin to consider these maritime experiences abstractly? I guess that's what I am always doing: reimagining my own experiences abstractly to write stories.

This process was involved in the writing of *The Ritual* and *The Reddening*. *Monumental* adds a third story to my predilection for writing horror novels of pagan terror, set outdoors. My own experiences outdoors inspired and informed all three of these stories. The first two were informed by hiking and camping, the third by sea kayaking.

These three novels have other similarities too: each story involves a confrontation with the supernormal at a remote location, before deteriorating into a quest for survival. Each novel also features a near-forgotten pagan god. And if I promise the reader a god in one of my stories, then I will deliver one. But the entity should not resemble what the reader is expecting. Editorial suggestions that *The Reddening* didn't need the god were key to my decision to publish the novel independently.

So I'd been hearing the call again for a few years – the call of the wild – and I answered it by writing *Monumental*. 2024 was the year in which, imaginatively, I needed to go back outside and enter the undeveloped rural world – in this case, a rewilded natural landscape. In 2023 I had three strong ideas for novels brewing, and my dilemma was which one to write next. While having a beer and looking out to sea, I chose *Monumental*.

Readers of my novels *The Reddening*, *Cunning Folk*, *The Vessel* and now *Monumental* may also recognise a more formal intention by the author, in the latest story, to develop a regional pantheon of supernormal entities. I've never written books in series, but I do like a network of interconnecting ideas. After making a start on *The Reddening* in late 2016, this synthesis has occurred as I've gone along.

Each book can be read as a stand-alone title. Collectively, however, they suggest a greater cosmic evil, concentrated in a part of the world in which the very ages of the earth are visible in the cliffs. Many of us also write in the long shadow cast by H. P. Lovecraft.

And though I am adding a length of coastline and new locations and habitations, these four novels are very much Devonian stories and based on, and around, the place where my family and I have lived for the last ten years. Some of my first two years were also spent living in Plymouth, though I don't remember them as I was too young; but maybe destiny has played a part in my return to the south-west and my revelation of its hidden horrors? Will I dig up more pagan terrors down here? Probably.

It might also be worth mentioning the form the story took, as I've written in previous iterations of 'Story Notes' about my flirtation with screenwriting. Although this novel did not begin life as a screenplay, the structure was guided by cinematic conventions. So in *Monumental* I've mirrored some of what I have learned from writing screenplays.

Firstly, there is the ticking clock; the entire story occupies around fifteen hours and is dictated by tidal cycles: two high tides and two low tides in twenty-four hours. This worked as a framework for the action of the story. Time added compression and produced an effect of real-time horror. Also, there is a single location – the valley – containing various stages within itself for different parts of the story. So, a form of block-horror with a limited cast, but set outdoors, is what I aimed for. Fewer movements through time and space, and fewer locations, I find, add a claustrophobic tension.

Story Notes: About This Horror

As with *The Ritual*, I didn't want cutaways or flashbacks or life before the story begins. Expositional detail needed to be imparted and contained within the chosen timeline. On this matter, I blew hot and cold on the inclusion of Briar's Journals. I pondered writing the history of the valley, using an epistolary technique, and including excerpts from Briar's records in between the chapters. Though Briar is only seen as a dead man, in the gloom of the temple (in which Sophie treads on his lifeless face), he is an important character off-screen, as a kind of oracle who had the misfortune of incrementally translating and piecing together what a terrible mistake Clement Colman had made.

I imagined Briar as one of those men, and I've met a few, who speak with authority on any subject that you could name, while never seeming to have accomplished anything. In fact, despite their loquacity and deep reservoirs of knowledge, their lives are often festooned with mishap, and are chaotic. But I decided against including interludes in which Briar narrated what he had discovered, by interpreting secondary texts and documented evidence, about the valley's history. My reason for not using this device was tempo. I simply preferred the pace and tempo of the story with less elaboration and lore. A taste thing.

Almost infuriatingly, as I wrote *Monumental*, I thought of another three stories set in the same valley. I would need years of research and writing, however, to compose these expansion stories, and I am not a quick writer; meanwhile, other unrelated ideas press at me daily and demand their turn. I am, however, finally at peace about how I might include so much of the time that I have spent on the water in a kayak within a horror story. We all have bucket lists.

Folks, thank you for coming on another journey with me. And please always check the weather before you set off.
Manes exite paterni
Adam L. G. Nevill
Devon, December 2024.

Acknowledgements

*R*itual Limited is a one-sided endeavour because the press is all about my books. I write the books that the press publishes, and project manage the publishing and critical path that extends from a finished, typed manuscript to five completed editions of each book. But I don't create those editions, not physically.

Peter Marsh handles all of the design: text, artwork and jackets. Sam Araya paints the covers. Tony Russell edits out my clumsiness. Eleanor Abraham has proofread the last two books. Anne Nevill now does another pass. Sometimes I even add a design proofreader. Kris Dyer and Suzy Wootton Voices created and produced the last audiobook and Greg Patmore has been kind enough to narrate this novel. TJ International do the offset printing; IngramSpark and Amazon KDP handle the print-on-demand publishing. Ebook Launch Inc now take care of all of my eBook editions. ACX, Ingram, Amazon and Publish Drive distribute my books worldwide. Anne Nevill also handles the growing and groaning business administration with a firm of accountants, designs the newsletters, maintains the website and fulfils the limited edition hardback orders with me. Helen Turner is web mistress.

So, Ritual Limited, over our first ten years, has grown as a business and into a press with many moving parts and contributors. Quite simply, I could not do this alone, and I remain immensely grateful to everyone who plays their considerable part, and adds their expertise and knowledge, to turn my mad stories into actual books.

I often say: I used to be a writer. And, sometimes, that's exactly how it feels. From start to finish, it can take five months plus to create and painstakingly check each generation of each edition. Indie publishing is no cakewalk, but it is worth it, because you readers read and collect the books, appreciate them, review them and boost their signals. And those who were especially kind to *All the Fiends of Hell*, and many others of my titles, deserve more than a mere mention here. But I record my immense gratitude for the attention and the thoughts of Olly Clarke (*CriminOlly*), Kayleigh Dobbs (*Happy Goat Horror*), Michael Wilson and Bob Pastorella (*This Is Horror*), Gavin Kendall and Steve Stred (*Kendall Reviews*), Tony Jones (*Horror DNA* and *Gingernuts of Horror*), Sadie Hartmann and Ashley (*Nightworms*), Steve Sangapore (*Specularis Conversations*), Neil McRobert (*Talking Scared* and *Esquire*), David Simms (*Cemetery Dance*), Wyatt Towns (*Vogue Horror*), Michael Wertenberg, Jim Moon (*Hypnogoria*), Anthony Watson (*Dark Musings*) and the multitude of kind Bookstagrammers of Instagram, like Mark (*oneconstantreader*) and Mers (*Harpies in the Trees*), who are but two examples of that fine social media horror community.

A special thanks goes out to my peers in the paddling world, with whom I've traversed so many miles on the water. Scores of people, but most often: Tim Durrant, Jon Roberts, Hannah and John Bagby, Ems Freemantle, James Yarham, Shaun Richards, Graham Reynolds, Kyran Ryan, Sam Kite, Robert Cox, Jez Baillie, Caryl Bickle, Gill Bowles, Angela Pearce, Henry James Ward, Bridget Greet, Colin Ellis-Winter, David Ching.

And readers, of this book and my others, you will always come first. You keep me afloat and make this endeavour worthwhile. Thank you and beware the Blood Worm.

About the Author

Adam L. G. Nevill was born in Birmingham, England, in 1969 and grew up in England and New Zealand. He is an author of horror fiction. Of his novels, *The Ritual*, *Last Days*, *No One Gets Out Alive* and *The Reddening* were all winners of The August Derleth Award for Best Horror Novel. He has also published three collections of short stories, with *Some Will Not Sleep* winning the British Fantasy Award for Best Collection, 2017.

Imaginarium adapted *The Ritual* and *No One Gets Out Alive* into feature films and more of his work is currently in development for the screen.

The author lives in Devon, England. More information about the author and his books is available at: www.adamlgnevill.com

More Horror Fiction from Adam L. G. Nevill and Ritual Limited.

Available in eBook (and included in Kindle Unlimited) at Amazon, and in paperback and audio from major online retailers. Signed editions are available from www.adamlgnevill.com

All the Fiends of Hell

The red night of bells heralds global catastrophe.
Annihilation on a biblical scale.

Seeing the morning is no blessing. The handful of scattered survivors are confronted by blood-red skies and an infestation of predatory horrors that never originated on earth. An occupying force intent on erasing the remnants of animal life from the planet.

Across the deserted landscapes of England, bereft of infrastructure and society, the overlooked can either hide or try to outrun the infernal hunting terrors. Until a rumour emerges claiming that the sea may offer an escape.

Ordinary, unexceptional, directionless Karl, is one of the few who made it through the first night. In the company of two orphans, he flees south. But only into horrifying revelations and greater peril, where a transformed world and expanding race of ravening creatures await. Driven to the end of the country and himself, he must overcome alien and human malevolence and act in ways that were unthinkable mere days before.

All The Fiends of Hell is a novel of alien horror from the four times winner of the August Derleth Award for Best Horror Novel.

"A broad, electric, and brutal story that goes for the throat with no remorse" *Cemetery Dance*

The Vessel

"A watcher may remark that after sleeping for so long, the building appears to have been roused."

Struggling with money, raising a child alone and fleeing a volatile ex, Jess McMachen accepts a job caring for an elderly patient. Flo Gardner – a disturbed shut-in and invalid. But if Jess can hold this job down, she and her daughter, Izzy, can begin a new life.

Flo's vast home, Nerthus House, may resemble a stately vicarage in an idyllic village, but the labyrinthine interior is a dark, cluttered warren filled with pagan artefacts.

And Nerthus House lives in the shadow of a malevolent secret. A sinister enigma determined to reveal itself to Jess and to drive her to the end of her tether. Not only is she stricken by the malign manipulation of the Vicarage's bleak past, but mercurial Flo is soon casting a baleful influence over young Izzy. What appeared to be a routine job soon becomes a battle for Jess's sanity and the control of her child.

It's as if an ancient ritual was triggered when Jess crossed the threshold of the vicarage. A rite leading her and Izzy to a terrifying critical mass, where all will be lost or saved.

'In refining the tale of supernatural horror to its essence, M.R. James increased the terror, and among his living inheritors is Adam Nevill' - *Ramsey Campbell*

Cunning Folk

No home is heaven with hell next door.

Money's tight and their new home is a fixer-upper. Deep in rural South West England, with an ancient wood at the foot of the garden, Tom and his family are miles from anywhere and anyone familiar. His wife, Fiona, was never convinced that buying the money-pit at auction was a good idea. Not least because the previous owner committed suicide. Though no one can explain why.

Within days of crossing the threshold, when hostilities break out with the elderly couple next door, Tom's dreams of future contentment are threatened by an escalating tit-for-tat campaign of petty damage and disruption.

Increasingly isolated and tormented, Tom risks losing his home, everyone dear to him and his mind. Because, surely, only the mad would suspect that the oddballs across the hedgerow command unearthly powers. A malicious magic even older than the eerie wood and the strange barrow therein. A hallowed realm from where, he suspects, his neighbours draw a hideous power.

A compelling folk-horror story of deadly rivalry and the oldest magic from the four times winner of The August Derleth Award for Best Horror Novel.

"*Cunning Fo*lk gets under the skin from the first page, the story infused with mordant humour and grotesquely apt images of confinement, frustration and otherworldly power."*Toronto Star.*

The Reddening

Winner of the August Derleth Award for Best Horror Novel, 2020.

One million years of evolution didn't change our nature. Nor did it bury the horrors predating civilisation. Ancient rites, old deities and savage ways can reappear in the places you least expect.

Lifestyle journalist Katrine escaped past traumas by moving to a coast renowned for seaside holidays and natural beauty. But when a vast hoard of human remains and prehistoric artefacts is discovered in nearby Brickburgh, a hideous shadow engulfs her life.

Helene, a disillusioned lone parent, lost her brother, Lincoln, six years ago. Disturbing subterranean noises he recorded prior to vanishing, draw her to Brickburgh's caves. A site where early humans butchered each other across sixty thousand years. Upon the walls, images of their nameless gods remain.

Amidst rumours of drug plantations and new sightings of the mythical red folk, it also appears that the inquisitive have been disappearing from this remote part of the world for years. A rural idyll where outsiders are unwelcome and where an infernal power is believed to linger beneath the earth. A timeless supernormal influence that only the desperate would dream of confronting. But to save themselves and those they love, and to thwart a crimson tide of pitiless barbarity, Kat and Helene are given no choice. They were involved and condemned before they knew it.

The Reddening is an epic story of folk and prehistoric horrors, written by the author of *The Ritual*, *Last Days*, *No One Gets Out Alive* and the four times winner of The August Derleth Award for Best Horror Novel.

Some Will Not Sleep
Selected Horrors

Winner of the British Fantasy Award:
Best Collection 2017.

In ghastly harmony with the nightmarish visions of the award-winning writer's novels, these stories blend a lifelong appreciation of horror culture with the grotesque fascinations and terrors that are the author's own. Adam L. G. Nevill's best early horror stories are collected here for the first time.

"Great storytelling, but across a wider palate and range of styles than you might have expected, leading to some delightfully unexpected visions and hellscapes." *Gingernuts of Horror.*

"There is not one single tale which feels less than the others, none which seem to be mere 'filler'. They are beautifully crafted, original and complete works." *This is Horror.*

Hasty for the Dark
Selected Horrors

Hasty for the Dark is the second short story collection from the award-winning and widely appreciated British writer of horror fiction, Adam L. G. Nevill. The author's best horror stories from 2009 to 2015 are collected here for the first time. "These tales are dark, starkly violent, but also subtle and ambiguous, often at the same time." This is Horror.

"The nine tales are cleverly varied, exhibiting varied pace, chills which deal with the supernatural in both every day and altogether freakier situations, and other curve-balls which drop feet into other genres." Gingernuts of Horror.

Wyrd and Other Derelictions

Derelictions are horror stories told in ways you may not have encountered before.

Something is missing from the silent places and worlds inside these stories. Something has been removed, taken flight, or been destroyed. Us.

Derelictions are weird tales that tell of aftermaths and of new and liminal places. Each location has witnessed catastrophe, infernal visitations, or unearthly transformations. But across these landscapes of murder, genocide and invasion, crucial evidence remains. And it is the task of the reader to sift through ruin and ponder the residual enigma, to behold and wonder at the full horror that was visited upon mankind.

Wyrd contains seven derelictions, original tales of mystery and horror from the author of *Hasty for the Dark* and *Some Will Not Sleep* (winner of The British Fantasy Award for Best Collection).

"This is a different collection, one that might remind one of Peter Straub, Thomas Ligotti, or even Robert Aickman in its exquisite weirdness. It is well worth the read. Recommended reading for any serious horror fan or for speculative fiction aficionados who crave intelligence in their weirdness."*Cemetery Dance.*

"I can't recommend this collection of stories enough. This is experimental literary horror and the experiment has exceeded all expectations. Read this and enjoy the horrific scenes Nevill has laid out for you." *Horror Bound.*

Free eBook

If you like horror stories, missing chapters, advice for writing horror, articles on horror fiction and films, and much more, register at www.adamlgnevill.com to seize your Free Book today.

www.ingramcontent.com/pod-product-compliance
Lightning Source LLC
LaVergne TN
LVHW041619060526
838200LV00040B/1346